LOVELIGHT

"Get ready for love," he said. "I intend to have you tonight."

The warmth of his hands sent a sizzling sensation along her arms, down her spine and into her legs. She tried to pull away, but only in her imagination. In reality, his touch was too magnetic to deny.

He traced the shape of her face, her lips. "So delicate," he murmured, "so full of hidden passion. I could awaken that passion. Like this . . ."

He pulled her down to lie along his supine body. His nakedness beneath the blanket tempted her, called to her, teased her. Before she realized it, her lips were brushing his. He held her tighter, as he ran his tongue around the rim of her mouth arousing the desire inside her, deep down within the center of her womanly self. . . .

UNDER THE WILD MOON

UNDER THE WILD MOON

DIANE CAREY

A SIGNET BOOK

NEW AMERICAN LIBRARY

NAL BOOKS ARE AVAILABLE AT QUANTITY DISCOUNTS
WHEN USED TO PROMOTE PRODUCTS OR SERVICES.
FOR INFORMATION PLEASE WRITE TO PREMIUM MARKETING DIVISION,
NEW AMERICAN LIBRARY, 1633 BROADWAY,
NEW YORK, NEW YORK 10019.

SIGNET, SIGNET CLASSIC, MENTOR, PLUME, MERIDIAN
and NAL BOOKS are published by New American Library,
1633 Broadway, New York, New York 10019

First Printing, March, 1986

1 2 3 4 5 6 7 8 9

PRINTED IN THE UNITED STATES OF AMERICA

To my husband, Gregory Brodeur,
who guards every word I write with unbelievable care
and insight—You are still my magic.

And, of course, to Errol Flynn and Patric Knowles,
who brought life to Robin Hood and Will Scarlet
long before I did.

Last night, where under the wild moon
On grassy mattress I had laid me,
Within my arms great Solomon,
I suddenly cried out in a strange tongue
Not his, not mine.

. . . Yet the world ends when these two things,
though several, are a single light,
When oil and wick are burned in one;
Therefore a blessed moon last night
Gave Sheba to her Solomon.

—William Butler Yeats,
    "Solomon and the Witch"

• *Prologue* •

It is the year 1192, deep in the core of the land known as England. The ruling class are descendants of the Norman conquest of 1066 under the Duke of Normandy. The monarchy carries the Norman name Plantagenet, and the king is Richard, called Lionheart. Absent from England on a Crusade to free the Holy Land from "infidels," Richard has clumsily allowed himself to be taken hostage by the king of Austria. His brother, Prince John, called Lackland, has declared himself Prince Regent and set upon a reign of terror to wrest taxes and land from those of Saxon blood, whom the Normans conquered earlier and with whom they have been sharing the land and its fruits. Ever hopeful, the Saxons remain loyal to Richard while the Normans find profit in loyalty to John; John, in turn, is loyal only to himself.

Within this larger struggle are the day-to-day struggles of the people—the same struggles men and women have undergone since the beginning of civilization. And behind every struggle there is a story....

• PART ONE •

LUNASA

• Chapter One •

"Edward Chenoweth, if you die, I swear I'll follow you to the grave."

A bloodless hand slid across the sheets, a hand of memories. There had once been power in that hand, power for the forge and for loving. Power to hammer metal into blades and draw wire to make chain mail and armor for King Richard's armies. But the Lionheart was gone, and the Gentle Heart lay dying. Oh, Edward.

Katie caught her husband's hand and refused to tremble. She leaned over him with her body half on the bed and half off, her gray eyes searching for the last dust of life in his. Edward heaved a rattling breath, nothing at all like the laughter and booming voice that once thundered from his body, now an eaten-out shell of white skin and wasting bones. Even now his eyes glittered each time a breeze carried the odors of brimstone and bog iron from the forge where Gaston and Nick were pounding away their anguish. The rhythmical clank of the hammers seemed to soothe him, so Kate had ordered both apprentices to work hard, hoping Edward's soul might be carried to heaven on the sounds he made in life.

"Edward," she spoke, then held her words. Her voice cracked; she wasn't going to let him see her hopelessness or hear her agony. She had beaten death away from him with doctors, Druids, and every manner of chant until the neighbors cried witchcraft, until Edward could no longer bear it and Katie drove the blood-letters away. Then she had tended him with love and common sense, sponging cool water over him, replacing the oils of his body with herb baths, but nothing would bring back the rosiness of health. Soon Katie could only ease his pain with mandrake root, and it took all her strength to keep from ending the torment with a measure too much of it.

She caressed the gaunt, black-bearded face and thought how much a dying man resembles his own ghost. Today she wouldn't speak to Edward of the smelter, the wheel rims, the bellows, how the month's delivery of mild steel was late coming from Scotland, or how Nick took a chip out of the anvil stump with a bad swing.

Today Edward would finish his dying, and not even Katie's threat to follow could beg him back.

At the very moment anyone else would have pronounced him dead—when the breath fell from his lungs and they had no power to draw more in—Katie held on to his eyes, still seeing the old passion. Edward wasn't going to die alone. Katie Chenoweth put his life in her eyes and held it there.

His fingers tightened on her hand once, twice, three times. I . . . love . . . you.

She squeezed back once, twice, but before she could finish, the luster faded from her eyes. Certainly it was gone forever.

There were eyes more beautiful in the world, but none more intense. Some perfumed maiden's locks were more like the sun, but Kate's thick hair added a yellow glint to the sooty furnace yard. There were women more compelling and more graceful, but Katie had a power of spirit about her that matched Edward's, a determination that grew stronger when Edward's illness took his hand from his hammers.

She was no flaxen-haired Helen, she knew, nor any heroine or temptress from the tales of Delilah, Ishtar, Athena, Antigone, or Guinevere, but she had listened to those stories with every corner of her mind and all the while had felt her heart grow. Beauty of nobility, the nuns said, was holier than pride of the body.

Of course, the nuns did not know a husband's touch, did they?

As she walked from Edward's deathbed, her lips still numb from the last kiss, Katie was aware of how far her belt hung down against her tunic. It had lengthened as her waist narrowed through Edward's illness.

Pity me that I couldn't draw from your lips the disease that took you, my love, so I could die too. The same scourge kept my womb barren from your seed, and now I must go on as your widow without even your baby to hold. I would rather have withered with you, but I still live.

And still living as she was, her first task was to tell Nick and Gaston. Neither she nor Edward was much older than the apprentices, who were seventeen. Edward was—had been— twenty-four, and Katie was twenty-one.

A very old twenty-one.

They had been married for seven hard and profitable years, seven years of growing up hand in hand, struggling through Edward's apprenticeship with Master Dermott, the smith's son, vying for membership to the guild when they opened their own furnace works, finally earning their place in Armorer's Alley here in Southwell. None of it had been easy; all of it had been satisfying.

This was not easy, not satisfying.

Katie felt Gaston's small, alert eyes piercing her shell of strength as she entered the furnace yard.

"Oh, Lord, be merciful," he whispered with a groan, letting his hammer clunk to the packed dirt.

Nick reached out a hand out to him, pain crossing his own deep-set eyes as he read Katie's expression.

Katie leaned on the anvil stump, glad of their wordless acceptance. There were no tears to distort the shallow-water grayness of her eyes; she had cried herself dry long ago. The crying was over, the work was finished, and more was still to be done.

"Oh, Katie, what will become of us?" Gaston said, sobbing.

Nick's voice sounded frighteningly like Edward's. "Would you mourn for us when Edward lies there?" The rolling Scots tongue added spark where he intended none.

"It's Edward on my mind," the sloe-haired lad replied, his words clipped by the faint accent of Anjou. How different he was from the child Edward had dragged back from the Brittany border, a starving street puppy without family or direction. How hard Gaston had worked for them, and how he had come to love Edward's storytelling, even though he understood few of his words in the beginning. "How will we keep his dream alive?"

"The guild will nae deny us membership," Nick said. "They cannae."

"They may," Katie said, bitterness rising in her words. "They owe us nothing. While Edward lived we could keep the forge going, and I could make trade as Edward did—"

"Aye, so you could," Nick agreed. "You're as clever a merchant as any man."

"Man or maid, it was Edward's name on the guild ticket, not his wife's or his apprentices'. Edward and I have no son to pass the shop on to, but you are like his brothers. Whatever becomes of me, we're family, and this furnace will stay afire."

"But—"

Katie closed her eyes and waved one hand, knowing the two lads would understand her signal. The silence weakened them all. In moments Gaston was sobbing again. Nick grasped Gaston's arm and stared absently into the blazing furnace. No doubt he saw Edward's face dancing between the flames. Katie knew that hope would have to grow from the ashes. She

would live again ... later. But for now she
was as dead as Edward. Now was the time for
thought-bare duties. A public crier would have
to be hired to walk the streets, calling the hour
and place of burial. The doors and death room—
Edward, my adored, our marriage bed—would have
to be draped in black. She would summon the
abbey to send Friar Ghent and Friar Cadmus
to wash the body with rosewater, anoint and
enshroud him, and stitch him in elkskin. As
well-to-do burghers, Edward and Katie could
afford to buy a coffin and actually go to earth
in it, unlike the cooper's second wife. A coffin
had been rented for her funeral, but she had
been buried without it.

There were no other worries beyond those
the guild could lay upon her.

Aside from the question of her membership
as a master smith, the guild officers would do
what they could to help a member's widow.
They would pay part of the funeral expenses
and donate a token to charity in Edward's name.
Still, it was a struggle not to be bitter. Katie
couldn't help but recall the fight they'd had to
convince the smiths' guild to let them hire
Nick as a second apprentice. She'd been angry
at them since, and it had been almost two
years. Edward always paid his dues early, always offered discounts to guild members and
their relatives, and Katie figured he was owed
an extra courtesy or two. Edward's will had
long since been prepared, and endowments had
been given to the church ahead of time to
insure Edward's quick journey through purgatory. In deference to his faith, Katie had en-

couraged Edward to do whatever comforted him.

She didn't go back into the death chamber. Edward wasn't there.

Instead Katie went to the tiny garret, a bright place with shuttered windows—oh, how she and Edward had delighted in those fine shutters—and opened them onto the bustling business of Armorer's Alley. She could see the shops of the helmet-maker, the harness-maker, the armorer, the locksmith, the swordsman, the buckle-maker, the old clothes-mender, the oil merchant—and she could smell the butchery. People shuffled busily up and down the narrow street. At the alley's end Katie could see the stand of trees that skirted York Street Abbey, and in her mind she heard the Gregorian liturgical chants that always made her sleepy.

She unbound her hair and fingered the yellow plaits until they fell loosely over her shoulders and past her waist. Suddenly she thought of her mother. Inanna of the Willow, her people called her, plain of face and beautiful in her communion with the trees. She was always able to tell the farmers when to harvest, that perfect day when the corn was ripe and could not ripen more without beginning to wither. Katie had often heard the villagers comment that her mother must be the handmaiden of the Mother Goddess. But today was August twenty-first, and soon, after the food-gathering, the Goddess would give the countryside over to the Horned God and the land would begin to darken. For those of the Old Religion, like Katie, today was the first day of Lunasa.

*   *   *

Katie wore her best gown for the funeral—
her wedding gown, in fact. It was long and
simple, flaring below the hips, and the color
was the green of new apples. The draping
sleeves were embroidered with roses and vines,
and she had a matching embroidered belt that
rode on her hips. There was also a wonderful
bluebird stitched on the skirt near her knee
where the old clothes-mender had closed a tear.
Guild rules prevented him from making it look
like new, lest he compete with the new clothes
merchants, so he had disguised his work with
this pretty bird. Katie liked the bird. She called
it "little minstrel" and often pretended it was
singing to her. A smile touched her lips even
now. Edward used to hide in her wardrobe
and twitter a tune, whereupon Katie would
say, "Is that my little minstrel calling? What
can he want of me?" And the tune would get
exciting.

Today she put a wimple on her head and
wore a black shawl, and she walked behind
Edward's bier to the chancel. Nick and Gaston
walked at either side of her, wailing the loud
laments expected of the family, but all Katie
could do was make her feet go in the proper
direction. If they'd said her soul was in danger, still she couldn't have squeezed up a single tear. Her pain was too deep for display,
and her mother had taught her that public
keening was a showing off, not a true measure
of love for the dead.

The procession continued to the burial grounds
with candles lit and monks leading the way.
There were many mourners: sincere friends
and colleagues as well as a group of beggars

whom Katie would pay alms to for carrying candles.

There, in a shallow cross-shaped trench, Katie Chenoweth left the body of her beloved Edward. She gave him to his Christ or to the Horned God of her own people, leaving it to them to decide where his soul would spend Eternity. In these strange, detached moments Katie felt charitable toward neither of these nearby religions or their gods—neither had helped her keep Edward at her side. Edward's Christian beliefs had comforted him but had done nothing more, and all the comfort had been within himself. He had tried to share it with Katie but had always understood her choice, her decision to remain part of her mother's Old Religion. He hadn't tried to make her pretend toward Christianity, though he might have felt safer if she had. So Katie had found no solace in belief; even the Horned God, who would take over the year as autumn began, refused to turn his divine ways toward changing the inevitable. The gods must not care to alter the lives of men, she concluded, and looked inside herself for strength. She called upon that strength now, at this moment of true aloneness.

All that remained was to go home, to sleep alone.

But as she and the lads turned back, they realized they were being watched—glared at, in fact—by the shopkeepers and patrons they passed.

"What is it they want?" Gaston whispered.

"Ignore them," Katie said.

"Look," Nick pointed out. "See hae Mistress Heloise glowers at us. Why would she?"

"I care not. I only want my home, a warm fire, and some of your leek-and-shallot soup."

They continued to walk, but soon the whispers surfaced.

"There she is."

"Shed not a tear for him."

" 'Tis said she cannot weep, or she'll burn in it."

"Did you know her mother is a Druid?"

"She's always worked hard. . . ."

". . . always speaks kindly to me . . ."

". . . loved her husband?"

". . . not a Christian . . ."

". . . Druid . . ."

". . . pagan . . ."

"That's why he died."

"They say he had no blood to let."

". . . punished for marrying a pagan . . ."

Katie burst away from Gaston and Nick, running through the arbor of eyes until the door of her own house clapped shut behind her, but the echoes wouldn't die.

"Katie! Katie, come quickly! There's a crowd gathered out your door!"

The shutters of the garret clanked open seconds after Nick called. Katie went boldly out onto the loggia. Yes, there was a small crowd.

"What do you want, neighbors?"

They seemed startled by her firm voice and lack of shyness. She took the moment to survey the torchlit faces. There was Sally, the cooper's third wife, and there was the cooper. Behind him was a collection of merchants, a few nuns and monks, some peddlers, Henry the Chandler, Beatrice Johnson, Albert Gilmore, Roland Taggart, and many others she knew.

And at the head of them all, Abbot Godfrey. She didn't like Abbot Godfrey.

"A word with you, Mistress Chenoweth," his round face said.

"I'm listening, good sir."

"We have a concern."

Katie shifted her feet. "Then speak it."

"It's said you shed no tears nor mourned at all at the mastersmith's passing. Many of this company think this may be because you haven't accepted our Lord Jesus Christ as your Savior."

" 'Tis true. I have not. It's no secret to any of you."

"Then you cling to your mother's pagan ways?"

"My mother is a gentle and educated woman of the Old Religion, and I have no shame in finding her wise."

The crowd buzzed among themselves until Katie tired of their sudden suspicion. These were her neighbors! Why this childish behavior? Katie silenced them with her voice.

"What is it you fear in me? Have any of your babies disappeared? Have I not worked beside you all these years? Is there one of you who hasn't a link or a hinge hammered in this shop?"

There was another shuffle in the group, accompanied by nods and shrugs. She pushed on. "If you come here looking for tears, you'll go home empty-handed. My sorrow is within me and not yours to see. Or are you vultures that you hunger so for a woman's agony?"

Evidently she had chosen good words.

"She speaks truly," someone said.

"Yet if we let her continue in business, will God punish us?"

Oh, what silliness!

The abbot considered this. "We shall leave it for God to decide. If you prove yourself worthy, and if this community will do well to have you here in your husband's stead, your success will show that God is not against you."

The crowd rippled its approval, but Kate narrowed her eyes. "And what deed have you in mind that I must do?"

Abbot Godfrey turned to confer with the cluster while Katie could do nothing but wait. How exasperating! Why must people allow their ignorance to drive them to fear? Was it easier to fear than to learn? Did they get some joy from crying witchcraft when they knew better? There was no one here whom Katie hadn't traded with in some capacity, but the whispering had started, and like the first falling leaf of autumn, it had signaled a rush.

"Come down here," he said then. "Face me in person, unless you quake at the nearness of divine extension." His small, deep-socketed eyes narrowed and grew ugly.

Katie tapped her toe against the inside of the balcony in disgust. The abbot was no mystery to her. "I'll come down."

Nick followed her down the stairs to the solar, vying for her attention and hissing, "Dinnae trust him, Katie. He's a demon in cleric's robes! He'll skin you and eat you and rape your bones, dead or not!"

"Nicholas, for pity's sake."

"His mouth is a gate into hell."

"I can't be sent to a place I don't believe in," she said calmly. "Believing is everything, Nick. Terror lives there. Stand out of my way, thank you."

In a moment the abbot was pacing around her solar, fingering her possessions and raising his eyebrow at Edward's small iron crucifix, which hung over their table. "You have fallen under the watchful eye of the Church now that your husband is dead. That eye may protect you or burn you for a heretic, for such is the ultimate power of the Almighty. His hand shakes the earth beneath us, and if the earth parts, you may find yourself tumbling into hell if you cannot make recompense with the Lord and His followers here in Southwell."

Katie looked at him. Unlike the townspeople who waited, she didn't see the abbot through a religious shroud and had no worries about his divine powers. She knew he was just another piece in a complex puzzle, another bit of evidence that her world was fading. A new force was moving in. This was a time of change. Edward had been dead now for over five weeks; in a way Katie had accepted his death many weeks before it had actually come. She knew she would be on her own, and she had been ready. Her neighbors had shown no qualms about working with her. But in that time the abbot had clearly been chiseling away at their security with her Old Religion. He had made them afraid of her.

Still, she couldn't resist saying, "That means you and those others out there?"

There was no merciful deity involved in his

glare as he twisted his head like an apple on a stick. She saw the truth, cold and knifelike, on his face. She wasn't a threat to his god. She was a threat to *him*. "Take care, woman," he breathed. "You know what the law dictates we must do to proven heretics. They must be made public. Their bodies must be purged of demons. By blade, spike, or screw, the devil marks must be found. There is talk in the higher clergy of declaring heresy punishable by death. Do you hear? This, to me, means burning. For only fire can consume itself, and fire is the drowning water of devils."

With quiet sickness at the realization that peaceful ideas of comfort could become so perverted, Katie muttered, "There are no devils." She never knew whether he heard her or not. Cannily she moved to the door and nudged it open, allowing in all the curious stares from the street. These people were willing to condemn her or defend her on a whim, and if they could hear what the abbot was saying, he might be tied a little more securely to fairness. "What recompense"—she almost choked on the word—"do you require?"

"There is a task to do. It will benefit our town. Four men have died in the attempt. But even outlaws must answer to God, and I think they may not murder a woman."

Outlaws! Murder?

"The Cart Road across the River Trent has been under siege for three months, and trade is suffering. You will go there, find the thieves who commit travesty against the Crown, and negotiate with them to open the road."

"What?" Nick bellowed from behind Katie. "Daft ould man!"

"You expect me to deal with murderers?" Katie stared at him.

"If God is with you, you will be triumphant."

"If God was with me, my husband would not be dead!"

The crowd gasped at that, forcing Katie to cap her insult and fury. She knew her future was down there in the street, to be spared or trampled at their whim.

"If I do this task," she began, thinking as she went, "I want an oath from you in return." Her gray eyes locked with the abbot's, mesmerizing him and specifically telling him that the responsibility had shifted.

"You dare make demands upon the church?"

"Nay. Upon *you*. It is you to whom the tithes of trade are paid. If I go to the outlaws and open the Cart Road, you will insure my name in the smiths' guild membership. You will see that my shop is not inspected while I am gone, and my apprentices will receive a nominal wage to make up for me."

Moments passed. Katie could only hear the roar of her own breathing, the thump of blood in her ears. The abbot's dour face was a carving—unreadable.

"Those are good terms," someone called.

"Aye, they're fair."

"Give her the bargain!"

"Aye!"

"Aye, give it!"

Clerical robes dusted the floor. It was well known that the abbot desired the approval of his parish, and desire showed plainly in his eyes as they darted back and forth to the ca-

dence of the shouts. He knew that his words—
yea or nay—would have to be calm and correct
enough to quell this storm. These people paid
tithes to him, his percentage of their sweat
kept him in mutton and silk. He knew it, and
so did Katie.

"I give it," he said.

Very low, she murmured, "Then I agree."

• Chapter Two •

Sssstthok!

One-quarter buried in oak bark, the shaft hummed an inch from his nose. He closed his eyes and swallowed the closeness of death, refusing to let the shock in his body show up on his face as he turned to glare at the arrow's source.

"Pox on you, cousin," he said, gripping the thick branch he was perched on. "You might have made me fall out of this hank of God's hair."

From the tree on the other side of the road, his cousin tugged a green cowled hood up over his head, revealing only a few light curls, a trimmed beard, and a mustache surrounding his grin. His eyes danced as he strung another arrow on a yew longbow and quietly called back, "You make a fine bow in God's hair, Will. Cover those red stockings or they'll give us away."

Will pulled deerskin boots higher on his legs, hiding his stockings, and muttered, "Be hanged."

"Someday I want to shoot like he does," Alan said.

"You do, boy, and this hand'll help you to hell."

Alan laughed, careful to keep his voice down, and eyed an approaching group of horsemen and a wagon. "Looks like a juicy treat for us, this one. I wonder what the wagon carries. It might be food. Or clothes. Do you think it could be clothes?"

"That would do well by the children of the wood, but for my cousin's sake, let's hope it's a booty of silver to add to King Richard's ransom." Will was talking, but his mind was occupied with something entirely different. In seconds he had the horses counted, their positions noted, and had guessed the sizes and weights of the riders plus the two men in the wagon. He made the appropriate signals to the other tree.

"How many?" Alan asked. "Six?"

"Seven. On the large side. Hired men, no doubt. The merchant means to get his wares by us." Will adjusted the brown cloak that hid his bright clothes so his sleeves wouldn't show. The cloak had a simple design, as good as a cape but without no opening other than a hole to put his head through. It was a large circle of fabric, and the hole was off center, making the back hang long and the front hang exactly to the wrist. The cloak was a little tattered on the hem after a year of vaulting through trees, but he loved it anyway. Will's frequent emotional attachment to pieces of clothing was a constant source of entertainment for his rascally relative across the road. He took great joy in seeing how much of Will's clothing he could put holes in without actually putting holes in Will. "He's either wealthy enough to take such precautions," Will said thoughtfully, "or we've hurt him before. I don't recognize the wagon. Ah . . . what's this?"

"What?"

"Behind them, at a distance. It seems they have a rearguard. One lone rider . . . not as big as these . . . armed. He'll bear watching. As it is, we're outnumbered."

"Told you we should've brought Reynold and his sons."

"I'll listen next time."

Alan smiled his appreciation at the more experienced man's approval and loaded his own bow, waiting for a signal from the other tree. They fell silent. Will reached up and tested a rope strung from tree to tree, then slipped the loop of a short leather thong over his hand. On one end of the strip of leather was the loop; on the other end was a plum-sized knot. It was an ingenious invention, the brainchild of the huge-boned man in the other tree. The loop went around the wrist so the thong could be gripped like the long end of a hangman's noose. Will secured the loop on his wrist, hooked the knot over the rope, and grasped the thong, bracing his other hand on the knot. He breathed slowly and was still.

The plodding sound of hooves and a creaking wheel filled the air around them. The forest mother concealed them in her leafy boughs, in the darkness of her shadows. Here, the sunlight came only in dusty shafts, confusing to unaccustomed eyes.

The merchant's party clip-clopped nearer. Yes, Will could see now, the horsemen were hired guards. They all wore the blue gloves that were typical of this shire's mercenaries, making them easy to find and providing an obvious threat to robbers. Will almost laughed out loud. Surely these men knew their gloves would be more bait than he and his friends could stand. No man of spirit could turn away such a challenge.

When the wagon was fully beneath them, Will put his weight on the rope, aimed, and pushed off. Like a great tiercel, he flew downward. Twigs snapped as he crashed through the branches, his weight pulling the rope groundward, matched by the other man coming down on the other side.

A horse screamed and reared up, meeting Will's body in midair. Only by lifting his feet did he clear the horse's head and catch the rider in his legs. The world tumbled around him. Something hard rang against his head, making him fight for consciousness as he grappled his quarry flat to the ground. His vision blackened for a few precious seconds. His arms felt weak, but he gritted his teeth, willed himself not to pass out, and freed the hand with the thong. Leaning to one side, he backhanded his opponent with the hard leather knot. Will stumbled to his feet, dazed and fighting for balance in a gaggle of crazed horses. Twice his feet were stepped on before he cleared them and shook his vision almost back to normal.

"Hold! Hold still or you're pigs on a spit!" his cousin's voice ordered from high above. Will knew arrows were aimed on them, no

longer hidden. Across from him his bearded
friend and two others had unhorsed their share
of guards. Only two of the hired men were
still saddled. "Throw down your swords.
Down!"

Metal clattered. Will's ears continued singing long after. He tried to look steady and
threatening, but it was hard just to stay on his
feet. In an effort to keep his balance he snatched
the reins of a riderless horse and leaned on
them, hoping it looked like he was holding the
horse and not the other way around.

"You're taking a horrid chance, vassal," one
of the guards said. "You're tangling with worthy foes."

"Aye, I hope you're worth much," the tree
said. "Take back the cover on that wagon, will
you, fearsome foe?"

"If I refuse?"

"Refuse away, lordling, I've plenty arrows.
One for each toe at least. Johnny, help him
take that cover back."

"You common bitch's brood, you'll pay with
your blood for this."

Something in the guard's voice was troublesome; it wasn't the voice of a man on the short
end of destiny. Will fought to understand it,
but the buzz in his ears confounded him, so he
kept silent while his cousin spoke.

"Nay, piglet, it's King Richard's blood we'll
pay for when we buy him back from captivity."

"I was unaware the king of Austria was taking merchants' wares in trade for royalty. You
ask me to believe that none of this finds its
way into nearer pockets?"

"Farther away than yours, Johnny."

The big bearded man jolted the guard around as a child tosses a doll, forcing him toward the wagon. Will watched all this with practiced calm. His head was still ringing, but at least his eyes had cleared and he could focus on the lumpy burlap cover on the wagon. It helped him stay balanced to focus on one lump and think about sending the pain away. Doing better ... better ... the lump was only moving slightly now, not undulating like everything had when he first got hit. He blinked and—something registered.

"Johnny, it's a trap!" he shrieked without thinking. His leather knot thwacked on the horse's rump, causing a storm among the beasts. He dodged between horses and men, snatching up a sword. The burlap came alive, and the wagon was suddenly full of swordsmen, all bearing the crest of the shire. Deputies!

"A trap! Run!" Fear gripped him—a cold insanity that knotted his muscles and made him expect the slice of a blade through his body. Beyond the wagon the vicious glint of Johnny's felling ax took sunlight and traded it for blood. The trees came alive as the outnumbered thieves scrambled to escape with their skins. Will himself took down two men before the sword was wrenched from his hands, now bleeding from hacks and near misses. All around him swarmed the shire crest, striking panic into his heart.

"Run! Johnny, the horses!"

Will vaulted onto the nearest horse and prayed the others would follow his lead. The animal pranced under him in confusion, then gathered and bolted for freedom.

The ferns and rushes peeled away under shod hooves. Will put his thoughts in front of him and concentrated on escape, forcing himself not to look back. It wasn't easy fending off the urge to guess which of his companions would live and which would die. Perhaps the archers in the trees would turn the odds in their favor, he could only hope.

He caught the mare's rein and steered directly for the ravine, a great gouge in the rib of the land where the River Trent cut a path between steep cliffs. Hoofbeats thundered up behind him, but he didn't look. Looking would only throw him and his horse off-balance, losing them precious strides. The ravine came up before him. The earth fell away. He felt the mare gathering for an impossible jump. Death laughed from two directions.

Will wasn't a man to be laughed at. With a wild shout he hauled up on the reins. The beast screamed in protest and veered, hooves beating on the loose ground at the edge of the ravine. Bits of grass and soil flew away, careening downward to crash along the crags to the river. Will dug his heels into the mare's flanks, yanked to the left, and urged her into a gallop. He followed the cliff until the river bent eastward, until the trees on the opposite side were thick and tall, skirted with man-high rushes. Plenty enough to hide in. Another few strides and he saw what he was looking for.

The horse never even stopped running. Foam from her mouth flecked her hot flanks and spat in Will's face as he leaned treacherously to the right. In her confusion the mare pushed her head forward, seeking a hand on the reins, and pounded faster.

Will held his breath, forced his body to go limp, and released the horse. The rushes whipped his face. The ground crashed up against him like a giant hand slapping him insensible. His hands clutched at the rushes, barely preventing him from tumbling off the cliff's edge. Somehow his feet found solidity, and he was running, gripping the leather thong still looped around his wrist. With an insane yell—part panic and part victory—he tossed the knotted end over a line of hemp that reached from a root on his side of the river to a tree on the other side. Without breaking stride he grasped the knot and flew off the cliff. Momentum carried him downward, outward, in a flight over the river into the rushes and headlong into a birch tree. Shaking himself, he got to his feet.

Just in time to be smashed silly by an immense body.

"Get off me, you great ox!" He grunted as Johnny rolled to one side. Will made a headlong dive, knife in hand, and slashed the escape rope before their pursuers could join them. "That'll do it. Let's hope the others made away as cleanly as we did."

The big face with black whiskers nodded.

"How many men came out of that wagon?" Will asked.

Johnny's eyes widened. He held up all ten fingers, then two.

"That many? We'll have to make sure this doesn't happen again."

The mute nodded agreement, his thick eyebrows raised in amazement that they had been attacked, yet had managed to get away against such odds. He flipped a rag over his head, clutching it to his chin, and imitated a doddering beggar.

Will grunted. "Yes. Next time we'll manage to peek in the wagon. Come on." He clapped a vast shoulder. "Let's hie back to camp and see who lived. Or didn't."

Since they were on the wrong side of the river, it took Will and Johnny some time to get back across without attracting the deputies. But in the forest the advantage was theirs. Here, the trees, moss, rocks, and ferns worked for them. Will's brown cloak and Johnny's green-and-buff clothes and jerkin made them as good as invisible. Johnny looked more like a bear than a man as he trundled out of the bushes. In an hour the familiar clutter of their camp broke out before them, and Will started anxiously counting heads.

The camp was abuzz with familiar voices—Bluestocking, Will Stutley ("the other Will"), Roger Reynoldson and his four brothers, and the women who stayed with the band and provided for their many needs. A stew pot gurgled on a fire, and the bowers of the oaks provided a perfect ceiling. It was a symphony of welcome sights and smells for Will, but heart's ease didn't come until he spied the face he was looking for.

"Will!" His cousin hurried toward them. "Johnny. We feared for you."

Will inhaled a breath. Oh, that stew was savory! "And we for you," he said, sighing his first breath of relief. "What a folly, Robin. Did you know there were a dozen men in that wagon?"

"A dozen and two," Robin corrected. He touched the sore spot on Will's head. "I saw you take a nasty hit. How do you feel?"

"Like a lucky man. How are the others?"

"Oh, well enough. Alan took an arrow in his thigh before I noticed they had an archer, and Stutley got a blade at his shoulder, but we've been hurt worse, and we sent some of Prince John's puppets to hell."

"With our fright more than our skill. That was a poor show for us, Robin, to be cornered so easily."

"Verily. My soul is sick within me to think we came so close to chains, or worse."

"There *is* nothing worse than chains for this crew, cousin. And I—Robin, have you sacked a roedeer?" They approached a large sack writhing on the ground, and Will circled it. "Taking prisoners?"

"More like an uninvited guest. This one was following you."

"Me?"

"Aye, lurking after you and Johnny just before you reached the river."

"So why didn't you dispatch him with the others?"

Robin folded his arms. "Against my morals."

Will laughed. "Since when?"

"Open the guest room and see for yourself."

"It must be something to see indeed. Let me stand away for a good view. Oh, no, you don't. . . . You stay within arm's length in case I end up needing revenge. Bluestocking! Come over here and open this strange haggis, will you?"

A short curly-haired man laughed his agreement, unsheathed a dagger, and ripped into the wriggling sack.

Will was still chuckling as he pulled the cloak over his head and hung it on his arm. When Bluestocking finally yanked the stitching from the sack and pulled it free of its captive, the smile fell from Will's lips.

For an instant, for eternity, the world stood still.

• Chapter Three •

When Katie shook herself free of the awful, smelly bag she'd spent at least an hour in, her hair was tangled, her wrists raw, and her temper was in an even sorer condition. There had been a dirty rag stuffed in her mouth, since her captors had grown tired of her complaints. Now someone sliced the bindings on her wrists; she yanked the rag from her teeth and spat away the taste. Oh, it was rank too. She perched on the remains of her sack—as if her experience hadn't been downgrading enough so far— staring at a pack of jackals in rags. And a stinking lot they were, too; unclean and untidy and unapproachable. A few steps away bubbled a pot of something very rank. Did they mean to eat it or boil her in it?

She coughed the dust from her lungs and tossed the one long braid of hair behind her back where it belonged. For too long she'd been tossed around with that braid under her nose. She opened her mouth to shriek her opinion, but no sound would come out. Instead she merely stared. It was all she could do.

He was standing before her. The Horned

God himself. See, Edward? You should never have tried to convert me. I was right all along.

She stared dry-lipped at him.

He was clad mostly in scarlet—deep like blood, not bright like a cardinal's wings—scarlet hose, shirt, cowl, and belt. His jerkin was of soft, mustard-colored deerskin, laced from belly to chest and without sleeves, allowing the floppy sleeves of his shirt to move freely on long arms. His boots were more like knee-high slippers than the sturdy brogues Katie preferred and were also made of deerskin. They seemed perfect for secreting about the forest.

But even the startling scarlet against dark greenery couldn't draw Katie's stare from his face. His eyes were an unremarkable brown, but their rectangular shape made them captivating, and they stood out from his frame of golden hair. While Katie's hair was platinum, thick, long, and too wavy, this man had sleek locks any woman would have envied. They were the color of brass and brushed against his collar rather than stopping at the jaw like most men's. And he was completely beardless. It was odd that his face could be so bare and smooth yet remain so manly. His nose was long and had a slight slope, distinguishing his profile and providing a line that carried her gaze right back to those eyes— but not before she noticed a set of thick, half-grinning lips. Not a classic face at all. Not even handsome, yet . . . spellbinding.

Yes, he must be the Horned God himself. His eyes were hunting. His antlers were heavy, dipping his head, and his shoulders sagged a little from the weight of legend.

He was an incongruity here, among thieves. Part of him belonged, but only part.

After a blink or two she decided the antlers might really be a white plume in a scarlet cap.

"Saints take me," he murmured. "A changeling."

Katie got the feeling he wanted to laugh at her—her clumsiness at being caught and the way she had followed him—but it seemed he couldn't make himself do it. She jolted to one side as another man, very stocky and carrying a dagger, moved next to her and cut the bindings on her ankles. In spite of the pain of cramped legs and the retarded flow of blood in her feet, she struggled up and stood proudly before them, looking around her. The Horned God was standing next to a man of his own age who wore quite different clothing. This one was dressed more like the others: in logan-green foresting clothes, leather jerkin, broad waist belt made for holding weapons and water skins, and a long strap with a hunting horn. His hair and beard were blond, too, but this was a duskier blond, like the last glimpse of sunlight on a sandy road before sunset.

"Are you the leaders?" she asked them firmly.

"Leaders, little dove?" the Horned God asked.

"You know what I mean."

He pursed his lips and scratched his ear. "Care to admit to it, cousin? Seems we have a vixen in our bag."

"I'm the leader," Robin said, rather tersely. "Who are you?"

She drew a deep breath. "My name is Katie Chenoweth. I'm a blacksmith from the town of Southwell. I've been sent here to negotiate with you to reopen the Cart Road to the shallow crossing of the River Trent. Tell me your price and I'll tell you if we can meet it."

The men before her stared. The scarlet-clad man couldn't resist a snicker, and suddenly the silence fell away in waves of laughter.

"God-a-mercy," a tall, brown-haired man murmured from her right side.

The one who had called himself leader grinned and turned away. "Take over, Will. I shan't deal with this."

The scarlet one grabbed his leader's elbow. "Stay, coward. I've seen you face bigger foes."

"Bigger but more beatable."

"Lady, don't you fear what price we could demand of you?"

"I must hope that even thieves have some code of honor regarding how much they steal," Katie said.

"Oh? We have a right to steal a person's goods—"

"But not a person's very soul."

"I'm always amazed at the variety of places God may hide a woman's very soul." His companions laughed with him, at Katie's expense. "What say you, friends? Which one of you wants the first taste of this sweet morsel? Or *saucy* might be a better word."

This joking had gone far enough. Katie squared her shoulders and clenched her jaw. "If you're going to rape me, then do it and be done, so we can bargain as equals."

"You . . . *want* us to rape you?"

"If it will keep you from killing me, yes. If it will hurry along your ability to think with your heads and not your breeches."

Again there was laughter all around, but this time it was with her, and the peacock's cheeks soon matched his sleeves.

"She's got you there, Will," the leader said.

Katie shook in her shoes, hoping her ruse would work. If they thought rape wouldn't cost her much, perhaps they wouldn't consider it a weapon. She only hoped they wouldn't consider it an offer. "At least do me the courtesy of knowing the names of those I must deal with."

The two men shared a comical shrug.

"Fair enough," the peacock said, and one by one he ticked off the men who stood in the clearing. "Yonder is Will Stutley. Next to him are Roger and Padraic Reynoldson; beyond them, Alan o' Dale and Edmund Bluestocking; and the big, fuzzy, silent one is John Little Naylor. This beside me is the one to whom our fealty is paid. He is my cousin, Robert Fitzooth of Locksley. Here we call him Robin o' the Hood."

So. That one. He was well known in this part of England. Katie had always assumed the stories were bigger than the man himself. He wasn't actually a tall man—hardly the snaggletoothed, winged giant he was made out to be by imaginative tongues. His scarlet-clad companion was almost a hand taller.

The measuring brought her attention back to the dynamic one. "And your name, sir?"

"My name I left on a tract of land now claimed by a false crown. In these forests I am reborn," he said, "as Will Scarlet."

Carefully she noted, "I see why."

"Why should we do business with you?" Robin o' the Hood asked.

"Why should you not?"

"Lady, I don't like games."

"I don't offer any."

Will Scarlet put a hand on his cousin's shoulder. "I'll play with this one for you, Robin. She makes me . . . curious."

Katie allowed the anger inside her to rise on her face at last. "Scum, if my Edward wasn't—"

"Oh, spare me!" Will implored, mocking her. "All I need is a rattling of 'Brave Edward' stories. Surely were he here, he'd tie us to a tree and tickle us nigh to death with the end of your braid. If Edward be such a fearsome knight, why are you here in his stead? Of course! Edward must be off on Crusades with the Lionheart. That explains it, doesn't it, fellows? Any man gone crusading on the shirttails of a king should leave such a woman behind. Lady, I've heard it all before. I'm sure Edward is brave. He's gallant, he's noble, he's brutal, he's gentle, he's—"

"He's dead. These past five weeks."

The air between them went stone cold.

The moment belonged to Katie.

Will Scarlet had trouble defining what stirred in his chest at the sight of the pale vestige of womanhood before him. He was used to lovely women being either shy or vain. Lovely? Yes, she had a corn-pure loveliness, but there was no character flaw in this one, none so plain as vanity. She stood before him with her feet buried in the torn folds of that sack as though in a mound of rubies, and each time he tried to make fun of her, that pointed chin would go up a little more. She had deliberately let him rant, knowing exactly when to let him cut his own throat. He didn't like being made a fool before his friends—always loyal yet so eager to taunt—but something deep inside told him this was worth looking foolish for.

Her eyes were gray, like dark diamonds, if such gems could exist. And unflinching. When was the last time a woman had met his glare like this?

His lips went dry. He couldn't blink. His fascination with her blunt courage was nearly enough to choke him. He felt Robin's concerned grip on his arm. Probably Robin thought the bump on his head had dazed him. Will told himself he'd have to shake out of it or look even sillier than he already did, but it would take more than a clunk on the skull to make his chest pound and his legs tingle like this.

What was her name? Katie . . . Katie.

Simple, like her.

Brave and womanly. Like her.

Reputation be damned!

"I . . . " he began, then corrected the emptiness of his voice. "Forgive me. That was thoughtless."

She dipped those intriguing, bold eyes for the first time. "You are a gentleman." Her eyelashes brushed his very soul.

Will was used to women who were combed, curried, and perfumed. This one was plain, even musty. And he couldn't understand what she was doing here, taking this deadly ravage-wish among thieves. "Come, milady fox. We have a scrub pail just your size."

Katie frowned at the insult, wanting to spit in his face. But . . . she did tire of the grit between her fingers and thighs, grinding each time she moved her legs. Still, her stubbornness clung. "I'm here to bargain."

"Robin, she's here to bargain."

"I don't feel like bargaining," the Hood said.

Will turned to Katie with a look of false concern. "He doesn't want to bargain."

Up went the little chin. "Then I stay till he does."

"Walk with me, then, and I'll introduce you to a cloth and water."

It was a courteous enough invitation, even from a highwayman. Katie turned to follow him and winced, perplexed when she felt him feel the end of her long braid. Was he so fascinated with her hair? It was hair, nothing more. Why were his fingers in it?

The tingle of his touch rippled from her spine to her scalp and lay there shivering like a bird; yet within her mind the only reaction was a strange, foreign question, as though she had forgotten something she was supposed to know.

"Tell me again your lovely name," Will Scarlet said as they walked past the aromatic stew pot. Suddenly he was hungry and gave the pot a longing look.

"Katie Chenoweth," she said, holding her breath until they were past the cauldron that smelled of dead fish. "You aren't the only one who may leave a name behind in the folding past."

His engaging brown eyes, in their cuffs of gold lashes, took hold of her. "You have another name?"

Katie blinked. She hadn't told him that, had

she? She'd never told anyone, except Edward and her mother's folk, who already knew it. The foreign stirring moved within her again. Her lips parted. "My . . . name is . . . is Cerridwyn. When I married Edward, we knew he had poor future in Gwynedd—you know it as North Wales—and we migrated to Southwell. We thought it wise that I have an English name, so I took the name of a woman who helped me when I was ill with Edward's child."

"You have a child?"

"I had a quickening, but the baby was miscarried." Time's slow hand kept that old sadness from tainting her voice. "I know now it was the illness that killed Edward. His seed was as sick as he was and died with him."

If there was empathy in Will, he didn't show it. "Cerridwyn. So musical. Tell me"—he interrupted himself then—"why aren't you afraid of us? Surely you know we kill on a whim. No one has ever left these woods who wasn't loyal to Robin from hair to bone. What magic or faith keeps Cerridwyn unafraid?"

"No magic. It doesn't matter if you kill me. There is no life left in me to take away. You would only be doing for me something I can't do for myself. I've been dead for many days, and I'll be dead for the rest of my life."

"Dear lady!" He spun before her, a wave of buff and scarlet, and took her by the shoulders. "All this for a dead love?"

Was he surprised that it could be so? "He died in my arms," she said.

Will glanced down. Her body was draped in a belted white tunic and stockings, her breasts like round dewdrops clinging to a flower. "I

know of less succulent places to die. Come.
Have supper with us. I may be able to soothe
the heart of fair Cerridwyn with a melody. I
can sing a little.''

For the first time her rowanberry mouth
curved its corners upward. ''I can listen.''

The greenwood was abuzz with human life.
Katie would never have guessed from the road
that the thick ferns, foliage, and trees could
hide so many people. Were all of these bandits
and their families? She didn't ask. The path
was rootbound, vines and low boughs making
walking difficult, and she followed Will in silence as he plowed the way for her. He was
strong and sure, step after hacking step, through
oak branches and tangled overgrowth so thick
that Katie was sure they'd lost their way. Shame
at her clumsiness in the forest sneaked up on
her. Her mother, they said, was tree-wise, and
Katie wished she could be too. Yet she had
been more at home at Edward's anvil than in
the greenwood, despite her childhood in the
countryside. Her home had been on the coast
of the Irish Sea, near Drenwy, and there the
land was rocky and sparse, not lush like this.

A branch rife with serrated brown-green
leaves whipped out of nowhere, caught her
across her throat, and knocked her into a bush.
She reached outward to save herself but crashed
down, feeling foolish. It didn't matter; he would
come back for her.

And he did.

''I should've left you in the sack and put you
over my shoulder.'' His long, scarlet arms
pierced the green curtain and hauled her to
her feet. ''Can you do it?''

"I'll do it," she shot back, disgusted both with his tone and her own clumsiness. A Druid should be more graceful. "I need no one's shoulder, least of all a thief's."

His eyes flashed. "Hold your tongue until your mind knows more."

When the woodlands released them into a clearing, Katie's belt was loose, her stockings torn, one shoe was missing—was this weedy thing in her hand a shoe?—and her hair was wrenched to a half-braided mangle. She stumbled after Will down a hill into a tree-bare hollow. Overhead hung a thick canopy of boughs and vines. Katie imagined it would keep out even a good rain.

And here there were children. Ragged but well fed and clean, with bright eyes and curious, unafraid glances. Some of the smaller ones—beautiful, rosy-faced, and healthy—approached her and tried to touch her. Katie drew her hands away.

Will noticed.

He said nothing of it. "Marian," he called through the cluster of men and women also quietly looking, "I have a changeling for you. Marian, where are you?"

"Here! Behind the tree."

"Come with me," he said to Katie, and led her on, past people sitting and working here as though the greenwood were the most common place to live. A thin woman smiled as she held a wriggly newborn to her breast. Katie returned the smile and continued to follow Will.

Splashes. Laughter. The laughter of children.

They came upon two children. White-blond, twin girls, maybe two summers old. And a woman, her sleeves pulled back, sponging clear water over them in a small washtub. She brushed back a tuft of very curly dusk-black hair that was tamed by a single bronze circlet around her head. Her eyes were black and full of delight as she greeted them from across the hollow. The gown she wore was finely embroidered, like a bit of silk tapestry clinging to her body, but she seemed not to care if it got splashed or if the hem was muddy.

"She's Robin's lady," Will told Katie. "Marian Fitzwalter."

"His wife?"

"Nay . . . his lady."

"Ah."

"You disapprove?"

She looked straight at him. "Not at all. Marriage is in the heart." Well, that silenced him.

Marian lifted one baby from the tub, Will the other. The two naked bottoms wobbled off into the hollow, glinting in patchy shafts of sun, toward the arms of an ugly little man who clearly adored them.

Marian came to Katie, saying, "Welcome. It feels wonderful to see another woman of my own age. Most here are younger with babies, or older with many children. You look tired, dear! And your clothes are torn. Is this your shoe? Sit down and I'll mend that rip in your tunic. Will, comb out her hair, will you?" She handed him a comb and fluttered her hand at him.

Katie began, "I don't really need—"

"Oh, Will doesn't mind, do you? He's always happy to have his fingers in a woman's locks, aren't you, Will?"

He opened his mouth. "Sometimes it's—"

"Sit down now, dear. I think I have a needle and thread right here ... oh, where is it? Yes, right here. Go ahead, Will, comb."

Will smirked knowingly and motioned Katie to a stump obviously used as a chair. Katie did as she was told; she was too exhausted by now to do otherwise. The journey from Southwell had been day-long and tedious—nearly twelve miles—and Robin's men had been less than hospitable. Of course, she'd fought them and even done some damage, but there had been four of them and a bag.

Oh—that sensation! Hands undoing her braid, fluffing the never-cut lengths of hair. Her eyelids began to shut. The comb moving along her scalp, raking the thoughts from her head. Feeling *so good*! She lost herself in it, in the tenderness coming from Will's hands. The comb began on her head, went down into the curve of her neck, over her shoulder, down her arm, her back. She felt the tent of wavy hair bloom out around her. In the darkness behind her closed eyes Edward was combing and plaiting those tresses as he used to, but this touch was nicer than Edward's.

Will Scarlet. These were his long fingers against her back. Mmmm ... he was good at this. He was enjoying it. Long after the tangles were gone he continued combing.

"... and it was a wonderful afternoon for bathing the children. Oh, I do hope the deputies all got home to spend this evening with their own families. Poor Robin. He so hates having to shoot them. It's such a good-smelling evening, isn't it? The warmth makes the wildflowers release their scents. By the way, I haven't been told your name, dear, so would you tell me? I hope it's not Bridget. You don't look like a Bridget. But then, you don't look like a Rosemary or a Modena, either. People tell me I look like a Marian, but I've never thought so. I always thought I looked like an Eliande. If I have a daughter, I hope she looks like an Eliande. What did you say your name was?"

"Hm?" Was someone talking? Katie opened her eyes. A slight tug near her knee made her remember. Oh, yes ... Marian. The pretty woman was pulling a discolored thread through Katie's tunic.

"Her name," the washing tide murmured from behind her, "is Cerridwyn."

Marian lit that ready smile. "Welsh! How romantic. Are you Welsh? I hope you're Welsh, because that probably means you'll know lots of stories for the Greenwood children. I've told them over and again all the stories I know, and Will's told his and Alan plays his harp for them—Alan's songs are wonderful, but his stories are boring. You haven't been here very long, so I don't suppose you've heard any of Alan's songs yet, have you, Cerridwyn?"

"No, but I—"

"Oh, well, he'll just have to play for you at supper this night. We usually wait until late after dark to eat so the bugs have a chance to come and go. They come out mostly at dusk, you know, but they don't like the torches we light after sunset. You can wait that long to eat, can't you?"

"I did pack a—"

"Because if you can't, Cerridwyn, I'm sure we can find you a nice loaf and goat's butter—we have lots of goats, you know, milk for the children—and we have berries aplenty. Rowanberries, strawberries, blueberries, even apples. That's one good thing about—"

"Katie."

"Excuse me, pardon me, what?"

"Katie. That's what I call myself. Katie."

Marian blinked. She glared over Katie's shoulder at Will. "Will Scarlet, you told me a lie."

"I did na—"

"If I ever forgive you, it won't be in this life. A person has every right, as well you know, to call herself—"

"He didn't lie," Katie jumped in, starting to get the rhythm of conversing with this hummingbird. "My real name is Cerridwyn. But since my marriage I've always called myself Katie so people in England wouldn't be suspicious or frightened of my past. You see," she added, thinking of Will standing smugly behind her, "I'm a Druid."

Marian's face lit up. "Oh, my goodness! Why, my goodness! A Druid! Why, I didn't know there were any of those—of you—left anywhere at all!"

Katie smiled at Marian's obvious delight and curiosity. "Oh, yes," she said, "we're still here. There are many pockets of the Old Religion in the countryside, though we've retreated to the oak hollows for privacy and safety. It's difficult to paddle uphill against intolerance, and my folk are not the kind to rally and fight. We merely go quietly farther back into the land."

"Was your Edward also a Druid?" Will asked, his voice heavy with her beloved's name.

"No," she said, tipping her head. "He was

Christian. My father was also, but I chose my mother's teachings to guide my life."

"Likely you would have made a better choice if you'd been raised properly."

Katie leapt to her feet, taking his comb and Marian's needle with her. She spun to face him and had to smother a gasp as his bright form and dynamic face struck her anew. "You speak of something you know little of."

"And what do you know of the church?"

"Enough to know it spawns too many half-headed opinions like yours, Sir Scarlet."

Marian waved both hands. "Oh, please don't argue! I hate arguing. It's so unpleasant!"

After a deep breath Katie grasped Marian's hand and said, "I'm sorry. You've been hospitable, and I'm being rude." She made quite sure that Will Scarlet had heard that last word.

She refused to look at him, making her look a weapon, and took command of the comb hanging in her hair with an old skill. It wasn't the world's best hair, but it was incredibly long unbraided, and it hid the unsureness in her eyes as she split it in back and pulled it across her shoulders, covering that unsureness. Katie hated to have her weaknesses pop out for the viewing; call it unmaidenly, call it its own kind of cowardice, but she despised having to display them. Yes, of course, it went against all the codes of chivalry and courtly love, knight wooing maiden under a prescribed set of rules, maiden presiding daintily over his puppy-doggish persual of her through song, poem, and prowess, only to turn him away because he hesitated two steps before plunging through a wall of boiling oil for the right to wear that little favor hanging from her belt. Katie didn't need that anymore. She'd had it once; Edward had done all of it to win her hand, and no one would ever do it better, so why go looking? Will had combed her hair and it felt wonderful, it felt delicious, but she was here for a reason and that wasn't it.

"When may I speak to Robin about opening the Cart Road?" she asked.

His fine locks slipped off one shoulder as he tilted his head thoughtfully. "It's to our advantage to keep it closed."

"I don't see how. If the road is closed, who will come by for you to rob? You'll have no booty to hoard."

"Suffice to say that it works for us to cripple the merchants of Nottingham these days. Those people keep the shire in taxes, which feeds the sheriff and others in the grip of the Crown, a reign as corrupt as a maggoty corpse."

Katie bristled. After all, she was loyal to that maggoty corpse. It did rankle that King Richard pranced off to foreign soil to defend the Holy Land, though it wasn't his land to defend and only the Goddess knew why he was defending it, only to get himself kidnapped and stuffed in an Austrian prison for ransom. Even among royalty there was indirection and blight to be found. Richard had made a mistake, and now England was paying for it. The king's brother was no replacement of any quality. No, none at all.

Katie couldn't deny that she was curious to know what made Will and these others so bitter about Richard's quest, since they obviously shared his religion and probably his cause, to some extent. Why were they using his absence as a chance to cripple his economy? Of course, she couldn't dismiss greed as a motive. There was always greed, and rare was the man immune to its embrace.

In the warm breeze rustling above them, carrying messages from tree to tree in oak language, Katie felt a challenge rise between Will and herself. It would have to find some resolution, since neither of them was the surrendering kind. She volunteered, "It makes me wonder how many prejudices you bring upon yourself, using wrongs to correct wrongs as you do."

Looking at his face, she thought he would lash out in fury, so burning was the icy fire behind his eyes. After an eternal unblinking glare, his one eyebrow crawled upward, followed cagily by one corner of his mouth. She could see he was accepting the gauntlet's slap. She swore his cheek reddened from it.

His head raised and tipped back grandly, again giving the impression of antlers.

Will watched her, particularly struck with the mote of differences between the familiar, lighthearted Marian and this thoughtful, unblushing woman whose courage was of a sad kind.

In a single motion he swept the feathered cap off his head and brushed his hair back with his wrist, deliberately looking away from Katie's intelligent face. He stepped around the stump, took the comb out of her hair, and firmly steered her back to her seat. "Come along. I'm not finished. I always finish what I begin."

There was more than duty in his hands as

he ran the comb down, down all that sea of hair, imagining the question surely smoldering in her eyes. What was she really doing here? To bargain for the Cart Road? Why would a woman risk her life for a road? Part of him believed her, but there was much in him that cried of something else, another reason.

Had she come here looking for a straight path to her Edward's side?

And so, my soul, what will put the light of life back in Katie's eyes? Is there a corner, a taste of me that might do it? No matter how I search for the immortal vitality a young woman's eyes should have, I find only a yawning sorrow. Beneath skin of an impossible whiteness I see only the echo of life, a tarnish coming out as that ruddy tinge on her cheeks, as though, in some former existence, a hand had stricken her in anger or agony.

As her head gave back slightly beneath his hands, he made a picture of her face, relaxed yet troubled, in the front of his mind, trying to make himself understand her. But he couldn't. The man Will had become, this carelessly free person called Scarlet could too easily shift away from anger at the force staining these ivory cheeks; his fingers brushed them as he collected creamy strands into the comb. Deep within himself he still wanted to know everything about those around him, without divulging his own secrets, like a wizard watching eternity pass in a glass ball.

Yet, to know a woman like this, glass is worth the shattering.

• Chapter Four •

Night fell. Mist descended into the forest.

Torches glowed orange in the night, crackling and spitting. Lunasa, she had called it. A time of changeover. That was all she had said, she who claimed to be dead.

Will was grateful for the company he shared tonight: Alan, Will Stutley, Johnny, and Tuck with his round, full-bearded face circled with silver hair; he said it was fur from God's very arm. And, of course, Robin.

"How do you find the morsel we trapped for you, Will?" his cousin asked over the jangling noise of lutes, flutes, bells, and drums near one of the several camp fires.

They sat at the fire, a little apart from the people who depended on them. It was here, at supper, that Robin o' the Hood and his band planned their strategies and reaffirmed the strengths that made them a unit. Will sat beside Robin, wrapped in his cloak. They were sharing an overspiced leg of boar.

"She was chewed at before you trapped her for me, and sorely she's attached to the life that did it," Will said.

"A tainted woman?"

"Nay . . . taunted."

"By you?"

Will chuckled. "Give me time, will you? Ah, Robin . . ." He sighed, his mood abruptly shifting. "It's sorrow that's tainting her. But I've never seen it rear up as it does in her. Did you see how brave she was? Still, it wasn't bravery as you and I are used to seeing it."

Thoughtfully Robin studied him in the firelight. He was used to Will's excursions into philosophy and his way of sifting through everyone else's habits, searching for reasons behind them. Since they were boys together at Gamewell, Will had always wanted to know what made the sky blue, the wind blow, a dove warble, a woman weep. He spared no one this scrutiny, Robin had long ago found out—least of all himself. If any man knew himself well, Will Scarlet did. So it was no surprise to Robin when the clouds he now saw on his cousin's eyes began to gather; that meant Will had stumbled upon some untrodden corner in his mind or soul which would plague him until he had mapped it out. Robin had seen it happen before, this thorough picking away of feelings; he had seen it occur both outwardly, when Will applied it to others, and inwardly, as he applied it to himself. It was a merciless process that had often made him enemies.

By way of a helping hand, Robin encouraged, "Then what is it?"

Will's deepened eyes grew narrow. Several descriptions came and went, touching then fleeing his lips because they were inaccurate—he wouldn't take those. Eventually it came: "Surrender."

Poor at this game of hearts Will relished, Robin ducked back. "I can't believe I hear you, of all men, complaining about surrender in a woman." Only after he said it did he realize that this was no time for jokes, that Will was serious to the core.

"You damned well know what I mean," Will growled, staring askance at him as a wounded wolf does.

Robin cleared a grape of its pit and lowered his gaze, then looked at him. "Yes. Forgive me. I do know. Forget about her, Will, if it causes you pain not to." He touched the stiffened arm beside him. "It's not God's will that you carry her burden for her."

"God isn't watching her face grow cool as I am. I *don't* understand what she's doing here!" He slammed a chunk of bread wastefully into the fire.

"Are you suspicious? Do you think she's involved in a plot?"

Clearly this had touched Will's thoughts. "A pawn, possibly. An expendable bauble with a soft armor. Women just don't ..." His voice trailed away. "Curse me, Robin, I can't bear to see a woman hurting."

"You're too used to Marian."

"It's true, I am. We see too few girls here of a kind I circled with in Gamewell. I began to think they were all like Marian ... you're right there. I understand why you love her. She's untouched by the scurvious world we live in. What is it, Rob? What is it about me that I've never given my heart? Have I no heart to give?

Is this"—he thumped his chest—"empty and barren?"

Robin turned on his knee and squeezed Will's wrist firmly until he felt the pulse rushing strongly there. "Will, don't let her do this to you. As much as you can't stand to see her in pain, I can't stand to see *you* in pain."

"I thank you for that."

"I want no thanks. I want your smile. And," he added, cannily picking up a soup spoon, "if I don't get it, I'm liable to ... dig it out by force!" He threw himself at Will, the force carrying them both backward into a leggy tumble. Robin tried in earnest to cram the spoon down Will's mouth, which encouraged Will to fight back without feint, all to the roars and hoots of the others at their camp fire. Unable to hoot, Johnny rang his dagger blade against the stew pot hanging at the fire.

Will's legs flailed out, seeking to twist in Robin's and yank his cousin off, but he kicked into the fire logs and succeeded only in sending red ashes sparking into the night. Robin was tenacious as the fog and twice as hard to brush away; when he wrestled, for fun or for life, he did it with all his being.

"Take care, Robin," Tuck warned after a clearing swallow somewhere within his massive beard, "you'll mar him. He's had a rough day, poor Will."

And Robin, being on top, did have an advantage. Though Will had a few pounds on him, Robin was that much quicker and had twice the fighting grit of anyone there. Will himself had said that the latter trait made Robin their uncrowned woodland king and welded their

loyalty to him. Will's own feelings for Robin
had begun in a fight, when, at the bonny age of
fifteen, they had first met at Gamewell. Years
later, when Robin's parents were dead and his
title stolen, and Will's own fortune had also
fallen prey to corruption, Will had come looking for him and ended up beating Robin in
another fight in the forest. They hadn't even
recognized each other at the time, and with a
quarterstaff, Will was deadly.

But not at wrestling.

In seconds he was pinned by the throat, and
Robin had his knee wedged neatly into Will's
stomach, keeping him from breathing.

"Rob-in . . . I . . . c'nt . . . brith. . . ."

"Say again? Confess to your sins, grouse.
Admit you're ruining a perfectly happy meal
with your complaining."

"I . . . c'nt . . . br—"

"What?"

"He's telling you he can't bloody get air,
man," Will Stutley, a lanky, brown-haired forester, said, translating. "Robin, get off his gut
before you kill him with that knobby knee."

"Eh? Oh. Sorry. Up with you, Scarlet." He
rolled to one side and hauled Will up, gasping,
beside him. "Did I hurt you? Are you hurt?"

Will rubbed his ribs and his throat. "By the
Virgin, Robin, you play too rough."

"I do lose myself in my work, I admit."

"Which is why we're all eating instead of
starving," Tuck pointed out, adjusting the huge
wooden cross that dangled on a leather string
from his wide girth. The Friar's round haircut
had grown out since he took up life in their
band; except for that cross and his monk's

brown robes, he looked like a rounder, older version of Johnny.

Robin rubbed and patted Will's back to get him breathing again. "All right?"

"I swear you take pleasure in my pain."

"You do make rather a teasing target. You always have. At least I've managed to distract you from your dark ruminations."

"Squeezed them out of me is what you've done."

"Here." Robin reached for the goblet in Alan's hand. The quiet young bard handed it over, and Robin held it to Will. "Drink."

"Never! You've probably poisoned it to see how sick I'll get."

"Oh, Will."

"Do you blame me? I can barely keep my blood in my body with you around, and when you're not around, it's your blasted arrows biting at me constantly. Someday you're going to miss," he warned, wagging his finger in Robin's face, "and instead of impaling my water skin or my money pouch, you're going to put a hole in me and I'll die as you agonize over me. That'll be your hell, Robin, and you'll deserve it."

With this, evidently, he succeeded in nulling his cousin's cheerful mood. Robin wasted no time retaliating. "And your hell will be a closed room with eyes in the walls which will watch you as you watch the rest of us." He turned back to the fire. The other men grew quiet. Some used the tension as a cloak to sneak away to more lighthearted quarters. Only those closest to Robin and Will's strange tourneys chose to stay and weather it out. Will

Stutley stayed, but only because he was too drunk to walk away. Alan o' Dale stayed because he was too much of a coward to risk Robin's disgruntlement if he left. Tuck stayed, mainly because of his own vulturous curiosity about the machinations of men's minds. For a man of God, Tuck wasn't much on pity. He'd never made any pretenses about his "calling" to the church, admitting that the distance between himself and the Almighty had been nudged closed by the gloomy hand of poverty, which was all he had before joining the monastery. As the gap grew slimmer Tuck's waistline had grown wider.

For a time the only sounds were those of the crackling fire and of laborious chewing and swallowing. No one would speak, until Robin or Will did; no one dared turn loose either of those tempers.

This went on until the fog thickened. In an effort at diplomacy Tuck filled the wine goblet and sent it around the fire. It went around, hand to hand, to Robin. He refused it.

Back around it came to Alan . . . to Tuck . . . to Stutley . . . to Will.

Will took a sip, quite ceremoniously. The warm liquid filled his mouth, chased around his tingling tongue, and flowed down his gullet, taking most of his pique with it. He reached out to send the goblet back to Tuck, then hesitated. In the firelight glittered the careful etchings of the silver goblet, and unbidden memory of how they came by it flooded into his mind. Part of a booty, it was, and Robin had paid dearly for that wagonload of silverwork. The silversmith, it turned out, had brought the wares as a donation to the king's ransom; like today, though, they had been followed by the hirelings of Guy of Gisbourne and the shire's officials. Robin had fought his way out. He'd saved three lives that day, one of them Will's, and he'd lain near death himself for most of a month.

The memory dissolved, and Will's hand stole tentatively upward, over, to Robin's shoulder. He felt the sandy grit embedded in green broadcloth and, beneath it, the play of his cousin's trim muscles as Robin turned questioningly.

Will brought the goblet around, leaning a little on Robin, and rotated it in his hand to show his cousin the fire's dance in silver. He waited until the glow filled Robin's eyes. "Take a sip of atonement, my friend. From my hand to yours."

No one alive could have doubted the remorse in Robin's expression, though it was sketchy and rife with injury. No matter how rude he was, he was always well intentioned and didn't understand getting rudeness hurled back in his face. Yet he kept spitting into that wind.

Robin turned fully, scooted closer to Will, and accepted the goblet. It touched his lips as he tried not to flinch from the healing wounds he and Will had cut into each other. Cold wounds, many times healed, often reopened, seldom with quite so ragged a blade as that which had swung tonight.

"I accept your apology," he said.

"My apology!" Will roared.

"If you'll accept mine" was hastily added.

Tuck bellowed, "For the sake of Jesus Christ

Our Lord 'n Savior, hurry up with it before you set me sobbing, the two of you.''

Will and Robin exchanged surrendering smiles, then Will said, "Tuck, you're a compassionate man."

"Compassion's for prelates and nuns."

"Well, you're no prelate."

Once purged, the tension stayed away.

Until the women came.

Marian led Katie down the secret path where the forest's arm bent away for them, then closed behind them to hide their passage. Every step put memories into Katie's mind, filling her with tidbits of woodland lore her mother had taught her, stored away behind the life she and Edward had made together. Now she needed them, and they were obligingly returning.

As Katie and Marian approached a soft glow of firelight through the night-black trees and bushes, Katie took note of the music and the sounds that came through the woods. Lively music it was, unrefined and folksy, not like the abbey's haunting chants with their trumpets and high, echoing halls. This music was cheerful. The prioresses had always told her that cheerful music was the voice of sin.

She had never believed them.

The aroma of food awakened her appetite. At least she was clean and the grit was gone from between her thighs and in her elbows. Her hair felt like hair again, though it would have pained her to admit that it still tingled from the touch of a particular highwayman.

Marian parted the saplings before them and stepped aside to make room in the clearing for

Katie. Katie stopped short, the air stilling in her body. Before her, around the fire, were the men she both sought and feared.

A handful of legends came with her through the bushes. They swarmed and clouded around her even as the moonlight met firelight on her freshly washed white linen tunic. Her face was scrubbed to an alabaster glow, and her hair made a lemony fan around her head, separated in back and draping over her shoulders, where it was bound loosely by twining silk strings—Marian's touch on Will's handiwork.

Some of the men actually moved aside. Tuck rolled his eyes and crossed himself, then resumed chewing. Robin watched Katie, then Will.

Will was staring.

It was as though the ghostly sadness, so absorbing, so like ecstasy in its way, had come to life and materialized in this airy specter before him.

He had seen a sculpture once. At the castle of Baron Forsythe near Tynemouth, part of the baron's collection of artifacts from his participation in the Crusades. It was a statue of a Greek woman called Pandora. Will knew her story, how she had opened a box filled with disease because she couldn't bear not knowing, but only when he saw the statue and its incomparably simple beauty did he fully comprehend the story's import.

Now he understood, for there she was: simple, mythological, as cool as stone.

He had to work to finish swallowing the

gulp of wine he'd swigged and somehow managed not to choke on it.

Robin covered for him. "You're late, both of you. Come. Eat while it's fresh and hot."

"You stay, dear," Marian said to Katie.

"Aren't you eating?" Katie followed her across the clearing and tripped over a sprawled pair of legs. The drunken man groaned but didn't move. "Marian?"

"Oh, yes, sweet. Of course I am, but I have to go to the next camp to help Edith feed her children. Robin, Will, you be gentlemen now, won't you?"

"Us? Of course."

"Did you ever doubt it?"

"Take good care of Katie, then," Marian said, and dodged skillfully into a clutch of overgrowth so dense and black, Katie would have sworn there was no way through it.

Katie watched the leaves close behind Marian and knew there was no hope of finding her way through. Evidently Marian wasn't worried about leaving her alone here with these men, so she resolved to act as though they couldn't intimidate her. Hoping her helplessness could masquerade as aloofness, Katie squared her shoulders and stood her ground, looking at the red-gold shapes surrounding the fire. Robin was a shadow with a golden beard, the fire flickering on his face. Beside him, the scarlet lines of Will's arms and legs rested below the corona of long gleaming hair. She was clutched by his penetrating eyes, a little sleepy-looking as they scanned her. Here, beside the fire's inherent calm, she could feel his masculinity. He was so much taller and slimmer than Edward, presenting his sensuality in a totally new form. Until now, no man other than Edward had stirred the warmth below her waist with just a look.

The challenge was entirely real, as she and Will shared a bizarre moment of standoff, soaking in each other's physical shapes as knights study a landscape for gopher holes or dangerous ground. The thrill was undeniably there: a tug-of-war was beginning between them, at once horrible and sweet. Katie brushed her palms on her thighs. They were moist.

His lips parted.

She watched the men. They seemed hardly human. More like works of art.

"Lady"—Will's voice grasped her—"join us on this side." Katie seemed to float around the fire, spiritual and fluid.

She picked her way across the dark clearing, rooty ground distorted by the fire, being especially careful not to trip over any more legs. She didn't want to appear any clumsier than she had to. She wanted, more than anything, to appear competent, cunning, and quite able to act as proxy for the people of Southwell. These men had to see her as more than a trapped woman, out of place and helpless, if she was going to succeed at her task. Their view of her had already suffered enough damage with the absurdity of her entry on the scene earlier today, and Katie worried that respect might prove irretrievable.

She stood over Will just long enough to establish an air of aloofness, making it clear that she wasn't in any hurry to sit next to him or share their ill-gotten dinner. Was it victory or failure when he stood up?

"Are you planning to eat on your feet as part of some ritual?" he asked, cocking his hip. He obviously wanted to sit down again, but something made it hard for him to look up at a woman.

"Nay, I'll sit," Katie said, her tone of voice ridiculing him soundly. Her small prize won, she sat down, leaving him standing there foolishly.

Tuck snickered and winked at her. Will frowned, then took his seat. "My lady, do you drink wine or water?"

"I'll have wine, thank you."

"Ah. I knew there was a Christian in you somewhere."

"Because I drink wine?"

"It is the blood of our Lord."

"And why would you drink the blood of your Lord?" she countered.

Only after several moments of sizzling quiet did she realize that her counterattack had found a tender mark, and another second or two went by before she felt sorry about it. After all, it wasn't these people's fault that she had been persecuted about her choice. Will's strong, masculine, thoughtful face beside her, with its heavy-lidded eyes and draping of golden hair, was not the acid face of Godfrey, nor the suspicious glare of the citizens of Southwell when they were led to doubt her. It was cruel of her to imply that she didn't understand about the Christian sacrament, because she did; Katie, more than most folk, understood that all beings were entitled to their own beliefs. She was using their ignorance against them. She must be more frightened than she felt. For all his abrasiveness, this Scarlet had been nothing but kind to her, and she wouldn't for all the world's truths hurt Marian's childlike happiness. If Marian had heard her, Katie would have felt terrible.

"Forgive me," she said, looking from Robin to Will. She had planned to look back at Robin, but something in Will Scarlet's haunting, hot-cold gaze held her. "I'm rude to disturb your peace at suppertime. I've had quite a tiring day, and my nerves are on edge. Please . . . go on with your meal."

There was an uncomfortable shifting of limbs before the meal resumed. Will wordlessly passed her a slice of day-old bread, which Katie arranged carefully on her knees, then she waited while Tuck ladled capon brewet into a bowl and passed it to Will for him and Katie to share, as was only courteous. While Will reached for a thick chunk of bread with a hole in it that was their salt shaker, Katie took a moment to wash her hands in the water basin beside the fire. The wine goblet started to circle, though Katie suspected it had already seen plenty of circumnavigations. The boar's meat went around as Robin hacked civets from it, and when Katie received hers, she placed it on the old bread on her knees and waited for the lettuce, soft cheese, and shallots to be passed. They also had pears and apples and something that looked like—yes, it was. Raspberries! Since she'd lived in Southwell she'd had precious little fruit. It wasn't prevalent in the towns.

Now that she thought about it, these men

weren't behaving at all like the brutes they were reputed to be. They ate slowly, with small bites, swallowed before drinking, and always wiped their lips before partaking of the shared wine. Except for Tuck, who bit his bread instead of breaking it, there was hardly a social grace left unobserved. They didn't even talk while they were eating; Katie expected at least that from men who robbed for a living and scurried underbush when they wanted to sleep. It must have been Marian's effect on them, she surmised. These thieves were lucky to have a gentlewoman to teach them civil ways.

"Would you like some frumenty?" Will asked her, passing a bowl of custard that was piping hot and smelled of figs and honey. Amazing that foresters could live so well!

"My compliments," Katie said. "This is fine food. The only things missing are eggs and wafers."

"We get those from time to rare time," Will said, "when the right farmer happens by."

"It seems the Cart Road feeds you as much as it feeds us," Katie said.

"Aye," the Hood said. "There's less and less bounty coming our way these days."

Katie didn't flinch. "You can't expect merchants to bring their trade down a road where they'll surely lose it, can you?"

"Not all must pay our toll, mistress."

"How do you make your choice? I've known many people of many oaths who've felt the bite of your arrows."

"We are free people, lady. We make free choices."

"Your freedom will fill few bellies when the

merchants of Southwell and Nottingham find a route around you or throw more ambushes at you as they did today."

Will had been listening carefully, watching the faces of his bombastic leader and their curious guest. "You understand us so little, Katie."

"I see little to understand. You cut off trade, and your own throats bleed."

"The Cart Road is a game fowl between ourselves and Guy, Baron of Gisbourne, who suffers when we damage the trade flow. He supports the new Crown, and it's he who has appropriated the lands we cherish. He says we squat on the king's land, land that used to belong to honest men. These people who live with us in the Greenwood depend on us to clothe and feed them. Or have you no sympathy for the children you saw today?'

"Can they eat and stay warm if the road is abandoned to you?"

Will's tone was acrid when he said, "We'll go hungry if it means starving one carrot from the mouth of the false Crown."

Tightening her lips in a thin line, Katie managed to keep her anger to herself. True, she had taken the Old Religion from her mother, but it didn't take being a Christian to be loyal to King Richard, and Katie was fiercely loyal. The England made by King Henry and kept by his heir, Richard, was a good, profitable, civilized England where a young landless couple could found a business and become well-to-do burghers. It grated on her to listen to Will badmouthing her king.

"Your tongue is free with barbs for a ruler

who loves England more than his life," she defended, her voice rising in pitch despite her efforts to keep it down.

"He loves England enough to steal it out from under our very plows," came the answer, twice as gruff and fired by the light in his glare. "How can you be so blind?"

"I'm no more blind than any honest person who works for a living instead of pillaging the sweat of others."

"The Cart Road stays closed," Robin said, "until *we* decide to open it."

"And what price will persuade you to open it?"

"When England is again a land for all men, Norman and Saxon alike," Will said, bristling, "when nobility no longer depends on favors done to a despicable Crown and betrayal after betrayal of men who refuse to grovel."

Meeting his attack, Katie hurried in with, "Seems to me you're groveling pretty well, hiding behind a tract of trees and skulking like lizards to steal the goods of Normans and Saxons alike."

"Are you calling us cowards?"

"Are you denying it?"

The ground shook as Will thundered to his feet and stood over her, eyes blazing, fists knotting and unknotting, the muscles in his legs locking all the way up to his groin.

Except for the fact that she was utterly terror-stricken, Katie appeared unfazed.

"I don't have to take this from you!" the sky roared. "By the breath of Christ, I don't!"

His hand launched back to strike her. Katie stiffened but refused to duck away. She would never know if it was pride or pure horror that kept her from moving, but she expected the rock-hard blow and braced for it because there was no time to do anything else.

She *thought* there wasn't.

In that instant, though, there was a flash, a crack, and Will reeled backward.

Katie blinked her eyes clear of fear's fog in time to see Robin leap over the fire, grasp Will's forearm, and pull a dagger from behind Will where it had pinned the red sleeve to a tree and yanked him off-balance.

"Damn you!" Will howled, his face gnarling.

Robin twisted the blade from its deep bite and tightened his grip on Will's arm. "Never strike a lady in my presence. You're a better man than that."

"I'm a better man than one who takes insults from a politicking woman!"

Katie used the moment to scramble to the other side of the fire, tripping—again!—over Stutley's legs and openly gasping with fright. She'd come close to a bruised face; there was no doubt. His strong arm, driven by rage, would have rocked her from here to Nottingham. Had he known Robin would intervene? Would he have gone through with it? Would he actually have hit her? If the shattering in her legs was any measure, yes.

"You'll take what I say you'll take," Robin commanded. Immediately Will's arm was torn from his grip.

"*In hell!*" It was a cruel, hushed promise.

The chief forester sheathed his dagger without balking from his cousin's fury. Only when he looked at Katie did he speak again. "You I want out of my Greenwood. Evidently we can't speak in peace with you here, mistress. Johnny . . . Johnny, hang you, wake up! Outfit her with bread and a water skin and deliver her to the edge of Sherwood while you still have moonlight to see by. Lady, I bid you good night and, above all, good-bye."

What? He was sending her away? She'd never find her way back here, and her task wasn't yet accomplished! She *had* to succeed. Her blacksmith shop, Edward's dream, Nick, Gaston —aye, her very life depended on making these men listen to reason.

Will had started to leave, but at this he spun around and declared, "You have no business sending her away!"

"I'll send away whom I please! You'll have to quench your loins at another fountain."

"She's my concern. You said it yourself."

"No longer. Johnny."

Katie didn't miss the reference to Will Scarlet's sexual satisfaction, and it might have been just that which drove her next move. She stepped into the glow of the fire and announced, "I am my own concern, Sir Hood, not yours and certainly not his."

"Johnny, by the sword!"

A huge, hairy hand caught her waist and propelled her sideways and into a clutch of bushes that sagged away under her weight to reveal a hacked-out path. The massive beast called Johnny then lifted her to her feet with the complete antithesis of his previous force, a gentility that wouldn't have flushed a sparrow.

"Robin, you'll rue that!" she heard Will bellow behind her.

"It's out of your hands."

"I'll put my hands where I please."

"Then stuff them in your mouth."

"Robin, come back here! Robin!"

Katie was hauled away, and the ferocious argument faded behind her until all that filled her mind was the strange image of Will Scarlet's hands venturing toward her.

• *Chapter Five* •

The forest's edge was damp and cold. Katie sat where Johnny had left her for more than two hours, shivering under a wool cloak and waiting for Will to get the better of Robin and come back for her. He *would* come. Something inside her knew that. He wasn't the kind of man to leave a woman defenseless on a deserted road in the middle of the night, and he certainly wasn't the kind to take orders. Why did he stay with Robin? From what she'd seen, they didn't seem to like each other very much. Will was haughty and Robin was willful, and they were both stubborn, not to mention the difference in their social standings. Will Scarlet was running with outlaws, but Katie knew a nobleman when she saw one—she had made many a nobleman's armor and sword at her forge. Will was one both in blood and manner. Spoiled but noble. Why, then, was he keeping company with this motley collection of brigands?

As much as she hated to admit it, his threat to strike her had been thrilling—not because she would have actually been stricken, of course, but because of the bizarre wonder she found in knowing she held the key to his sea of emotions, in watching his muscles ripple with raw anathema. He was a fabulous sight, roaring over her. There was majesty in a powerful man. She'd felt it, seen it, loved it every time Edward's glistening arm and shoulder had flexed to raise his hammer, every time his thighs braced against the ringing anvil while coaxing iron to bend to his wish.

Her chilled limbs ached to feel those hot, blood-flooded sinews, Edward's or . . .

Or—

She got up and started to walk in an effort to get warm. She scanned the rim of bushes and trees, certain that she was being watched. They hadn't given her anything to make a fire with, hoping she'd be discouraged from keeping camp here, but she knew—well, *guessed*—that they weren't leaving her unobserved. Someone, somewhere in those leaves, was keeping an eye on her. Not likely Will; someone else. Johnny, maybe. Or Alan. They would report back to Robin that she was a woman of her word: She meant to have her say and get the Cart Road open again. Perhaps she hadn't gone about it the right way. Antagonizing them evidently wasn't the way to get them thinking. Pointing out the harm they were doing themselves hadn't worked, either. It seemed they had more complicated reasons for wanting to raid the Cart Road's travelers. Revenge against the Baron of Gisbourne? That seemed to have much to do with it.

It was cold, much colder than she had realized while she sat with Will at the campfire and shared his wine. Now that the heat had passed, she was able to remember the easy grace of his hands as he served her supper, the depth of his gaze as he questioned her and answered her blunt accusations; she imagined the wheels turning in his mind and was fascinated by them. Of all the personalities she could have encountered on this adventure, his was the least expected. Never in a million guesses could she have predicted all the unique puzzle parts that came together to make Will Scarlet. He was an unusual man: a noble among thieves, a gentleman thorn.

If only she knew what to do. Suddenly she wished she'd let Nick come with her as he had planned to. It hadn't been easy, stealing out of the town under midnight's cloak just to be sure that Nick would stay behind. She'd insisted he not come with her—over and over, she'd insisted—but he also insisted. After a day-long argument Katie decided that she'd like a nice quiet middle-of-the-night breath of fresh air. Her outing had been somewhat strenuous.

And now the bugs were settling on her ankles. She tugged the wool cloak tightly at her throat and wished Robin had at least provided her with the horse she'd come in on. It wasn't even her horse. Now she would have to explain to Roger Gervais why she wasn't coming back with his favorite pack gelding.

That is, if they let her back into town at all.

If the abbot hadn't stained her beyond repair in the eyes of her neighbors. If she wasn't condemned as a witch. If Nick and Gaston could keep the radicals from burning down the shop. If . . . if . . . if . . .

"If only I was warm!"

The moon gleamed blindly down.

Clop . . . clop . . . clop . . . clop . . .

She whirled, squinting.

Large black shapes. On horseback.

Katie wanted to duck back into the forest, but to her horror she realized that her walking had brought her out into the middle of the moon-bathed road, and unless they were as blind as the moon, whoever they were had surely seen her. She was a pillar of dark cloak in a dusk-blue road, a target for any two-year-old to delight in.

She stood staring facelessly at them for a good minute and they at her. The challenge became so intense, Katie nearly screamed with frustration. Only the breath catching in her throat and a choking, cold breeze held her silent. Then, sensing it more than seeing it, she knew one of the riders had nudged his horse forward.

Clop . . . clop . . .

The horse's left forehoof was uneven; it needed a shoe. *Edward, there's another customer around back. A hoof filing might help, but I'd put a half shoe on it. Edward? Do you hear me?*

Closer they came on the chalk-blue road.

Coming after her. By now she knew it wasn't Robin or Will or anyone she wanted to talk to. She inhaled sharply. The intruders passed under an overhanging bough. Its shadow obscured their outlines and shocked Katie into action.

With a strangled yell she yanked up the cloak and bolted down the road, angling toward the trees at a dead run.

And they bolted after her.

The horses drummed down on her, and she dared not break her stride to glance back. She'd gotten a slight edge while the horses gathered to break into a run, but now she was rapidly losing her advantage. The dirt plumed out beneath her hammering feet as she put every bit of energy she had into running away toward the trees—if only she could find an opening in the brush. If not, the tangled boughs and vines would become a great net, catching her like a fish. She angled wildly to her left, only to have a dark rider lumber in to cut off her escape, the horse's hoofbeats vibrating up through her wood-soled shoes and into her legs. She veered away and ran harder. Wind tore the cloak from her shoulders and mangled her combed hair, whipping strands of it at her face as she dared a look to her right.

Three riders, and they were surrounding her.

Horses' hot breath rippled on her neck, her shoulders, foam flecking on her hair as she let out one more yell, a fearful shout that flooded her body with energy. But not enough energy. Terror descended and clutched her heart. They were upon her.

An iron band coiled her waist, bruising a rib, and the ground dropped away beneath her. Her only awareness beyond panic was the incongruous, flexing warmth of a horse's shoulder against her back. She kicked, but there was nothing to kick against.

In a wave of panic her tortured mind called, Edward! Edward!

Will!

The music of defeat blasted from her lungs,

and the wide blue night closed in on her fading scream.

The human hand is a marvelous thing. Its fingers fold inward to make a fist, straighten to form a salute, and may work together or separately to perform intricate tasks. Each finger can work with the thumb, sensitive enough to feel an unborn pulse, yet strong enough to draw a bow and sense the exact moment to let an arrow fly. The palm is a curving cushion of feelings, capable of seeking out hidden passions, coaxing them to the surface. Yet, turn it over, and there, like rocks jutting from a mountain slope, will be knuckles hard enough to ring a deadly blow.

Open.
Closed.
Open.
Closed.

Strange . . . it didn't seem like such a danger as it flexed, harmless, here in the shadows. So what part of him had made it a weapon?

Over and over Will turned it in his mind, crushing his cap in that hand until the feather was worried, but he could find no answer. Only an echo—no excuses and no disclosures. Would he ever find and kill the beast within him? Through half the night, as the moon arched overhead, he had searched and failed.

"I almost struck her," he said, speaking to the emptiness just to see how it sounded, to see if perhaps there could be an excuse for his behavior hidden there. All that was left was the bald reality: he had almost hit a beautiful, intelligent, gentle woman.

And for what? Over a petty political disagreement. This was shameful. How many times
had he sat calmly at supper in Gamewell and
parlayed ideas on religion and affairs of state
without even raising his voice? Will had always been the envy of his peers, the only man
in the shire capable of debating difficult issues
without becoming emotional. With this skill he
had taken the prize in almost every argument
with barons and masters and manor lords ...
yet one sedate and lovely girl had splintered
his composure and driven him to violence.

And, to top it off, he had been angry with
Robin for stopping him. Robin had done him a
vaulting favor, and he had very nearly turned
this hand on his cousin, rewarding him with
insults and rage.

How could Katie have unsettled him so much,
so quickly?

Perhaps there was more. He had never before stopped to ponder the effect living in the
Greenwood was having on him. Was he becoming like one of the animals, given to fits of
anger and moodiness? Had he left more than
his name and title behind?

His mind began to drift. Defenseless, he followed it.

The family house at Gamewell ... his father, the tall, graceful source of Will's sultry
looks ... his mother, plump and thoughtful,
from whence Will's yearning for knowledge
had sprung. Their big stone house—almost a
castle—with its many passageways and para-
pets and the big main courtyard overlooking
the demesne. Out there were the crofts of the
families his father protected as lord of the

manor, who in turn supported the lands of Gamewell. In the haze of memories and wishes Will imagined a girl, linen-robed, corn-haired, quiet. He saw himself approaching her. There were flowers in his hand—daisies, sorrel, bluebells, violets. He felt her small white fingers take the gift, her head tipping as she smiled. Oh . . . a smile to melt a man's heart! She gave her reward: one cool kiss on his cheek just under his eye, and another smile. As the dictates of courtly love required, he could give her certain gifts to call him to her mind—a mirror, a gold wreath, a tassel for her belt, a handkerchief, a fillet to plait in her hair—but if he gave her a ring, she would be honorbound to hide the stone on the inside of her left hand, keeping his pledge of love tight to her heart and away from curious eyes.

Will watched from miles and years away as his self-vision parted the daisies from the bouquet, braided them into a circlet while reciting a poem of love, and, in the poem's last couplet, placed the circlet on her pale hair. A daisy crowned with daisies she was, with her white robe and yellow hair, and she charmed him to his toes.

In those days he would have taken her riding, giving her his favorite horse, Palermo, and taking her on a tour of Gamewell. How grand he would have felt with her, calm and happy at his side, her skirt flowing over Palermo's flank, the stallion wearing his best silver-mesh bridle and reins. Were there shadows in his eyes now that hadn't been there then? For an instant he felt the movement of the horse beneath him, the softness of a small hand in his own, and his imagination strayed to the contours of melon-firm breasts beneath a lace bandeau, legs as eager as his own to find the entanglement of desire hidden deep under the rules of etiquette. Yet a twinkle in her eyes told him that rules could be broken, desire could be unleashed, passion could be found.

With disgrace nipping at his conscience Will wondered how time had vagabonded away that young man of courtly ways who would never in a thousand Christmases have raised his hand in violence to a lady.

So who was this stranger borrowing his skin these days?

Whoever it was, Will wasn't too fond of him right now.

A rustling in the bushes nearby shook him from his thoughts. He leaned back, hoping to remain out of sight. He was sitting on a fallen log and suddenly realized how foolish it was to sit in the very place he always sat when he wanted to be alone—Robin could be sure to find him and help him be alone. Today, though, it would be too trying to see the amused sympathy in his cousin's face. Will leaned a bit farther back, but unless he moved away completely Robin would surely see him whether he wanted to be seen or not. His chest grew more hollow with each rustle the bushes made behind him.

"Will? Will, are you there?"

Marian.

He almost stayed quiet. Marian wouldn't be able to find him. A portion of his mind wondered why Robin hadn't come here yet.

"Will Scarlet? Are you here?"

What was that tremor in her voice?

His tone sagging, he called, "Here, Marian." When the bushes kept rustling, he repeated, "Here."

"Oh, Will!" Marian appeared and hurried to him. "I just heard that Robin sent Katie away! Where will she go? Did she say anything to you?"

"She wasn't speaking to me at the time."

"But this is terrible! Where can she go?"

"I suppose she'll go back to her town. What else is there for her to do?"

Marian's face took on a distraught crumple. "This is awful ... horrible. Will, you must find her and bring her back!"

"What? Why do you say that?"

She wrung her hands at her small bosom and paced back and forth.

Will stood up. "Marian? Tell me."

"Before supper ... she ... she said—"

"Marian, for God's sake—"

"She'll be persecuted if she goes back!"

The air around them grew suddenly cold, forcing a bone-deep shiver through Will's entire body. "*What?*"

A tear snaked down Marian's cheek. "Because of her beliefs. If she fails to negotiate with Robin, she'll be accused of not being in God's favor. As a woman of the Old Religion, she'll be accused of being a witch or a heretic. Can you think of anything so heinous? You have to bring her back, Will. It's her only chance! We have to keep her safe, with us, until some solution can be found. Please say you'll do it. Oh, why can't everyone just be a Christian? Everything would be so easy then!"

Will only half heard her. He was looking up through thick branches at the moon and was reminded of a haunting face calling to him through the veils of night. He had only just discovered her. Was he to lose her before he knew what she could mean to him?

Katie . . .

His chest was no longer empty. Now there was an icy lump in it. He knew all too well what the charge of heresy could mean in these times of change, of misunderstanding. She would be publicly humiliated. Tortured. Drawn and quartered, left to die before a hooting crowd. Soberly Will admitted to himself that he was to blame if she came to trouble out on the open road. She was in danger because he couldn't hold his temper. His shame redoubled as he glanced at Marian, her hands knotted and pressed to her lips in dire hope. She, too, had obviously fallen under Katie's spell.

Will clenched his fists, only to find them dry and numb. Blood began to race in his body, his heart to thud out of control.

"Get me a horse!"

• *Chapter Six* •

She was dying. She knew she was because she couldn't breathe. A terrible weight oppressed her body until she could no longer inhale. The hard earth bit away her helpless squirms and bruised her shoulder blades. A rocky force crushed her lips, and there was nothing but pain and black shadows against the dark blue night; there had been only terror and hurt for untold moments, longer moments than Edward's last breath. Yellow-and-red light flamed over her, blinding her. Weakness made her arms go thready, and the darkness closed over her eyes. Suddenly a gust of force blew the weight off her body and sent her rolling.

"Get off her, you crude lout!" There was a slap of flesh against flesh.

Katie gasped for air and tried to crawl away from the strong, deep-toned voice that had blown the weight off. Soon she gave up, though, and concentrated on sitting up and reclaiming a measure of dignity. If she had to die in the hands of highwaymen, she wanted to do it with dignity. That was reasonable, wasn't it?

Hadn't she had enough failures? Did she have to die sloppily as well?

"Girl, get up," the deep voice said. Resonant. Like the moan of a clear night wind. "Let me see your face." A hand pulled her hair away from her cheeks. She looked up, willing her body to slow its desperate gasps, and found herself staring into a black shape framed by the cloud-laced moon and obscured by torchlight that flickered in patches of gold and orange from behind her. She stole a glance back and saw a horseshoe of men surrounding her, each holding a torch. When had they found time to light torches? She looked back at their leader. As her eyes adjusted she found a face in the shape, smoke-bearded and edged in silver. She could see his eyes. "Who are you, girl? Outlaw or victim?"

She thought quickly. "Victim."

"Prove it."

"How?"

The moon peered at her. "What's your name? What were you doing on this road at night?"

"They left me here," she lied carefully, formulating the story as she went. "They robbed me and put me out here when they were finished with me."

"Finished? Did they rape you?"

"No."

"And lucky you are, then. Did you tell them you were sick or leprose or something, to keep them from you?"

"I told them only that my husband died in my arms some weeks ago, and they left me alone."

He grunted thoughtfully. "Superstitious rabble" was his comment. "Do you have a name, or are you one of those barefoot barbarians calling yourself after your most obvious habit?"

Katie drew her shaking legs under her, ignoring the eyes that watched her from the sides and back, knowing she was dealing with the man in charge of these others. She wanted to stand up and square off with him, but her legs didn't feel as though they would hold her yet. "My name," she began, insisting that her voice carry all the power her legs refused to, "is Katie Chenoweth of Southwell."

"You assign yourself that name as though it's a title. Are you a noblewoman in that case?"

"Nay, sir, I'm a merchant, a tradeswoman. I came here to bargain with the outlaws to open this road, but they saw fit to reject me. Who are you and why have you manhandled me?"

He stood up, clearly not ashamed of his identity. "I am Guy, Baron of Gisbourne, and I have rescued you, not manhandled you. It's a cold, naked night for a lone woman with a nightshirt on and no man."

"Men have put me here," Katie replied indignantly. "I have nothing to thank any man for, least of all rogues who pluck me from the ground I'm on and give me a ride into terror, then throw me down and sit on me."

Guy of Gisbourne fingered his beard. "Yes . . . for that I'm sorry. My man Urlan has more muscle than manner. Come. Stand in the torchlight. Let me see you. Kenneth, bring that light around." He reached out for her. In that single motion the width of his shoulders beneath a glowing ermine half-cape became visible. Only then, when he mentioned the torchlight, did Katie notice his clothes and the sweet scents of cleanliness she hadn't encountered since leaving her mother's people. The Druids were scrupulously clean, bathing often in chilly herbstrewn pools, while in Southwell, as in most towns, bathing water was scarce and the smell of dirty bodies was the smell of the town. Guy of Gisbourne didn't smell like a town. The soft moon glowed, and the fires moved across a rich man's clothes of blue velvet and brocade, a belt of knotted flaxen strands, fine slippers of the kind preferred by nobility. Borders of stitched yellow threads in a design of interlinked ram's heads ran up his sleeves to vanish under the white fur, and the same design hemmed his blue tunic.

"You're not a child," Gisbourne said, making no attempt to avert his eyes from her unbound breasts beneath the soft, flowing tunic. His comment was one of discovery more than arousal, and it made Katie wonder if he'd missed the statement about her husband. After all, it was common among the upper gentry and the nobility to marry off their daughters when they were young as eleven years old, and Gisbourne probably thought nothing of it. Among the Druids—at least in Inanna's tribe—a girl's marriage ritual could wait until she herself felt the tug for a man's touch. For some it came earlier than others, but Katie couldn't recall any of her friends choosing to leave her parents until at least thirteen, and even that was considered early. Katie, herself, might not have married at fifteen if her father hadn't brought the young blacksmith's apprentice home to Gwynedd. Her father was a shoemaker and therefore well-to-do, and he wanted his daughter to be educated.

He and Edward had met while traveling on business—Edward looking for new sources of raw metal for his master's forge, and Meyric Chenoweth marketing his successful cobbling talents. Edward never suspected that the conniving glitter in Meyric's eyes had to do with a feather-light Druid girl waiting by her mother's side at their tribe's hill fort back in Gwynedd. The friendship had grown into a kind of partnership; Meyric could borrow a portion of Edward's master's shop whenever he came to Southwell, and there he would sell his shoes and do his customers' repairs in comfort and shelter, in exchange for access to the ore deposits within the Druid tribe's hill fort. All was well, for Edward happily agreed never to desecrate the *drunemeton*—the sacred oak grove where the turf altar lay and where the Druids held their invocationals. This Edward had scrupulously obeyed, respecting to the last detail all that was important to Katie's tribe. From Meyric Edward had learned how to love a Druid woman while remaining a Christian man, realizing that two beliefs could join in peace and wonder. He never challenged the beauty born of their joining.

Edward had learned to read and write Latin in the monastic schools, and Katie's father hoped Edward's knowledge would fascinate Katie enough that she would willingly go to the priory even though the nuns were so different from the Druid women. And Katie had gone happily from the priory to the young craftsman's bed and into his short destiny, a destiny she inherited and that now led her to Guy of Gisbourne. And here she stood, wondering where the next wind of whims would blow her.

"Katie Chenoweth," Gisbourne began, "lucky you are to be alive tonight. I can only imagine the constitution behind your quiet eyes that you managed to survive capture by the Hood. What is it you're not telling me? Much, I think. Shrewder than you look is what you are. Come with us and I'll see that you fall into no more danger this night of your life." His large hand gripped her arm gently, but to break the hold she would have needed help. This wasn't the moment to resist. Will hadn't come for her as she waited on the cold road—no, she hadn't forgotten that—and Guy of Gisbourne was offering what Katie could only hope would be protection; a fire, some food, more time. Time to think and to plan. Time to be warm again. Then she would be able to think. Her head would become clear once her toes had feeling again.

Gisbourne and his men took her to a shallow place between three interlocking hillocks where they had set up their tents. Katie's first thought when she saw the elaborate temporary dwellings—even more plush than most people's year-round homes—was to wonder whether or not Robin knew they were camped so near the rim of Sherwood. The big nobleman let her into his tent, the largest one and the only one with candles inside. Because it was lined with the hides of cattle, the tent could have light inside without it shining through to give away their location against the dark fabric of night. Katie had never known such splendor existed. Cushions of silk filled with goosedown lined an entire wall, made of colors Katie had never seen before. What dyes could combine to make these colors? One glowed as deep and rich as blueberries, but there was a cast to it more like part of a summer sunset over the great sea beyond Gwynedd. Here, in candlelight, it shone and writhed like something alive, drawing her hand until she couldn't resist.

Gisbourne's voice rumbled beside her. "It's called purple. I had it dyed for me, enough fabric for an entire room, while I was in the east on the second crusade. Is it not a color for kings?"

"How do they make it? What kind of berry or bark can boil up such a color?"

"None can."

"But then . . ."

"This comes not from the land but from the bowels of the sea. Great horned shells with animals inside must be boiled, and this is what they spew. So rare are the shells that only the very wealthy can afford to own or wear this color. Happily for me," he added, "I am very wealthy." Thick, arching brows, black as his beard, lifted to make his point. "Your hair is finely plaited and you're clean. You wouldn't be if you were a woodland scamp or an outlaw's whore. As such, I believe your story for now. Are you hungry?"

She wasn't. As brief and bombastic as the campside meal had been, the food Robin procured for his people was filling. Still, it wouldn't do to make any more enemies tonight. "Yes, some," she answered.

"Urlan! Wine, bread, and some fruit!"

"Aye, coming."

Gisbourne pulled the ermine cape from his shoulders and tossed it aside as though it were broadcloth. Katie watched it go with awe and some envy as she let him lead her to a seat amid the fat cushions. They were so soft! She almost slipped between them before she got the knack of sitting *on* them. Gisbourne also sat, reclining against a dais, his silver hair and black beard falling into the glow of the nearest candle. His eyes were small, dark, and animal-like but rimmed in thick ebony lashes and full of intelligence. He used them on her but said nothing as Urlan came in with an armload of foodstuffs and a carafe of red wine. Katie stole another glance around the tent, this time looking past the cushions to a vast tabard with a crest and castle stitched on it so realistically that she might have been peering at it through a clutch of trees.

"Castle Gisbourne," he supplied, and Katie gave up trying to hide the fact that she was gawking like a peasant. "And my clan crest."

"You're not English?"

"The last twenty years of my life I've called myself English. Before that I was of the Scottish borderlanders. Little more than a cowherd. Everything you see or lie upon I have earned for myself. Tell me," he said, his tone changing as he poured the wine into a pair of stunning silver goblets, "who told you Robin o' the Hood and his thieves were of a bargaining kind? And what do you care for this road to risk your life as you did?"

Katie ran quickly over the truth in her mind

to see if telling it would do any harm—at least up until she discovered kindness among the thieves. Finding no danger there, she told him about Edward, about Abbot Godfrey, about her quest to save her forge from persecution and her town from economic leprosy. The Cart Road was Southwell's link to Nottingham, and the merchants depended on trade coming from that larger and more prestigious town. Gisbourne nodded his understanding and offered his sympathies and encouragements.

"But why," he began when she paused, "would your town find you a threat?"

"Because I am of the Old Religion, and they cannot understand it."

"Indeed? The Old Religion, say you? Do you mean to say you are a . . ."

"Druid, yes."

"I thought there were none of that ilk left."

"Very few of us remain. Those who do are sequestered away in isolated pockets. Many are converted to Christianity as it grows more popular and knows its popularity, but still more of us simply hide our beliefs away and keep them in our silent hearts."

"But you?"

"I chose not to hide. I now pay the price for it. I must go on this quest when my body and my soul wish to be home mourning in my Edward's cold bed."

Sir Guy nodded, but Katie couldn't tell if he agreed or was merely comprehending.

What kind of man was he? He gave out no clues, no signals. Katie sought his eyes and his voice for windows to his heart, but all were guarded. Only when the subject turned to Robin

Hood, himself, did Gisbourne show a raw feeling. "That Locksley demon," he called him, and every description was consecutively less kind. Katie listened, guarding her own expression and etching out a plan of action. She knew she was as much a prisoner as a guest, for only the dark, cold road would receive her again if she tried to leave, and what excuse could she give Guy of Gisbourne? In the midst of his hateful description of the Hood's crimes, could she tell him that she needed to leave these warm cushions, to go back into the Greenwood and take up company with the outlaws her host loathed and was sworn to destroy?

No. She was safer appearing to be their victim. That she did see in his careful, confident glare. As she conversed with him Katie took care to express relief at being rescued but not to prattle on about the horrors of her woodland experience. Gisbourne was no fool. He continually searched her face for that flicker of description she kept hidden from him.

"Tell me," he asked as he refilled her goblet, "how is my old nemesis Robin looking these days?"

Katie sipped, using the goblet as a mask. "Looking? You mean, you know him personally?"

"Of course. How has life in the rotting mulch treated him? Last I saw, his beard was long, and his hair untouched by the sun. Is it the same?"

Katie doubted his word as she remembered Robin's trim, dust-blond beard and hair. She shrugged, disliking the position Gisbourne was edging her into. She dared not refuse to speak at all of the outlaws, but neither dared she argue that they were kinder people and nobler than he cared to say. "He is much like that," she said, "but I saw him only once and then only in the darkness. I could tell you things I saw, but night and fear much distorted the world for me then, as you might guess. Certainly a man of power like you can hardly rely on the view of a frightened woman, and I can't ask you to try."

His goblet turned in his thick fingers. One eyebrow raised, a black animal arching over its prey. "True, I am seldom caught by fear, but that in itself is only a habit. Sometimes a bad one."

"Can it be so?"

"Oh, yes. And you were lucky to fear them and let them see your fear. Had they thought you cocky, you may have found yourself hairless and half skinned. I suspect your husband's death, so recent and his ghost hardly settled in purgatory, was what kept you safe and finally made them exile you from the Greenwood. They're a sorry herd of derelicts, and it's a pity the countryside is at their mercy. Not for long, though. I've contained them in this section of Sherwood. Not long ago the Hood's domain reached considerably farther. Many men died to push them back, many families giving up their fathers to safeguard their king's land. Many go down even yet in cruel ambush by Hood and his nightcrawlers. They pleasure to destruction and taunting, as if plain thievery were not enough. Are you still hungry? Perhaps there is something you lack?"

"I lack nothing, thank you."

"Then tell me. Is Will Scarlet still soiling himself with his cousin's company?"

Katie's heart jumped. She almost squirmed to one side as Will's image bolted into the tent—she and Gisbourne were no longer alone among the silk cushions and warm tapestries. "I ... I may have seen someone of that name. . . ."

"Him you wouldn't forget once you'd seen him. He wears red clothing with a broadcloth cloak, or sometimes he dresses in black trews, a black tunic, and black cap with a sarcastic red feather. Nothing at all like a gentleman should dress. He's taken to looking like the rats he runs with. Did you meet a man of such description?" His small, artistic eyes bored into her and gave him his answer before Katie could blink away the ache in her own eyes. "I see you have. I see he affected you. He has a history of that."

"Do you ..." She found her throat dry and had to swallow. "Do you know him yourself?"

"I know he's an intelligent pirate." At first Gisbourne seemed almost unwilling to answer her question, and Katie pressed her lips together in contempt. "That one and I knew each other as youths, when he spent his summers in the north of England. Even then he was brash and rebellious."

"And headstrong," Katie muttered.

Black eyes flashed. "So you did meet him."

The blanket around Katie's shoulders failed to keep a chill from running up her spine. She wasn't really afraid of Sir Guy, but by now the numb bravery that landed her in the Greenwood had been diluted by all the hard riding, the hard tearing of her mind as she shifted from the life she knew into the company of people who seemed more mythical than alive. The danger had done something to her, and she was still full of its chill.

Quietly she admitted, "I saw many men. He was among them."

"Lady, you have been in the hands of a monster, then. However, luck was with you. You're safe here. I have warm clothes that will hang well on your body. I shall sleep in my guard's tent and you shall have this one for yourself. It's the warmest and most private. Sleep well," he bade as he rose, a giant in a sea of purple, "and when the day dawns, you and I will speak more of Robin Hood and Will Scarlet, and we'll see if you know anything that can help me end their siege on the road once and forever. With God's help we'll wash the road in their entrails."

With God's help, Katie thought, but not with mine. My concerns are for my forge and apprentices. Robin and Will may win or lose their private war with you, Sir Knight of Gisbourne, and you are my rescuer tonight and a learned man, but this political tugging at straws makes my heart hurt. My king isn't here to defend himself against insults, and I'm not strong enough to save my town and my king as well. I envy Richard the Lionheart that he has men like you to fight for him, but Robin Hood and his fiery cousin have done me no harm yet, and I'll do them none. Not yet.

"You will find me a generous host," Gisbourne said. "I take great pride in the art of hospitality." He opened a decorative box and punctu-

ated his claim with a fine-toothed ivory comb,
a bottle of body oil, and a thing he called a
sponge. "Another profit from the distant sea,"
he said as he handed it to her. It was coarse,
brown, and ugly, like a chunk of rotting wood,
and Katie couldn't imagine what it was for.
Gisbourne didn't explain. He ordered a pitcher
of water and a washbowl. When it came, the
water had the scent of roses and spice as he
poured it into the bowl. "Put the sponge in."

When she did, the water soothed her hand,
feeling like the very silk of these cushions, and
for a moment, she was shocked that water could
be made soft. Then she realized that something was happening to the sponge in her hand.
It was still pocked with holes, still brown, still
ugly. But moments ago it had been stiff and
scratchy; now, as she squeezed, the sponge
compressed and reinflated, and it was as soft
as the water!

"You may bathe yourself," Gisbourne said,
"then anoint your body with this libation to
keep you as supple as rose petals in spring.
Sleep among these pillows and remember where
you might have been sleeping had we not found
you."

"Good night to you," Katie said. "I am in
your debt."

"Many are," he replied, the silvery hair
around his face gleaming like clouds above the
sun, "but you may find there are worse debts
to bear."

In a ruffle of velvet he was gone. She sat in
the golden candlelight, keenly aware of her
aloneness, her hand still in the water, still
holding the sponge. Was this her destiny?

Soon she overcame her discomfort with the strange surroundings and stripped out of her tired tunic. She washed herself with the sponge and found it kind to her skin, the rosewater glistening on her in a million droplets, each of which held a minute reflection of Will Scarlet's questioning face. Why hadn't he come for her? Why had he left her helplessly pacing in the cold dust of night? She didn't imagine him to be the kind of man who was easily brought to heel, not even by a power like that which Robin possessed over his ragtag army. Yet, perhaps she had perceived Will incorrectly. Maybe he did bend knee to Robin's orders.

Katie shook her head. The sponge plopped into the water, quickly grew heavy, and sank. There must have been some other reason. She thought a man like Will would have come for her if only to defy Robin and assert his own identity amid the Greenwood rebels, but he hadn't come.

And she was warm now and clean, so why should she care?

She sat on a cushion and carefully unplaited her hair, length after length of it, the candleglow making it seem much yellower than its true apple-meat color. That done, she slowly drew the ivory comb through the strands, letting her head loll to the sensation. Slowly her eyes drifted closed. Hands drew the comb. Not her hands. The strong, gentle hands she'd felt before among the dark trees—combing, touching, smoothing, arranging—returned and caressed her head again. The lengths of her locks reached out luxuriously, falling off the comb in a great white-gold fan, brushing her naked body strand after strand, and she felt the rustle of leaves in the wind above her, around her again. The wind was singing, and on its howl was a name she longed to whisper.

Her eyes snapped open.

She spun around.

She was alone. With a sigh she wrapped herself in Sir Guy's ermine cape and soon was fast asleep in a sea of silk.

Morning came quietly, but it came too soon. For a few foggy moments the strange surroundings confused her, and she struggled up on her elbows among purple clouds and murmured, "Edward?" Then she remembered, and immediately the curtains dropped on that pain, separating her from it, and she was able to reassess all that had happened to her on her quest. How could she ever find Robin's hideaway again? His men were as elusive as foxes, and now they knew she was looking for them. If only Will had defied Robin as Katie had thought he might. She'd be willing to endure his fury for a second chance at success.

Her cheek stung with just the memory of the time Will had nearly struck her. She'd never faced the possibility of being roughly handled by a man, and the prospect enraged her. Her father hadn't had such a temper, and neither had Edward, there could be no excuse for it. Will Scarlet was—or had been—an aristocrat. He should have been able to control himself. Evidently life in the wilds had bestialized him and taken the sheen off his nobility.

Katie shook off the muses of awakening. With a dizzying stretch she got to her knees and looked for her tunic, but it was missing. In its place was a shimmering gown, spread out over the cushions beside her. It was flowing and grand, the color of yellow apples, the sleeves gathered at four points between the shoulder and wrist and tied with gold twine. Beside this finery was still more finery: soft leather slippers; stockings; a gold-mesh headpiece for her hair; bejeweled belts for her waist and hips; and an over-tunic with short sleeves, hemmed short in front and draping to the floor in back. She touched it gingerly. The underside was velvet in the color of raspberries, and the overside was rose-pink with a pattern of velvet-lined squares. Inside each square was a stitched design of gold rose leaves. Never had Katie seen such intricate work. Surely someone had spent many months creating such a masterpiece. How could she wear these? She was a blacksmith, a common merchant. How could she put someone's pride on her body and wear it like day-to-day robes?

But there was nothing else to wear. Her plain white tunic was gone. Gisbourne obviously knew how to achieve what he wanted.

Gisbourne and his men were breaking fast by the cold ashes of their camp fire when Katie emerged from the main tent in the clothing he had provided. She could tell from their faces how she looked. Truly she felt beautiful. The cream-yellow gown was warm and fleecy against her skin, the rich velvet tunic reflected its rosy color in her cheeks, and the jewels winked along her waist and draped around her hips on the gold belts with their silver links. Luxury carried her; she scarcely lifted her legs as she floated over the stubby grass. It was strange to feel the ground so near the soles of her feet! All her life, except when she was very small, she had worn the hard, cobbled shoes typical of the gentry. These supple leather slippers were a new experience.

Gisbourne stood up. "A princess has risen from a peasant's ashes," he announced, nudging away the gawk on Urlan's face to make a place beside himself for Katie. He offered her sweet bread and honey and a parcel of tender, spiced meat that she didn't recognize.

"What is this?" she finally asked. "Is it a bird?"

"Swan."

"Swan! Here in the wilds you indulge in roast swan? Such things are only for the richest of feasts!"

"Yes, it's so in the towns," Gisbourne admitted. "In the open spaces it's easier to find wild swans to kill, and I can afford the best of huntsmen to do the hard work for me." He indicated a thin, white-haired man with long features and quick eyes. "Marcus is the finest stalker of waterfowl and nesting birds coin can buy. He keeps my household in swans. His next bird earns him an extra gold piece for each from now on."

Marcus' eyes flickered. "Thank you, my lord!"

"Deserved. I believe in paying a prime wage." Sir Guy unfolded his thick legs and stretched them, then poured goat's milk from a pouch into Katie's cup. She was about to ask where he had gotten that when she spied the nanny goat tied near the horses, peacefully grazing. This man liked to travel in comfort and spared no expense for it. "I've found I get the best quality, both in product and in loyalty, when I pay well for it."

"A wealthy man's prerogative, my lord," Katie pointed out. "People of the merchant class must be shrewder bargainers."

"Are you a shrewd bargainer, Katie Chenoweth?"

"When I must be. I learn quickly, but I learn well."

"Who was your teacher? This husband who died?"

"Yes. My husband who died."

"He also taught you smithing?"

"He did, and taught me well. I intend to continue in Southwell as a blacksmith as was my Edward's dream."

"And where on that willow's body do you hope to grow the muscles for hammering and bellows work?"

"I have two strong apprentices for my muscles."

"Shrewd," he said, "and with foresight as well. How unique in a woman of delicate nature."

"Not so unique in the working class, Sir Guy. Many wives continue their husbands' trades when the men are taken from them. A wife is her husband's first and best assistant before he can afford apprentices. We work our trades and grow and learn together of necessity. Glad I am of it, as well, for as wonderful as I find these clothes you've draped on me, I have not earned them."

Gisbourne chuckled. That eyebrow once again

stalked prey. "Beauty is its own earning," he said.

Aching for honesty, Katie said bluntly, "I've never colored my lips or kohled my eyes as ladies of your standing do. Where in my simple face do you find beauty to compare with theirs?" It was an open question, full of knowing and suspicion of his compliment. She could see the shock in his stare that she was so world-wise at her age.

"One finds beauty where one looks," he said simply, and she could tell he was admitting the truth in her words and her self-evaluation. "To judge all women by court women is to judge a flower by a painting of a flower. There is no comparison, Katie. And the fine dress you wear you've earned by gracing my camp with your company."

"Would you be proud if Castle Gisbourne came to you by way of your company?"

Again he laughed. "Nay, you're right. So, ragged nymph, would you like your tatters back?"

It was Katie's turn to smile. "I'm shrewd, sir, not foolish."

"Good. It's unrefined to refuse a gift. And these clothes look so suited to you—the lemon of your hair in this dress, the pink of your cheeks in the tunic, those gems sputtering about your waist, so like the glittering in your eyes. I love to see a woman in good clothing. It does my disillusioned heart a kindness."

"What has disillusioned you?"

"Lady, the world."

"But you've had such success."

"Success of the purse. Not of the spirit."

"And what would give you that?"

He thought about it. "Will Scarlet's head on a pike." He thought some more. "And Robin Hood's corpse crying on a spit."

Will Scarlet's head, with the rest of him behind it, peeked from behind Sir Guy's tethered horses. Tracking Katie hadn't been easy. Her footprints had been difficult to find in the darkness, and waiting for the first thin rays of dawn before the small prints became visible had been damning. He followed them up the road and back. She had wandered. She had paced. He read turmoil in the road; he read a chill in her limbs. He felt that discomfort in his own. And when hoofprints tore the echo of her tread into clumps of dust, some of his heart was torn as well. What had happened? These horses were in full gallop. Had she been trampled? Had her murderers taken her body and disposed of it? Had she been kidnapped? He would have to wait to find out. But the rest of the story was here, etched in the dirt. These hooves were large, larger than those of wagon horses, so these weren't townspeople. They weren't as large as the hooves of plow horses, so these weren't farmers. Will glanced back at his hunting horse, Palermo, and knew who had stolen the woman he, himself, had stolen against her wishes—a woman who had proven more than worthy of the challenge. These were the hoofprints of horses of the nobility, hunting horses for well-to-do folk. His own kind. And no one else but Guy of Gisbourne would have that kind of horse in this area of Sherwood.

So Gisbourne had her. For her that could be

lucky or not. Unlucky either way for Robin's secrecies, and certainly no good for Will, since he would have to rescue her. Tracking the footprints to Gisbourne's camp hadn't been necessary; Robin's scouts had long watched the baron's every move and knew his every camp. Gisbourne favored four prime camp locations, each of which he was sure was secret, and Will had checked two of them before he discovered the familiar tents. He scouted the camp at dawn, scoffing Sir Guy's habit of traveling with so many luxuries. It made him predictable. A man who didn't like discomfort tended to settle for the best in camping areas, and there were only so many of those. Unlike Robin's men, who would camp inside a rotting log, Gisbourne often sacrificed good military judgment for personal comfort.

Will had no trouble hiding amid the horses. Knowing he was in for a day of stealth, he had changed out of his red clothes into his black tunic and trews and blended with the shadows of the horses and nearby trees. From there he watched three men build a fire and warm a plush fur cape there, until Gisbourne himself emerged, but not from his own tent. Why was he coming out of his guard's tent? As soon as Will posed the silent question, he knew the answer.

At least he's treating her like a guest, he thought as he crouched behind a shield of autumn gold, and not a prisoner. She should do well in that case. At least she's not dead. With luck she'll not be injured, either. If only I had not to ask myself *why* she's being treated like a guest instead of a prisoner. I hate the answer.

As Gisbourne dressed and his men prepared to break fast, Will formulated excuses for why Katie would be enjoying the comforts of Gisbourne's main tent and found all of the possibilities unpalatable. He vacillated between feelings of fury and protectiveness. He had let his poor judgment and his uncontained anger land her in this position, which wouldn't have happened at all, had she known a gentlewoman's place. But if she had known and had kept her place, Will would never have become so fascinated with her. He was sick to death of vain noblewomen with their decorated faces and their empty heads, and Katie intrigued him. She was a thinker, a surviver. Something within her was tough enough to hold back the floodgates of grief so that she could attempt her courageous quest; yet she was wise enough to know that there was life to be gotten on with in spite of a beloved husband's death. Will had seen women waste away to corpses after such a death, having no inner strength to keep the light of life afire. It was a sad kind of cowardice, Will thought, to give up because someone loved has died. Katie hadn't given up. She hadn't . . . yet she had. She was unique unto herself. She was . . . dangerous. Unpredictable.

And as he watched Gisbourne and his men at their morning meal, no emotion flew in Will's breast until the main tent parted and agony emerged. Agony in angel's garb.

Katie.

In clothing fit for a queen.

Will watched the cream gown and raspberry tunic move on her as she approached Gisbourne

and accepted company beside the arch nemesis of Robin Hood. What had she done to be
rewarded with such elegance? What information had she sold him? Or worse, what favors?

Will's teeth cut into his lower lip. The idea
of Katie defiling herself just to survive was a
writhing snake within him, and he bent over it
like an illness, clutching a hawthorn branch to
keep from retching. She had gotten more than
survival, though; she had gotten payment. It
glittered in the golden net that held her hair,
in the gems at her waist, floating like a thing
alive in lemon and pink on her body. Will had
never cared for Gisbourne; at this moment he
wholly loathed him.

Ducking his head, Will retreated and let the
russet leaves swallow him as he made his way
back to Palermo and the wad of supplies he'd
snatched at the last minute, before defying
Robin.

He had to get her back. Bitterly he changed
the noble idea of rescue to the distasteful idea
of kidnapping, a necessary alteration. He had
to accept the fact that Katie might not come
along willingly. Seldom had his heart steered
him wrong—he had a supernatural gift for judging character—but evidently this time it had.
Ringing anew within him came the awareness
of how vast the difference was between Katie
and the women of his class.

Class. Will sneered bestially as he fumbled
with a tangled rope. How preposterous the no-
tion seemed to him now, after all these months
of living with paupers and dispossessed nobility. Who could compare a woman like Katie
Chenoweth with court women? They were ei-

ther too vain to think a two-edged thought or too conniving to keep a friend. None he'd met had worked a day or striven for an ideal; why, they even hired wet nurses to raise their babies for them. They might as well forfeit womanhood.

How much I've changed to be thinking this way. Not long ago the man I was at Gamewell would've preferred a silent, painted face at his side instead of chasing after a chameleon who defies possessing. What is it she wants out of life? Nothing, she claims, without her Edward, yet her yearning to survive seems well enough intact. By the Cross I'll slit Gisbourne's gullet if Katie was taken unwillingly and those raiments she wears are compensation for his loins' dishonor.

The oath would've sat better in his chest if he'd seen regret or shame or defilement on Katie's face when she'd stepped from Gisbourne's tent. If there had been the slightest trace—some twitch, some hint of displacement, some flicker to tell Will she was here against her wishes—he would have found his hands less cold as they tucked the rope into his belt and his other tools into other places. He would need his hands free.

If only he could free his mind.

He put anxiety behind and moved stealthily into the hawthorns to take his place in Katie Chenoweth's future.

That future was vague even to Katie as she sat before the foreign fire, warming her toes on one of the big rocks they had used to circle their burning kindling. Sir Guy plied her with

questions about Robin's manpower and land-
marks to his hideaway deep in the bowels of
the Greenwood, but Katie shielded herself and
Robin—however wisely or unwisely—with
feigned ignorance. No, she wasn't protecting
Robin; not really. Robin Hood needed no protection with his natural cunning and men like
Will Scarlet at his side, but Katie was unwilling to give over information to Gisbourne or
anyone yet, even as craftily as Gisbourne posed
his questions. He asked her things as though
he already knew the answers and merely would
be amused to hear her speak them. In his own
way, he was as cunning as Robin.

"I hear old Rob and his cronies have no
comfort in the woods in this outcast life they've
chosen," Sir Guy mentioned as he watched his
men stoke their small fire and warm a clay jug
of wine to ward off the morning chill. "I tell
you," he said, chuckling, "at times I wish things
could be different. I'd like to be a ragged
bandsman of his for a day or so, just to look at
how a man survives living as a rat does. Ah,
but I'm being caustic, aren't I? Robin must be
superhuman to convince so many people to
follow him into squalor."

Katie shifted her feet to a warmer rock. "I
believe many didn't follow. It seems they may
have been pushed."

The big man's eyes narrowed. "Pushed by
whom or what?"

Coolness washed through her. She'd already
said too much. "I don't know. I know I saw
children being fed who had been hungry. I saw
men who seemed honorable, at least to me."

"They grow fat on royal deer, deer held in

trust for the Crown. And I told you why their hands stayed to their sides where you were concerned."

"Sir, the kind of brigands you think them to be aren't the kind who would shy off a wanted woman just because of a dead husband . . . but perhaps I'm wrong."

"You are."

"Then I'll decline to your experience."

"Wisely put."

Katie held her breath, begging luck that he would end his questions before she gave herself away entirely. She needed his help if she was ever to find Robin and Will again, and she needed him to believe she was simply another of the outlaws' victims. She'd fielded his queries well enough so far. Foolish defense of the Greenwood outlaws would destroy what little advantage she still had, and the moon would hang on a stick before she would forfeit her edge.

If Gisbourne suspected anything, he didn't show it. That didn't stop Katie from assuming him to be suspicious. He wasn't a man who could be easily fooled, and she wasn't a woman who was quick to underestimate men of power. Even as she exchanged glances with him over the crackling fire, she felt they understood each other; a strange rainbow of fascination and distrust, admiration and caution. Certainly he would expect her to back down. So she did. She lowered her eyes. Now all the pieces were in place. He was in charge again, and she was his meek, grateful ward. With luck, Katie calculated, this arrangement would turn in her favor. It would depend, finally, on which of

them could be more skillful in the delicate art
of manipulation. It would depend on Katie's
decision, yet to be made, about Gisbourne himself. Was he her enemy? Was Robin her friend?
And what label would she stitch to the firm
chest under scarlet fabric? If the answers came
from which of them had treated her kindly,
more gently, more honorably, the choice was
easy. But Katie couldn't find simplicity in her
heart today, no matter how deeply she dug
into the clouds and smoke twisting there. So
she rubbed her toes on the warm rock and kept
silent.

"We'll break camp," Gisbourne was saying,
"and move to a new location. It doesn't do to
stay in one area too long." He leaned back, his
massive chest heaving a sigh beneath the black
beard. In the creamy white light of morning he
was even more imposing than he had been last
night in torchlight. Clearly he was used to
having power at his fingertips. "I will forfeit
my best packhorse, the bay mare with the broad
back, and Urlan will escort you to Castle
Gisbourne until I return. Then we'll decide
what to do with you."

Katie glared at him. "Do? I'm a free woman."

"Nay, you're not. You're a foundling under
my care, and care for you I shall. You can't
return to Southwell—isn't it true?—until this
road is broken of the Hood's siege, else you
face the, may I say, brutish wrath of your
fellow merchants. I swear, I had thought such
shortsightedness was gone in England, but I
see it's very much alive, and you have no place
to go, have you, until I can quell the cause. If
you'll give me your favor, I shall act as your

champion." When he saw her brow knit with ignorance of this courtly rite, he added, "A trinket. A bit of cloth, a ribbon from your hair, a brooch, a piece of garment which you give with your blessing, entrusting your fate to me and giving me the right to act on your behalf."

Disturbed, Katie stood up and paced halfway around the fire, her fingers laced in quandary. It was true that she had no place to go. "And yet . . .

She inhaled slowly, trying to puzzle it all out carefully, line by line, before she finally spoke.

"I have no favor to give," she stated, a blunt set of words considering that they covered evasion, "for you have taken my clothes, and all I now wear you already own. I have no blessing to put on a favor, because I'm not a Christian and don't believe in blessings. I have no fate, for I died when my Edward died. And you have no right to act for me because I will not transfer myself to your charge. I only hope you take no offense, for I mean none, but"—she turned to face him, her arms falling stiffly to her sides—"you cannot send me away. I *am* a free woman, in charge of myself, Sir Guy. For your care I thank you profoundly, most profoundly, most heartily, but I'm staying here to fulfill my obligation. That much I owe to myself and my husband's dream. I can't shift the responsibility over; indeed I've no desire to do so. These hands, these limbs you see before you are numb and aching for death. In every breath of wind I wish my breath would cease, and this quest of mine, no matter how much I didn't want it, is keeping me alive. Castle

Gisbourne, I'm sure, is grand and warm and princely, and your offer is as gracious as your treatment has been, but, sir, I must decline."

"And I must override you."

"Sir, you can't deny me possession of my own destiny!"

"Nay, nor do I. It's obvious you're over-wrought, unable to make a clear-eyed decision, my dear girl. As a lady of means in my shelter you'll find quietude and solace. As for occupying yourself there is much to keep a lady busy. If you can read, I have a library with no less than twenty books, or I shall *teach* you to read. If you yearn after music, I employ two fine troubadours who will play for you or instruct you in the lute and flute and bodhran. You won't be bored."

"I won't be there! I'll be here, doing what I came to do."

He gestured at the empty air. "How? Do you plan to be robbed again? The Hood is no such idiot, Katie. You'll never find him again."

"I will. I will, somehow."

"You won't. You're talking about an elusive snake. The more you chase him, the deeper he roots under the moss. I know, believe me. You'll be safe at my castle, as a lady should be, and a lady you are despite the forge soot under your fingernails. Yes, I've seen it. It'll go away in time. You'll have a servant woman to rub lemons on your fingers every morning and night until you glow like ivory. Face reality, Katie. Your days as a smith are finished, aren't they? Did you go to the coals out of love for the coals or for your husband?"

"For my husband, of course. Why—"

"Then what are the coals to you now? Soot and an income. Your quest is better off in my hands, I think. A woman requires a guardian. I shall keep your fingers clean and provide for all your needs. You will be the great quest of my days. I shall make a queen of you, Katie!" he promised, his small eyes wide, his voice as deep as smoke, and in that moment of offering he was an awesome force. Consumed with what he called a quest, his sudden, intense involvement with Katie made her wish to retreat, and retreat she did, mentally, into a new caution. She wouldn't misjudge him again. The price for that error would be too dear.

In the few seconds she had, Katie scoured her conversations with Gisbourne, seeking a word or phrase that would move him, something that would have impact on a man of his kind of thinking. What would make him see indignity in what he was doing? She knew he couldn't stand to be undignified. What could she say to parry off his "protection"? It had to be good or she would soon find herself riding off to Castle Gisbourne on a broad bay mare, and that wouldn't do at all.

"Katie, Katie," Gisbourne muttered through her calculations, "such an unaristocratic name, a street name. I think I shall call you something else. I'll call you ... Catherine. Yes. A name befitting the woman, the goddess I'll make of you. Catherine is what I'll call you."

If Katie had been intimidated before, she was now enraged. She balled her fists. "Call me Cerridwyn, then, for *that* is my name!"

"Cerridwyn, Catherine, they're close." He wagged that hand again, trivializing her identity and her self-possession all in one gesture. "Druidry is dead, Catherine. Let it die. You need a Christian name to be anyone these days."

"I am who I choose to be," she said firmly, struggling against the small quake in her voice. Men, men controlled everything! How could she get away?

Gisbourne stood up, filling the countryside with himself. "You are Catherine Chenoweth of Gisbourne Demesne. In time you'll hardly remember wanting to be anything else."

Curse me for being myself! she raged internally. What is it he sees when he looks at me that he has to possess it? I don't know what he sees or how to blind him to it! Edward, why couldn't you have simply gone on living?

Reading her thoughts, Gisbourne looked at her askance as though he knew her well and lowered his voice to say, "Katie Chenoweth the blacksmith wants death. Let her have it." Quietly with great significance, he added, "Be reborn today."

Never before had she faced an obstacle as ominous and as appealing as Guy of Gisbourne. Standing there like some grand monarch, he offered her no small thing. Any person of the gentry would sell a piece of being for what he was dropping at her feet; indeed, what he was forcing upon her. Strange that he considered such dictates within his power. To take control of another person's whole self? When had she ever heard of such a thing before?

Carefully and with gambling forethought she uttered, "Yes, yes . . . you may be right. I must think . . . but what you say of me is true. A woman needs a guardian. Perhaps . . . perhaps you will give me time to grow used to the idea." She quaked to the pit of her bowels but remained steady on the outside, her twitching hands hidden behind her.

Sir Guy rolled back his head and laughed until it ended in an amused moan. "Oh, I'm so discouraged! I had hoped you would fight longer. I do so love a woman who tugs at my wits, Catherine. In time I hope to kindle a desire in you to tug at other things, but until then I'll wrap you in a cocoon of silk and fineries and wait to discover the winged creature lying in that dirty Druid worm that holds you captive. There's a butterfly within you that will be a towering addition to Christendom when I tear away the damaged outer skin. Ah, glorious! Catherine! Glorious!"

The hills echoed. The sun made no comment. The rubicund trees of Lunasa glowered nearby, arguing. High overhead one lonely cloud smoldered its way across the morning sky in a stiff wind, and Katie's soul followed it. But the worldly rest of her was still here and raging against a terrible truth—she *wanted* to sink into the placidity he described. Yes, it was a guilty truth. To put behind her the wrench of Edward's love, his death, the responsibilities she had borne, to cast off like a filthy cloak the collusions of her life. The abbot. The outlaws. The Cart Road. The Old Way. How easy it would be to drown into the conquering religion and pretend to embrace it so all the arguing would subside, so no one would look at her in fear or disgust; no one would scour her face for pockmarks of the devil they had themselves created. Oh Horned One, oh, Goddess, push away this interlude! It would be death of a most horrible kind to retreat with him to Castle Gisbourne. Death, useless death. No! No! I won't. No one is master of my entity but me, this woman I choose to be, this Katie, once Cerridwyn, never Catherine. Forgive me, Gisbourne. You're a tough tree for the cutting, and deceit is a keen ax.

"Speak no more of this for a while," she requested, making sure it sounded like a request. "I must adjust my mind to it all."

His brows raised. "You *are* wise, on more than one level. How unique. What a Cleopatra you are. What a Hatshepsut. Can you read and write?"

"Yes, your grace."

"How is that possible?"

"My father is a shoemaker. He sent me to a priory for education. My mother, being of the Old Folk and because Druids revere knowledge above all, agreed even though the education was of a different religious order."

"Marvelous!" He clapped his hands, rubbed them, and laughed out loud.

Katie pressed her hands to her temple and interrupted. "Forgive me . . . forgive me . . . your knowledge dazes me."

His knowledge was abrasive.

She went on. "Please, allow me to be Druid a little longer. I must. I'm still too entwined in the Old Way."

"I understand. Not to worry. God will make himself known to you. I will see to it."

"In the meantime . . ."

"In the meantime you may practice your

pagan ring-singing. You'll wean of it eventually."

"Until then . . ."

"Speak. Go ahead. Say what I see in your eyes."

She stopped walking and faced him, deliberately keeping the hungry star of freedom out of her eyes. "This is the time of year we call Lunasa. At this time we make preparations for the changeover from the reign of the Goddess to the harvest and hunting season of the Horned God, which will come at Samhain. In order to prepare our minds for the twice-yearly march of the Sidhe—our Faery people—we stand morning vigils among the oaks. Would it be possible . . . might I have that time this morning? One of your guards may go with me if he doesn't stand too close and if he knows enough discretion to keep silent and avert his eyes while I meditate."

"Little enough to ask, isn't it?" Gisbourne took her arm and they strolled again. He seemed indulgent to the point of condescension, which turned her stomach. "You'll have your vigil. Of course, I must warn you about Urlan. While you're meditating, best you not try walking about at all. The slightest rustle of leaves or the snap of a twig may bring Urlan's sword out slashing. We wouldn't want him to accidentally dice an arm off you, would we now, eh?" His meaning was unmistakable.

Her throat tightened. "No . . . no."

Could she make her plan work now?

It depended on Urlan. If he was too bright or too stupid or the wrong combination of the two, all would go awry. Sir Guy's advice was

also a threat—there was no doubt about it—
and now all her chances rested on the gullibil-
ity of a mercenary manservant.

Sir Guy bade her a reluctant farewell, his
uplifted eyebrow reiterating that subtle warning. The gleam in his eyes showed enthusiasm
for his new toy and their future at Castle
Gisbourne, as Katie waded into a froth of ferns
with Urlan tramping behind her.

"Your master told you why we're here?" she
asked him, leading the way deep into the trees.

"He did, mistress."

"Do you understand it?"

"I don't, mistress."

"Things will happen that you may not understand, that may frighten you. Are you brave
enough?" She could almost feel his eyes widen.

"I'm brave, but . . . will there be spirits?"

"There may, I confess. I am of their own
kind, but I fear for you. The shades may not
recognize you. I've awakened from my morning trances to find my hair braided or undone,
my shoes displaced, boughs gathered around
my legs—I never know what to expect. They've
never hurt me, though as I said, I'm one of
them. There are tales of mistaken identity or
antagonism . . . oh, not to worry. The spirits
may not mind you if they sense you're here to
guard me from harm. If you were here to keep
me prisoner, things might be different."

Urlan's big body shook as he walked. "I . . . I
am here to keep you . . . safe. Is there a charm
that might be put on me to keep them away?"

Katie shrugged. "Druids don't extend charms
or curses, Urlan." She stopped and turned to
him. "But there may be a way. If the spirits

think you can't hear or see them, they may only touch your face from curiosity and pass you by.''

"I could blind my eyes with this cloth! I can hold my hands over my ears!"

She licked her lips, holding back a laugh. This was childishly easy. No wonder Gisbourne kept Urlan around. The confusion in Urlan's mind showed quite clearly in his eyes, making Katie hope his fear of heathen spirits could outweigh his fear of her escaping. She counted on his not quite comprehending all the facets of her acquaintance with Gisbourne or Gisbourne's specifications about whether he was to guard her from harm or keep her from getting away. While Katie was sure it was both, she hoped she could steer Urlan's thoughts with a little help from pretend magic. She would also have to invent a ritual that didn't exist and invoke spirits that were powerless outside of myth.

"Best not go farther, mistress," Urlan said nervously when she had led him down a steep, leaf-covered incline into a thick stand of trees. Not oaks, but they would do. Urlan wouldn't know the difference.

"All right," she agreed sweetly. "Why don't you sit there on that fallen tree? Face away from me."

"I will!" He put his hulky body on the log, breaking two twigs that were in his way, and tied a cloth around his head over his eyes. "Tell me when the spirits come and I'll cover my ears."

Eerily Katie said, "You'll know."

He shivered. His hand clutched and unclutched the hilt of his sword spasmodically.

Katie moved several paces away, glancing back at the big man and shaking her head, trying to think of a frightening enough invocation. This pretense would be laughable if her life didn't depend on it.

She passed by a broken branch half the length of her arm, decided it would add to the effect of her fakery, and scooped it up. She turned toward the dawn sun as it pierced the trees and raised her stick over her head with her hands grasping either end of it. If Sir Guy happened to be watching, perhaps this would allay his doubts and he would look away.

For Urlan's sake she tugged references out of her memory and chanted away:

> O great Aristotle, fill the morning,
> ride on the wings of Osiris,
> in the pit of a sea flower.
> Give me Cleopatra's wings
> that I may fly like a lizard.
> Cast away the eons' dust and call forth
> The ghosts of the barrows and nooks
> Deep in Beowulf's Grendel.

Urlan was holding his arms rigid and close to his body. Katie stole a glance at him, then surged on with her advantage.

> Come forth, Gwydion.
> Come forth, Mathonwy.
> Come out, come near us, Arianrhod.
> Bran, Artemis, and Thetis!
> Let the wryneck feed on willow-tree nests

and ants, she-bear, crane and fish
merge and move in our limbs
that we will climb the four idols of rock
and deliver to us the horrible spirit
of Cromm Cruich!
Danger! Lament! Enchantment!

She stole another look. Urlan had clapped his hands tight over his ears and was breathing hard and fast. Katie laughed, then covered her mouth and fought to contain it as she crept through the leaves to where Urlan sat trembling at her absurd cacophony of invocations. She peeked to make sure he truly couldn't see or hear, then leaned close and blew softly in his face. He sucked in his breath and shook. She ran her fingers lightly up and down the outer fabric of his sleeves, making sure he felt it but not too much. Poor Urlan drew his arms tighter to his head and actually whimpered. She picked up a leaf and ran it down his nose, then blew in his face again. Nothing, *nothing* would make him open his eyes or uncover his ears. Katie giggled at her victory and looked around for a rock big enough to hit him with; the stick she was holding wasn't heavy enough to render him senseless. There wasn't a suitable rock nearby, and knowing she had little time, she sneaked a few steps away.

There was a muffled thump behind her.

She whirled around. Urlan lay on the ground in a heap, the position of his arms telling her that he was unconscious. Katie stared, holding her breath, then realized the danger she was in. Baffled, she looked around. There was nothing. She heard an unnatural rustle and looked up, only to be blinded by the sun. A huge, silhouetted shape moved above her in a tree, then dropped out of the sun and knocked her to the ground. Involuntarily she let out a wild shriek. An arm choked her, killing any further outcry, and a horrible, smothering curtain dropped over her head like a mask without eyeholes or room to breathe. Seconds later her arms were immobilized and she was flung into the air over a hard shoulder. The force pushed the air from her body and left her dizzy as she was carried on a rough ride through the trees with the point of that shoulder ramming into her stomach at every step. She tried to move her arms, but it was as though she were wrapped in a carpet. Her magic stick was pressed along her rib cage, crushing one breast and scraping the side of her head. She tried to yell for help—even rescue by Sir Guy would be better than this—but that shoulder beneath her bent body prevented her from taking a deep breath. She squirmed, but her legs were held immobile. Terror clawed at her heart and roared in her ears. Her hands and feet began to ache as the restriction kept her blood from flowing into them, though she tried to kick wildly. High on the hill, rapidly growing more distant, she thought she heard shouts of fury and threat. Sir Guy must have heard her cry out and was coming after her. In her confusion Katie couldn't distinguish one hope from another. Who was kidnapping her and who did she want to save her? No logic could pierce the chaos of this ride. The wind howled in her head. Or was it her own blood pounding there?

Suddenly she was shifted on her assailant's

back and flung high in the air to land hard over a wideness with a spine—a horse. It must be—a big horse. Yes, she felt it tramp and rear beneath her, grunting its fury and snorting as a body crushed up against her on the animal's back. The reins snapped tight near her ears. The vast creature balked beneath her, then vaulted clear of the tangled bushes and they were off. More horrible, more bone-crushing than the last had been, this gallop left her gasping. Air wouldn't come into her lungs fast enough to keep her from feeling ill. Her breakfast lurched within her and came up to choke her, but she reacted with anger, forcing it down again and putting all her strength into one concerted thrash.

Swish—thunk. An arrow shot by and lodged in a tree. She heard more arrows come, but she didn't care. One hand was free!

Somehow her hand had wrenched through an open space, and she inhaled, working the stick through the hole until it, too, was free. Immediately she began hacking at the man who steered this stretching beast. Hooves drummed the ground, lurching and fighting the uneven land. Wider and wider the strides became as Katie thrashed harder and harder. The arrows swished past faster, like hungry horrors after meat. Her stick found flesh, and she beat at it, ignoring her crushed ribs and the ringing in her head. Her tortured lungs screamed for air. Fury and pain merged into one blinding explosion, driving her to hack harder and more viciously. A hand caught her wrist, but she wrenched loose and struck high, landing a blow on something firm. There was a cry of pain.

"Katie, stop it!"

It was Will's voice. And no surprise. Out of plain insult she kept hitting him, forgetting the thunder of Sir Guy's horses behind them and the buzz of arrows all around her. The horse was now grunting with every stride. Foam from its mouth flecked back onto her hand, and an instant later a stab of pain numbed her entire arm. Terrible forces—branches probably—whipped her head and legs, telling her that trees were closing in around them. The Greenwood. The air was suddenly cool as they left the sun behind and Gisbourne with it.

Her arm hung limp. The stick had been torn from it. The pain brought tears to her eyes when the numbness started to fade, but she was helpless again. Helpless to know what she wanted, whether or not to be insulted, whether to thank Will for rescuing her or deride him for coming so late. And why now? Why had he come at all?

• *Chapter Seven* •

The ride seemed endless. The horse carried them deeper into the sweet moss-smell where the woodland shadows were cool. The sound of hoofbeats from behind had gone entirely. Katie tried to let her aching body go limp, but the awkward position prevented it. She could only suffer. When the horse shifted from a full gallop to a trot, the ride became bumpy and agonizing, making her certain that Will was doing this to her deliberately. He didn't have to keep the animal trotting so long; a canter or a walk would have been easier on her.

By the time the mossy-moist scent of the deep woods became entwined with the aroma of bubbling stew, telling her the Greenwood encampment was very near, Katie was nearly hammered senseless. She felt bruises spreading on her ribs, and with every twinge she cursed Will for treating her this way. When the horse stopped, she didn't even realize it.

There was a tug on her legs. The world spun in the darkness of her cloth prison and she slammed to the ground in a heap. The moans she heard were her own, and the very sound of

132

them ignited her wrath, forcing her to push aside her pain. A few thrashes freed her head and shoulders from what appeared to be the same rotting sack she'd first been captured in by Robin's band. In a blind rage she gritted her teeth and wrenched the thing from her body, kicking it off and stomping it in abject revenge. Then she looked around for a better target for her fury.

And there he was. Dressed all in black, except for brown boots and a red feather in his hat. Leaning against a tree, Will was apparently catching his breath.

Barely able to walk on her tingling legs, Katie planted her feet and swore, "I'll disembowel the next creature who puts a sack over my head!"

Will gazed at her, panting in fatigue, his breath coming too deeply and too quickly, not bothering to respond but merely watching her with practiced disregard.

"I have never *been*," she raged, also gasping, "treated this *way* in my *life!* You are a barbarian! Is this your version of chivalry? Might you not have asked me to go with you? Look at me! I'm all bumps and bruises. I'm sick of being dragged off against my will, and I say it won't happen to me again!"

"Oh, cease your bitching," Will snarled. He was still breathing hard. "There's gratitude. Ask you to come with me indeed. How was I supposed to know your answer? I'm not ready to offer up my life for yours." He pushed off the tree and limped to her, plucking up part of her skirt. "What's this?" he demanded, ruffling the finery in her face, "Payment?"

She yanked it back. "A gift."

"From captor to captive? Hah! Or can it be you weren't a captive at all? Could that be it?"

"I certainly was! Do you want me to say I wasn't glad to be warm and dry last night? I'd be lying."

"I don't doubt it."

"Why didn't you help me last night when Robin ordered me left by the roadside?"

"You weren't by the hanged roadside! You were in Gisbourne's coverlets, eating Gisbourne's swan by Gisbourne's bedamned candlelight! How much did you tell him about us? Manpower? Location? Provisions?"

"I should've at that."

"I wouldn't put it past you. You're all out for Katie in the end." He limped away.

"Who *should* I be out for? I had no one else to give my loyalty to when I was alone and waiting for help that never showed a face in the darkness."

"Am I responsible for you? Where did you get the thought that I would come for you at all?" Will leaned on his horse's foamy flank, irritating her with apparent lassitude. "I recall no obligation."

"I recall crawling out of a burlap coffin twice like some trapped animal within one sun's circling because of you and your fellow cutpurses. Still the stench clings to me—I swear I'd pay for a cool breeze through wildflowers to take the stink away! Why, why, why would you handle a person so?"

Will coughed the dust out of his lungs, his eyes icy and accusative. "For one who was happily chumming with my enemy, you're quick to expect fealty from me, woman. Seems you little know the concept yourself."

"For one so slow to give it, you're quick to expect it."

"What did you sell Gisbourne for your lavish treatment?"

"For a thief you concern yourself too much with the price of integrity."

He glared at her, his shoulders slumping, heaved a lungful of exasperation, and shook his head in disgust. His long golden hair flared like a lion's mane. After stalking around in a circle he waved his hand at the firmament and mourned, "Is this the last stronghold of decency in Christendom? I begin to think that the entire country has gone as corrupt as the landless ape who runs it."

Katie had already endured too many slurs against her king from Will Scarlet; this was one too many. Her anger was ripe and seeking prey, forcing her forward into controversy despite its ignobility. "Landless? He lives for England."

"To feed off England."

"How can you say such things? While he bears the weight of the Crown you think yourself high for leaving your own lands behind to live like a pirate."

"The head beneath that Crown is a worm-pot and doesn't fit that despot by birth or temperament, and you're coming very close to insulting my principles."

"You have no principles!"

"What has made you insane?" Will narrowed his eyes as though to look through her skin and into her heart itself, hoping to catch and kill the sickness eating her good sense before it turned this intelligent woman into a misguided wretch. The pause was one of abject befuddlement, but it gave him time to hear the echo of their words. He had to shake off his assumptions and remember that this woman, more than most, was unlikely to be steered away from good sense by passion or promises. His eyes narrowed further. He rested a hand on his hip and forced his breathing to slow as though to keep the kindling from catching fire again. Katie's glower was not honed of thoughtless ire—well, perhaps it was justified—in spite of her animus of his treatment. Will shifted his weight from an aching leg that bore bruises from a tree Palermo hadn't quite cleared, and asked deliberately, "What is the name of your liege?"

Katie broke the spell, turning from him to stalk about on stiffened legs, no longer willing to bear his contemptuous gaze. "Can there be a need?"

"Name him. It matters."

"England has but one true monarch."

"Blast you, Katie, name the man!"

"Richard! Who else should it be?"

There was a long, stiff pause. Then Will rubbed his eyes, turned away from her, and grumbled, "Bless me."

"What's the matter with you?" Katie asked, bluntly. Whether it pleased her to admit it or not, anger was all that stood between her and racking sobs of belated fear and relief and a cartful of other sentiments that tore at her, fueling this friction between them.

"I hate wasting wrath," Will said dryly.

"What?"

He turned to her. "Misty waif, we've wronged each other."

"Tell me what you mean!" Even as her fists struck her thighs the meaning came through the sieve of emotions, and she put it together herself, urged on by his expression. She muttered dully, "You thought I was loyal to Prince John."

"And you thought I was insulting Richard. And you think me a common thief after all. Katie . . . Katie, how can you misread us so? Christ's holy bones, girl, you know us not at all."

In his simple statement about injustice lurking too near home—a duplicity Katie could never endure in herself—anger fled. She felt weak, placable.

When Will moved toward her, he was as imposing as a tree lifted from its roots and suddenly animate. She couldn't move away; the injustice wouldn't let her. She had to take her punishment—but for what? For his condescension? He *was* just a common thief, was he not?

Reading this in her eyes, Will caught her elbow and led her through the trees until they emerged into the Greenwood encampment. "Let me introduce you to the people behind the thieves."

The gaggle of men and women offered her their surreptitious glances and shy stares. Katie knew at once that the discourse between herself and Will had met no obstruction coming through the trees. They had heard; they had heard it all. Who had looked the bigger fool?

"You weren't listening when I introduced you to Robin, were you?" Will said as he moved to his cousin and touched Robin's arm. Robin accepted Katie with his eyes, his arms folded. He said nothing, his expression filled with purging both for her, whom he had exiled, and Will, who had defied him. Yet he leaned into the tactile gesture Will offered, a signal that they had been forgiven. "This fine leader of rabble, dear Katie," Will began, "is no rabble himself. This is Robert Fitzooth—remember my telling you this? Robert Fitzooth of Locksley Demesne, First Earl of Huntingdon and son of the Ranger of the King's Forests at Barnesdale and Sherwood. When he defied Prince John's right to go beyond the regent's post in King Richard's absence, Robin's lands were confiscated and are now held by John. When Robin insisted that John provide ransom from England's coffers to free Richard from the King of Austria's prison, the good prince saw fit to have him denounced as an insurgent, formulated a crock of lies about treason and sedition, and had him thrown into a dungeon at Walthamstow. He spent three months in that rat's cesspit with whip welts festering on his back and the misery of righteousness in his soul."

Katie felt her own face tighten in empathy, though Robin only sighed at the true account of his past, never looking away or down.

Will composed himself and pointed at the lanky, brown-haired woodsman known as the other Will, who looked at Katie baldly and without shame, just as Robin had. "Will Stutley is second son of the Baron of Broadweald, an area of land extended to him by Robin's father in gratitude for loyalty in battle, as feudal law dictates. Both Will's father and older brother were beheaded as traitors after the raid on Walthamstow that freed Robin from one pain into another. Over there is Alan o' Dale, a minstrel—a troubadour of so fine a talent that he was brought to the court of Henry the Second as a favorite of his queen, Eleanor of Aquitaine. There he strummed until the king's death and the crowning of Richard. When Richard struck off on the Crusades, Alan refused to compose ballads in honor of Prince John. So here he sits, with us. Beyond him, Katie, you see a besmudged vassal. Can this have once been the great landed knight, Reynold of Tickhill? Can those four men near him be all that's left of his nine strong sons? His lands, all earned by sword, were taxed to ruin and sold to nobles who favor the sick rule of Prince John. And Marian—dearest, kindhearted Marian—Marian Fitzwalter, daughter of a manor lord and ward of King Richard, refused to cast her lot with Prince John when he declared his brother legally dead and announced that he would himself be crowned king. Only through political pressure have friends of King Richard in high position been able to obtain a grace period until it can be substantiated that Richard is dead. In the meanwhile," Will said, gesturing toward the clearing, which was full of ragtag, dispossessed nobility, "we, victims of devotion to a king we believe alive, struggle to keep his England of honor alive in the wake of corruption. All the nasty things you thought I said of my king were meant for his brother, a true despot."

Katie let it all sink in. The eyes regarding her were filled with shame. Those who once had been great were driven to become paupers, filled with bitterness toward their persecutor. They were a sad crew, they were beaten down—she could see it in their faces. What noble blood had not been thinned in their veins was pumped, she could tell, by the one tremendous heart at their core—Robin. She looked at him now, not in defiance or disdain but with respect and pity. Robin saw the look and turned away, moving behind Will. His arms tightened about his ribs as though holding in what little was left of integrity.

"We mistook each other," Will said to her. "I don't apologize, for I said what I said in good faith."

"None expected," Katie said weakly. "But I do owe you one."

"No."

"Yes. I do. I judged you before I knew you, and for that I have shame. Even I would go to stealing to feed my loved ones if I had to. You must endure terrible dreams to see yourselves this way, but please rest a little better for this: I don't approve of Prince John, nor does any honest merchant in the town I come from. None of us are as close to the royal court as some of you have been. I am amazed and in awe of anyone who can hold his head high and defy an anointed prince to his face. You may be beggers now, but you're higher than those who sold themselves to John's corruption and kept their land. Please, accept my apology—"

"No!"

She stepped back, caught in a wave of unexpected anger. Will Scarlet towered like a great charred tree above her, his brown boots planted in fallen leaves, his long, gilt hair still a mess from their ride. His face was suddenly shocked and shocking. "We'll take nothing from one in whose eyes we've gone from thieves to beggars. We're soldiers, Katie, men of a cause. *Richard.* Richard is our cause!"

She found herself gazing through his anger with the same pity she had felt for Robin.

He saw it. "Sweet Mother of God! What proof do you need?"

"I need nothing. Will . . ."

"Do you think we steal for ourselves, our own greed? We eat, certainly, but only enough to live and we feed our children and our sick. As for the rest, every bauble, every coin, every shard of any value we can put aside is stored, dear blind Katie Chenoweth, stored for King Richard's bloody ransom! While his scurvy brother steals England from itself, we steal to free our King!"

Her body stung with the echo of his words, new shame flaring to life as she looked at Will. Her cool fingers touched the lips that had trangressed on the echo of their own apology, doing the same wrong all over again. Her teeth broke the skin of her lower lip, so hard were her hands pressing her mouth, until she tasted a trickle of blood. The juice of her own life, it reminded her of many things. Sad, true, unfortunate things—things that could be changed.

"Well, that's enough," Robin said then. Katie couldn't see it, but she sensed his hand pressing against Will's twitching back.

The black-clad nobleman let his head drop slightly.

He said quietly, "I wish I could cut the word *outlaw* from our language and cast it to perdition." He made his way across the clearing, men moving to either side of his powerful wake. His back was to Katie, a sea of raven fabric. She could almost feel his heart pound.

Katie clutched her hands into fists, gathering her courage. But she didn't have enough of it to deal with the humiliation rattling between her and these exiles—everyone felt it—so her solution was to ignore them. She would divorce herself from them completely until there was no one but herself and Will in the entire clearing. In all of Sherwood. In all England. In the world.

Heart in hand, she approached the quivering coal-black wall and spoke to it. "Now I know who lives in the Greenwood," she said. "All but you. Am I beaten down enough to be told . . . who *you* are?"

Even under the loose-cut tunic she could see, or sense, his shoulders knot. He didn't move. She couldn't see his face. His hair looked darker in the shadow, except for one small patch of gold glowing in a bit of sunlight.

He wouldn't answer her.

Katie stood behind him, waiting. In those tortured moments she had already learned much about him. Maybe too much. If he never spoke, she would still know him better than most people ever came to know each other.

Another voice pierced the killing silence.

"He is Will Scarlet," Robin said, approaching Katie to stand on the oblique between herself and Will. "The man he was died of agony. The corpse was called Geoffrey Montfichet of Gamewell, Squire of Sandwell and Sherwood. But he died, that man. . . ." His solemn eyes turned to Will, then back to Katie. "You'll find naught of him here."

Will said flatly, "Robin, I tire of this." He took what appeared to be a step, but his feet didn't follow him. His knees buckled. Katie gasped in shock as he toppled to one side. Robin's arms shot out, catching Will by the shoulders and keeping him on his feet. His friends gathered around him quickly, but Katie was too stunned to move.

"Will," Robin said urgently, "what is it?"

"There's blood under his shirt," Stutley pointed out, pressing the back of Will's tunic. His hand came up a sheet of red.

"It was an arrow," Will told them. There was no pain in his face, only exasperation and weariness. "Behind my shoulder. I plucked it out."

"You might have been killed," Robin said soberly.

"This is nothing." He shook off their hands and stood on his own.

"Nonsense. Where's Marian? Tuck, will you find her? Quickly now, quickly."

"No—please." Katie shoved her way through the small crowd. "Please, let me tend him. I owe him that."

Robin's glare cut her in two. He held tighter on to Will as they both looked at her. "In faith you do," he said. His natural protectiveness for those he loved was in full color, as was his sense of fairness. He looked at Will. "Do you want her?"

Will leaned on Robin and half smiled, looking like a black shadow against the deep greens and browns of Robin's clothes. He crossed his legs and said, "Are you selling her?"

"She's free."

"I like the price. I'll take her, then."

So she was forgiven. Forgiven for things she hadn't done. Quite aware that she'd done only what was best for herself, Katie forced herself to forgive them for doing only what they had to do. It all came down to that. Whatever she had done in her life in hurt or ecstasy had come down to that. Even her marriage to Edward in its way, as wonderful as it had been and as full of joy and hope and sturdiness. And, oh, it had been joyful. But no memory or past truth could prevent this twinge of guilt as she looked at Will and Robin and saw only her misconceptions of them. As much as she wanted to, she still couldn't smile.

"Take him someplace warm," she said.

The morning settled back. Clouds gathered overhead, and sometime later, in the quiet of the coming storm, Robin and his cousin waited for it together, alone.

"There you are." Robin tucked the blanket in at Will's sides. It was a warm morning, almost clammy. They were in one of Greenwoodside's makeshift timber dwellings. Deer hides surrounded them, keeping the wind out. A small fire burned nearby. The first few drops began to fall.

"Where's Katie?" Will asked, shifting the

damaged shoulder as he looked forward to appearing much sicker than he was. His bloodied tunic was off being patched, and beneath the cover he was comfortably naked, lying on a bed of straw and grass.

"She's making a poultice of some kind for your wound. Says it'll pull out the dead blood or something like that."

"Druids are skilled in the medicines, I'm told. Did someone pick up my hat? I must have dropped it when I fell over."

"Yes, we got your hat."

"And the—"

"*And* the cursed feather." Robin watched him for a moment, then sighed. He tucked the blanket even closer at Will's left side. They could both sense what would come next. "Ah, Will," Robin said on another sigh, "why didn't you ask for help?"

His arm folded casually across his body, Will felt a swell of honesty and couldn't look away from Robin. Nor did he want to. "If I had, what would the answer have been?"

Robin put his palm on Will's arm and felt the life there. He seemed to take both strength and distress from it. With some difficulty he opened his mouth to speak. "Is there more than one answer?"

Will clasped his cousin's hand. Now they were close. Their relationship had its ebbs and tides; this was one of the tides. Before long something would come around to ebb them apart for a while, but neither of them would let it in yet. Those were the rules, and they obeyed them; the rules let them have this moment.

"You'll let her stay, won't you?" he asked softly.

Robin gripped his hand as though it were an anchor, as though the tide were sucking him away. "She's trouble, Will."

"We've had trouble before, God knows." He could see Robin's resistance. "She's brave, Rob. She's intelligent. She puts up a fight. She's rare."

"Rare danger. I see her filling your eyes. The disaster she brings. I see your having to choose, and the choice is rending you apart. Soon she'll ask me again to forfeit the road. She'll lure you into trying to turn my mind. Disaster, Will, I can feel it. You know I can't give her what she wants. I can't give her the road if we're to collect enough funds to free Richard. Even just to survive, I can't. She'd be saving herself and her smeltery and we'd all be sacrificed to it. You, me, Marian, Alan, the children ... is she worth that? By the Holy Mass," he pleaded, "don't let her bewitch you."

"She's no witch. Nor am I any saint."

Robin's mouth curled up at one corner. "That you're not. And that's another thing, isn't it? You take care not to make her a victim of herself."

"What do you mean by that?"

"Will, she's newly a widow. If she turns to you in love, why would she be turning to you so soon if not to soothe her loneliness? It would be unmanly and unchristian to take advantage of her."

"Well, unchristian it might be, I'll give you that."

"You're drawn to her."

"I won't lie to you of it. It's my business, Robin."

Intensely Robin said, "And I pray you never make it my business. Take care, is all I'm saying. If she meddles too far, I'll have to take a hand."

"Would you have had me leave her to Gisbourne?"

Robin's shoulders sagged. "No ... that was my fault. I should have spared the men and means to deliver her safely to her town when I ordered her out. I'm glad you freed her from him."

"If you're not impressed enough with her, she almost freed herself. Quite a feat if that was what she was doing. I'm not sure. If only I could know the secrets of her heart, know the truth of her meeting with Gisbourne. She had no reason to be loyal to us, to be sure. If only I could know!"

"Will, Will, calm down. You're hurt."

"Oh, bull's pissle. I've been hurt worse stumbling in the woods. Robin, let her stay. I promise on my life she'll make no more trouble. I'll see she doesn't. She has nowhere else to go, nowhere at all."

The intensity softened Robin quickly; Will had freshly risked his life on his own. The Greenwood band was based on unity, and Will had been left to think he had to act alone. Robin would feel that thorn for days. "Next time she makes trouble," he said quietly, still holding Will's hand, "ask for help."

Will felt the heat of emotion rise in his cheeks. He whispered, "God bless you, Robin."

Robin smiled. "God bless you, Will."

*   *   *

A moment later, Katie hurried in carrying a large steaming stone bowl and shook the rain from the hooded cloak she'd borrowed from one of the women. "It's raining so hard!" she said, putting the bowl down near the fire. The hem of her expensive gown was a rim of mud and rain. Soon the soaked cloak was hanging up to dry, and Katie crouched down beside Will, working the hot poultice to a smooth consistency. "This will make you feel better."

Will winked at Robin, then acknowledged, "It may, but I'm hurt pretty badly, you know."

Her sense of obligation, or at least her awareness that she was the cause of all this, stung her again. Right or wrong, it was an important consideration: her inner drive putting other people's lives at risk—indeed, their very lives being pushed to the brink of death on her account. The idea was as sore as Will's shoulder must be. She owed him, and she would pay.

She asked Robin to help Will sit up while she plied the poultice to the swollen arrow wound, all the while hoping Robin would stay long enough for her to talk to him about the Cart Road. As the minutes passed she came to feel this was not the right time to bring it up. The casualness in Robin's face, the tolerance for her in his eyes—obviously on Will's account—demonstrated the extreme wrongness of turning this warm rain-surrounded hut into an arena. Better and smarter to wait for a real arena. If she spoke now, she would ruin any opinion Robin had of her as anything other than a one-problem annoyance. After all, she had plenty of time to cultivate Robin's respect and sow the soil for success. Robin was crafty; she vowed to be craftier. Making a mind-turning tool of her silence and the job she was doing on Will's shoulder, she covered the poultice with a rag and strapped it with a strip of cloth around his chest and over his shoulder. "How does that feel?"

"All right," Will said, "but I'm in great pain. Agony, nearly."

"I'll change the dressing in a little while," she said, refusing to make a fool of herself by oversympathizing before she knew how much discomfort would really hurt a man like Will. More than he was in, she guessed, but such a wound could certainly be painful.

Robin stood up. "It's nearly my hour of prayer. May I take a wish to God's ear on your behalf, cousin?"

"None. I'll speak to him myself at Tuck's evening mass, but I thank you, anyway."

"Then I'll say good morning to you. And to you, lady." He obviously wanted to curtail the amount of time he was at risk to Katie's confrontation, one they all knew would come eventually.

"Have a good morning, sir," Katie replied with a solidity that made Robin tip his gaze at her with a suspicious little grin before stepping briskly outside. He soon disappeared behind sheets of rain into the empty encampment. The storm had driven everyone into their meager shelters. In the scowling grayness the inner forest became almost as dark as night, leaving only a few puffs of smoke from the openings in wood-and-hide dwellings to show anyone lived here. Katie began to see how

Robin's people managed to remain elusive ghosts to the law enforcers who sought them. Even from where she was, in the very midst of these huts, Katie could barely pick them out. If not for the smoke, she might never have seen them at all. If it was her mother's people, Katie wouldn't have thought it odd, but these folk were gentry, nobility, farmers—not Druids. They were not naturally of the oaks. These men and their families had been driven here or found refuge here; survival brings strange moods into a person's life. Katie wondered, as she turned rather tentatively back to Will, what it would bring to her.

"Early this morning a wagon was taken on the road, Marian tells me," she said, pulling a flask from her belt, "and it was loaded with seven casks of fresh mead. I thought it would do you good to drink some. The driver says it was made with honey from rose-fed bees. Perhaps I could pour you some?"

"Perhaps you could pour us both some," he said. "Then come sit by me again. Your nearness will warm me even better than a swig of mead. But I'll take the mead too. Here, sit here. This is dry. I can sit up against this tree and we'll talk. I have to say Gisbourne has a magician's sense for dressing a woman. You look stunning. Those colors were etched in heaven above your name. Look how that velvet on the tunic is the color of your lips. And this gown—I can hardly tell it from your hair. Your hair ... where is your hair? Christ's wounds, it shouldn't be hidden, not even in gold net. Why did you undo my braids?"

"*My* braids," she corrected, smiling. "You only held the comb."

"My girl, that was purely artwork I did on you, practically sculpture, and I want credit."

"Yet you have no beard for me to trim, so I have no means of reciprocating."

"Ah, beards I gave up on years ago. The beard I get is a pitiable fuzz at best, so I do without." He shifted uncomfortably. "This poultice is very sticky. What's in the recipe?"

"Mud and moss from a running brook, some medicinal herbs, and the lichen that grows on young trees. I'm not a physician nor even completely a Druid, but all the children of my mother's tribe were taught enough healing arts to save ourselves if we were ever injured in the woods. It came in handy to have this knowledge even in Southwell. Blacksmithing can be a dangerous business."

He thought about that for a moment, then slowly asked, "Was it an injury of the forge that took your Edward to his death?"

If only it had been, she thought, perhaps I might have helped him, even cured him. Yet I was helpless.

She decided to answer, even though her throat was suddenly dry. "My . . . my Edward died of no wounds to his body from our forge. The malaise that withered him came from within, to eat away his healthy body and purloin his strength until he died. I could . . . there was nothing to be done about it. He's gone. He's over with. I can only wish to join him in oblivion once my task is done."

Will stared at her and actually fielded a shiver. Nothing was eerier than this, few things more tragic to his way of thinking. There was something residing deep within her, uglier even than the disease she spoke of. He found it distasteful. Not only the ugliness itself but also her acceptance of it. Her giving in when she gave in to nothing else.

"Your husband has been dead now these six weeks," he said, "and still I've seen no tears from your eyes. Is it that you did your mourning earlier on?"

"Too early. I mourned before he died. I mourned his sickness and its grip on him. I mourned the withering of a firm young body whose touch not so long ago was vibrant and intoxicating. I mourned its fading. If you would have more weeping, you may have to hire professional elegists, because I have no more to give."

"Is that all a man can expect of you, then, Katie? A bedside troth and nothing afterward?"

"You're mocking me." She touched her throat, expecting it to tighten as it had so often before Edward died, when she had to stuff down the grip of weeping because giving in would have anguished her poor husband. Daily she had seen the shame and sorrow in his wasting eyes, the bite of helplessness, of humiliation when he could no longer rise to relieve himself, and finally when he lost control entirely. Never had she wept in front of him. Soon she wept not at all. So her throat didn't knot now as Will wanted it to; no wetness came to her eyes. What must he, a man so involved in sensation, think of her? And wasn't it curious that Will's approval had suddenly become important to her?

"I don't intend to," he said with flatness.
"Mockery is a children's game. Curiosity,
however—that's another story."

"Nor am I fodder for your curiosity. Please
speak no more of my husband."

Will's heavy brown eyes grew serious. Something about his relaxed posture, bereft of the
usual lively clothing, made it an honest intensity. "Katie."

"Please don't."

"Katie, you must realize that he's gone."

"I do, I tell you. Again and again, haven't I
said it?"

"And all but your heart listens. Katie, a person needs release from those bonds of love that
become shackles after a death. Katie, you have
to cry for him or he'll hold you and you'll hold
him. How can his soul depart if you continue
to keep him clinging to vestiges of life that
will never catch flame? Sooner or later you
have to admit you're still alive. Else how can
some other man reach out"—his hand flexed,
stole slowly toward her, cupping the outer swell
of her breast beneath the shimmering tunic—
"find you, and discover that gem which Edward prized?"

He seemed so unimposing, so much the poet,
so little the aggressor as he lay propped up.
His gold hair clung to the tree that sheltered
this hut, his eyes were unremittingly tender,
his face rosy as his body rushed to heal itself.
His hand held her covered breast without pressure, and Katie could not force herself to lean
away from his touch.

The warmth of his hands sent a sizzling
sensation along her arms, down her spine, and

into her legs. She tried to pull away but only in her imagination. In reality his touch was too magnetic to deny—an unbelievable pull she hadn't felt in months and expected never to feel again.

But she did feel it. She felt his fingers firmly caressing her arms, kneading the fleshy parts of her shoulders, ushering in Will's own brand of comfort and desire.

He traced the shape of her face, her lips. "So delicate," he murmured, "so full of hidden passion. I could awaken that passion. Like this . . ."

He pulled her down to lie along his supine body. His nakedness beneath the blanket tempted her, called to her, teased her. Before she realized it, her lips were brushing his. He held her ever so slightly away, not letting her weight fall upon him entirely, a tactic that worked all too well.

Katie swallowed hard, unable to keep down a breathy gasp as his tongue ran along the rim of her mouth, resisting the throb of thick desire growing inside her, deep within the center of her womanly self. Was he proving to himself that he could arouse her? Surely there was no victory in what a man could do to a woman simply because she couldn't help reacting like a woman. She told herself over and over again that he saw nothing in her beyond a man's satiation, and even as she thought it, she knew it was a lie. The short time she'd known Will Scarlet had filled her with a secret admiration for him, and somehow she knew that his kisses held a genuine fascination with her, a genuine desire to feel the power of her womanhood. She sensed his knowledge of that buried passion in the way he moved his legs against hers, his knee caressing the inner part of her thigh as he drew her into another, deeper kiss. His gentility surprised her, a softness too captivating to resist. She had always expected him to be rough in love, powerful and demanding, but his unpretentious kisses crossed her face and her throat as softly as the brush of a bird's feather.

"Will—" she began.

"Hush," was his answer as he buried her protest beneath a moist conquest.

Once again his hand stole away to her breast, cupping the globe and squeezing it, but Will didn't realize that he was insulting her, encouraging her to remember his words, until she pressed his bare shoulders and pushed herself up again, away from him.

Ignoring the most disturbing element of what he had said to her before—whether Edward was holding her or she holding him—Katie grasped his hand and crushed it against her breast. Recklessly defiant, her glare was twice as guileless as his. "There," she said. "Touch all you like. You see? I have no virginal fear of you. You can't hurt me or steal any of my strength away, no matter how it would please you to whittle me down to a sobbing wretch. My tears are dry. All that's in me is dry. Edward took the warmth with him, and if truth be known, I'm glad to see it go. Passion and pain are one and the same to me, and if I have no passion, I can stay free of pain. So paw me as much as you like."

Her iciness shocked even her. A blast of cold

wind outside echoed her words, its shimmer of rain framing her head like a shroud.

Will's hand stayed put beneath her unflinching gaze.

For Katie the omen struck through soul and bone, thudding like heartache. This was not anger she heard venturing out, nor was it defiance, nor aggression to topple a foe. Her words were anemic, washed-out, vacant of anything but their own hard truth. If Edward had not already been dead, these words might have killed him.

And yet . . . there was a spark in her eyes. A deep flicker, far back, beyond the ugliness. In that unbridled moment Will caught sight of it, trapped it, and held it in his heart. There the light could be kept alive until she could nurture it herself.

Katie almost saw it go, almost heard the swish of joy as her life's light passed into safer hands than her own. In an instant the unnatural communion was over, and she never could have said for sure that it happened at all, the odd and ethereal joining that fused her with Will. But she knew it, and he knew it. Neither could have put it into words except to say that it was true, that it had occurred.

He withdrew his hand from her breast. A singular statement; within was the pledge to return.

The episode left them both weak. Not only weak but cleansed.

"Oh, Will." Katie sighed. "Why do you test me so?"

"Only because you beguile me."

She shook her head. "What am I that I should become the vagary of two men?"

"I can help you."

She slapped her own leg in exasperation. "And both stuffed with vainglory. Do I appear so helpless? I think not, if you would stop tearing open my wounds as they heal."

"Ah, but Katie, they are not healing."

"Who are you to say?"

"One who looks within."

"My wounds, like my body, are fully clothed. You may stop your looking. I resent this tampering and tossing about between you and Gisbourne as though I'm a shuttlecock. My personhood is intact and not your toy or his."

"There's no pain in true passion, Katie," Will said, "unless you insist there be. Your body will believe what you tell it. Muscle is slave to the mind. A man may think himself to death. Or think himself alive. Or a woman may."

"I think myself alive until I'm done with myself."

"Then prove it. Let me feel the life." He touched her face. "Kiss me."

It was, in its way, a fair challenge. If she turned it down, she would be admitting to a lack of control. She had to show him. Katie, not Will, not Gisbourne, was in charge of her own integral self. The best gift of Edward's love was his respect for her when she had never asked for it, and now—spoiled or vain, some would say—she had learned to demand it.

She bent down, unblinking. Lips touched, cool and dry. As they transferred warmth a moisture came between them. The sensation was disconcerting for a woman who knew the taste of only one man's lips in a lifetime, but Katie drove through the barrier of unfamiliarity, determined to show Will that she was strong.

His arm moved around her and drew her against him. She didn't pull back or resist him. At first this was part of her show, her strategy. She had expected him to be rougher, though, but he wasn't; he was gentle—searching, questing. Once again she winced at the sting of being someone's quest, as though a woman's destiny was ultimately possession by a man or at the least guidance by him, bringing up her resistance from the sweet juices of Will's kiss. Up from surprise, from a new awareness of men. So used to Edward, she always assumed other men's touches—all other men's—would be distasteful. Will's mouth was supple and receiving. Inwardly she was grateful that now she could believe in a different substance of touch, since she had always wondered about a strange touch and could never try it. Oh, some had been offered, but she had wanted none.

Pulling herself away—how difficult to cleave from his warm, bare, healthy, full chest and strong arm—Katie asserted herself. "There," she said, even though she knew her voice would crack. "You've had all of me you will ever have. Dead or alive, I belong forever to another man."

A small moan rumbled from Will's throat. "Your song is tedious. I find little nobility left in that doleful dirge, even if you do sing it with your chin up."

"You're mocking me again, and I won't have it!"

"By God, I will! You do Edward a bigger injustice than you do yourself. You spit courage as well as any viper, but, Christ, you'll choke on it!"

"Let go of me."

"Let go of Edward! Let the poor man die."

"My arm!"

"Arm be damned. It's your spirit needs releasing."

He had her one arm, but he certainly didn't have the other. She wrenched around, her free hand connecting with the bowlful of muddy, mossy poultice. "Mock this, you ape!" And she swung.

"Oh, no—!"

• *Chapter Eight* •

"I have a solution."

Escape was on her mind: escape from herself and from her unnatural bonding with Will, which she could no longer deny. They were alike but in calamitous ways. Time would take them onward through trial to disaster if she allowed it to do so, to control her life and the flow of its events, and all this pushed her into dangerous logic: the flow of events must change, and she would have to change them.

Robin paced away from her. "There is no problem."

She followed. "There is. I see it in the eyes of people here when they give more food to their children than they give to themselves, or when three people share a blanket meant for one. Your supplies are depleting. And winter is coming. Soon there will be less game to hunt, and the rare stag you do bring down will be lean and stringy. What will you tell your people when you're starved out of the Greenwood and at the mercy of those you've mocked?"

For a few long, thoughtful moments Robin searched the treed surroundings for something to distract him. "Gisbourne taught you well the art of offensive maneuvers."

Had Will said it, she would have been furious. But this was Robin's cunning nature at work. "You know better."

"How do I?"

"You're a better judge of character than that. You know I think for myself."

"So you do." He pondered but had already admitted it. "We fared all right last winter. No, there was nothing easy about it. But we survived. We'll do so again. It is my pledge."

"Will you feed them your pledge or wrap them in it?" Katie approached him then. Her tone had become accusatory, and she knew he would never be moved by adversity any more than she would. Quietly, with special intensity, she said, "Robin, *Robin*, I see the anguish when you turn away from me. Your raids on the Cart Road have made merchants seek other routes or other places to sell their wares. When you have no one left to steal from, how will you do yourself any good, much less Richard? If you can't feed your children, you'll certainly have nothing to set aside to ransom a king. Listen to me. Perhaps I see your situation a little more clearly, being a newcomer here and being a merchant myself. Won't you hear me out?" In deference to him, his position of importance in these woods, and the wisdom he had to have in order to have led these folk successfully for so long, Katie made it clear with her expression that she wouldn't say more if he didn't want to listen. He was, after all, Robin of the Hood, and he deserved courtesy.

He didn't let her down.

"Speak," he said. "Say your thoughts."

Careful not to seem too eager lest she insult him, she explained. "Though it may seem otherwise to you, secluded in exile as you are, the biggest part of England's people are with you in favor of King Richard. Prince John is unpopular. The people squirm when his dictates come down to us because we know King Richard loves England and John loves only John."

"You paint a pretty picture. Too simple, though."

"True, there is a struggle. John's reach goes deep, and threads run everywhere. Many men's loyalties hide in their purses, or, even worse, in their hunger to rule others. This shows up in the towns when some who need favors are denied while others are given two portions, or when one business is prospering while its competition wallows, all because Prince John's minions have changed guild rules or tax laws in exchange for support or payment. So, you see, Robin, you're not alone."

"I appreciate knowing this," he said, "but how does it—"

"Cooperate. Work with the people rather than against them."

"You forget the noose around my neck. Mine, Will's, Johnny's, we're all condemned men. We'd be hanged, butchered, and burned were we to show our faces in Southwell or Nottingham or any town at all."

"There's no need for that."

"We cooperate by sorcery, then?"

"No. By a business proposition. Presented by you and carried to the towns by someone who has no death sentence waiting."

"This proposition is—"

"Christ in God, Robin, I'm sorry!" Will stumbled out of the ferns, coming to a halt between them. He was wearing only his red shirt, which was beltless and hanging loose, nearly to his knees. "She slipped away while I was sleeping. I'll watch her more carefully now on, I swear. Katie, when, when, when will you tire of making trouble? Have you not had your fill? Back to the hut before my promise is ruined entirely."

Indignantly she pulled away from his grip. "I'm talking to Robin."

"And it's up to me to see you talk no further." His eyes widened emphatically. "On with you, right now."

"Will—" Robin began.

Will swung around. "It's my fault. She'll learn to leave you alone."

Robin laughed. "Then I'll never hear the end of the story."

"Story?"

"Yes. Whether John wins or we do."

"What?"

"What do I see in your hair? Is that mud?"

"Don't touch my hair."

"Were you standing out in the rain?"

"Robin, I'm trying to save you from aggravation herself"—his glare hit Katie like a lance—"and you're giving me trouble."

"Still, I'd like to hear her out."

"Well, damn you for the south wind! One minute you cast her out, the next you hear her out. On one hand you warn me to keep her reined, then it's me you draw back! What is going on?"

"Nothing," Robin said with a chuckle. "Nothing, cousin, no conspiracies." He clapped Will's shoulder and looked at Katie. "Oh, we argued when she first caught me here, off-guard, so soon after my prayers, but Holy Communion mellowed my spirit and gave her an edge. And she put it to wise use. I begin to see what intrigues you so about this pretty problem. Go ahead, Katie. Now I'm curious."

"Are you!" Will huffed.

Silent until now, Katie was surprised to find herself hesitant. With Will here, speaking candidly to Robin seemed impossible. Will, who *hadn't* been at his prayers, wasn't in a very amicable mood at all. He would ridicule and chide and discount everything she wanted to say; she could see that in his eyes behind the blue fire.

"Go on," Robin said again. "Your solution."

She shifted and tried to hide her nervousness. "A proposal to all merchants still loyal to King Richard."

"Comprised of . . ."

"Of a donation. A toll for use of the Cart Road. A percentage—say a fifth—of what they carry, to be held in trust for Richard's ransom, minus some to feed and clothe the folk of Sherwood."

Robin's brow furrowed. He folded his arms.

Will took a step inward, saying, "This is abs—"

"Don't you see?" Katie shoved past him to Robin. "Tell them! Tell the people who you are, why you're here, that you're not just thieves. They misunderstand you as I did when I first came here. Robin, Will—think! You preach on the mettle of English stock, so let Englishmen show what they're worth. Let us be part of your struggle!"

She barely breathed. Waiting for a reaction from either of them seemed eternal. Only when she realized Will was holding his breath, too, staring at Robin with the same clutching anticipation, did she feel the first pinch of victory. If she convinced Will, perhaps . . .

A single brow raised on Robin's forehead. His gaze flipped to her. "The Welsh are of no mean stock, either, I see," was his comment, "and may the saints be tender if we fail."

Katie began to shake.

Will was staring at her now, then back at Robin, then at her again. With each shift his expression changed, as though parcels of logic were fitting and arranging in his mind somewhere within the astonishment that Robin was giving in to her. But Katie wasn't astonished. Nor was she peeved at Will. He wasn't, for all his strength of character, the leader. He wasn't the one upon whom the burdens ultimately rested. Perhaps if he had those decisions to make—whether the children of the woods would have full or empty bellies—he, too, would give in. Evidently Katie's observations about the coming of winter weren't new to Robin. Yet, even as she and Will watched, one weight rolled off Robin's shoulders and another rolled on in its place.

"Say we try this," he began. "Who would be our emissary? Who can we trust who isn't one of us? And all of us are outlaws, to be hanged on sight."

"I thought the choice was obvious," Katie said, her voice heavy with indication.

Robin stared. "Oh, no. No. I'll not risk a woman's life. Women are sacred under God and must be protected. I won't risk a woman."

"As opposed to risking the children?" Seeing the impact this had on him, she pressed it. "Edmund's children and the four orphans and Edith's boy and girl, not to mention Edith, herself, who must nourish a babe yet unborn? And the sickly one in that hut over there? And what about Glynna and Samuel Mondsey, who already know the loss of three children from starvation?"

"You can go. God take me . . . you can go."

"But not alone." Will's voice cut through Robin's distress. "I'll go too."

"You'll be hanged."

"I'll disguise myself."

"As what, a tall bagpipe?"

"We'll think of something."

Robin inhaled slowly, once again paced between the trees. For the first time Katie noticed his left shoulder drooped slightly, probably from the chronic strain on shoulder and spine after years of drawing a longbow. He was known far and wide for the skill his body had adjusted to, having gained far wider note as an outlaw than he ever had at the archery butts during games when he was younger, when times were better for him. Distinction had its price. "I don't know," he thought aloud. "It seems too simple. I don't trust simplicity when so many people must be involved in a scheme."

"The simple logic makes the plan workable," Katie said.

"Don't downplay the danger," Will warned her, "or underestimate our foes. The lawkeepers in both Nottingham and Southwell are bastions of Prince John's men. He *is* Prince Regent, he does have the right of rule in Richard's absence, and as such, neither you nor anyone, Katie, can undermine his power. If we overtly defy him, we'll simply be killed."

"But that's the beauty of it! We'll act not overtly but covertly. "We'll address not the lawkeepers but the townsmen themselves." She pulled up her skirt to step over a fallen tree, putting herself strategically between Robin and Will, so they would both have to look at her in order to exchange their own thoughts. "We'll go into the merchants' bazaar and speak to the shopkeepers and tradesmen themselves, individually and in private."

Her first indication of Robin's being drawn in was his suggestion: "Perhaps the wiser course would be to address a guild meeting where no town officials are allowed. Then you would be assured of at least being heard out."

"Before we're arrested," Will added cursively.

Katie shot him a growling look.

"You'll go first to Nottingham. Katie will need no disguise there, but what will we do with you?" Robin strolled around Will, scanning him.

"I'll go ... as a wealthy nobleman in town for a visit. I'll take money and purchase clothing—which, of course, I'll bring back for our folk here—and things for 'my' children, so the townspeople will think me genuine."

"Will," Robin said, "with that shining hair and beardless face you'd be recognized by the first deputy of the shire who sees you. We can dirty you up and send you as a dung peddler."

"If I go as a pauper, I can return with nothing for our people." Clearly that was not the aspect of Robin's suggestion disturbing him most.

Seeing Will standing there with his legs showing, still postured in his usual aristocratic manner and expecting to swagger into Nottingham with all the flamboyance of his Gamewell upbringing, Katie felt an idea form in her mind, which at first she rejected as preposterous. When Will raised his eyebrow, she suddenly decided the preposterous was fated for him.

"Robin," she said, using him to degrade Will ever so slightly, "I have an idea just right for his gold hair and bare face. No one will guess who he is."

"It's perfect." Robin stood back, watching as Katie and three of the camp women worked on Will. "Not God himself would recognize you. Will, I had no idea."

"No idea *what?*"

"That you were such a beautiful woman."

As Katie plaited yet another strand of gold hair and attached a blue ribbon at the end of it, she nearly had to move out of the steam rising from Will's bejeweled ears. His legs were buried in a red woolen skirt, and one of the women had donated a large bright blue tunic with an embroidered belt and tassles. Beneath colored eyelashes and lines of kohl, one eyelid drooped in cold rage. His glare followed Robin, daring even a snicker, though the rest of his face remained a statue beneath green eye shadow made of parsley, oil, and beeswax, and lips carefully drawn and colored with beeswax and alkanet root. His fingernails had been painted with a paste of henna powder and his fingers adorned with rings from King Richard's booty. Katie, who had never worn cosmetics herself, was fascinated by the process and watched the women with intrigue, delighted to use it on this of all men.

Will sat still and rumbled with abject indignation as a chain of gold links was placed around his neck and someone dabbed his cheeks with berry juice. "I'll slit the first throat that laughs," he warned, seeing a grin rise between Robin's sandy beard and mustache.

"No one's laughing, cousin," the Hood protested unconvincingly. "On the contrary, I'm stricken with awe. Why, you look as proper a whore as ever marched an alley. Had I known you could appear this way, I might never have been able to contain myself."

"Assassination is not beyond me."

"Hush and be still while I finish your face, Will Scarlet," the woman called Alva said.

"Yes, hush, Will Scarlet," Robin parroted, "or should we say Wilfreda."

"I hunger for fish, and guts make good bait."

"Don't pull," Katie complained. "Your braids may be uneven."

"Can't have that," Robin said.

Will lunged for him, but Katie's firm grip on a hank of hair gave her the leverage—namely pain—to hold him back. She winked at Robin as Will yowled his opinion and arched backward to get the pressure off.

"Turn loose of me! I've had enough!"

"You go this way or Katie goes alone." Robin leaned back on a tree. "You'll need horses, but better that Palermo is not among them. Tales of a big yellow hunter hold on too long. You'll go into Nottingham by the east gate where the paupers' quarter is. People there are concerned only with eating from day to day and may beg from you but will tell no tales of your passing through. Oh, and I'll see you have coins to give them and a few loaves of bread for the hungry children. They may not be of Greenwoodside, but they're still children of the true realm and deserve our help if we can give any."

"Take care you don't spread your generosity too thin to really help anyone."

"Fear you not," Robin dispensed. "God will provide."

"Then pray he feeds your bow," Will reminded.

Robin's glance at Katie was full of memory, of the words she had used to convince him. She glanced back, in agreement with Will rather than repeating what had already been said. Robin was bothered enough by his responsibilities, by the scowling shroud of winter hanging on his horizon, and by the danger into which he knew he was sending Will and Katie. All three knew, perhaps even felt, the danger locked within the personalities of the two people he agreed to send together. Without doubt Robin had weighed those aspects too. A wisdom hewn of long use made him both glad and apprehensive of Katie and Will's ability to draw together efficiently in the crises they might face. Katie could see those doubts and hear them in the little worried sighs falling from Robin as he planned their errand.

By the time they were finished with Will— the most unbearable part for him coming at the end, having his tunic stuffed across the chest so he would seem womanly in more than face—two drab-colored horses had been prepared for them and loaded with bread and drink for the journey. Katie put on a brightly embroidered cloak to add to her rich clothing so she wouldn't appear too dull riding beside Will. She allowed Johnny Little to lift her up onto her horse in time to giggle softly while Will argued, "I'll be hanged if I'm going to ride like a woman! There's too much bulk between my legs to ride all on one side, and the misbalance may make the steed go sideways."

"You're dressed as a woman, boastful rogue," Robin said. "You'll ride like a woman."

"I'm dressed like a whore, I'll ride like a whore. With my legs open."

Robin threw his hands up. "Get him another saddle." He turned back to Will and wagged a finger. "But be warned. Remember you are on a mission and supposed to be a woman. You must *be* a woman. Your life, Katie's life, in fact all our lives are resting upon you and your ability to convince Nottingham's folk that you are indeed just a courtesan. Forget none of the importance of this. Your success means nothing less than our survival."

Will flushed beneath the color on his cheeks. Quietly he vowed, "I will not forget."

Katie watched solemnly as a silence befell the group. She suddenly felt the heavy goal shift from Robin's shoulders to her own.

Carrying on the tone Will had just used, Robin said, "Keep your thoughts level. Show little exuberance. Speak less than you have to. And look into a child's eyes from time to time."

Any more words would have been extravagant. Luckily they were spoken by a man who knew that.

Moments later a different saddle, a man's saddle, was brought for Will. He paused before climbing astride, still looking at Robin, and the exchange was that of two leaves hovering in an updraft before floating apart.

Katie watched. Before long, as their discomfort swelled, she laughed out loud enough that the horse started beneath her. Johnny held its head down, but even the big mute shook with soundless laughter.

Robin finally broke down. "Pardon," he said, chuckling. "Will, I'd hug you, but with you trapped in ribbons, I can't bring myself to do it."

"Charming!" Will rumbled. He yanked himself up onto the horse, only to end up tangled in skirt lengths and hanging over the saddle with one leg caught on the horse's rump. Johnny stepped around and freed him. No one else was in any condition to do so.

Thinking the worst was over, Will became thoroughly livid when he realized that the path out of Sherwood was also the path directly through the Greenwood camp and that so far only a handful of people had seen him this way. Katie rode beside him, keeping resolutely silent as word spread and people piled around them to view the spectacle. The women grinned, the children laughed, but the men—the men were merciless.

"Edmund, look!"

"I see! Why, it's a *scarlet woman!*"

"You must be wrong. See how tall she is? See how her breasts stick out as though never used? She must be an unsqueezed fruit. Will Stutley, do you see?"

"I see a woman of high stamp, or at least high," Will Stutley replied.

"That's the horse."

"Aye, the horse is hung better."

"Say, girlie, how much are you?"

"Give us a look under."

"Those lips look like rough terrain to me."

"That's a big woman, lads. *Big.*"

"Big enough to crush me."

"*Will* you?"

"Aye, she *will.*"

"We always knew his love for pretty clothes would soften him out of sense."

"Are you soft, Will?"

"Look, I can prance too!"

"Ah, you're still ugly, but you smell better."

"Don't get killed in those wraps, dearie, that's not your best dress, y'know."

"God'll have to go a-hunting at the stews for his soul, then."

"*I* wouldn't want a woman who sits a horse with both legs, would you?"

All the while Will rode through them, enduring rolls of laughter, hoots, mimicry, and mockery of theatrical proportions, and the look on his face quite tersely said, "I'm going to die now. Do not bury me in a dress."

Then one man shouted, "Say, Katie, is that your bodyguard or your mother?"

Another responded, "She don't need no bodyguard, so it *must* her mother. I'll prove it." He came up beside Katie's horse and made a high grab for her breast. With an indignant sound Katie blocked him with both arms, hardly sooner than Will launched an arm right past her and swatted the man a good blow.

"You touch her again, and I'll piss on your grave," he swore.

The icy rage in his voice had an edge of truth to it which they apparently recognized because the teasing soon wore off to a few whistles and farewell-dearies as the two of them were finally allowed to go on their way. Katie stifled a last giggle, though she made less of an effort to hide her smile. His scowl beneath his now-pretty face was satisfying. They rode in silence through the edge of camp and into the deep woods, and only when they saw a small huddle of tents around a single fire, several women tending it, did Katie break her train of thought. The women looked, exchanged comments with each other, along with a spare smile or two, and when Katie waved, one of them did wave back.

"Will, who are those women? I've not seen them at Greenwoodside."

He looked, then seemed to search for words. "They are in real life what I pretend to be."

He refused eye contact with her until they were well past the annexed camp. She took this to mean that he didn't want to describe anything in detail and asked nothing further, but the women in the woods would remain in her thoughts for many miles.

Just as they were leaving Sherwood, as the canopied froth of trees opened its arms and released them to the bright afternoon sun, when both their minds had long left the woods, a buzzing sound trilled in the air, causing them to rein in slightly out of pure caution. Will identified the sound—Katie could tell because of a small gasp from him—before she did, but not soon enough. Not before it struck. Will bellowed and tugged against the shivering arrow that pinned his sleeve to their food bag. A quick search found Robin's grin high in a tree far off at the edge of arrow range. He waved elfishly, a gesture, unmistakably, of good luck and great affection.

Will huffed his response, then gave his cousin a fist shake before breaking down and returning the wave.

They rode easily but steadily, resting only once before reaching Nottingham town. By then it was dusk. Most families were either at supper or closing up their shops, and the streets were rapidly emptying. No one bothered them as they made their way to a small, nondescript tavern where they had a meal under the skulking eyes of the innkeeper. He might have been merely curious, and rightfully so, as they made an odd pair, this delicately pale girl and the large harridan at her side, but he made no trouble. Soon his curiosity lost its edge, and he once again retreated into the dingy shadows of his dingy inn.

A few carefully planted questions around the tavern's patrons, fetid people looking for a coin's worth of warmth for the night, soon yielded profit for Katie and Will. This being the time of year for many bi-yearly guild meetings, luck had it that the carpenters' guild would assemble the next day at noon. Exhausted from the day-long ride, they needed little persuading to fall into their beds for a fitful night's rest.

Katie never would have believed she could sleep so soundly with Will so near. His sheer power of being was imposing, confusing, disturbing, and decidedly scintillating. His regular breathing told her that he, too, had been tired by the long day on horseback, and for that she was glad. The temptation to touch him, to kiss him again, had grown in her since their lips had met that first time, when her kiss was given not in affection but in response to a dare. His lack of satisfaction had stayed with her and rested like a stone in her now, though she knew its source. As magnetic as Will was, she could easily have resisted him before, when her husband was alive and her mind had no reason to scream for him in its mourning darkness. For months now she had been as good as alone, perhaps worse than alone. Her wish to rest in Will Scarlet's arms came from that. Yet for this night's rest by herself she was grateful. Her body ached from ankles to nape after sitting sideways on a horse all day, and all she could do to relieve it was to lie on the opposite side and stretch her aching leg out behind her. The straw mattress was worn but didn't smell, and they had their own blankets for extra warmth, so she was quickly oblivious to the other bed's song of sleep.

In what seemed only moments the sun was warming her face through a small, unshuttered window. Katie groaned softly and rolled over onto her back, even stiffer now than last night. She had slept soundly enough not to move all night long, and her body took it as another day-long ride. Will, who was sitting and stretching on his own mattress, apparently had the same motionless sleep. His braids—oh, they looked odd on him—were still intact, even the blue ribbons in place, and the cosmetics on his face required only a touch or two to bring them back to yesterday's perfection. For all his griping Will was fastidious about every detail of his appearance now that he was away from the men of the Greenwood for whom he had provided such jest. Now he tucked and tied and pecked and preened like a peacock or, more accurately, like a woman. Were his braids even? Was his hem muddy? Was his bosom on straight? Was his face smeared? Where was his belt and was it tied right?

"I thought you hated this ruse," Katie said.

"I hate it," he assured, "but it is the ruse I'm bound to, thanks to you and my dear cousin. I'll live up to my portion of this, if only to show you two vainglorious goblins that you're not dealing with an incompetent. If it's a woman I must be," he said, shaking the wrinkles out of his skirt, "then I'll be the best damned woman in creation."

Katie laughed. "That's an altogether different kind of bravery than I've ever seen."

"I have no lack of bravery."

"But plenty of modesty."

"Oh, hush, you coffin nail, or I'll make you

dress like an ugly little man and clean up after my horse." He chased her across the small room, up onto the window ledge, and pinched her until she cried out for mercy and squirmed away in laughter.

Not to be outdone, being the troublemaker he thought she was, Katie ducked around him and swatted him on the rump before he turned. He jumped away, hitting the wall, caught her sleeve, and propelled her sideways, but she grasped his arm and used his weight against him. Together they spun around and crashed onto the bed, both tittering like children, and for a few precious seconds Katie utterly forgot that Will was dressed as he was. She saw only the unique man beneath the makeup, the man of unparalleled sensibilities who at times could look into her eyes and see her soul.

"Oh, Will," she said, sighing, "do you know how much time has passed since I laughed out loud?"

He knew. She could tell he did. "Katie, I yearn to see you laugh and laugh again. But not until I've seen you weep."

"That's a fine thing to say."

"You know my meaning. Don't be angry."

"Then stop giving me cause. My soul needs no keeper."

"Fair enough. The sun is high. We must go soon. Are you ready for this?"

"I have no choice but to be ready. I'll go before them armed with the truth and hope it will be enough."

"It's a good thing you're already dead. A live woman would be quaking in her shoes."

She paused before they went out the door. "I must be alive, then."

They went as quickly as possible through Nottingham's bustling streets. Like Southwell and most small towns, craft shops that depended upon each other tended to gather in the same areas, shoemakers near the leather-wrights, tailors near hatmakers and weavers, saddlers near harness-makers, cutlers near chandlers, wood-sellers near wood-carvers. Shuttered shops lined the streets, flanked by open stalls, all bustling with business. The odors of the town were sweet to Katie, even after so short a separation from her business. Perhaps it was knowing that she might never be able to return, to keep her forge operating as Edward wished. Smells of animal dung, horses, and fish twined with savory aromas from homes, taverns, cook shops, and herb gardens. Shimmering linens, hung up for sale beside spun-wool skeins and loom products, waved beneath the sun. People of every size and shape, dressed in every color a cloth could be dyed to, mingled everywhere, their voices raised in bargaining as Katie and Will deliberately passed by tempting pastry-makers, spice merchants, and wine-sellers. Katie could see why the Cart Road was so crucial to Nottingham as a trade route. This was a craft and trade town, and there were many things to sell.

But soon they arrived at the carpenters' guild hall, a sizable building those men had built for themselves. Evidently the meeting had already begun. There was a gray-bearded foreman at the door when Katie gathered the nerve to rap on it. He took one look at Will and said, "No tramps allowed here. We're in meeting."

"I am a tradeswoman from Southwell," Katie spoke up, stepping forward. "I wish to address the assembly."

"Your trade's plain. You can wait out by the stable till we're done."

"I am a blacksmith," she said firmly, correcting him, "and I wish to address the assembly."

" 'Bout what?"

"About a way to open the Cart Road to trade again."

He tipped his head, his eyes squinting. "Serious?"

"Very."

"Done. In this way and ... bring your big friend. She can stand in the back. You'll have to wait till our orders of business are done and the magistrate asks for new business."

"I promise to."

Moments later they were led inside. The big room was dim, a maze of small windows and rafters, filled with rows of benches and several large wooden tables. At the far side a seller of mead and ale had been brought in to supply the guild members who filled the hall today. Katie and Will endured curious stares as various bits of business were discussed. Finally, though, the moment came when Katie was invited to the platform in the front of the hall. She marched to the front alone, and turned boldly to the rumbling, curious carpenters.

"Good fellow tradesmen," she began, "my name is Katie Chenoweth. I am a blacksmith, and my forge is in the town of Southwell, which, as you know, is the nearest center of trade to Nottingham, linked by the Cart Road. I know your trade of carpentry has suffered since the occupation of Sherwood Forest by outlaws. I know you cannot receive as much timber from the woodcutters because it cannot be safely transported. You also suffer indirectly when merchants are robbed in transit, since they then can afford less carpentry and other needs and luxuries bought by coin or kind. But I am here to tell you that I've been in the thick of Sherwood these past few days, talking with those highwaymen, and I believe I know what is in their hearts."

"Greed, that's in their hearts," someone called, setting the assembly abuzz. "Robin Hood would steal the hide of an old ass."

Katie pounced on it. "Right you are to think so from what you've seen, fellow. Let me say this: Without speaking aloud, so no one among you will seem less in the eyes of another, think to yourselves the name of the ruler you're loyal to, he whom you prefer to see under England's crown. That done, I'll risk telling you the truth about Robin o' the Hood and his men."

A gasp rippled through the crowd. What truth could there be, they wondered, except that thieves are thieves? They listened, though, being fair guildsmen and willing to hear her out, willing to give ear to the thoughts of a fellow crafter.

"Deep in the bowels of Sherwood, where I was taken against my will, I found not a coven of thieves but a sanctuary of exiled noblemen. These are men who were stripped of their lands and rights because they defied the regency of Prince John and upheld the Crown of

King Richard in his absence. There are women there with small children, living in a camp they call Greenwoodside, existing like outcasts while the men who sustain them are branded traitors against the Crown. But how can they be? Fellows, I saw with these very eyes a horde of wealth and worth being held not for these people, but to ransom King Richard from his Austrian prison. It's that to which your goods and coins are going!"

There was a great wash of shock and disbelief, for they had never before heard of this possibility. A dozen arguments broke out through the guild hall, and Katie could see the danger rising. They were divided in their loyalties— some for Richard, some for John, some in turmoil, some disgusted at Richard for leaving England when it needed him.

"I bring to you," she went on, "a proposal from the Hood himself. The Cart Road will be open from now on to any merchant who wishes to use it, and Hood asks only a contribution of one-fifth your load, or that value in coin to be added to King Richard's ransom and to support the cause of freedom."

A roar crashed through the hall as the men argued and clamored. A large man in the middle of the bench rows stood up and shouted, "Fancy stories to cover a lie!"

"Aye! How do we know the booty would ever reach the king?"

"Better to have a promise than no hope at all," another argued.

"It was Richard himself who left John in charge, and I say leave well enough alone and let kings free kings."

"It was primogeniture, not Richard, that put John in charge," Katie cried. "You have a chance to open your major trade route and aid your liege king at the same stroke. Robin Hood is honorable, a nobleman and a gentleman. I've met him myself and you may believe my word."

"We could if we knew you," one man said from the crowd.

"Aye, what good is your word?" agreed another.

"How do you know you weren't lied to, woman?" still another demanded.

"And her in the company of whores," chided the first man.

"Look who's talking!" His companion slapped him hard on the back.

Laughter rumbled throughout. From where she was Katie saw Will slug off an ill-advised squeeze, and his strike actually put the offender out of sight.

"It's a fair bargain, an offer made in good faith from Robin Hood to his fellow Englishmen," Katie called over the noise.

"My goods'll be in the woods, that's all I know!"

"He's right," someone else called, starting a roar of dissent.

"And I say it's worth trying."

"I'd say *she's* worth trying!"

"Robin Hood's a pirate and a murderer, and I say his messenger is too.'

"Here's a chance to take a hand in our king's salvation. I vote we take it," was the first shout in Katie's favor.

"There's still no proof. We've no way to be

sure she speaks for the Hood. Go to Sherwood and, by faith, you may find your throat cut."

"He's right!" shouted a fat man, and many others with him.

"If you trust no one," Katie insisted, "how will you ever succeed?"

"She's right too," said a female guild member in the first row.

"She talks like a merchant . . ."

"She talks like a love-struck girl."

"Is that it, girl? Did the Hood fondle you right, eh?"

The accusation was loud, and they wanted an answer.

It came. But from the back of the hall. A strong, familiar voice.

"By God's beard! You animals, know you not an honest deal when you hear one?"

The noise deadened, pounded down by the single strong voice and flowing figure who now stood atop a rickety table. "You petty bug-brained cowards! Here's a chance to help yourselves and your homeland and free your king, yet all you can do is beg for proofs while you cackle among yourselves! Is it proof you need? Take this for it!"

A wool skirt bellied over a dozen heads. Blue ribbons fluttered like birds. A belt landed on someone's head. Golden hair shook out its plaits. A cloth flew down, smudged with colors. The bright blue tunic bled red and fell to the floor.

The crowd swarmed.

"It's a man!"

Will's foot lashed out at the voice and connected with someone's shoulder. "It's more than a man, Sammy suck-egg, it's Will Scarlet of

Sherwood!" Horror flushed through the hall, a hush of realization, but Will needed no notoriety to bolster his words, and he plowed through their reaction. "Never have I listened to the talk of such slop jars! Did you people catch the simples or what? You've the wit of a bunch of fleas and half the courage. Where's the England Richard expects to come home to? This woman appears before you in good faith, offering a chance to do the right thing, and you're friendly as bramblebushes. You want proof? Here's proof, in this shell where my heart lies, a heart as true to Robin Hood as he is to Richard Lionheart, and may I die with dogs before I count myself a countryman of yours!"

They knew his name. They knew his reputation. Arguments erupted throughout the hall as some men cried for Will's arrest and others demanded his defense. Katie watched helplessly, her hopes guttering, as fists flew and Will was swallowed in a series of brawls. Order broke down. Soon she, too, was lost in grabbing hands, but not before she saw the doors fly open and a handful of the shire's deputies pushing through the crowd. Katie shrieked a warning but doubted Will could hear it, leaving her only with the silent wish for them both to escape this folly with whole skins. Escape was a chaos. No sooner did one set of hands grapple her down than did another yank her free and send her spinning into more hands. Only once did she catch sight of Will, and as near as she could tell, he had just slammed two men backward into three others, taking down a whole flank of them. The vicious power in his face, the raw anger, frightened even her.

Then world went ablaze with angry faces, smelly armpits, breathy shouts, and bone-jarring action. Twice she was driven to the floor and twice hauled up by the same wrist, helpless in the sea of strong men with carpenters' muscles. Will? What happened to Will?

Suddenly a blinding light broke before her, attacking her senses and driving out the last vestige of control she had over this situation. She continued to thrash, often striking flesh, but a second later she was flung toward the brightness. It was sunlight reflecting on a line of white linens for sale across the street. Long before she reached it, a solid force smashed against her body—a wagon full of bales. She found, when her eyes adjusted, that she was hanging on to the wagon, gasping and confused. Just as she collected herself and turned around, a form flew out of the doorway at her.

"Run, Katie!"

She pushed off the wagon and ran. Will stumbled after her, and after him came a crew of deputies. Whether they knew it or not, they were minions of Prince John's tyrannical web, and it was into those sticky coils that they would deliver Katie and Will.

If they caught them.

Since it was the busiest point of the business day, the two of them quickly became lost in a traffic of brightly clothed artisans, merchants in fur-trimmed tunics, women doing business at countless tents and open stalls. Because she'd been a city woman since her sixteenth summer, Katie easily led Will on a twisting escape around food shops and between peddlers, through one quarter of the town and into another, until finally not even a hound could have trailed them. They were breathless and aching, but they were still free.

Behind a cooper's shop they collapsed, not speaking until their bodies stopped the hearing of exhaustion.

When she could breathe easily again, Katie let her thoughts out, hoping to understand.

"What happened to us, Will?" she asked, her voice somber. "Were we thrown out or did they deliberately save us? Did we succeed?"

"We failed," he told her tersely. "They saved us, some few of them. At least they kept us from being arrested before they were sure of our guilt. Some in that hall would've preferred to see our blood flow."

"But some ... some believed us," Katie murmured, "didn't they?"

"Well," he grunted, leaning back and wiping the remnants of berry juice and beeswax from his face, "I'd be loath to put my money on it. They had a valid worry, curse me for admitting it. They had no reason to trust our bald words, now, did they? Who were we to them?"

"But it was the truth! It was good sense."

"To us. To them it was a spineless offer."

"Oh, spare me this, Will! I'm a tradeswoman. I know their minds from inside."

"Perhaps so, but now you are what I am. A fugitive. First order of business is to get out of Nottingham with all our limbs."

"More disguises?"

"It pains me to say so. By now we're branded as insurgents against the Crown, and our guilt or innocence means not a whit."

"But are we guilty? We *are* against the legal regency. Does that make us criminals?"

"If the regency is Prince John, it does."

"Why must it be so? People should be free to speak against unfairness, even if it comes from royalty."

"Divine right of kings."

"Then divinity should go. Folk should be able to say their thoughts and demand even-handedness."

He chuckled. "You'll be one of us yet."

"Is it untrue? A king is not king for his own delight. He has people beneath him who should be nurtured and guided. For all his faults Richard cares in his heart for his subjects. If only he understood that England needs him more than the Holy Land does."

"Aye." Will sighed. "At first I lauded him for attending the Crusades. Then the bite of John's fangs broke through to Gamewell and things changed. England began to bleed. And after all that, the news from the Holy Land was bad. Richard on his way home, ineffectual, then tossed in an Austrian dungeon and there he sits ... ah, blast. Things may change but not today and not for us. We must get out of this town and do so cannily. Let's see what disguises we can find."

Never in his tone of voice would she have found the revenge he was planning, and not until he returned from his adventuring through the alleys did she realize his plan. He carried a large bundle of rags, and at its core was a cloak of cow dung and stagnant water.

"What—" Katie held it away when he pushed it toward her and waved the air. "Oh! Reek!"

"Your disguise."

"*My* disguise?"

"Yes. If you dress as a leper, you should smell like a leper."

"Leper? No leper is this . . . aromatic! Will Scarlet, you'll not do this to me."

"Then try to escape dressed as you are."

"You know I cannot."

"Then a leper you'll be, if a whore I was."

"Can you expect me to wear these stenchy rags?"

"You'll wear them."

"Will!"

"Come, come, Katie, be a true soldier."

"Soldiers do not smell!"

"I endured my costume. Can you be less tolerant than I?"

"Your costume smelled like a costume."

"Here. Here's a sack to put our clothes in. Strip from your gown and tunic. That way your good clothes won't smell like—"

"Like I will. All right! You'll have your revenge, if you're small enough to need it. But I get a bath in the first pool we come to!"

And, oh, she did long for it as they wended through Nottingham toward the east gate and freedom. People shied away from the pauper and his tangy companion, so they had no trouble. Will had disguised Katie's bright face and hands with smears of muddy dung and dusted himself liberally with street dirt until Robin himself never would have known them.

And thus they got out of Nottingham. Without horses, without hope.

When they reached the woodlands under the cloak of evening, guided only by the full moon's creamy light, Katie had emptied her mind of thoughts about Nottingham and that awful question: What would she tell Robin?

There was little passage of words between as they hurried deeper and deeper into the leafed density; this forest was not Sherwood, and going was difficult without the familiar paths and aromas of cooking pots to guide them into safety's bosom. Tonight would be a survival time, a time of animals, of night's cool breath, of sorrows, shames, of wound-licking and new plans, all under the wild shroud of the full moon. England's moon; King Richard's moon—the Plantagenet moon.

"Oh, water!" Katie gasped when the unmistakable bell of a running bourn touched her ears beyond the crickets' whistles. She stumbled through the ferns and saplings, scratching herself on hawthorns but heedless of the pain. Will followed, wordless, quite ready to get free of Katie's pungent punishment.

Yes, there was a brook of clear water rushing over rocks, glittering in the moonlight, running into an onyx pool. Here the trees parted. The moon shone down without obstruction, except for the haze of its own cloudy veil, which took the bright cream glow and spread it in a soft, sparkling halo.

"I'm bathing," she announced. "I reek beyond tolerance. Can you be a gentleman?"

He flopped down, exhausted, beneath a clutch of young maples with his back to the pool. "Have your bath, have it alone. One body is like another."

She cast him an irritable glare. "Fine, then." Gladly she shrugged off the layers of fetid rags, baring her white body to the white moon, only her face and hands still smeared with refuse. The night chill tightened her skin and caused her breasts to contract and their nipples to stiffen to nubs, but the obsidian pool still held the warmth of late summer and today's sun as her feet found its edge and disappeared in the dark, glossy mirror.

The moon's reflection lay before her on the surface, a great eye looking at her nakedness, jealous, for it too was naked and unashamed. But for all its beauty it was without arms to spread across the onyx water, without breasts to rise softly afloat, without the lengths of flaxen hair that fell earthward as the leper transformed into a woman. A woman, a chrysalis—the lines of definition blurred tonight. Who could have said what manner of being, spirit or dryad, woman or godling, moved in that sable water? The cool wetness lay on alabaster skin; Katie's lips fell open as she filled her hair with water and lifted its heaviness from her back. Her eyes were closed, no matter how much the moon entreated her to look up. And other eyes watched, eyes ringed with mischief and filled with wonder, absorbing her long back and hips disappearing at the water line.

What had she called those mystical beings of Faerie? The Sidhe, he'd heard her call them. *Shhheeee* was how the word had come from her lips, and they were pale beings hanging between worlds. A warrior race long ago faded to illusory shades. And she was one of them now. Her pearl skin, argent hair—or was it only the moon—soft angular shoulders, her long hands, made Will desire Cerridwyn more than he thought possible.

The bones beneath her shoulders rolled in ecstasy as the dirt floated into rushy shadows. Katie let her head drift back, her chin tip high, as she pressed the warm water from the sides of her hair. It drained down her spine, keeping her from knowing for sure when his hand actually met her skin. Slowly she opened her eyes. Slowly she realized and turned.

He stood before her, naked, the water lapping at his belly. His broad chest and arms glistened from the wetness. The dust of Nottingham ebbed away. The moonlight on his hair was sulfurous, and in his eyes it was splendor. His want of her was there.

Katie only half tried to cover herself, crossing one hand to the opposing shoulder. An acre of hair lay over the remaining breast, gleaming and dripping. She was a woman who had been married. A man's seeing of her body was less shame to her than when she was a girl, but the flattery of Will's hopeful eyes was marred not by shame but rather by surprise. Her bond with Will was ethereal and beyond the flesh, yet flesh now called between them, pulsing its earthy desires in the very blood flowing beneath it, and drew them nearer, nearer, deeper into itself.

The siren and the goddess within her met and argued. She may have been any woman in that moment, any incarnation of all things female, seeing his manhood reach out for her. She might have been any woman living, dead, or dreamed. She was plain, simple, but her surroundings were kissed by the great Goddess as she prepared to give over the year to the Horned God, the he-thing that was both lover and foe. And that temporal fight was fought between Katie and Will, a wordless, nameless fight that tore Katie to bits as a part of her entered the water.

"I was dirty too," he whispered. "Let us cleanse each other."

"Will," came her helpless murmur, for truly she was at his mercy now, "be my friend. I so dearly need a friend."

He held his hands sideward, his palms questioning. "Must I be to you what I am to Robin? Friend of the heart and soul without being friend to your body?"

A small sob caught back her response. Her fingers brushed his chest but at arm's length. "Will ... oh, forgive me—I do want you ... but is it my loneliness that wants you? I'd sooner die than hurt you with a false need. I need you as a friend, as food for my heart and soul while my body heals and remembers that I am still young." She thought to explain further but failed.

"Katie!" he gasped. His voice cracked as he caught her hand and pulled her flush against his chest, caressing her head. "Katie, that's the first hint you've given of thinking yourself alive and young. Praise God, you've stepped forward! Out of the pit, out of the grave ... you may live the life you were born for after all. Can you hold on?"

Crushed tight against him, feeling the strength of his arms around her, Katie melted deep into his security, the realness of him, the thickness of his healthy body and his rushing aliveness, and even more into his true care for her. He did, he cared. He was in this water for her body and her spirit. So rare! Not for just any woman would he be here—not Will Scarlet, not this man.

The warmth of his body showed her how chilled the water had made her. She hadn't realized it. Her arms coiled inward against his chest as he cradled her there, skin to skin. With his arms he kept her warm, his broad hands spanning her back and hips. "I could love you," he offered softly, his lips against her shoulder hot and moist.

"It would hurt me," she said.

His sigh quivered. "I almost struck you once. May I die before I hurt you. Tell me when you feel pain." He lifted her face to his, and their lips touched. With gentle urgency his tongue outlined the shape of her mouth but made no inward venturing, as though he knew she had not lied. She could be hurt. Robin's warning echoed in his ears and, like a hand on his shoulder, held him back. His masculinity reached against her, but a single, eloquent shiver down her legs and arms told him there could be no loving tonight, not good loving. He could take her—with a little force she would give way—but he would be making love alone. The Katie he wanted was still not here.

He dipped down and lifted her legs from the water, rocking her in his arms for a moment, giving him time to admire the peaked domes of her breasts, the soft nipples reacting to him as her coiled arms hugged them together, and when he felt her accept the intimacy of his body against hers, he returned her trust with seductive pliancy. He asked nothing of her and gave everything, put no burdens upon the alluring white heat in his arms but rocked her gently as he nuzzled her throat. One hand softly grasped her creamy, supple legs; the other supported her neck as she curled against him in something quite beyond the friendship she'd asked for earlier.

Katie lay in Will's arms, giving in to a temperate yearning as his lips grazed across her skin, letting her know that she still could be loved, could be wanted, and with each kiss he filled her with a placid intrigue of what the future would be like. Yes, she had a future; perhaps even a future with Will. The prospect charmed her in spite of the tensions that often ran between two such strong-willed people.

He kissed her ear, making her shiver. "Cold?" he asked in a whisper.

"Part of me burns," she whispered back. "Part is cold. The night air makes me cold."

"And I hope I make you burn." He smiled and pressed his lips to hers.

"Oh, Will," she moaned, "you help me so much. I do need you. I never thought I'd say it."

"Nor did I. Forgive the pleasure it gives me." He held her tighter, covering as much of her nakedness as he could with his strong arms, warming her with dulcifying kisses. He enjoyed those short, roving kisses as much as he might enjoy the wholeness of making love; indeed, on this particular night, he enjoyed them even more. His tryst was not boorish, not demonstrative, but only a clement stimulation, a love song of chivalry as he rocked her over the glassy water. The water reflected the moon's ivory light onto his peaceful face as she gazed up at him. He moved his hand from her neck to her back, coiling his arm around her in such a way that his fingers could fondle the soft outer curve of her breast, and he found great triumph in the fact that she didn't recoil from his touch or mock it as she had once before. A hundred years ago, it seemed. And would it be another hundred years before she could let him give more than friendship?

He put away hopeless thoughts. Katie was strong. She would turn to him someday soon, and he would be there, ready to carry her beyond the boundaries of her injured heart.

"I have not meant to lead you on," she said, "or tempt you unfairly."

He shook his head and laughed a little. "Ah, Katie, dove, you lead me on by your very being. Something about you calls to me even when we aren't together. I sometimes think I felt it before we even met. Magic, don't you think? Destiny? Tell me you don't feel it. Tell me you feel nothing special in this. . . ." He hugged her close and enveloped her in the kind of deep, wet kiss all the others had been leading to, slackening her resistance with sheer force of passion, rolling her body against his chest in rhythm with the kiss, and almost in prophesy.

Only when he felt the tears press between their cheeks did he release her and draw back to gaze into her moist eyes. It was a moisture of happiness, but of still great quandary. He knew then the depth to which he could love her and also knew that he could wait for her love. When he felt her shiver delicately in the night's chill, he turned and strode through the muck to the dewy shore.

There he set her down and covered her with his chest. Knowing she could see his filled-out nakedness in the moon's wash, he hovered a little while over her before drawing on his tunic. She would have that memory of him to go to seed in her mind.

He built a fire. Soon they were huddled by it, staring not at each other but into the crackling flames. Will brought out bread from the sack of provisions he had somehow managed to keep during all that happened to them, and deep inside it he found a block of goat's cheese and some raspberries, all most welcome. And though not wine, the water from the rushing brook was sparkling-sweet if taken where it ran over rocks. Will did something with the bread that Katie had never seen or heard of. He sliced the cheese, placed it on a slab of bread, then skewered it on a stick and held it over the fire.

"Why are you doing that?" she asked once the cheese grew dangerously soft.

"Hot food is best for the soul."

"But the cheese is melting."

"If I do it just right, yes."

"But—"

"Show a little faith. Ah, yes. There . . . perfect. The milk of the gods. Look at it in the moonlight, Katie, and see cheese for all it is capable of becoming in this world. And notice how the bread is warm and soft again, with this crunchy coating beneath? Here. Take a taste of it. It'll heat your ribs."

Katie took it, catching a long, dripping thread

of cheese just before it joined the grass, and steered the odd food into her mouth. It was warm and soft and chewy.

He saw the pleasure in her face and laughed. "When will you learn to take me at my word?"

"Will your talents ever end?" she countered, smiling back.

"They don't. They go on indefinitely. Even I cannot count them. In fact, I often surprise myself. Once, with some feat or other, I shocked myself into a dead faint. Scared my father nigh to perdition that I might die and deprive the world of me. I'm all he had, you know. Once there was me, how could a wife, two other sons, three daughters, fifteen horses, and Gamewell Desmesne hope to compete? I nearly glowed with worth. Is the moon out or is it me?"

The prize came. She was laughing, a sound so much like the rippling stream that Will almost looked in that direction, so easy was it to confuse her with the animate forest. The leaves, the soft, breathy wind, the soul-freeing beauty all reminded him of Katie.

She was no classic Cleopatra, nor, as he had reminded himself, one of the painted pretties of higher court. Her face was rounder than those classic mythologems, without the upswept eyes or angles, her hair neither ebony nor perfect honey. She was ghostly, nymphlike in her pale loveliness as the moon glowed down on her, a loveliness so simple that he never would have expected himself to perceive it. A new capability entirely. Sweet-tasting.

"Katie," he said softly, "keep your hopes, eh?"

"We failed," she reminded. "I gave my hope to Robin, and now I must face him in defeat and assure him the winter will be as ugly as the picture I forced on him to make him send me on this quest. If the children starve, may it be my fault?"

He moved to her and cupped her face in both hands. "No—oh, no! Where's your grit? Give me that stubborn, fighting Katie. We'll try again."

"In Nottingham we're outlaws. We can't go back. We can't."

"In Nottingham. For now. *Only in Nottingham.*"

"But not—in Southwell! Oh, Will! Could we? Dare we?"

"I think we must."

"Southwell . . . home . . ."

"Indeed, dear brave Helen of Troy. Home."

• *Chapter Nine* •

"Does Robin always use a longbow?"

"Exclusively."

"I thought the preferred weapon of archery was the crossbow." Katie limped along the side of the road on a sore foot, a gift from Nottingham's lumpy streets. At her side Will walked, looking like himself again in black clothes and brown boots and cloak, having unconditionally refused to dress like a woman anymore. They had come a long way already, having traveled a full three days, cutting directly through wild territory to the Cart Road and were now well past the area haunted by the Greenwood band.

"It is," Will said, answering her question. "But Robin has perfected use of the yew bow. Or says he has. He hits his targets square center ninety-five times out of a hundred instead of sixty like most crossbowmen. The yew allows the archer to shoot from the eye instead of the waist or chest. Robin says it will be the weapon of the future. Here. Stand in front of me. Let me show you."

Glad of a chance to break their relentless pace, Katie did as he asked. He put his arms on either side of her and took hold of her wrists. "With a crossbow your arms can be no higher than this, unless you're very strong and can hold the heavy wood high for a duration. Few can. So the crossbow can be no more accurate than a man's aim from here, at the chest, or here, at the waist."

When he took his hands away and stepped back, she felt empty. The feeling of him was a throb in her breast, like life itself. "Its range must be better than a yew bow's."

"Usually, though, the strength in the archer's shoulders makes a difference with the yew. Though it requires a shorter distance, it is that many times more accurate. It's also faster to load and draw. A crossbow requires winding up. So says Robin, at least. I'm no archer, so I seldom argue about such details."

"He impresses me with his skill. Is he as good with the sword?"

"God! Put a sword in his hand and you could defeat him with a ball of spit. And in your sleep too."

They began walking again.

"Are you and Robin true cousins," Katie asked, "or is it a term of affection between you?"

"We are true cousins. Our mothers are sisters."

"He said your name was . . . George. . . ."

"Geoffrey."

"Yes, Geoffrey Mon—"

He sighed. "Montfichet," he said, not willingly. "Geoffrey Montfichet of damned Gamewell, if you must remind me."

"Then why are you called Will? What has it to do with Geoffrey?"

"Nothing, praise God." After a strained moment he decided to tell her. "My mother named me Geoffrey, but my father called me Willie after a character in a favorite song. Robin has called me nothing else since we were boys, and I was glad to have it handy when my title soured on me."

Katie nodded. "I understand. Sometimes I long for a shroud to hide behind."

"You carry a thick enough shroud now."

"Yet I wish I could shed Katie Chenoweth and her burdens."

"And the torch she carries?"

"A sweet and heavy flame, Will. Perhaps you've never loved as I have loved. Such flames endure."

"They also consume."

"I wish to play no games with you today."

"No games? A shame! And here I am beside you with a game you'll enjoy, I trow."

"What game? Tell me."

"No games you said."

"Geoffrey, Geoffrey, Geoffrey—"

"All right! Here it is. We'll shed ourselves and be some others. If you could be anyone, any figure of history or legend, who would you become?"

"Anyone? Man, woman, or beast?"

"Well, there must be some limitation for common sense. You're no beast, nor a man, so be some woman. Or a goddess you may choose. Say . . . Aphrodite or Artemis."

"And will you be man, woman, or beast?" She grinned. "You've played all three parts."

His eyes flashed brighter than the sun on his long hair. "I will be a man. Now and for good. And don't forget it."

"It's the way you looked with ribbons on that I won't soon forget."

"Yes, yes, on with the game. Who will you be?"

"I'll be . . . Hypatia."

"Hypatia? Who is that? A goddess?"

"No. Hypatia was the last scientist to study and publish and spread the great knowledge of the ages at the Library of Alexandria."

"And when was this? Before our Lord Christ?"

"After. And therein lies the tragedy."

"Say what you mean."

"Hypatia kept the integrity and value of the Alexandrian Library until early in the fifth century. Rome was crumbling. Christianity was gathering strength. She defied all convention to preserve the writings of a citadel of geniuses—mathematics, astronomy, medicine, literature, biology. The library was the brainchild of the Ptolemys of Egypt. They collected manuscripts from every known culture. The library itself was eight hundred years old, a repository of wealth of the human mind, and Hypatia was its last guardian. I wish often that I could lance through time and walk and read in the halls of that place. Imagine the treasury!"

"What has Christ to do with this?"

"Can you endure the truth?"

He waved a limp hand. "I have faith. Truth cannot hurt me."

"Keep that in mind," she warned, amused. "Hypatia was a bastion of science, which was and is still linked to paganism by the church.

The Archbishop of Alexandria sent a mob of his believers to destroy her."

"God save her."

"He did not. She was dragged from her wagon and sliced to death with razor-edged seashells."

Will held his breath, wincing. "Misguided fools," he murmured. A shudder went through him. "What became of her work? The manuscripts?"

No longer wishing to pain or tease him, Katie spoke plainly and hoped the harshness of truth could be eased by the centuries. "Lost. Destroyed when the library was burned to its floors after her death. With it went immeasurable knowledge. A half million scrolls. A hundred or more plays of Sophocles, works by Euripides, Aeschylus, Aristarchus, Democritus. Who knows the lengths of that list? Who can reassemble the lost knowledge of the ages? It may be lifetimes before we gather once again that guttered brilliance. It was the greatest tragedy of all time, to me."

Stopping short in his tracks, staring at the road before him, his lips pressed flat. "This game was meant to ease your heart. Now it has flayed your mind. Knowledge is precious to you."

"More precious than anything. It is my Druid heritage."

"In that I agree with you. I was never comfortable with the clergy's teachings that their simple philosophy is enough, that truth should cease to exist beyond the church. But God created all truths, and what he has made I have no fear of." He shook his head and grimaced again. "Frightened, inept fools! I give you your identity as that woman, Katie. A noble selection. Tell me, was she beautiful?"

"It's said she was."

"Then some man would have pursued and married her."

"Many pursued. She turned down every one."

"Then who shall I be? Who would Hypatia love?"

Katie shrugged, trying to keep up with his long-legged stride now that they were moving again. "Is there no one you ever dreamed to meet in those twilight moments when time is fluid? Hypatia, for me, is the zenith of what a person may achieve. Philosopher, mathematician, star-watcher, recorder of civilization, and, best of all, teacher. Is there no one who is that to you?"

The brown cloak lifted as he whirled. In a flash he was upon her, clutching her hand by the arms, leaving her gasping with unexpected fear as he spoke through clenched teeth. "Who do I have to be? What man will fit my clothes who can move you? Alexander to conquer you? Caesar to possess you? I cannot become Edward for you. I cannot compete with a legendary lover. How can I beat a man I'll never challenge face-to-face? Perhaps if he were here, I'd find it easier to quell this churning you've made in me. Who must I be to make you love the woman you are? To make you love *me*?"

"Will, don't frighten me!" She leaned away from his forceful stare, wincing as his hands bit into her arms. "What . . . what brings this on? Will!"

"Hypatia! Indeed. How can you know these things? You're a blacksmith, or so you say!

And how old are you? Twenty? Twenty-two? When did you have time to amass all this knowledge? When did you have time to bed your husband? Or did you at all? Were you dreaming of the past when he needed you? Are you a virgin? Is that why I can't move your heart? Don't look at me with those dry eyes and wonder why I've gone mad." He dragged her across the road as though to leave Edward behind. "Cry for him, damn you, girl! Your sobs will send him on his way and leave you free to answer these hands of mine on your breasts. Cry, Katie Chenoweth, and drive Edward home once and for all!"

Katie trembled in his grasp. She hoped he could see her terror so that he would regret it later, but before she could react, he cast her away. "Never have I known anyone like you! How you can embrace the world and still fend away the passion of a man when it's available is beyond my thinking. You make a man's rope rise, yet give it no anchorage—you are a witch and not the magical kind!" He stalked away, snarling. "Let's go. Southwell and all its ghosts are waiting."

His fury still nameless, he paced off down the road, leaving her in the dust rising from his heels.

Katie stared after him. The lump in her throat pounded. Blood rushed in her ears along with the searing echo of his words. Their confusing vulcanism left her weak. She shook her head, but it wouldn't clear of the smoke he'd blown in there. Dizzied, she made herself follow, but at a safe distance.

What beast am I?

She thought about it but got no answers. Did Will love her, or was he only consumed with beating Edward in some macabre joust?

Or was she the victim of impossible odds?

Could there be two great loves in one lifetime?

A day later Southwell came up on their horizon. Katie's heart thumped at the first puff of smoke from her town's craft quarter. It was morning now. They had been walking since dawn, but the steady, warm sun of yesterday had dried the land and left the ground warm, giving them opportunity for good sleep, and she felt refreshed.

"Shall we hide our faces?" Will wondered as the town gates drew near.

"I'll not hide myself in my own town," Katie said. "Never have I lied to these people of what I am. If I'm to survive here, they must know honesty from me. If you choose to hide your identity," she added, "do it."

He squinted in the morning light. "I'm done with that. Where do you want to start?"

"I want to see my forge."

Of course, the forge itself was secondary. The faces turning before her were those of two boys nearly grown, their cheeks ablaze with red firelight, wincing from the sparks as thick, black-haired arms raised and dropped hammer blow after hammer blow on the anvil, showing them the right way. When the hammer lifted high and disappeared like vapor, new arms pumped the bellows. Then the sound of hissing went away, replaced by the purr of a man's voice telling stories. Eager eyes widened. The rumble of Nick's laughter, the trickle of Gaston's.

But where was the sound she longed for?

She moved wordlessly through Southwell, searching her mind for the forgotten sound, ignoring the looks of people who knew her once she and Will were among them. Her heart lifted when she received a few courageous greetings from her oldest friends, though enough people shied off to make her self-conscious and wary.

But Southwell itself smelled and sounded wonderful. Citizens in their blues, yellows, reds, golds, strapped with leathern belts many of whose buckles Katie herself had struck. Girls with wimples or garlands on their heads. Striped flagpoles hawking each shop's goods. The farrier who traveled the town, tending horseshoes and tack that Katie had forged. It was home.

Then—Cistercians.

Two of them, walking toward the abbey, their white robes and brown tabards identifying them absolutely. Large crosses bobbed against their knees, hanging from rope belts.

Katie stopped walking, frozen as they passed. Her hands chilled. Will watched her, but he couldn't understand.

Katie bolted through the crowded street. She couldn't make herself warm again. Will had to run to keep up with her. Glad she was that he didn't call her name out or ask any questions of her.

Dread struck as she rounded the corner to her own street, passing the familiar two-sided staff-and-cane carver's tent and the hundred whittled faces staring from the tops of those goods, because it was usually there that she would first smell the charcoaly odor of her forge at work and hear the ring of iron on iron. Fifty steps. Thirty. Ten.

"Nick? Nick? Gaston?" Her vision blurred on her own belongings as she stumbled through them, past them, and out into the furnace yard. The smelter itself, hodded and backed, glowering like a thief, the anvil on its oak stump, the sets of tongs, the big leather bellows—all were safe.

She gasped as arms and bodies slammed into her, engulfing her.

"Katie!"

"Bless the Virgin!"

"Oh, you two! I didn't smell the coal or hear your working!" She pushed them back to look at them, at Nick's deeply set eyes and dirty red hair and new beard; at Gaston, shy, sweet Gaston, black-haired and pale-skinned.

"Thank the saints you're safe," Nick breathed. "What happened? Did y' find—" His Northern burr halted. He stared past her.

She turned.

Will stood in the doorway, in a shadow. Tall and narrow, he was imposing and grand, though his mysteriousness had returned, implicit in the fact that he didn't intrude. That alone was a method of control.

Anxiety stirred in the pit of Katie's stomach. She ignored Will and rounded on Nick. "Why is the fire so low in the smelter? Why are you both so tired and skinny? Tell me!"

Nick, being entirely Nick and answerable to no one, sometimes not even his Savior, touched her shoulder and in a voice too like Edward's said, "At the table. Over wine."

The wine was red, spiced, patient with them. Sunlight seemed unwilling to come in. They sat in Katie and Edward's solar at the square table, all four of them, each on a side. A lamp glowed in the center. Nick put out bowls, spoons, and a pot of frumenty, disturbing Katie with his unusual charge of her cupboards.

"We're all right, Katie. Business is a wee slowed down, is all. We're working mornings only, but only till things—"

"Business is off," Katie snapped. "That smelter's not been fired today at all. Don't lie to me, Nick. I'm no convent girl, and business should be good as ever. I saw it all the way here."

Taking a bump under the table as a cue, Gaston suddenly spoke up. "What about you? Where got you these marvelous clothes? Did you find the outlaws of Sherwood?" The faint French accent betrayed nervousness, as did that darted glance at Nick and the wink it got.

Katie bolted to her feet, grasping the edges of the table. "Child! You sit here with an outlaw of Sherwood! I've walked my feet to the bone these past days. I've been chased, pushed, kidnapped, sacked like a cheese, and I'm not in a mood to be lied to. Now the truth! *Nicholas!*"

Nick never flinched. His muscled arms flexed as he raised his cup and sipped wine, taking his time swallowing. His eyes met Katie's gray glare. "We were well for a week after you left. Then our customers started passing us by. We asked why but got nae answers. We've nae been getting the guild wage you made His Reverence promise us. The guild leaders willnae talk to me about it." He shrugged wearily, noticing Will's frown.

"Then I'll confront him with his ignobility," Katie said.

"He's counting on it," Nick told her. "The abbot wants you to fight him out, Katie, it's plain enough. He means tae squeeze you out of Southwell. First he promises you the forge'll stay afire; now he uses its failure to push at you. We're done for, Katie, we're finished."

She slapped his face.

Will lunged forward, grasping her stinging hand, but the deed was done.

More in fatigue than in shame, Nick averted his eyes. Gaston gathered his arms about his body as though he was the one who had been stricken. Katie could only see the top of his bowed head.

The hand on her arm said with its calm force, *Sit down. Think.*

She made the mistake of looking at him. In that instant his steady brown eyes clasped onto her, bolt-tight, preventing her from assaulting Nick any further when within herself she knew Nick was nearly as devoted to Edward's dream as she was. But how did Will know that?

The chair skidded under her as she once again dropped into it. "Where are my neighbors? They heard the abbot's pledge to me. Why are they silent?"

"Fear." This from Will, not Nick.

Katie yanked her arm belligerently at the smugness in his tone, but Will still had hold of it, and he pulled hard, lips pressed together and his glare abusive. Defiance roared in both of them, their private war lapping over into other troubles, but before their glares could consummate, Nick launched out of his chair. His big hands dragged Will up and flattened him against the hearth mantle. "Don't ever touch her," he hissed. In that moment Nick no longer looked like just a tall boy.

Katie started to interfere but never got the chance.

Will's arm moved, a flash so instantaneous that it nearly created sparks. Nick was thrown off-balance. He slammed backward into the rack of cast-iron pots and utensils next to the cupboard. In two strides Will was breathing over him, stone-faced, with one finger nailed to Nick's chest. Will put the other hand on his hip and let seconds go by.

"Don't ever touch *me*."

He turned to find Katie and Gaston both on their feet, statue-stiff and gawking in anticipation, and when he saw the meat ax in Gaston's left hand, he screwed his face into a grimace and snarled, "Oh, put that away, you chuffin head." He strode through the floor rushes to the front door, pausing once before leaving. "I'm going to buy horses. When you and your hot little boys decide on a course, let me know."

Effective. He took their energy with him and threw it in the street.

Nick rubbed his jaw. Gaston shamefacedly put the ax away.

Katie reprimanded them with a quick glance before rifling through the pack of supplies given to her and Will as they left the Greenwood, and she came up with the money pouch Robin had given her. Half of the coins spangled onto the table.

"Use that when you need it, sparingly and only to survive or pay dues to keep the forge going until I return. I will return, do you hear? Never stop believing that." She yanked the pouch closed and affixed it to her belt. She snatched up the provision sack without adding so much as a scallion to it.

"Where are you going?"

Her cloak swarmed. "To hell."

• *Chapter Ten* •

"I confess surprise at seeing you back in Southwell. I truly doubted those pirates would spare your life."

"You hoped not."

The abbot's white robe moved on the stone floor of his cell. His hands were clasped habitually across the hooded white tabard of the Cistercian order. His small eyes darted under their sharp gray brows. "Dear daughter, you misjudge. I delight in your safety. I do mourn, though, at the misfortune of timing. Your return so soon may hurt your business. People will see you've failed and decide Almighty God is against you, as he must be against all heretics."

Katie squared her shoulders. "The word *heretic* means "to know," and I would like to know why my forge is losing the business of steady customers and why my apprentices haven't been paid my surrogate wage when our agreement said you would protect them."

"In the days you have been gone I have prayed continually for divine guidance and have been told that our original agreement was an error on my part. Of course, you, not being in communion with the Holy Spirit, could not know this, so I had to take things upon myself. My obedience to God must take precedence. You entered into a pact with the Church, but such a pact is not binding upon the Church if made under the rules of paganism."

"I made no pact with your church. I made a pact with you! And I've upheld it. I sought and met the outlaws of Sherwood, and their leader has agreed to open the Cart Road under certain conditions that will seem fair to any who are devoted to King Richard. I am succeeding, do you hear?"

The abbot showed no effect from her words. "As long as you are here I foresee no hope for your smithery."

"What do you mean?"

"When you are gone and have been gone a long time and your memory has faded from your forge, then will your business succeed once again. That is my promise."

"I spit on your promise. I've seen your promises."

"Mine? Ah, nay, good daughter, I can but give voice to the Lord." Forcefully he said, "When no hints remain of you, when your apprentices become the smiths and are paying proper alms to those who protect them—"

"To *you*."

"Then ... will they prosper, only then. My holy mandate is to rid my parish of paganism. Such a seed as you represent might bear bad fruit. You wouldn't want to corrupt the religious purity of Southwell, would you?" Watching Katie tremble in rage and affront at his covert threat, he hardly gave her time to respond. "Your apprentices are young. Malleable. And both are Christians. In time They will fit nicely into the form of our community."

"Into your mold, you mean," Katie squeaked, unable to control her voice any longer. How could she fight him? Her mind begged for a way, but he was so steady, so proficient at this—and why? Why would he seek to harm her business?

Even as she asked it of herself the answer flooded in upon her, a twisted ball of Godfrey's personality and a dozen smaller realizations. Without thinking she spoke up. "You're reaping some profit from the closing of the road." Incredulity rang in her tone. When he turned, his eyes narrowed, his lips flat, she could see how right she was. "Can it be true?" she blurted. "Who pays to keep the road closed? It makes no sense!"

"Then . . ." he began cautiously, "you must be mistaken."

"I hear in your voice that I am not. I see it in your face. Why would you seek to harm our town? For money? You know we must trade with Nottingham!"

"It is only slightly more difficult to trade with the town of Lincoln. Southwell's guilds will soon adjust to the trading north instead of south, and the harm of the closed road will fade." He knew he had given himself away with those statements; Katie could tell he knew and could tell he didn't care that she had figured him out. He was not afraid of her or her knowledge of his traitorous bargaining. So she was right: Someone, some power or powers in

Lincoln were paying him for his influence in keeping the road to Nottingham closed! And Robin was playing right into his hands.

Katie nearly grew ill with the thought that Robin, so pious and good, was inadvertently playing along with this vile creature, filling the abbot's pockets while trying to do no more than feed and clothe the poor people of the Greenwood and save a vestige of England for King Richard. Robin would be crushed if he knew.

"You are a fiend," Katie said. Her voice cracked just enough to let her fear seep through. "Lincoln is half again as far to travel."

Hearing the flaw in her voice, Godfrey turned squarely to her with a gleam in his eye. His ruddy, red cheeks fired with victory. "Leave Southwell forever, daughter. Or the wrath of God may be swift and you will die at the hands of the devil you espouse."

Never in her short, young life had Katie felt so utterly victimized. Helpless and glassy-eyed, feeling as inexperienced as a hatchling bird, she stumbled from the abbey. She would never know how long she wandered, dazed, the streets she could never return to, the paths of home, before Will found her. In her desperation she turned to him without struggle. He put her on a horse, climbed on his own, and took her back to the Greenwood, which was now her only home, a sanctuary of outcasts among whom she would take her place.

As evening fell on the abbey that autumn day, the abbot's cell murmured. "Most Holy Father, forgive us our earthly sins and guide my thoughts. Mistress Chenoweth's success in

Sherwood undermines Thy Divine authority and will cut short the benefits we receive as long as the road is closed. Almighty Father, bless this Holy cause. You have shown me a vision that this infidel will find her death among the thieves. Give me the strength to aid Thy word to fulfillment, that she may soon stand silent before Thy countenance in repentence of her sins and know finally Thine infinite glory. In the name of Him who died for our sins, Jesus Christ our Lord and Savior, I pray. Amen."

• PART TWO •

SAMHAIN

• *Chapter Eleven* •

And thus came a vast change in Katie's life, a change about which she could do absolutely nothing. At first she was sullen for a few days. Then the defeat penetrated, and she once again became the bitter, futureless spirit she was when Will had first seen her, caring not whether she slept or ate. This mood lasted more days, extended because Will was gone for a long time on hunt and there was no one else in the Greenwood who could awaken Katie's senses. It was better, though, the days passing uneventfully, the burden of her forge and the Cart Road torn from her as abruptly as they had been forced on. Nothing. There was nothing she could do.

Days became weeks. Katie put her old life behind her, telling herself it was temporary, though some nights she dreamed of the pile of coins on the table between Nick and Gaston. She put her forge in their keeping, knowing they would fight for it to the last.

The Greenwood absorbed her, and soon it was that time of year her folk called Samhain, the time of changeover when the Mother Goddess gave up the year to the beast-god of hunt-

ing time. All Hallow's Eve. In the far-distant
areas of Ireland and Wales and, she had heard,
Scotland also, children would carve horrible
faces in empty gourds, put them atop torches,
and run about the countryside gleefully imitating the malevolent spirits they were driving
away. But the Greenwood children were Christian and played games quite different from
any Katie remembered: prisoner's base, blind
man's bluff, and other joys available while
weather allowed.

Whenever Will was able, he spent time with
her, even teaching her to skate upon the frozen
pond with horse's shinbones tied to her feet.
She was clumsy at it and never got proficient,
but she loved to be out among the children,
who were proficient as they propelled themselves around her with iron-shod poles. These
were episodes of delightful and romantic in-
terplay between her and Will, though the definition of love continued to elude her. Will's
friendly distance was disturbing enough. He
no longer clasped her forcefully, nor drew her
close to his body in those fiery moments she'd
experienced from him, not even when she found
herself wishing he would. Had he given up
just when she so needed his anchor to hold on
to, to keep her from drifting back? His lack of
effort toward her made her long for it. Oh, he
treated her kindly enough, and they talked
long hours away, and even sometimes their
lips strayed toward each other and sometimes
met, but fleetingly, briefly.

And she made other friends. As winter kept
the men wandering on their hunting parties,
she gradually sought out the company of other

women. This, after years with Edward, Nick, and Gaston filling her life, was a new aspect. She'd had some female acquaintances in Southwell, women with whom or with whose husbands she did business, but no real friends. But here she found sympathy from people who had been beaten down, folk trying to make their sequestered lives into some echo of what they had known in better times, and as time passed, she gave in to her displaced home and family, buffeted by Will's companionship and a nagging sensuality that showed her she was still alive. The short days and cold nights offered little time for her to see Will, and as their food and dry firewood supplies dwindled, she saw even less of him. That is, except one day when he sought her out and for once seemed rested.

"Katie, I've been looking for you all morning," he announced, tromping out of the woods, not using any of the paths. He found her shelling walnuts but was no longer surprised not to find the glorious queen he'd kidnapped from Sir Guy. These days, cold days, she had put away those fine clothes, trading them in for the dull-colored wools so necessary in the winter forest. Her braided hair was bound up around her head and ears like a hat, and a simple woven belt kept her tunic snug around her waist, and each time, though rare, he tromped through the bare trees and evergreens to her, she looked better to him. Each time it was more like coming home. Yet it seemed to Will that as Katie grew stronger, drew farther from her dead husband, her strength replaced the quiver of need she had for Will when they first met. In response he held himself away, hoping she would once again turn to him but more fully. He hoped the day would come when she dreamed of him. Until that moment he dared not approach her in love; if he did, might he not helplessly repeat the scene of near ravagery on the Cart Road near Southwell? There could never again be such crudeness. Once he had nearly slapped her. That time he had nearly raped her.

He saw the reflection of undeserved forgiveness in her water-gray eyes as she looked up at him now. "I've been right here all morning," she said, "nearly since dawn. Why?"

"Good news." He fastidiously brushed the snow from his boots.

"I'd like some."

"Recall our little jaunt in Nottingham?"

"I have tried hard to forget it."

"We had visitors on the road last evening and early today, merchants both. One had a load of wine casks and the other herbs, medicines, and wheat."

"And were they promptly robbed dry?"

"That's the marvelous part. There was no need to rob them. Both had come this route specifically to offer up donations to our cause and our survival for the winter. Each handed over a full third, mind you, of his goods—did you hear that? An entire third—and begged to be part of the movement to liberate Richard. Now, where do you suppose they got such an idea? And need I even say the value of wheat and wine to us?"

Sentences ago Katie had drifted down onto a nearby stool and stared at him in disbelief.

"You need not. Oh, Will, can it be because of us?"

He leaned on her barrel of shucked nuts. "Who else would it be because of? Slowly but steadily our proposal is spreading. Two wagons today, perhaps more next week, and more after those. I tell you, these men seemed overjoyed to participate in favor of their king. One jumped from his wagon and landed Robin a kiss right on the cheek, and that was a sight."

Katie refused to overreact. "Take care, though," she said. "A third wagonload is a huge amount for products of the earth like wine and wheat, and likely it was all those men could spare for the whole year. And it took them all these weeks to get here. That may very well be the end of it."

One gold-brown eyebrow cocked. "Well, I daresay. You are an ungrateful little animal, aren't you? Here I came dashing through with good news to toast your heart and you must play the devil. That's naughty and cruel, and I'm bruised."

She smiled but nodded wisely. "I've been bruised too. One learns caution after much of it."

"Ah! So serious. So dour. Such a settled mentality. Katie, you pain me. Even out here in these glorious woodlands, far removed from everything that ever hurt you, still you cannot be spontaneous. You cannot give in, can you?"

It was true, she acknowledged to herself, that she still awakened in the night now and then with her legs cold and her heart thudding and her arm reaching outward to her left, where Edward had always been.

She stood up. "Very well. I'll be happy and not cautious at all. You're right! It does feel better. The winter does look a shade or two brighter, doesn't it?"

"Liar," he said, the corner of his mouth tipping upward. He started to say more, but a sucking sound invaded the air, and he and Katie found themselves gawking down at an arrow stuck fast through the top flap of Will's boot and deep into the nut barrel. He looked into the trees and swore. "God burn him, he might've lamed me for life!" Then he raised his voice. "Robin, this game is *not* funny, hang your hide! Do you hear me? I see your green ass in that tree. Don't try to hide. There isn't a tree trunk in Sherwood thick enough to cover your swollen head! Come out of there!" There was a distant rustling in the pines, after which Will sighed in frustration. "Saints, there he goes. And he gave me the damnedest wink too."

"Apparently his mood is as cheery as yours is."

"As mine *was*." He yanked the arrow free of the barrel, worked it out of his boot top, and examined the hole in the leather, grumbling in smoldering disgust. "Ruined!"

"It can be mended," Katie said with amused sympathy.

"But never will it be perfect. Damn, damn, and damn my cousin's prankishness. Someday he's going to slip and hurt me, and both of us will be ungodly sorry."

"Has he ever drawn blood?"

"Not mine, praise the saints, at least not yet. The odds get smaller by the day. He's come so close, I swear there've been times I've felt the shaft buzz on my skin. A charming sensation, I tell you. Blast!"

"What's wrong?"

"He's coming back . . . yes . . . I see clumps of branches where there should be none. There— did you see it? A movement against the wind? That rot! He's going to get me again!"

"Have you tried running away?"

"That, Katie girl, would be deeply beneath my dignity."

"Oh? I'll save your dignity." She dug into the barrel of nuts and hurled a handful of them into his surprised face. "Chase me!"

Robin flushed out of Will's mind quicker than dust in a breeze when he saw Katie dash off through the trees, twigs pulling at her legs, just as freely and vibrantly as a bit of stray sunlight. He felt a sexual chuckle rise in his throat. To resist chasing her would be like a fox resisting the scent of a young hare.

So he did.

He chased. Branches snapped around him. Trees rushed by, whipping their bare branches, the pines dropping stiff needles with a faint sprinkling sound. Snow flew in his face from her heels, tempting him as her laughing eyes and bright face darted at him, but if she wanted him to catch her, she never made it easy. In fact, she led him on a true adventure, never giving any leeway, never faltering conveniently so he could gain ground. Her sportsmanship both aroused and confused him. By the time he'd caught up with her, he was warmer than he had been in months and in more than one way. And even then he hadn't really caught her.

"Katie," he said, stalking around the base of a tall young oak, "you come down from there."

The sun flickered, blinding him, glinting around a solid form. "I won't. I like it up here."

"That's enough. Come down."

"You come up."

Crustily he muttered, "Already have." He clasped low branches and hoisted himself into the tree. But no matter how high he climbed, she climbed higher, having the lighter weight and thus the advantage. Finally he stepped on a branch too high, too thin, and felt it crack. At that, he backed off and struck her with a heavy stare. "I dare not go farther. I'll fall if I do, and you wouldn't enjoy scraping me from these limbs, now would you?"

Hugging the tree trunk mischievously, she said, "You never know what I'm going to enjoy, do you?"

"I've given up trying to find out." Will settled on the highest branch that was willing to hold him without creaking and wedged one foot into a notch, casting only one unfocused glance at the disturbingly distant ground. Why would God create anything so tall? "Won't you climb down?"

"Don't you find the fresh wind pleasant?"

"I find it frightful when it waves this tree back and forth. This is dangerous."

"But Will Scarlet laughs at danger."

"Katie, you're being troublesome."

"Never. I'm only repaying you for all the times you teased me and embarrassed me and all those wonderful other moments. Remember those moments?"

"I cannot stay here forever, Katie. There's another hunting party planned, and I can't hunt from up here, can I?"

"Then climb down."

"What? And admit defeat?"

Adjusting her rump on her chosen branch, Katie looked across the trees. Will was collared by his heavy brown cloak as it draped from his shoulders to his hands, which clutched branches with wary firmness, again draping from one hand down across his body to the other hand. She admired how he looked. "Haven't you told me," she began, "that you're bad with an arrow?"

"I'm abominable with an arrow."

"Then with what sort of weapon do you hunt? A sling? Surely not sword or dagger."

"Of course not, and not a sling, either. I hunt with my head."

"You must be a good tracker to get close enough to knock your prey with your head."

He smirked at her. "You know what I mean."

"I don't, really. How could you hunt with—"

"When we go a-hunting"—he sighed, then stiffened as a breeze waved their perch sickeningly—"when we hunt, I help to flush out the prey and steer it toward our bowmen. But my best hunting talent comes during those long hours before and after the kill."

"Doing what?"

"Oh, I tell stories. I stave off the boredom and the cold with my tales and my poems, and Alan does the same with his songs. Anything to kill the misery."

"Do you know many stories? What stories do you know?"

"Oh, I recite what bits and pieces of epic poems I can recall. *Beowulf, The Phoenix, Caedmon's Hymn*, things anyone knows."

"Please recite something now! Please?"

"Well, why?"

"Oh, *please*! Or I'll go higher."

"No, no, stay where you are. Let me see . . . very well, here it is:

"He who shall muse   on these mouldering ruins
And deeply ponder   on this darkling life
Must brood on old legends   of battle and bloodshed
And heavy the mood   that troubles his heart:
'Where now is the warrior?   Where is the war horse?
Bestowal of treasure,   and sharing of feast?
Alas! the bright ale-cup,   the byrny-clad warrior,
The prince in his splendor   —those days are long sped
In the night of the past,   as if they never had been!' "

The tree waved. Branches clasped at nothing. Eyes full of enchantment took on a mystical glaze. Soon where there had been a man's voice now came, now whispered, a woman's:

"And now remains only,   for warriors's memorial,
A wall wondrous high   with serpent shapes carved.
Storms of ash-spears   have smitten the eorls,
Carnage of weapon,   and conquering Fate."

And again—his:
"Storms now batter   these ramparts of stone;
Blowing snow   and the blast of winter
Enfold the earth;   night-shadows fall

Darkly glowering,   from the north driving
Raging hail   in wrath upon men.
Wretchedness fills   the realm of earth,
And Fate's decrees   transform the world."

Tears welled. Gray globes became crystal as
Katie whispered the last refrain:

"Mere wealth is fleeting,   friends are fleeting,
Man is fleeting—"

And Will responded:

"Maid is fleeting;   All the foundation
of earth . . . shall fail!"

The wind shimmered between them, lights
of tomorrow and yesterday, live spirits he could
not believe in, that she knew existed, caressing
the bodies of mortalkind high in a tree of the
earth. A sound indescribable. An echo.

"Katie, don't cry. It injures me when you do."

She covered her face for a moment. After all
the demanding he'd done for her to cry she
gasped, "I'm not crying." No, she wasn't; she
was laughing. Her cheeks glowed. "I can't believe it—I never met anyone else who knew *The
Wanderer* well enough to recite it. Will, I'm so
glad!"

"And what about that is there to make you so
glad? It's a poem only, no thing of mystery. . . ."

"A poem *only*? Never say those words. A
poem is a special thing, Will, more than words
yet better than song. Were I nearer I would
embrace you hard."

His eyes grew sultry. "I'll hold you to it. But
I still don't understand—"

"Don't you?"

"You're not dealing with a peasant here."

"More than that! Literacy will save mankind from his fears. There is nothing grander than to commit to memory a great epic of times past, to be a living echo of some elegance gone by. If only all people could read and be taught the great stories of history and imagination and all the excitements that make people invent things to tell and write down. There will be more of literacy in the future."

"I see Robin isn't the only prophet in my midst."

"You disagree?"

"It's a charming wish, Katie, but how could it come true? So many are ignorant, so few are teachers. A book is too costly and too long in the making and the masses of the unread widely flung. There will always be illiteracy. Just as the aristocracy will always rule. It is God's well-planned natural order. Each to his place."

"Fodder."

"Katie, that is how the Almighty measures our mettle for the afterlife—how well we each fulfill our own separate lots in life."

"Trash."

"Katie!"

"I accept no preconceived lot," she said forcefully, but not without a pinch of arrogance, raw of any apology. "Nor do you."

"I? In faith I do. I accept my place."

"You accepted your station because yours was comfortable. Some of us have no Gamewell. The ancient Egyptians thought being born poor meant you must stay poor and be very good at poverty in order to earn better status in the afterlife. How convenient for the wealthy that the poor held themselves down."

"Are you intimating that I'm afraid of spreading literacy?"

"Are there not those who fear its power?"

"But are you saying I am?"

"Are you?"

"Katie!" He sat back, blown by indignation, and, forgetting he was in a tree, nearly fell out.

Katie hugged the tree trunk and laughed at his expression. He saw how easily he was falling prey to her teasing and appeased himself with a deep breath and a rearranging of his cloak about his shoulders. "Rude little wench."

Katie spent several indulgent moments enjoying the flurry of emotions, all the thoughts and depths and complexities meeting in the tawny eyes across from her, allowing the changes in his face to fill her. She enjoyed taking him by surprise. It almost always led her down a new channel of Will's personality. At times she suspected he was doing the same to her, yet she could still catch him off-guard, impish though the habit was.

"You have a pompous streak in you, Katie," he declared when his senses stopped reeling from a downward glance. "You do."

"Pompous?" she retaliated before she could hold back the pride in her voice, knowing one was the same as the other.

"You are."

"How am I?"

"You get a sadistic enjoyment out of using your background to tug down others, your mixed education and your off-center sensibilities—"

"Is this a nice thing to be saying?"

"Touting yourself as a great deliverer of literacy to the unread claptrappers of the world, nice? Nice, you ask? Who knows what's nice to a Druid blacksmith daughter-of-a-cobbler convent-student with grandiose dreams? Who can suppose? Christ!"

"Will, hang on! Hold that bough."

"Damned tree, must it bob so?"

"If you insist on dancing about. And your cloak is caught."

"Where—where—"

"Caught. There. On that—yes."

"My God, you're chilling. Even my cloak grabs for its life around you. It's not the wind rattling this tree, it's *you*. There's one dimension in you upon another, each always one fraction more out of reach than that before it, angles that torture the traveler and hurt and confuse and confound and weed up anyone who walks in there, in you—in you . . . what a sensual phrase—Katie Chenoweth, a house of mismatched ornaments."

She stared at him, hearing the cacophony of truths and half faults with their tickling bemusement and felt miserable, happy, noble, all those things he could make her feel with a glance. "Am I so skewed by my history?"

"A house of ornaments, all in the center of one room."

"You look at me through a watery surface," she said, loving her mysteriousness.

"*You*," he said with a finger up, "are the one drink beyond my tolerance.

Smiling in spite of herself, Katie tipped her head. The sunlight shined through her eyelashes, striating her lemony cheeks, a fringe upon surprise. "All this because secretly I wish to be a teacher instead of a blacksmith?"

The sound at the bottom of the tree was Will's tirade falling. He relaxed, sighed, having gotten it out; no telling, of course, how long the respite would last. "You can never be a teacher, Katie lass. Not in England, sadly."

"But . . ." Though the small hope had never budded, it worried her to have it slashed.

He saw it but was helpless. "In England a teacher must teach the Holy Gospel, Katie, and the Gospel and you apparently are poor bedfellows. There are no clutches of Old Religion learning. Our children who have the means are sent to monastery schools or—"

"Or convents."

"Or convents. They are allowed no—"

"Even in the convents my questions were encouraged, Will," she was compelled to say. "Even the nuns tolerated my imagination, my love for tales older than theirs."

"But," he tried again, "you must teach the Gospel of Jesus Christ as the only *truth*. All gods but the Almighty must be acknowledged as dead. Were you to do otherwise," he said, his gaze intensely sorrowful, for he had learned much from her, "the persecution would be far worse than anything you expected in Southwell from your simpleton fellowship in the crafters' quarter. Even your imagination can't race that of incensed clerics. Yes, I can admit it; my church is one of high-flown belief, and they hunger for exorcism these days. We must sort out our devotions or fall prey to them. But you, dear women," he added quietly, "must never dare to teach in England."

Was she destroyed? Will could not tell the

effect on her of his admonishing. Nor could he tell for certain the root of his drive to tell her these things, things she probably knew but probably never contemplated, and his fingers squeezed tight. The tighter they clenched, the slicker the dream he had grabbed for. Beyond Southwell, before Edward, into a distance. For once he had shot beyond her wounds to another time long before Edward's time, to something he, Will, could touch, could change—and he had ruined it at the root. Slowly he realized this, too slowly to fix it.

She didn't move, but her eyes altered. "You have no imagination," she said. And it came to her then, in just those few seconds, what had never occurred to her before. "Those things are true." Quiet, full words, but incomplete. "Everywhere but in the cathedral of the Greenwood."

The forest was still except for Katie and Will's even breathing as they sat huddled together in what had become *their* tree. Will watched her, wondering where his childlike imagination had gone. Katie certainly retained the wit and exuberance of youth; for the first time he thought about the decade or so separating them.

"I'm suddenly cold," he said, cringing against a stiff wind. He glanced downward gingerly. "Have we not stayed here long enough? If I remain longer, I may not be able to move these legs and go on the hunting expedition, and I'll have to blame you in front of everyone. 'Sat too long in a tree with that Druid,' I'll have to say."

"Then go down. I can't climb past you, can I?"

"Suppose not. All right, but you promised. Let's go."

Going down proved trickier than climbing up, he soon discovered as he fought branches growing in entirely uncooperative directions and having shrunken, it seemed, since he was a lad and did this regularly. His cloak was a hindrance, as were his hard-soled boots, and eventually he slipped. Reaching for a bough, his hands missed, a stiff force whipped his face, blinding him, and instantly the sounds of cracking branches and Katie's frantic shrieks filled his ears.

Thump.

Something hurt.

Yes, it definitely hurt. Will recognized pain.

"Will! Did you break anything?"

He opened his eyes one at a time. Katie was hanging above him, still fairly high in the tree, both hands braced on a branch as she stared down with held breath.

"On the tree or on myself?"

"Are you hurt?"

"I'm hurting, if that's your question." He was lying flat on his back in snow and late-fallen leaves, his long legs flung over a log. "Down with you now."

"No, I think I'll stay."

"Katie! Blast you, Chenoweth, you gave your word."

"I did not."

"Girl, I'm not climbing back up that weed."

"And I'll not come down until you swear I'm smarter, trickier, and prettier than you are."

"Never."

"Swear it."

"Maybe prettier. Maybe."

"You know, the breeze feels refreshing."

"Very well. I swear. Climb down this minute or I'll plait candles into your hair and light them as you sleep."

Katie felt a giggle rise in her throat and decided her victories numbered enough for one day as the chilly breeze encouraged her to accept. Unfortunately Will's fall had snapped off the branch she'd used as her main brace for getting up the tree, the one she'd planned to use, unfortunately, for getting down. She descended as low as possible without that branch, but she was still high up in the air, staring down at a limbless trunk.

"Will . . . I need help."

He folded his arms. "Do you? Can you not jump?"

"Do you truly expect me to jump?"

"It seems God has ordained it."

"I'll break my neck."

"You'll find some wise alternative. I'll be here to record the moment for posterity."

"Will Scarlet, it's no gentleman I see before me."

"Or more accurately, below you." He felt the slow warmth of another image seep under his skin and cooled it with a smile.

Katie edged her legs around the tree trunk and moved free of the branch she was sitting on until she was holding on like a tree toad. The bark bit into her flesh, hands, calves, and thighs as she inched down the tree—until her wool tunic clung to the bark and climbed up her legs, up her body, to gather around her waist in a tangle. "Oh! Oh ... no ... Will, *help* me."

"Now, I said posterity, not posterior. Moonrise is early tonight." He circled below her, appreciating the view of warm winter-rose flesh and trim lines, a tempting, artistic scene for a man who still considered himself young despite some wear around the edges. Looking at this pale countryside made him feel young and he felt consumed with a creeping vitality that had been so fleeting lately.

Will gazed up at Katie, suddenly finding himself drawing away mentally. She was beginning to want him, he realized, even though the shroud still clung and the prospect caused him pain. Pain for her. She was a woman shaking the tree of the world, forcing it to bend her way, while he had let his tree wither. She had built a life and stowed it carefully away for a moment when she could return to it. Yet if she loved him, he could give her only withered gifts. A barren winter's chill; memories of a titled estate; strenuous years of life with the animals. Life *as* an animal.

He finally went to the tree and pulled Katie's skirts down, freeing her to drop into his arms. For too long he held her with sadness in his eyes. When he bent to kiss her pale lips, it was the sadness that caressed her. It ran through her bones; he felt it.

Quickly he put her down and mourned at the sound of frosted leaves beneath her feet.

"There you are. Safe."

Katie mistook the doubt in his eyes for arrogance, and her cheer soured. She really hadn't been embarrassed, not too much, half bare before a man who had looked beyond her body, which all women had, to her deeply lodged soul, which was only hers.

He held out his hand to her, a completely empty hand. "Come, teacher. There are ears awaiting your stories."

Thus it came that Katie began to teach the children of the Greenwood community. Will's changed attitude did not fade after that day but continued in strange behavior and an icy edge Katie assumed to be envy, for she knew more stories than he did, as well as the histories behind them. She soon forgot Will's coolness in response to the faces of awed children. These little pauper sprites for whom her tales painted riches had wide eyes of imagination, and eventually even the children of those who had at first rejected her tales as paganistic gathered around her. When God did not strike Katie mute, the adults supposed He approved and sent their little ones to her to learn tales and letters. At first she taught them to write their own names, then to read each others' names, then to read other words of import to them in their woodland life, simply because those were the words of most interest to them. The girls wished to write names of their clay dolls, boys wished to know how to pass secret notes with crucial messages as they played games imitating their fathers' hunts and the activities of the men they admired—the only men they ever saw. Katie filled their insatiable minds with *The Odyssey, The Wanderer, The Battle of Maldon*, Helen and Paris, Brian Boru of Ireland, the Viking Pantheon of Asgaard, the plays of Sophocles and Aeschylus. She told them of the destroyed Tuatha de Dananns of Ireland, who became the mystic pale Sidhe when they could no longer fight the forces of oppression. As the slow, cold hungry days passed, others began to hover around Katie's small fire when there was wood dry enough for fires. Some were faces often unseen through the harsh days as winter fully encroached. Johnny. Alan. Edmund. Edith. Marian. Will Stutley. Robin.

And even Will, though rarely.

It often troubled Katie to see all the men grown gaunt and tired from their constant quest for food, feeding the womenfolk and children before themselves. They even fed their hunting dogs better than themselves, so valuable were those dogs. Will seemed unwilling to have her see him exhausted and thin, knowing it might very well be a picture of his future, his old age. His hair had lost its summer luster, his eyes their summer gleam, and more, the gleam of surreal hope. As he held the flicker of her life away from the guttering of her grief, Katie caught and held the bud of his hope and carried it for him through the harsh December.

It warmed her as she spun her tales for them to distract them, embellishing details until they moved beyond reality into some believable glory, and she became a better shanachie than ever graced her mother's folk. One day when she was reciting some pre-Christian bardic poems of Wales, "poems of being" they were called, fate took another quick turn that marred her time in the Greenwood. Some folk here were still uneasy with her tales, not knowing whether to take them as folklore or fact;

there were still grumblings, even here, about the fine line between truth and entertainment, which came to a head when one of the women, Nell Johnson, found the courage—or enough fear—to challenge her.

> *"I am smoke, I am fog,*
> *I burn away fog, I am the sun,*
> *I am a chariot, I am a harp,*
> *I turn to stone when I am loved.*
>
> *I am frogs, I am streams,*
> *I flow, I climb,*
> *I am wind.*
> *I follow antelope, I run with deer.*
> *I touch grass upon slopes,*
> *I become steam—"*

"You endanger all of us!"

Katie, and everyone, looked up into the face of Nell, smelling the fear. Nell had always been distant, and now her distance would explain itself.

"What do you mean, Nell?" Katie asked, using her calm tone as an example for the children clustered around her. She was especially aware of Edith Small's curious little daughter, Gwennie, whose desire to learn had forded every obstacle of weather or prejudice since Katie first asked to teach the Greenwood children.

Nell was a woman who would have been beautiful had she been born into a higher stratum of society. She had the long-necked, square-jawed elegance of a noblewoman of good stock and that same kind of autonomy; unfortunately

her birthplace had been the slum quarter of
Nottingham. She had moved upward only by
marriage to a fisherman, and then only from
beggardom to a hard life at the nets and scal-
ing boards.

Her independent drive had been downbeaten
until all that was left was a twitch in her right
eye and a crippling bitterness.

"You teach our children these myths as
though they are true," she accused.

Katie sat firmly on self-confidence. "They
are true."

"They are sacrilegious." The twitch went to
work, wrecking her mouth as it tugged her eye
into a blade. "Your words have dried the Cart
Road with God's wrath and kept the animals
from our hunters. We're being punished because we let you talk and corrupt us with your
heathen stories."

Had they been alone, Katie would have spared
Nell's feelings, but this public confrontation
put her in a difficult position, and backing down
would have made Nell's words true and de-
graded Katie in the eyes of all who watched.
"Nell, you have no children in my circle. Perhaps the emptiness hurts you into doing this.
Sit down. I will teach you too."

"Listening to you would put me at hell's
door."

"There have been hard winters before, have
there not?"

"We know why you're here," Nell continued, stiffening. The bite Katie felt from her
eyes was not hatred; it was fright. "You can't
go home or you'll be tested for a witch! God
punished you with your husband's death."

"But your husband died too. Are you also punished?"

This took Nell by surprise. She sucked in a breath and held it. The right eye nearly jerked shut now.

Katie used the chance. "Your life has been harder than any among us. I understand why you needed your god's hand to lean upon. In many ways we are alike, you and I, and I understand you."

"You are without God. It's a sin!"

"My god and goddess are not for that kind of worship. We go hand in hand with them, rather than in subservience to them. But I do not call you sinner for not accepting my gods. Why do you condemn me for being true to them?" She knew Nell could not think philosophically. She knew she was using her abilities to best the shortsighted woman and regretted that one of them must ultimately look foolish in front of those who were listening today. Fortunately Will and Robin had collapsed in their tents earlier after a four-day hunt and were not here to add damage, as surely they would. But Alan was present, as were the parents of some of the younger children, and Katie was concerned about the outcome. She was not here to set the Greenwood asunder. She was not here to cede her honor, nor to take the chewing of Nell's glare. She might someday die for it in this changing world, but she refused to lie to protect Nell's god. Nell would have to accept the existence of other beliefs beyond her own, no matter what the pain, or shame.

It became obvious immediately that Nell had no premeditated plan to use against Katie, for she faltered at Katie's calm steadiness. Katie could have prevailed by simply staring Nell down and waiting for her to frustrate herself into a palsy and leave.

Eventually this is exactly what happened. It only took a little more nudging, which Nell insisted upon provoking when she said, "Evil will be among us as long as you stay here. I can *feel* it."

Animosity moved between the two women where before there had been only a variance of pasts. The children watched, absorbed. Others watched, worried.

This is what it is to be oppressed, Katie thought. I always assumed it would involve pain. But this is pain. Pain for her and them. I cannot, I will not change what I am so she can sleep better.

"Soon it will be Christmas," Nell said, knotted up with rage, "and the telling time will be here."

"Let it come, then." Katie kept her hands folded sedately in her lap, though even the mindful lack of movement was testimony to her own unease. "Let your god strike me down dead at this moment if he disapproves of one word I've spoken in these woods."

The true wish was unmistakable. Here was a woman prepared to brave hell if she was wrong rather than compromise herself. It was the goal of everyone present to gain such integrity. They waited, breath held, for the lightning bolt strike.

They listened. Wind.

They peeked. Chill blue sky.

Nell struggled with the horror of abandon-

ment, choked on it, spun, and ran into the bare
forest until they could no longer see her. But
the memory of her eyes, full of astonishment
and prophesy, lingered.

She knew Nell would have her way, since
Katie's Druid people were fading away, refusing
to bloody themselves for their creeds. After
she was gone Katie could not remember a poem
to recite or a story to tell.

"Katie, come in!" Round-cheeked Edith held
out a hand to her. She was sitting up, plump
with pregnancy and having been the Greenwood's first-fed since her life sustained fully
three lives—hers, her unborn's, and year-and-a-
half-old Amlin's, who still suckled her body.
Edith had taken to Katie and become as close a
friend as Katie ever knew, admiring her knowledge and the bravery that had brought her to
the forest. "We're going to have our baby tonight," she said, using the plural for Gwennie's
sake.

Katie stared at her. Where was the agony?
Where were the moans?

"Will you take charge of Gwennie and Amlin?
They love you so." Edith fondled the tiny hand
of her infant son, asleep at her side. When
Katie nodded, she tacked on, "But stay here
for the sake of this new child. If you're nearby,
the influence will be brightness of wit. Stay,
will you?"

A reassuring smile disguised shifting, am-
biguous doubts. "I will." For her friend she
would stay. She would pretend no dull aches
of sorrow.

"Unbraid her hair," Ula said, handing Katie

a comb, "and comb it free. Labor will be easier. Melicent and I will go prepare the dried crane's blood for good luck."

"Yes, there must be good luck when the baby comes," Marian insisted as she wrestled to untie a knot in her own belt.

Participating in the sympathetic magic, Katie unbraided Edith's long, graying hair and thought how Christianity huddled with paganism in this tent tonight, but she said nothing, not letting her resentment show. Nell was not here tonight. These women were not her oppressors.

"We'll have to borrow a few things from King Richard's booty," Marian advised. "A few bits of ivory, a gold cup ... some spices ... and a leatherbound book or some other symbol of knowledge."

"Why would you do that?" Katie asked.

Both Marian and Edith looked at her strangely. Marian shrugged. "Don't you know?"

"I never attended a birth before. I know little of them." Sweat broke on her palms. Edith's hair stuck to them.

"To make an aspiring environment for the baby, of course," Marian said, distractedly working the knot. "It is important, every detail. Or else how can the child ever hope to prosper?"

None of these things were done for me, and I prospered, Katie thought. Though I am far from prosperity now.

"Is it uncomfortable to give birth, Edith?" The question was a surprise when it left Katie's lips.

"I don't find it so," the older woman said,

"but then, I have never been afraid. Fear is half of pain."

There was little time for talking when Ula and Melicent returned and prepared a table of herbs and a crock of warm water, not too hot, and swaddling for the baby. Edith became uncomfortable and elected to walk once around the camp to hurry her labor; Ula seized the opportunity to put Marian in charge of Edith's children, freeing Katie to go out after a lode of jasper. The gem was believed to have birth-helping properties, and the women wanted to hang nuggets of it in the birth tent. Katie readily agreed to go.

It was mid-afternoon. The sun wheeled, a great bright plate in the winter sky, shimmering the forest. The wind ran through the trees and played them as Alan's fingers ran the strings of his lute, music full of heart, soul, and English misty winter, a song without a voice, a high-hearted sound. And today Katie felt sure the wind from the west held spirits. The *sluashee* came down from Ireland, brushing North Wales, to her.

"Cerridwyn, Cerridwyn," a voice called, though the young girl paid it no heed, for in that moment the future was as clear as a glare of ice. Simple, everything was so simple. It was a world for a child to glory in.

Yet it was not enough. Every answer begged a new question, and the world was a simple future of pasts without the troubles of men. It was a woman's world, a planet of the female, where daughters of the great oaks who heard the Murmuring had sense enough to listen.

"Cerridwyn?"

The child watched the cocoon move. Life was within it. Cerridwyn held back the strand of her white-blond hair that the breeze tried to blow between her and the cocoon. She was determined to witness that unrepeatable moment when life first cracked the prison shell and first felt the touch of real air. It reminded her of the time her father's goat gave birth, and a fabulous power to be female; to think and dream and dare, *and* to grow life from nothing. From absolutely nothing!

There seemed to be no female involved with the cocoon as far as Cerridwyn could discern, and she puzzled over that until her eyes ached from the staring. She had watched it all morning, and now the cocoon quivered with life even though it had been as still as death when she first found it. This led her to a simple equation: She must be the female from whom this flicker of life was drawing its strength. So as the day wore on she refused to abandon it, sending her life forces at it and speaking encouraging words, words of the trees and flowers it would soon light upon; care with each description was critical. Otherwise the offspring might not recognize the proper food. It wouldn't do to have it light on a hawthorn when it needed to eat myrtle for who know what hawthorn would do to a being meant to eat myrtle.

"Cerridwyn!"

"Don't bother me. It's hatching," the young child replied.

The cocoon shivered in a light breeze. The insect within the shell picked its way free. Cerridwyn absorbed every movement of the ugly little body with its separate, swiveling head, segmented legs, and wet, crumpled wings. But like any mother, her wrinkled newborn looked beautiful to Cerridwyn. Her young, voracious curiosity forgiving nature its every grossness, she resisted the urge to help break away the cocoon and help the moth to better footing. That lesson had been hard-learned and had cost the life of a baby bird newly fallen from its nest, still in the egg. Cerridwyn, anxious to hurry inside, had picked the shell from the frail, blue-veined being within, piece by piece, slowly, with each pick telling herself one more would do no harm. Harm it did, though, and the world was short a life because of her. The guilt was crushing. It kept her hands off this cocoon.

Before the wings dried, a shadow crossed between them and the sun.

"Cerridwyn," said the shadow. "Your mother wants you."

"Don't block the light," the child responded, pushing against a yellow-and-green woven belt of the *túath*, their tribe. Her uncle's hair glowed red around his shadowed face.

"Your mother calls you," Desmond said again.

"I'm busy."

"Doing what?" He stooped down, shifting enough for the sun to reach those crumpled wings. "You mean that?"

"Yes. She needs me."

He laughed, and clean bright teeth flashed. "He doesn't need you. Go on, off to your mother's hut. Off with you, girl. I mean it. He's been fine without you until now, and he'll do fine when you're gone."

Before running off, Cerridwyn tossed smartly back, "*She*."

Inanna of the Willow waited in the myrtle grove, a familiar sight with her nettle robe, yellow-and-green belt, and bright red hair. Not a pretty woman, her close-set hazel eyes and thin lips brightened visibly when she saw Cerridwyn running toward her through the woods so eagerly. Rare it was that a girl of ten so enjoyed her own mother's company. Inanna hoped to keep it that way. Perhaps she should have been more strict with her headstrong little daughter, but perhaps then Cerridwyn would not approach her for answers but might go somewhere else. Children were like rivulets easily turned by a hand in the wrong place.

Cerridwyn gamboled into the smoky clearing, waving away a gray cloud from the fire, and planted her bony backside on the stump beside Inanna. "Did you hear from my father?"

"Not yet. Perhaps during the bright half of the month."

"Then it's a story?"

"Yes."

Cerridwyn squirmed until she was comfortable, brushed back her thigh-length hair, and said, "I'm ready, then."

And it was a story, a good story. A tale of enchantment about the son of Dagda Mor, DeDanann Chief, the prince called Midar the Proud and his mortal queen, Edain. Cerridwyn listened devotedly to the details; she listened about the Murmuring, a whispering of the trees to those who are *geas*, those who believe and have the ear of the Sidhe. She listened to details of the apple-round moon, of the trembling milk-

pale maid, of the silver bridle of Kieran Dark-
lake, of mystical obligations, called *geassa*. Of
D'yeree-in-Dowan—the world's end.

Cerridwyn took note of how deeply her
mother believed these stories to be history and
recalled how scrupulously Inanna observed the
needs of living in peace with the Sidhe, whom
she believed had followed her and her family
from Ireland to Gwynedd. Inanna believed the
DeDananns were adept at sorcery but betrayed
by their magic when they were conquered by
people called Milesians. She taught her daughter how the Dananns had retreated to the raths,
caves, waters and hills to live in immortality
as the Sidhe; they haunted gentle places, dells
where they conducted their midnight revels.
Yet they weren't true ghosts. "They migrate at
certain times of year, as all natural life is wont
to do," Inanna explained to the tireless mental
appetite listening, "and if your house lives on
a Sidhe path, you must at those times open
your doors so they may pass through on the
sluashee, the fairy wind."

Cerridwyn paid dear attention to her mother,
trying to sort legend from reality, but found
the two inseparable. She guessed the stories
might be inaccurate, having been told and retold so many ages past, passing from lip to lip.
Each time Inanna told them, they became a
little more embellished, a little more magical,
and Cerridwyn was unimpressed by magic. She
was determined to learn as much as possible
from Inanna without pointing out her mother's
limitations. Inanna knew woodlore but little of
the world outside.

"What's the difference between being Druid and being Christian, Mother?"

Her mother thought about this as the sun moved. This was one habit of Inanna's, this tendency to think for a long time before speaking, which fascinated Cerridwyn; she would watch her mother's face, the changes in it, and wonder if her mother found thinking to actually be that difficult. Cerridwyn felt guilty. Putting things together in her head was not so hard for her. Often she tried to find questions to ask that would be easy for Inanna to answer, and then the little girl would sit with feigned patience while the Druid woman puzzled out a response.

This was partially one of those questions and partially not.

The sun was higher when words came.

"Christianity," began Inanna, pausing over the word and thinking hard, "is a religion. It requires gods."

"A single god."

"Oh, no, they have several. And a goddess they borrowed from our Mother. They have a pantheon to worship, like the Greeks. Religion is religion. One cannot be what the next is not."

"But what's different about being Druid?"

"Druidry is not a religion. It is not of the blood or the belief."

"Then what is it?"

"A practice and a privilege. To be *drui* is to be friends with the oaks and all routes of this planet. It's not a belief. It is knowledge and search."

"But we have the Mother Goddess and the Horned God."

"We do not have them. They *are*. They are separate from the knowledge. To believe in them is not necessarily to have the *drui*." The tall Irishwoman hesitated, then looked squarely into her daughter's large gray eyes and said strongly, "Never confuse what you believe with what you know."

"Is it our medicine and herbs and the names of the trees that make us Druid?"

"Those. And a sense of life. Learning to feel magic, to direct a portion of it. To be able to hear the Murmuring and understand."

"The supernatural?"

"No, no. The natural. We have no control over the supernatural, nor they over us. To coexist is something very different from worship. Much more sensible."

"Don't we worship the Goddess and the Horned One?"

Inanna smiled. "Have we ever prayed to them?"

Cerridwyn thought about it. "We stand in a circle. We call to them and ask favors into the flame."

"Is that worship?"

Cerridwyn frowned in confusion.

"Then what is it?"

"You just said it."

"I did?"

"We ask favors of them. A little help. The winds to blow a certain way. The sun to shine. Do you ever hear us fill their egos with hollow compliments?"

A shrug. "I haven't."

"Have we given them credit for our own toils?"

"No." Another shrug. A smaller one.

"Do we ask for things we can work for on our own?"

"Not usually."

"It would be worship if we did. Strength from gods is false strength. Your strength must be *in you*. That is what it means to be of the *drui*. Never forget."

Cerridwyn smiled. "I never will."

Her mother nodded proudly. "Then I deem you old enough."

The little girl sat up straight, her eyes widening, and she inhaled sharply. "Today I am old enough for something, when yesterday I was not?" What could it be? Something tantalizing and frightening and wonderfully new?

"Today," Inanna said, "I deem you old enough to attend the invocational at my side."

"Oh, Mother! Oh!"

"Run now, and don your white cloak. Today you shall take the first step toward becoming *drui*."

At her mother's side, as proudly as a young sparrow at first flight, Cerridwyn strode toward the *drunemeton*. Others walked with them. This would be the invocational of the vernal equinox, a rite of spring. The Goddess would be watching.

In the dripping, oak-draped grove the *rí* of their *túath* had designated sacred, there was a turf altar. This was the leaf pavilion, the *drunemeton*, different from other *nemetons*, which meant "sacred place." This was the oak grove, where the great oak trees spread their ageless arms across the ground and into the sky and where the oaks opened to create a beautiful, draped clearing in the dark woods. Here the altar sat, and near it were ancient pilars of stone, more ancient than any of the seers could guess. Skull-niches gawked emptily from the pillars, places where, once, severed heads were placed in times when people were foolish enough to believe the gods had a taste for blood.

"Mother," Cerridwyn whispered, "the stones have eyes."

"All things on Earth perceive each other," Inanna said.

"And I see a naked sword on the altar. Will something be killed?" She waited anxiously for her mother's answer, since Inanna had always told her Druids of her people believed in peace with all life.

"Nothing will die here," Inanna said. "Gone are the days when the spirits were misinterpreted so. We understand now that it is better to change the world with living changes. Today we celebrate life upon an altar where blood sacrifices once occurred. Do you think you can see why?"

Cerridwyn puzzled it and answered, "Because we must celebrate that we have learned a better way?"

Inanna smiled her crooked, sweet smile.

All around the altar stood men Cerridwyn recognized: the *rí* of the *túath*, and others she knew were *aes dána*—people of gifts. Gleaming bronze torcs at their necks set them apart from the others. These were the special folk of the tribe, those who were craftsmen of things, of thought, of words. These were the artisans who made their jewelry glitter with scrollwork and inlays; these were the poets and bards who so carefully handed down the wonderful stories and traditions with their recitations; these were the wisest among all the tribe, the thinkers. Some of them had families, children Cerridwyn played with. Today, though, they seemed special.

Since it would soon be eventide, a small fire had been lit in the center of the circle, in a place where the smoke could twine between the trees of the leaf pavilion without gathering beneath the boughs and damaging the sacred oak leaves. Two iron fire-dogs held dried wood, and the gentle crackling of the fire eased Cerridwyn's excited heart.

The *rí* stepped forward, followed by the archdruid, who carried a bronze symbol of the crescent moon, and the brief ceremony began. The archdruid turned, and his breastplate glittered.

Cerridwyn was amazed by the quietness of the archdruid's voice when he invoked the Goddess and requested a warm and gentle summer. In return he promised to continue to learn, to teach, and to spread passivity in the world. It was all quite simple, quite unlavish. Soon the *aes dána* gathered around the turf altar and together lifted the huge naked sword, sliding it symbolically into its sheath, which was held by the *rí* and the archdruid. One final time the evening sun glinted on the blade before the leather sheath covered the metal.

Faster than a breath of wind, the invocational ended. Cerridwyn felt her mother's hand upon her shoulder and blinked. Had she dozed off? Had she missed something? Desperately she looked around. Cloudlike beings in white robes were drifting off into the oak forest, on their way back to their families, or to meditate privately, or to practice their special arts.

"Oh, Mother . . . I think I fell asleep," she admitted sadly.

"You did not sleep, dear," Inanna said. "The invocational has touched you. Perhaps you will be *geassa* someday."

"*Geassa?*"

"You know what it means."

"To be touched by magic . . . or called by someone who also has a *geas* upon him. . . ."

"And other things," her mother comforted. "Don't worry over it or you may never feel it. No one is born *geassa,* just as no one is born *drui.* Let's go back to our hut before the sun sets. I've made Glamorgan pudding and leek pie."

Spontaneously her mother shot out a hand and tickled her. In a moment they were rolling in the new grass, tickling and laughing, pulling hair and laughing even harder. Then they got up and ran through the meadow. The earth became not only schoolroom but also playground. The moths fluttered for cover.

The stories rooted firmly in her memory, but they had pushed away thoughts of a broken, abandoned womb on a twig. When Cerridwyn remembered the cocoon, the thought lanced her. She had forgotten entirely! She hadn't held the life in her heart until it was safe!

She gasped into the sun's glare and shot for the forest. Inanna never knew why.

But the sun shimmered on a cracked remnant. A single powdered wing, half-dried and broken, dangled from a rough bit of bark, flipping in a light breeze.

High above Cerridwyn's trembling hand as she reached out, a morning curlew bolted down its dinner, then sang.

By the time Katie returned with the jasper, she was in a strange mood. She thought about the baby she'd lost and about all the things born of fear which Nell had said. Katie decided fear was no excuse to be vicious and accusatory, and she realized life had begun to deteriorate for her in the Greenwood. She hardly saw Will anymore, and when she did he displayed either a glacial aloofness or a passionate fury that consumed any chance for love. Thoughts of him now possessed her dreams, her nights, confounded her guilt about abandoning Edward and the corporeal legacy he had left her; Nick and Gaston. It hurt to catch a glimpse of Will as the hunting parties returned for a too brief rest, then went off again in another vain attempt to wrest sustenance from the hibernating winter landscape. It hurt to look at his tired legs and wish they could find enough strength to engulf her, his arms a little more power before he collapsed to catch her up against his hard form and *demand* she give in to his tormenting ardor. It would be simple then, if he took away her choice.

Too simple.

Her body ached with desire and pulsed his name over and over as she wished to be free of love's pangs and the guilts it held for her.

Katie knew that before Nell's attack, she had been happy in the Greenwood. She had almost freed herself completely from Southwell, since she was helpless there, and the possibility existed that she and Will might start a new life.

Her heart thudded. She closed her eyes to quell it, pausing and placing one hand between her breasts, feeling their sudden swelling from need.

But now Nell was a threat for her attitude was dangerous, and Katie sensed her time in the Greenwood was limited. The air itself seemed less sweet, even oppressive. As she had searched out the jasper she had felt eyes upon her, following her, where before she had found peace here. How many people agreed with Nell? How many whispers fluttered behind her back? How long would it be before the children, one by one, stopped coming to her lessons?

How long before Will's original disdain was reawakened?

A shaft of anguish cut through her. She flinched and clasped a branch for support, her downward gaze blurring on two long, thick tails of hair hanging forward over her shoulders, bound loosely with crossed strands of hemp in three places. Very primitive. Very Druid! Mother, you never told me the complicated parts, she thought. Maybe you didn't know them. I don't want the responsibilities you put on me anymore! I am not *geas*. I cannot uphold the *geassa*. I was arrogant because I prospered and still could proclaim myself Druid, but now my luck is slipping. Edward's death—I see now—was only the beginning. It is a black tide I sail. No matter how I try, this storm creeps up behind me and rages at my ears. Will is at its center. I may never reach him.

Mother, I am more afraid of this than of an enemy with teeth to shred my flesh. At least such an enemy could be fought. But against blind prejudice, what am I?

"Katie, is that you? Get in here with that, my girl!"

She shook off her anxieties and hurried into Edith's tent.

Melicent was standing beside Edith, who was grunting on the birthing stool, the midwife diligently massaging her patient's bare, bloated abdomen while Ula tended to unseen duties on the underside of the birthing stool. Katie could only imagine what was going on down there. Marian was, for once, silent as she rubbed Edith's shoulders.

"Is it happening?" Katie asked, stiff.

"Soon," Ula said flatly.

It disturbed Katie to see Edith drenched in sweat, smelling of femaleness, working so hard, her hands gripping the seat of the birthing stool and pulling impossibly hard. Folk magic and prayers were muddled as she listened. Katie felt she stood at the very core of womanhood, feeling at once part of Edith's body and yet distantly alien.

"Take charge of the children," Melicent said, giving her a snap-out-of-it glare.

Gwennie and her baby brother were huddled in the corner. Gwennie was trying to keep Amlin from crying, but he hadn't been fed yet in all the confusion, and Katie was glad for the excuse. She appropriated a bowl of wheat meal

and berries and went to sit in the corner. The
sounds of the human trial as it unfolded were
impossible to block out completely, no matter
how she tried.

In time the actions across the hut grew
quicker, more anxious, and Edith made one
quick grunt out of tempo with the others. Then
things grew furious.

Katie clenched Gwennie's hand and shut her
eyes.

Voices filled the tent. Women's voices. The
sounds of humanity.

Then Edith's voice.

Jubilation.

"A boy! A little boy . . . a son!"

"Christ's name be praised!" Marian's voice.

"A miracle." Ula's hushed whisper penetrated the air.

Gwennie shot away from Katie, who held
the squirming Amlin when he tried to toddle
after. "It was supposed to be a girl!" She
squirmed through to her mother, who was holding and fondling the chubby, wet, clumsy newborn, and scrutinized his tiny male parts as
though she didn't believe it.

"It's a miracle," Ula breathed, staring. "The
Almighty Father changed it in the womb! He
must have a truly great purpose in His Divine
Plan for this child." She dropped to both knees.
Her face disappeared in her flowing headpiece
as she bowed her head and mumbled a prayer.

"Katie?" Edith called. "Are you still here?"

Yes, her mind choked. "Y—yes—" She stumbled over there, clutching Amlin too tightly.
"Yes?"

"Look. Look at my second son. A child of

miracle. Name him for me, Katie. An intelligent name. A name to be worthy of his place in God's scheme. Do you know any name that great, Katie? Do you?"

The bloodstained infant squalled at his mother's swollen breasts, a misshapen, purple head swiveling after a nipple he could not see, soft little lips squared in protest, nibbling and searching. Useless arms and legs quivered in unaccustomed freedom, a wriggle of new strength.

Katie stared at him until her eyes burned. His swollen testicles and tiny penis seemed to be a microcosm of all men, all life, all destiny that had ever touched her. To these women the small organs spelled a miracle. Did they observe a future king? A savior?

This was not her right. Her integrity made her wish a Christian name would come to her, but none did. Only Will, Will, Will haunted her. That would never do.

A great name.

She whispered, "Alexander."

Edith bent down and kissed the child, now quiet in her arms. He had found his sustenance.

Immediately began the rituals following a birth. The cord was tied and bitten through. The baby was thoroughly washed with salt, his gums and palate rubbed with honey, and his body comforted by warm oils before being wrapped tightly in linen swaddling. A meal of white bread—very rare here—rice, almonds, hazelnuts, and stag meat was prepared for Edith, to assure that her milk would be wholesome, not corrupt. Katie took care of the children during all this, but even though she sought distraction, she couldn't avoid being caught up

in the joy. In a while she could even smile at
Edith's delirious babbling, able to shut out the
hard facts; it would indeed be a miracle if the
baby survived this winter of desolation.

Honor came to Katie when Edith asked her
to take the baby Alexander on his first journey, his baptism needing to occur as soon as
possible, lest he become one of the many who
died at birth. It was necessary he be "churched,"
even though here they had no church. Whether
Edith asked this to make Katie closer to Christianity or to help her appear inoffensive to
God in these people's eyes, Katie would never
know. But she was grateful. Either way, Edith
meant well. To Katie it was a gem shining in
the darkness. She accepted the honor.

I've never held a baby, she thought. I've never
held a baby while all around me women my
age have three and four and five children. And
they want me to climb a tree with a newborn.
If only Will were here. I could look into his
eyes and—what's wrong with me? I am changed
between yesterday and today. Suddenly I need
him, can think only of him. Am I so shaken by
a frightened woman's assault?

"Here you are," Melicent said, adjusting the
swaddled infant in Katie's arms. "Follow the
steps."

With a deep, steadying breath, Katie turned
to the tent opening. Before her were a series of
stools, benches, and boxes, each a step higher
than the one before it. Outside the tent, folk of
the Greenwood waited. The gently strummed
notes of Alan's lute filtered in. She stole a look
at the baby. His crinkled, pink face twisted in
a yawn, then he opened blurry blue eyes and

followed bright torch flame as Katie walked by the tent's only light.

One of the men held her elbow as she ascended the array of steps. Many eyes gleamed their approval as the baby was carried upward, closer to heaven, rather than downward to earthly demons. Katie shifted the child to her left arm and pulled herself into the tree ending the makeshift stairway, settling gingerly on a branch without nearly the boldness of her climb with Will.

Then she smiled, blushing through a wave of polite applause. It seemed incorrect somehow for her to head this moment of pleasure in the Greenwood, where true pleasantry was so precious.

Tuck appeared below her. "He is purified. Bring him down now."

In moments she stood before the massive bulk and beard of the friar. He cleared his throat and dipped his thumb into a goblet of holy water, speaking, "Alexander Small, I baptize thee in the name of the Father, the Son, and the Holy Spirit. Go well in thy life as a true son of the Church of our Savior Jesus Christ, and when you die, may your soul ascend to sit at the right hand of God Almighty. Amen."

"Amen," murmured the small gathering.

Edith stepped forward and took the baby as Katie said, "He's so lovely, Edith, so beautiful."

"Bless you, dear girl," her friend said. "We will always remember you and your stories."

"You must rest."

"I will. Good night. Send Gwennie and Amlin in to bed, will you?"

"I will." As she said it Katie felt the cold knife of realization. Gwennie ... Amlin ... where were they? Desperately she looked for their little faces in the dispersing crowd. People faded into the night—when had it gotten so dark? "Melicent! Have you seen Edith's children?"

"Me? You were to watch them."

"But I was churching the baby!"

"Did you not assign someone else charge of them?"

"I ... I didn't ... I wasn't thinking—"

" 'Tis true, you weren't. Start looking for them. I'll be out to help you in a minute or two. Hurry! In case they've wandered away—"

Dry branches caught at Katie's shoulders. Frozen ground thudded under her running feet. In a panic she called, "Gwennie? Gwennie, where are you? Amlin? Gwennie!"

Tears streamed down her face, nearly freezing on her cheeks. Darkness engulfed her entirely as she pulled farther from the camp's torches. There was no moon. There were no stars. Her frustrations piled on top of new fears, clutching her by the throat, making horrid echoes in her head.

Her legs were heavy as iron. Running became slow, distorted, torturous. Purple shapes and black shadows blurred around her.

Where were they? How had she let them slip away?

Pride? Had she let the flattery of Edith's requests cloud her mind?

Suddenly everything truly important in life seemed to swell before her as she ran endlessly through the dark, grasping forest. Priorities gently taught by her mother had been lost beneath other concerns, like Edith's children now lost somewhere in the woods. Katie ran harder, faster, until she was gasping for breath. She would find the children. She would re-arrange her life in favor of the important things. In favor of loyalty. And love.

The children were so small, so helpless with-out her.

And someone else, someone strong, was weak without her.

He rose out of the darkness, and Katie in-haled sharply as her whole body wrenched to a halt. An irresistible force pulled her out of a stagger. Her hair was everywhere, blinding her. She tossed it off and stared through her tears.

"Have you lost something?" The voice was resonant, bracing.

Ever so gradually Katie's vision cleared, tak-ing in the purple darkness a blood-crimson obelisk with shimmering hair and eyes catch-ing moonlight as the clouds began to part.

She rasped out, "Will . . ."

Then she saw what was in his arms, cooing and hugging.

And at his leg.

"Is it these you need?" he asked steadily, mocking her even as he soothed her.

His warm, dark blue cape flapped lazily in the night breeze, dancing against Gwennie's narrow shoulders. She clung to Will's leg, know-ing she had done wrong to wander off, fearing what she saw in her teacher's ashen face, won-dering how she caused such horror.

Will absently rubbed Amlin's threadbare leg as he held him.

He glared at Katie.

She stared back, gasping.

Torchlight distorted their faces. Soon they were surrounded by helping hands who gathered the children from Will and spirited them back to camp.

Both were deaf to the muttered reassurances tossed their way before they were left alone with the parting clouds.

"You . . ." Katie's voice failed her. "You're . . . here."

His swaggering approach was killingly slow, measured, too casual to be fatigue. "Yes." Yes, Katie my darling unpossessable love, where else would I be when whispers fly against you? "Of course I am." His voice betrayed none of his inner quarrel.

In that moment of purging Katie could do nothing but stand before him, shaking, her mind repeating all the horrible possibilities this night could have become. Night or nightmare?

"Katie Chenoweth, you need a man tonight," he said, tipping her face up with a cupped hand. "You need me. Get ready for love. I intend to have you tonight."

There. He had said it. He'd spoken those rehearsed words over the fence, fully knowing she was not a woman to be taken, and he would loathe himself if he made good on that oath. But a drowning man must at last take that saving stroke or die.

He felt her quiver. For a moment he thought he had finally gone too far, forever strangling any chance of bringing his love to flesh.

Then a miracle was set in his hands as he felt his arms fill in the powdery darkness.

Within his own engulfment he heard the precious, impossible, unbelievable symphony of sobbing.

He lifted his face to the moon, clutching Katie against a chest grown lean and rock-ribbed in the harshness of winter. She burrowed deeper into his embrace, her whole body thundering with sorrow and gasps and tears.

Stunned, Will caressed her damp head and buried his face in her pulsing throat. "*Katie . . .*"

She dissolved in tears. Out came all the agonies that had sat in her soul's dark pit like ice rocks. Her voice barely made a ruffle in his collar. "My . . . husband's . . . dead . . . my husband . . ." The words tore her in two. She collapsed, sobbing violently in his arms.

Will gathered her up, sob by sob, lifting her from the ground, shaking, himself, with empathy and with relief and joy. "Oh, my Katie . . . yes. . . what a man he must have been to deserve you . . ." One by one he kissed away her tears with soft, searching lips, beginning a slow trek through the forest toward camp. He turned one fleeting gaze to the dark velvet sky.

"Bless you, Edward. She's free."

He adored the gift in his arms, adored her tears, all the way through the rolling forest to his own tent, a small hide-flapped, fur-lined twig dwelling not far from where Robin and Marian slept. Will had always returned here alone and cast secret envy toward his cousin's softly breathing tent.

This night, though, he needed no incorporeal secret wishes.

A single tallow candle twinkled as the air shifted when he dipped inside, Katie still in his arms, still taking her breaths raggedly.

He did not put her down. He whispered at her cheek, "You are my miracle. Tell me I can love you at your body's altar and make a dawn of our own light. Tell me you want it."

Katie buried her face in his soft, throbbing throat. "Take me away," she pleaded. "Out of the Greenwood . . . I beg you . . . take me from this place for a while. . . ."

"I will, my dove, sweet Cerridwyn, distant angel, I promise. Now, before I die of need, tell me you want it."

"I want it," she gasped. The tears began again, for new reasons. A sweet moist suction of kisses rolled between them. "I want you."

Her feet touched the rush floor. Instantly she plucked away his clothes, piece by piece, until his bare shoulders and arms gleamed amber in the candlelight. She unlaced his jerkin. It fell away. His leggings soon followed. His cloak was a dark blue ocean at his feet.

He lay his hands upon her shoulders. "I want to kiss you and taste and tempt you until your Celtic blood races." Slowly he pulled down the wool garment she wore until her swelling breasts gleamed fully in the candle glow, stained by remnant tears.

Crazed emotion flew through her, hot, spear-pointed, sharp as a man's penetration, a blazing anticipation. *Free.* In response she felt his chest, exploring the swells of his pectorals and thrilling as his whole body hardened, then melted at her touch, then hardened again. She had forgotten how it could be, this art of love, this sensitizing fountain. With all her being she waded in.

Her garment fell from breasts to hips. With a touch Will sent it to her ankles. The animal-fur rug across his sleeping place received those soft bone-shaped curves of her body as Will lifted her hair in a glorious rain, then lowered himself on top of her. Her arms accepted him; it was like drowning in silk.

His voice, hot and deep, filled her ear. "Take the horns of love and wrestle them. Cerridwyn, sun of my days, star of my nights . . . take *me*."

He kissed her breasts, holding the world at a distance, determined to protect her, and fill her with so much passion that she would no longer see her pain.

Katie buried herself in Will's haven. A moan from deep in her urged him on. She felt his sexuality grow stiff and glossy between her thighs and responded with fluid kisses and parting of her knees. Her body took over, curving, writhing, asking beneath his fullness, begging for that great human fusion she knew would be her salvation. The passion exploding between them was no selfish thing, for Will gave as much as he took. The true exultation was in setting free this caged swan.

Her lips butterflied at his until his mouth joined his loins in masterful penetration.

Katie had boarded a wild ship this night, she knew. More wonderful than simply making love was the fiery fountain of loving a man of wisdom. She used upon him all the tricks Edward taught her for bringing a man to his zenith, but it was new this time. Now she was an experienced woman, widowed and purged and pulsing in need of this one special man. She used her legs, her mouth, her hands to give him all the worship a man could endure, until the fountain burst high and overflowed, a great, flourishing victory for two people who so intrepidly risked its dangers.

They barred the door between themselves and the world and all its guilts. Within their tent a single candle burned, casting a golden glow on shining maleness, and he began to show her such joy as she had forgotten existed. His body was golden as the memories of new womanhood for Katie, the days when all things were golden, exciting, virulent with thrills some called sinful. Even in the coolness of winter a thin sweat of anticipation sheened over the sinews of Will's arms and thighs, making his lean torso and his man's vanguard sheer fantasy for a woman who desperately needed him, who had to have him every bit as much as he had to have her.

No doubts lingered. There was no one in this tent but a man out of place and a woman ready to provide harbor.

And so they loved. And the past melted. And the future was conceived: honor's womb, danger's seed.

"Dear children, I beg you to reconsider this dangerous folly. The Cart Road is a deadly place to go."

Abbot Godfrey's white robe brushed the ground with its dirty hem as he cajoled a group of four guildsmen, ironworkers from the forge district, who were checking the ropes on their two wagonloads of wares.

"We'll be all right, Father," a round-faced man said. "Mistress Chenoweth's friend told us what to do if we're confronted."

"And you trust a stranger? You know Mistress Chenoweth is not guided by the hand of Jesus Christ. He could have been an outlaw who turned her head against us. You may be walking into a terrible trap."

"Bless us, Father," another man asked, plainly determined to go. "We'll get the road open for you. For the good of Southwell."

"Somebody's got to try, your Grace," a third man said.

The abbot bowed in concession. "My heart swells with pride at such bravery within my parish. If you must go," he said slowly, "go with God."

"Thank you, Father."

Helpless to change the determined minds of bold, young merchants in search of a profit, the abbot prayed with them, blessed them, blessed their goods and their journey, and left them to their packing and harnessing.

He entered an alley from the main street where patrons and vendors bustled and soon felt the shadows close around him. Almost instantly another presence fell in step with his unbroken stride.

The abbot did not look at the man at his side. He needed no extra glances to remind him of the time-gnarled face in its dirty red beard, or the quick blue eyes, or the scarred hands. "You're late."

"I bin waitin' here since Vespers was over," rasped the familiar voice.

From him sleeve pouch the abbot took a small

purse of coins. "You will see to it," he said, "that they never reach Sherwood."

"And that they never come back?"

"If God wills it, it must be so. Do what you wish with their goods, as long as you don't sell them in Southwell."

"Wha' about the corpses?"

"See that they are left on the road, near the forest's edge, in plain sight. Go quietly. Leave by the east gate, after dark. Speak to no one. Instruct your men so."

The purse jingled. "This be not enough for all my men this time, Father."

"More waits in the coffers of the abbey. Upon your success you shall receive God's bounty."

"We'll succeed, all right, Father," the man said. A long blade made a brief appearance from under his cloak.

For the first time the abbot stopped walking and turned to the disreputable face at his side. His hand moved in the same cross pattern as had blessed the party of merchants. The man bowed his head and ran one finger lovingly along the dagger blade.

As the end of the alley the merchants clucked their donkeys toward the north gate.

• PART THREE •

IMBOLC

• *Chapter Twelve* •

Christmas came and passed.

It was a different time for Katie. Nell's glares and those of folk who listened when rumors rang followed her wherever she walked, haunted her nights, and destroyed her days, till she longed for Will to make good his promise. But for Robin's sake and the welfare of all who needed his help in the harsh January weather, Will could not leave the forest yet. The day did not come for them to leave until the light snow came to show the tracks of the game and two deer were hunted down. The camp would not gorge, but neither would they starve. Meanwhile Katie often visited Will's tent, less worried about their unmarried status and its implications than of a night without him to cling to. Their lovemaking was infrequent, as Will often staggered back to camp exhausted with other equally exhausted men after tracking those two deer and smaller game for days on end, but when there was strength left for desire, it was sweet and whole-souled and rhapsodic.

Will had not forgotten. Never once did Katie

have to remind him of her need to escape for a time, to let the Greenwood recover from its discomfort with her, spread by Nell and those with the same combustible notions. Will mentioned it several times, somewhat remorsefully because it was taking so long, and kept her holding on by saying he had a plan. He may have; she was not sure. For now, though, she found solace in Will's protection, content to let him care for her and adopt her worries. Soon enough, she knew, would come the reckoning day when she would have to thank him with her eyes and take her troubles back upon herself. She would do it, for she was Katie Chenoweth and not merely Will Scarlet's woman. Her own wraith awaited her in every shadow. The widowed blacksmith was still at the core of her being.

He did have a plan, anyway. Katie had begun to doubt it, but she was wrong.

In the second week of January, in the year 1193, three riders entered the city gates of Nottingham in time for the Feast of Fools. Gaiety was everywhere. Revelry ran wild in the streets under the winter sun. People danced with bells upon their sleeves, making laughter spill from the masked, heavily feathered riders. Christmas was dull compared to these festivities. In the churches as the three rode by, an inversion of status had put the lower clergy in control with a Bishop Fool in presidence, allowing them to ridicule their leaders and church life. Everywhere church bells rang out of tempo. Choirs wore outrageous costumes and sang out of tune. Liturgical plays lost every semblance of piety, becoming comedic, raw,

insulting, even licentious, with no holds barred
on bawdiness and sacrilege. Things folk would
never even have *thought* any other time of year
they actually *did*, physically and enthusiasti-
cally. And it all made Katie laugh. She had
had her crying time; now it was her time to
laugh. She and Will and Alan o' Dale, since
they were hidden in eye masks bedecked with
grouse and pheasant feathers, were free to roam
unnoticed through the crazily costumed throng.
Banners hung on Nottingham's houses, patch-
ing colors against the crystal blue January sky
as the three liveried their horses and walked
into the great bazaar at the city's center.

"It's all so rampant," Katie commented, adjusting her mask as they passed huckster after
huckster, entertainer after jongleur after en-
trepreneur, all clothed in harlequin gaudery.
"Feast of Fools in Southwell is not so pied.
Nor as immodest."

"Yes, we're spicy in Nottingham," Will admitted. "Rare's the chance for public ribaldry,
but there's something healthy about it. Unbridled behavior is good for the soul."

"Then your soul must be an ox," she tossed
back.

His eyes twinkled behind the garishly feathered mask.

"Will, there are the troubadours," Alan said,
pointing at a group of musicians in bright
clothes, entertaining a large crowd.

"Do you mean to join them so soon, Alan?"
Will asked. "You'll have plenty of time to make
a few coins later."

"Yes, stay with us for a while, Alan," Katie
added. "I see you too seldom."

Alan graced her with a low, silly bow, rocking the lute hanging on his back. "You charm me to my very soul."

"Liar," she said, laughing.

"Well, all right, then, you only get halfway to my soul."

Katie took a breath to respond but never got the chance. In seconds she had forgotten she was talking to anyone at all. Her attention was completely taken by the subject of Will's next breath.

"Bless me," he exclaimed with a strange dryness, looking deep into another end of the bazaar. "There's his very face."

Katie looked in that direction. There was a great noise—music from trumpets and drums. A herd of shining pikes wobbled through the crowd, carried by a garrison of men in chain mail. They marched on all sides of a bannered litter upon which sat two people, a swarthy, bearded man dressing in gold robes and a very much older woman whose blue gown had a field of white fleurs-de-lis. A cape draped her body, heavily brocaded and caught at the shoulder with a scrolled, boar-faced brooch; its amber eyes winked at nothing. They sat on chairs, huge ones, padded with bear hides. the backs cut in ornate frescoes of a castle. Several horsed noblemen rode beside them on fancy saddled horses, idly chatting. Never, not even in Southwell's finest circles, had Katie seen clothing more embellished, so many embroidered scrolls, diamonds, spirals, so many tassels and frippery. Each noble had his coat of arms emblazoned on his surcoat.

But not one was more dazzling than the young

man and old woman being carried high over everyone else.

"Who is *that*?"

"That, my dear," Will said slowly, affectedly, "is His Highness Prince John Sans Terre."

"John—" Her breath barely held the name. She looked at the gilt-robed man with new understanding. "Who is that woman sitting beside him?"

Alan answered, "It is his lady mother, Queen Eleanor of Aquitaine. Many's the time I sat at her knee and played my tunes," he said wistfully, as though he had much enjoyed those days. "She tampers much in politics. Once King Henry sickened of it and had her shut up in Salisbury Castle. But that was long before I came to her court. Now she meddles between Richard and John. You know, it was she who was responsible for bringing my kind—minstrels, troubadours, chanteurs—to England. She peregrinates about from place to place now, holding court and giving audiences."

Katie craned her neck for a better view of the elegant, withered face. The Queen laughed at some wittiness tossed by Prince John, showing brown teeth and a marked preference for his company. Inwardly Katie churned, guessing that Eleanor had once favored Richard likewise. She would favor Richard again, Katie silently vowed, if Locksley had a say. Her thought was a promise as much as a guess.

"Surrounded by Norman sucklings too," Will commented. "Look at them. Fattening the golden goose. I'll bet those thrones ate a good twenty thousand gold marks. I see Gilbert of Blois and fat old Sir Henry of Rheims. There's that Burgundian—de Ville he calls himself, I think—and Philip de Touraine . . . and his uncle, de Crespy. Behind him . . . well, may I die old and wretched!''

Katie inhaled sharply, seeing what Will saw.

"If it isn't himself," Alan snarled.

Katie shivered, not used to that tone from Alan but unable to tear her eyes from the stocky form in brilliant purple; his cape was ermine with two large brooches joined by chain beneath a smoke-black beard. Wings of silver framed that bold face.

Beside her there was a huff. "Happy to see your old friend?"

Her heart stomped nervously. Katie tried to wrench her gaze away, but she was too stunned.

Sir Guy looked as if he thrived on hard weather. His cheeks were rosy, his raiment ever so grand. Images of frilled tents outside Sherwood flashed in Katie's memory. Until now she thought the effects of that time had faded. Evidently she had underestimated the lasting dynamism of Guy de Gisbourne. Suddenly the heritage of Normandy was magnified. Great admiration flushed in her, met head to head by great fear.

She awakened from her shock upon hearing Will's waist belt and baldric complain as he pushed back his sword. She looked his way, seeing unabashed jealousy beneath his mask, and hated herself for comparing Sir Guy's clothing to Will's simple red shoulder cape and gray calf-length surcoat. Even masked in feathers he looked more forester than noble.

Will realized it too. His mouth twisted in a frown painful to Katie, unreadable to Alan.

"Let's off," he grumbled. "My stomach roils. Must be something I hate."

He strode away, wasting time over the wares of booths he passed, trying, not convincingly, to act interested.

Her eyes followed him and something within her ached.

It was then that she first heard the drums.

She thought the skies were parting. All around her people craned to see the source of a bone-penetrating rhythm.

And there they were.

The crowd parted for them as though stunned back.

Never had Katie imagined such people could exist.

Their clothes made all the other costumes around seem sedate. Colored fabric—black, red, yellow, white, orange—was stitched together in angular patterns, and broad, dangling blue sashes wrapped the waists of four men, two women, and two toddlers. They swayed to the beat of their own drums and the rattle of beaded gourds shaken by the women. Two of the men bent over big gourd-shaped drums, their over-size headdresses and inky beards bobbing as they flat-handed the drums. Metal decorations on their drums and ankles jingled a primitive beat. Another man struck a cylindrical drum with a long stick as it wobbled on his knee.

Katie simply stood there with her mouth hanging open. The urge to run away was beaten only by amazement. She was spellbound. Their skin—it was the color of chestnuts! Dark, gleaming, their faces had strange features, animate with black eyes and flashing white teeth. Their hands were long and large, pale-palmed and imposing. The men's hair hung in long inky ropes to their shoulders. How could skin be so dark, hair so pitch-black?

They bobbed and chanted, rattling their rattles and jingling their bells, drumming their drums in an intricate rhythmic pattern. They moved into a circle before Katie bent over their drums, and entered a trance of faster rhythm. The beat intensified, then sped up. The two women entered the circle and began a flat-footed, openhanded dance, a series of undulations and wide-armed sweeps, and sang foreign words sounding more like shouts and howls. Upon the women's heads bright bands rolled and huge earrings flashed. Soon the two children joined in, blowing wooden whistles.

Katie felt Will beside her.

"Ethiopians," he said.

A moment later, Alan unexpectedly said, "I'm sorry, Will."

Will looked at him. "For what?"

"They're not Ethiopians, I'm afraid."

Will cast him a teasing glower that showed even through the feathered mask, then clapped him on the back. "I'm not offended. Go on with what you know."

Alan shifted his lute, cradling it in his left arm, freeing his right arm to point out what he wished to tell them. "They are Malinké. The land of Mali is across the continent from Ethiopia, in West Africa. The drums with the stems are called *kotero djembé*. The others are *kotero sabaro*, if I recall rightly. Some words fade with time, you know. The curved metal sheets with the rattles on the heads of the drums are called *koshink koshink*, because of the sound they make. Can you hear it?"

"Yes, I hear the sound," Katie answered, "each time the drum is struck. What do the words mean, Alan? Do you know?"

His eyes brightened. Usually Alan had little to do in the Greenwood, and it pleased him to be able to share a knowledge that went largely unused. "Their chanting tells the story of how the Malinké people acquired the *kotero*. Listen to it."

> *I-aye tinkarinta*
> *kotero bekumela*
> *doto koto*
> *toluba mwayla*
> *naata djela*
> *I-aye tinkarinta*

"What does it mean, Alan?" Katie pleaded. "Tell me. I must know."

Alan smiled. "They say, 'I hear the music of the kotero but I cannot see it. Yet it is right here.' Then they find the drum hanging suspended among the trees, and they say, 'Aha! There it is!' "

"Oh, Alan—" Katie whispered, breathless. "Where. . . . how . . . where could you learn these things?" She stared, entranced, at the Malinké drummers and their dancing women, women who had once again taken up the bead-sheathed gourds that shushed and rattled and thunked to the drum and chant.

Alan placed his hand on his chest. "My lady, I have been a musician to the Royal Court. Such positions are not easily gained."

She thought she had insulted him and looked at him, but Will chuckled, knowing something Katie did not. "Our Alan studied his music in Timbuktu and Sankore. He is a traveler of the world indeed."

Katie's eyes grew large with amazement within the feathered mask. "You mean you've actually been to . . . to . . . "

"Africa, yes."

"Oh, I envy you . . . I envy you." She turned back to the wide smiles of the dark Malinké people. "I envy you . . ."

Will and Alan ghared a glance past Katie as she stared.

"It's *wonderful*," Katie choked out. All around people tapped feet, dipped and swayed, caught in the vibrations. Like a symphony of heart-beats, the blacks brought their culture into show, grinning and winking at everyone. Katie soon joined in when the crowd started clapping hands to the rhythm. The Malinké women danced and stomped, bobbed and turned, whetting Katie's hunger to see their homeland with her own eyes.

"How far have they come?" she called over the throbbing din.

"Many times farther than England is long," Will answered.

She shot him a scoffing glare. "I'm not such a fool, Will Scarlet."

He only shrugged. "Believe what you like."

"You know Alan would travel as far as man could go just to say he had done it," Will baited.

"You old stallion!" Alan laughed and cuffed him playfully.

The two men turned back to the Malinké, and only then did they notice—

"Katie's gone!"

"What?"

"Where could she go?"

"Do you see her anywhere?"

"No . . . no. You look that way—I'll . . . never mind. I found her. There she is. Christ save me."

"Where?" Alan asked.

An aborted gesture sent Alan's gaze through the ring of drums. There a pair of slippered feet stomped and spun between two pairs of Malinké sandals. The crowd roared its approval. The faltering slippers grew more confident, picking up the simple steps and gaining speed with the coaching of black feet and large brown hands.

The chanting continued. The crowd laughed, cheered.

Prince John and Queen Eleanor applauded.

"Poppets, love spells, charms, straw dogs, herbs, this way! You, master, a poppet for your lady?"

"Thanks, not today."

"Oh, they're adorable!"

"Don't do this to me, Katie. Never have I played with dolls."

"These be no dolls, m'lord," cackled the crone behind the wagon of herb wares and strings dancing with cloth and straw poppets in the shapes of humans. The "females" were quite plain; the males had tiny cloth penises and were slightly larger. They had no faces. The six-toothed woman explained, "These be love poppets. Effigies. I make 'um while y' waits. Aw ... I sees through the masks, m'lord, m'lady. I knows love when I sees it. Many's them what passes here not in love, married or not. Few's them what's love I can sense for true. Look at my lady's eyes—naw, turn not away! Oh, m'lord, there's love lookin' down an' love lookin' after love. You listen to mother, good master. At this a long time, I've been. Longer than you thinks. Here, here—" Crippled hands plucked off two poppets, one male, one female. "Two for the price of one."

He sighed, staring at the poppets the old woman held; then he looked at Katie. Her feelings for him indeed shined through the feathered mask. As he gazed at her he felt love swell in his chest. His victory was real. The nights together in the Greenwood had not been dreams born of fatigue and wishing. Pure as birdsong was his love for her. And finally ... a chance to show it in a lighthearted way.

He took Katie's hand. Gently he kissed it. "Make them," he told the crone.

"Wise you are, master."

In seconds the female poppet had a full head of spun white rabbit's fur, combed from the rabbit, the woman said, and spun on a wheel into strands. She snipped them long to imitate Katie's calf-length tresses. A corn-colored wig of flax soon adored the male doll. "My eyes be not what they was. M'lady's eyes be blue?"

Will gazed into them, enraptured. Was the old woman indeed charming them? "Her eyes," he said quietly, "her eyes are the color of a dove's breast. They glow like seashells. They are fog and sky and moon."

Joy's very glow filled Katie. She could only smile as her poppet gained eyes of gray yarn knots and a delicate red mouth. Will's poppet soon had brown eyes and a mouth and a red cloth tunic. In another minute he wore tiny black leather bands for belts, a stick for a sword, and tall cloth boots.

Katie chuckled. "It does look like you."

"Yes . . . I'm more precious than I thought."

"Them are stuffed with rosemary, valerian, chamomile, dittany, yarrow and jus' a pinch of lavender. The heads is stuffed with dried rose-buds. I sees you be a swordsman, master, so thy poppet wears a wee sword. Might I know a little thing about m'lady so's I can give a token?"

"Give her a book," Will said, still looking at Katie.

"My lady can read? And a pretty wee book it shall be too." The gnarled old fingers created a tiny bundle of pages from fabric bits, stitched them together and gave them a leather cover. Soon the book dangled from the belt of the poppet's cream-colored gown, a rag minia-ture of Katie's.

As she worked the old woman asked, "Have you each a bit of something personal to bring the charm to life? A string, a ribbon, a hank of hair . . ."

A little embarrassed, they came up with a Celtic brooch, a small circular adornment Ka-tie's mother had given her years ago, not a valu-able piece at all but certainly personal; its counterpart would be a strap of leather from the lacing on Will's shirt, retrieved from un-der his surcoat. The brooch was used to join a tiny cape over the girl poppet's shoulders; the strap made an extra belt for Will's effigy. While she busily stitched, the crone's withered hands moving much more quickly than seemed possible, Will cleared his throat and on a whim said, "Mother, do you travel the Cart Road?"

She never took her eyes from her work. "I have, master, many times for many years. Though tough it is to go there now. Highwaymen, y' know."

"Yes," Will said, chuckling, "I do. I happen to know, however, that *you* could travel the road unharmed but for a small donation—a few herbs or a loaf of bread—to those who keep King Richard's cause."

"I wouldn't know, master. It's old for politics I am, too old. My time's passing."

"Should you happen to stray eastward, though," he went on, "and anyone bothers you, mention the words *scarlet oak*. Your life will be in the best hands in England."

"Thanks be, master." She winked at him. "I'll not forget it."

"You might tell others with Saxon sensibilities, might you not? If it slipped out?"

"I might, master. I'll not forget."

Will gave her a rakish half grin. "Lovely young thing."

Ancient eyes twinkled as she laughed a tooth-bare laugh. "I was once, m'lord, once I was: Here now . . . All done and pretty, and potent they are too." The old one toddled around her wagon, putting the poppets together belly to belly, tied with a green ribbon. She put them in Katie's hand, folding her fingers around them. Katie tried not to flinch at the cool, wrinkled touch. The old woman grasped Will's hands then, folding them around Katie's. "Speak two truths about each other, one first, then the other."

Conscious of the old one, Katie and Will fought blushes beneath their masks. But after a time Will did speak.

"You are the Artemis of my night's sky," he whispered.

Katie warmed her heart in his eyes. "You are my life's rescuer."

"You are a true heroine."

"You keep intrepid knowledge."

"I love you. . . ."

"And I you. . . ."

For all the effect of the milling crowd, they might as well have been standing alone in an endless meadow. The scent of flowers wafted up from the poppets, the spell took hold, and they were united in each other's eyes and in fun.

"Master will now keep his lady's image in his keeping." Crinkly hands tucked the miniature Katie into Will's belt. "And my lady must keep her lord's image near her heart." The little Will went into Katie's sash, below her breast.

"Go well in love, m'lord, my lass," she crackled, though there was a timbre in her ancient throat not there before. She held their hands together. "Many a danger you'll have to ford, many a rock in your path. Hold tight on to each the other and fight with every tooth, for the likes of us are a long time dead, and life together too rare."

Many moments passed in silence.

"How do you—" Will began.

"Ah, now, be done wi' me, master, too short's the day." The grandmother hobbled back around the wagon, accepting Will's payment—enough for two poppets and an extra few pennies for the charm. "Thanks be to thee, master. Off with you both now. Look not too long at grizzled faces like mine. Go away and enjoy. After all, 'tis Festival!"

Curiosity almost made them pursue her. On a breath she had forgotten them, shooing them off with her hawking. "Poppets, potions, herbs, and straw dogs, this way, three pennies each, no waiting!"

Seeing only each other, Will and Katie walked together, touring the bazaar and great courtlike area with its entertainers and folk hawking wares. Their arms went around each other's waists. They felt like children partaking of a wonderful game of secret identities and secret knowledge. Many smiles, too, beneath feathers. Katie wished they could become lost enough in the crowd to take off their masks and look into love's own face, but for now they were less conspicuous with masks than without. Danger still lurked. She saw it renewed each time Will glanced through the crowd to keep an eye on Alan. The minstrel was also masked, but his familiar lute as it swayed on his back made him easy to pick out. Also constant was their awareness of the shire's deputies haunting the area, recognizable in chain-mail hoods and blue tunics. Katie had no idea whether she and Will might still be wanted in Nottinghamshire after all this time, but chances were that the officials had long memories.

But she was not here for thoughts like that.

Dancing with the Malinké had made her feel jubilant. The old woman's strange ritual had heightened her ardor for Will. Thoughts of danger distanced themselves with her every step. After all, 'twas Festival!

Katie and Will strolled the pleasant lanes of booths and wagons, tasting or examining all the wares offered here. Master Henckel, the beekeeper, sold his sweet honey, Kirwan the Witch spelled out the futures of any who dared to know, Gwyl the Sculptress made clay castles and animals, Marcus the magician entertained the children with his sleight-of-hand, and the Wandering Poet stopped patrons in midstep and invented poems on the spot for whoever would grace his palm. The staff-carver, the hatter, the weaver, the leather master, the jeweler, the maker of the feathered masks Katie and Will now wore—all these found profit in the Feast of Fools. And Katie drowned herself in it and in Will's presence at her side, giving in to every distraction, every whim. It was a time for whimsy.

She tugged Will to a stop at a booth of linens and silks. After a moment he strayed to the next huckster, a seller of knives and weaponry, busying himself with those wares. In particular his interest wandered to a small doubleedged dagger with a staghorn handle and a bone sheath. He removed it from the sheath, turning it over and over in his fingers, checking sharpness, balance, other properties, then decided he liked it and went about haggling a price.

Katie left the array of shimmering fabrics only via keen self-control. With a sigh she moved along to Will. He was handing over a few coins. She said nothing as she came to his side, for he was already speaking quietly.

"Scarlet oak."

The blade-maker nodded. Discreetly he went on with counting his coins. Discreetly Will turned away.

"Believe I've found the trick to this," he muttered to Katie. "No more guild meetings for us. Here." He held out the hand-sized dirk, folding her fingers around it. "I want you to carry this."

"A weapon? Will, I couldn't stab anyone."

"Do as I say. Put it behind my alter ego there in your belt." He leaned down quite spontaneously and kissed her cheek. "It'll forever remind you of my cutting personality."

Her smile was uneasy. She sighed. "Well . . ."

"Do it. Keep it hidden and with you always."

Her eyes touched his with the truth. "I'll love it because of the thoughts behind it. Why you bought it for me."

Suddenly they were alone on an island. Will's hands caressed hers as he pulled her against him. "Love it for keeping you safe for me."

If only the crowd of Nottingham could dissolve away! They consumed each other, bonded both in love and in hazard, fused to the acute shortness of life.

"If I live a hundred years," he murmured, "it would not be enough. My only pain is knowing I cannot always protect you. Sooner or later I shall have to trust you to your own care. Those moments will show me hell's doorway, Katie, Cerridwyn, Hypatia, and I'll take anything that comforts me. I'd give you a broadsword if I thought you could wield it." His eyes grew sharp. He held her hands against the rough wool tunic over his heart. "Love that blade if you love me, Katie."

With her eyes first and then a deep embrace, Katie mortised the promise. Between them, the staghorn handle pushed into her ribs.

So the festival continued with dances, plays, music, acrobats, jugglers, games, wares and food. Church bells clanged out of tune, lesser clergy ridiculed their superiors, costumed entertainers passed their hats for coins. And so also began a whisper soon spreading across a vast underground of Saxon ears.

"The scarlet oak," one murmured.

"Scarlet oak for the Lion," another answered.

"Cart Road. Say 'scarlet oak.' "

"Scarlet oak. In Sherwood."

"A percentage . . . " one man explained.

"For the Lionheart."

"Scarlet oaks."

"It's the scarlet oak."

"*Coeur de Lion.*"

"Scarlet oak, that's the word."

"God save King Richard. The scarlet oak."

"Long live the King."

Alan rejoined Katie and Will after a morning of songs on a wooden stage with several other minstrels, his money pouch jangling nicely by then. Immediately he pulled them both aside. "Four times I've heard a thing I don't understand. This scarlet oak business. It comes only from intimates who know I'm Saxon." He clasped Will's shoulder accusatively. "I have certain suspicions about it."

"Do you?"

"I do."

"Thrilling."

"And what's this? Playing with dolls? It looks like Katie. Naughty, Will. You've got the real thing. Why do you need a pretend Katie?"

Will flopped the legs of the Katie poppet and smiled at the real Katie. "We got them from that old poppet-maker over there."

"Over where?"

"Right through there—"

They looked, but only an empty space remained where the herb wagon had been.

"Gone," Katie said, her brow furrowing half in suspicion and half in understanding.

"All's the better," Will decided. "She was a strange one."

"Not so strange," Katie murmured.

"Oh, look!" Alan called. "A swordsmanship demonstration! Come on then, let's watch."

"Do we dare?" Will commented dryly. "Katie may join in."

"Poor sport," she countered, following Alan.

They shouldered through the crowd, finally reaching an area roped off with triangular banners strung together. Every other banner was blue with the numeral 4 emblazoned upon it. A memory flickered for Katie; a single glance into the oblong arena confirmed her guess. Four people about her age parried and sliced at each other with heavy broadswords, displaying an art well practiced. There were three young men and a young woman who looked quite at home in similar black kneeboots, trews, shirts, and matching blue tabards. Some pieces of their garb were unalike, their differing belts or cross belts, for instance, evidently individual bits for decor or function. One of them had a special belt for a coiled whip, another a heavy crossbelt for a fancy Spanish sword. The woman's shirt had a lace collar and lace cuffs, dirty from fighting, and she wore black gloves.

"I know them," Katie murmured.

"What?"

"Will, I know those four!"

"Do you?"

"They call themselves the Four Swords. They were performing in Southwell two summers ago. They stayed at my home. One of my apprentices was friends with Master Brian—the tall brindle-haired one with all the flamboyance. They're more showmen than swordsmen, really. They go about to castles and feasts and festivals, performing their sword fights. I'd like to greet them."

Will held her arm. "Nay, Katie, wiser not to." He peered at the one she called Brian, deciding whether or not to trust the beardless face with its Roman features and casual mop of hair as he clashed swords with the serious blond woman who met his slices with alarming boldness. "We're not beyond danger if we're found out."

"Oh, not from them! I have a few friends after all, you know." She waded through a round of applause, up to the flagged barrier. Over the noise she called, "Brian! Nicole! Michael! Christopher!"

They turned her way, curiously finding her in the crowd. The one called Christopher brushed dust from thick, dark brown curls and smiled, but he couldn't possibly have recognized her behind her mask. He did swagger over to the flag string and, at her beckoning, leaned down for her to whisper in his ear. In delight he jumped back, spread his arms wide—gauntlets, sword, and all—and threw a joyous embrace around her. Only then did Will relax, though not completely. He and Alan stayed silent as Christopher beckoned to his companions. All came over.

Michael, the only bearded one of the three men, took one look at Katie's light hair, her stature, and her gray eyes through the mask and exclaimed, "Grand day! It's Ka—"

Christopher clapped a gloved hand raucously over his companion's mouth. "Now, now, gossip, some folk like to play different roles from time to time. Take care, eh?"

Not understanding but willing to play along, Michael said, "Makes sense to me." Then Christopher whispered into his ear, also allowing Brian and Nicole in on Katie's identity, after which she got hugs from every one.

"How's that scurvy dog you're married to?" Brian asked jovially, fondling the whip on his belt absently.

Katie spared him embarrassment with a fond grin. "I'm sorry to say my Edward grew ill and lingered long before dying last August. No, no please! No sad faces today. I'm so happy to see you four!"

"Are you in town for long?" Nicole asked, leaning on her sword, tossing away a strand of unbound straight hair, honey-colored and gritty from many rolls in the dirt today.

"We don't know," Katie said, lowering her voice. "The High Sheriff and others will be unhappy if we stay long enough to doff our masks."

"Ah." The girl nodded, her companions echoing her comprehension. They eyed Will and Alan but kept their secret.

"Then at least we'll dedicate a sword fight to you," Michael offered with a gracious bow.

Alan leaned toward Will. "An honor I can well do without," he whispered. "I see an old friend yonder, a troubadour I knew in London. His name is Gibbon, and I think I suddenly miss him."

"I suddenly don't blame you." Will turned and squeezed his arm. "Take care, you hear me? If we get separated, never mind us. See to your own welfare. Are you listening?"

Alan smiled. "You don't want me to fly in on a flaming arrow and save you?"

"Alan, I swore to Robin I'd take care of you. It's good enough that you sing your way into a few extra coins for our sakes. You needn't risk your life. So please don't." His sincerity was effective. Will had always felt like an older brother to Alan. The respect the young minstrel showed for Will fostered the emotion, though Alan was easy to like.

"Worry not. No one ever harms a minstrel. Give or take the odd lettuce in the face, that is." He flashed a wider grin, then added, "Go cannily yourself, old friend."

With a meeting of hands they parted. Will watched him go.

He turned back to Katie. She was inspecting the handle and quillons of Nicole's sword. "I'm glad to see the pommel has held all this time," she was saying. "The metal blend worked."

"It makes a perfect counterweight. You did a good job mending it," the swordwoman said.

"Can we meet later over a mug?" Michael asked, reminding them that the Four Swords still had a crowd to entertain. Christopher responded by touring the flags and kissing every woman he could reach. Brian followed him around, insulting all the men.

"My love, my adored, tell me your name and I shall cherish it."

"Say, sirrah, is that your face, or did your neck wretch?"

Christopher spun around. "Is that nice? To say that to such a comely fellow!"

"Comely? Crumbly, perhaps . . ."

"And you with that graceless gait. How you could criticize another—"

"Shut up or I'll strike you senseless. Oops— too late."

Christopher addressed the people. "I hear he was rejected by the monastery. Seems the sacramental wine kept vanishing."

"A mere he-say!" Brian claimed. He swaggered forward, removing his glove, and swacked his companion full in the face with it. "There, vassal. You're provoked."

"I feel it not." Christopher scratched his nose.

"Feel this, then!"

A blade flashed, and it was begun. For the tenth time this day, for fun, for profit, for the odd coins tossed into a bag hanging on the flag barrier. This was their brand of adventure. Brian's sword came down and was met by Christopher's. The clang was biting; the force of it drove Christopher to the dirt, but he kept hack-

ing, defending himself as the crowd cheered
him on. Brian moved forward, a rehearsed move
that didn't appear so, allowing Christopher to
grab his tabard. Christopher's foot caught
Brian's chest, and he was propelled up and
over his companion's head and on into the
dust. He made a convincing "Oof!" as he landed.

Nicole rushed in then, landing a showy head
hit—or at least what appeared to be that and
which also appeared to hurt—lunging and re-
coiling as her blade danced with Christopher's.
They tumbled to the dirt, recovered, and in
seconds shrieked the noise of metal on metal.
A circular parry neatly divested Christopher
of his blade.

In came Michael, the dangerous one.

Katie clapped and laughed, cheering along
with the crowd, once again happy to be with
old friends. She glanced at Will, thrilled to
have him at her side. He grinned reluctantly,
then chuckled, unable to escape from her delight. He watched the sword fight without generosity, and Katie noticed that.

"They're good," she said.

"They're fair," he corrected.

"Snob," she accused.

"Connoisseur," he advised.

By now the swordswoman had appropriated
Christopher's fallen sword and was wielding
one in each hand. Michael had doffed his tabard, leaving, under the sunlight, a linen shirt
as bright as the glints from their three darting
weapons. His speed was blinding as he flew
forward, hacking and parrying, his slices a true
challenge for Nicole to return. Had Katie not
known them, she would never have guessed it

was a show. There was no mercy in the action, yet endless grace and disturbingly violent skill. Perhaps that was why it looked so real.

The fight escalated, a cacophony of scraping steel and clacking attacks, until—

A whip cut the air. The crowd pressed back, for it had sliced too close to the arena perimeter.

The leather serpent coiled Michael's knees, taking him down. Nicole was left breathlessly grinning as both swords dangled.

Brian paraded about, taking more bows than his share while retrieving his whip.

Michael rolled over, spitting dirt, then shrugged. He stood up and dusted his legs.

"Another day, another dashing performance," Christopher tossed to Katie as his arm hung around her neck. He had "recovered" and come over to them to watch the rest of the act in peace instead of pieces.

"You've all improved so much since two years past at Southwell," Katie said. "You're so fast! I could hardly keep up watching."

Christopher, ever the charmer, swept her forward into a kiss. "I always knew I loved you."

Will plucked her back. "Love her at a distance then, good infant."

The dark-curled young man smiled his winning smile and held up both hands. "Wise advice, m'lord."

Michael, still in the middle of the arena, addressed all the people watching. "Would any brave soul care to put forth a coin for the privilege of challenge? Any one of us will take on any one of you. The price is a silver. The prize is two."

A jovial dissent breathed through their audience. The Four Swords meandered about, offering insults, compliments, and challenges, but no one entered the ring to take them on. Then Brian strode over to Katie and Will. He addressed her. "How about your feathered friend here? What say you, sir? Or do you fear mussing up your pretty self?"

"Take care, cockerel," Will said. "You never know when someone may pluck out a tongue as it wags."

"Ah! I hear thunder but I see no lightning—"

Katie interrupted, "Unfair talk to one who knows little of swordsmanship."

Will raised an eyebrow. "Yes," he blurted, "I know so little of all this."

"Worry not!" Christopher assured.

"Nay," agreed Nicole. "We'll show you how." She pulled Will's own sword from his baldric and presented it to him. Some time passed before he took hold.

"Oh, no!" Brian swashed to him. "Not like that. Hold it *this* way. There you are . . . perfect." He walked away, rolling eyes and shaking head. The crowd laughed.

"Come along," invited Michael.

"Yes, go along, Will," Katie urged, burying a giggle at his expression. "Let them teach you to defend yourself."

The crowd applauded the prospect.

Will's lowered gaze hit Katie.

"Katie," he droned, "I'm not going to swing steel with these children."

Then he was dragged to the arena's center. Brian stood before him at attack stance, sword up, his mouth twisted slightly in a canny grin. Ever cocky, he bounced both eyebrows at Will.

"Oh . . . lad"—Will chuckled, raising his own blade slowly—"don't do this."

"Talk is easy, m'lord." The grin was joined by a twinkle of olive eyes. "My cutting edge does my arguing."

"Then speak."

They went after each other.

Brian advanced brashly with bold strikes, or at least strikes that looked bold. He drove Will backward all the way to the line of flags, then turned and sauntered away, milking the crowd. "He must be a scullery cook. He handles his blade like a soup spoon!"

The crowd roared laughter.

Only when Brian turned to the finger tapping his shoulder did the laughter fade to a howl of approval.

A blade sung.

Brian's eyes widened. He launched into defense, stumbling away from a flashing weapon.

Will was lithe and relaxed, lean of body after the harsh winter. His blade wheeled upon the air, ringing on Brian's as the two forced each other around the arena. A few swipes and the game was over. The crowd trumpeted.

Brian sat flat in the dust, disarmed. A blade toyed with his nose. Will grinned down at him. "Did I do it right?"

Brian communed with the sword point for a moment, then raised a finger. "Oh! I understand now." He pointed at Will. "*You're* in charge. No one ever explained it to me before!"

The blade reflected sunlight as it rose away. Will got a saucy round of approval from the patrons. He took a tolerant bow, then tried to exit under cover of applause.

But the way was blocked.

His sword tip brushed the dusty ground. "Must we?" he asked.

"We must," Nicole said.

"We should," Michael said.

"We shall," Will said.

They did.

Knowing better than to advance straight on, Nicole and Michael separated, circling Will.

However, they did advance at the same time, from two angles, never expecting Will to be as ready as he was. He waited for them to get into sword length, then dodged suddenly forward, leaving them facing empty air and each other. Years in the Greenwood had made him quick, and it paid. Before the two could readjust their momentum, he was upon them. Blades chimed off one another, a carillon of strikes, first Michael, then Nicole, then, incredibly, both at once. The two grinned with enjoyment, and that delighted spark soon lit Will's face too. Blue tabards, gray surcoat, red stockings, and leather boots made a collage against the flying dirt as the swords flew faster and wilder. As the two realized Will's ability they gave up going gently and attacked joyously, but he also was enjoying the game and, taking out his long dagger, fought one with one hand, the second with the other. Blades were everywhere. The air sang with their voices.

Then Michael erred. He moved too close to his adversary.

Will's foot flew out, catching the younger man behind the knees, than a well-landed elbow caught him in the chest and he toppled backward, his weapon flying away. Instantly Will spun to meet Nicole's descending sword. He changed balance, and out went his other foot.

Nicole fought for balance, but there was no chance. She twisted, hoping to land on her hands for a quicker recovery, and *whack!* The flat of Will's sword disciplined her.

She turned over, rubbing her backside.

"Had enough punishment?" Will asked, grinning.

She laughed. "I liked it!"

The people cheered and hooted.

"I love an honest woman." He stepped back, shaking dust from his sleeves and smiling.

Katie watched, consumed with pleasure. Never would she have plotted for herself a course of such happiness. If there was only peace with her conscience about her forge and apprentices, the world would be impossibly bright. Edward's grave was finally quiet. If only she had understood earlier that the dead prefer to remain dead, would rather move forward in death than cling to a film of unreachable life, perhaps she could have spared herself and Will all that misery. But a hard lesson learned: the past was exactly that. Better so.

Suddenly something crossed her mind, not a thought, but an awareness took over her entire being.

Katie had never thought of herself as *geas*. But was there any other explanation for what she now felt?

Many a danger you'll have to ford. Many a rock in your path.

Hold tight on to each other.

Cautiously she looked to her left. She saw what she had seen all morning: Feast of Fools, with pikes incising the sky where before there had been only sky. Her heart jumped. She looked, slowly, to the right. More pikes. Mail-hooded heads. Chests large with the chess-board emblem of the shire. And, on a vast white horse, danger dazzled.

Will was a perfect target for those unblinking eyes as he stood unaware in the ring, joking and sharing challenges with the Four Swords. He seemed so happy, so relaxed. His presence in the ring's center and the wild swordplay had attracted unfortunate attention, including the wrong eyes.

Sir Guy sat on his horse like a stone. He seemed to be peering straight through Will's feather mask, dissolving it down to the features he knew well, assembling all the bits of evidence. Collar-length gold hair. Long legs. A nobleman's polished stance. Quick movements and a tendency to hold the sword low to the body. Such peculiarities were better identification than a coat of arms.

Before Katie could think of a way to warn Will, the laughter in the ring faded to uneasy smiles, which soon faded also.

The pikes became obvious. The crowd shifted nervously.

Then Will saw Sir Guy.

He inhaled deeply and took a few casual, measured steps away from the Swords and toward the white horse. The enemies exchanged expressionless looks. Will sheathed his dagger, though not his sword, and, in the same motion, peeled back his mask. His hair bounced forward again. He shook it out, never flinching from Sir Guy's glare.

The white horse stomped nervously. Gisbourne never moved. Will's presence in this shire insulted him.

"I greet you again, old friend," Gisbourne spoke.

Will cocked his head slightly to one side and smiled. "How long has it been?"

"Some months. Nigh onto years, I think."

"Yes. So it has." Will's calmness disturbed Katie as she watched helplessly from the other end of the arena, lost in a curious crowd. She realized with some horror that Will had deliberately walked toward Gisbourne to draw attention away from her. "I see the higher taxes have kept you well fed and fashionable," he was saying.

Gisbourne frowned. "You know Leopold of Austria has demanded one hundred fifty thousand silver marks for the king's release. How else are we to raise it?"

Bile rose in Will's throat. "Is Leopold in the business of receiving gilded robes and ermine capes in lieu of coins? Or have your deputies simply polished their rusted armor to make themselves gleam so? And I don't remember that sleek white in your stable. Do you think Leopold will like a desert horse?"

"Your words are treasonous, Montfichet. Too long drinking sedition's milk at Locksley's side. I expected better of you, Will. One of Norman blood should have a better sense of honor."

Katie visibly flinched. *Norman* blood?

Will remained nonplussed. "My heart is

Saxon. So is my honor. In Sherwood we believe blood should be kept sacred, Saxon and Norman alike, and not be poured to see which is the redder."

Gisbourne's steed swayed under him. Without moving he kept the animal in check, the reins snug, not tight, in fists resting on the steed's withers. "So," he began slowly, "it is finally over."

"You think prematurely."

"Look around."

"Yes, I see your men." Will changed from one foot to the other. It was an innately casual move, putting him on his strongest leg. He leaned on his sword, truly unaffected by Sir Guy at all. Though he felt Katie's anxiety eerily from far at his back, he could not muster an ounce of fear. If anything, there was a strange pool of calm at the center of his being. He would live or die in the next moments. An odd peace flowed over him as he gazed at Gisbourne and saw Gisbourne's hatred of that peace. "I warn you against killing me, for what good it may do."

"Why?" bellowed his adversary. "I think I am in control here."

"Your life would be worth precious little in my cousin's eyes."

"You overestimate Locksley's sense of revenge."

"You underestimate his sense of personal loyalty."

"Yes," Gisbourne drawled, "and I have been trying fruitlessly to draw him out of Sherwood for a fair fight. Even you shall have to agree that you make tidy bait. This is sad, Will. I'd rather have met you on the field of battle than have you hand yourself to me so unceremoniously. Not like the old days, is it?"

"Good thing for you." Will laughed. "I've been leaning my ribs on grass-fed deer while you've grown stout on grain-fed pig. Could you beat me, do you think?"

"We never shall know. Urlan, seize him."

Will spun around, already aware of the big man's approach from his left. Somehow the dagger was back in his left hand. His arm made a swipe at an impossible angle. Urlan stopped in midstep, gawking at Will. A great gasp rose from the stunned crowd; some even screamed. Urlan looked down at his chest, amazed at the dagger hilt protruding from the coat-of-arms as though it were part of the design. He looked up at Will. Blood began pouring from his mouth and gushed into the dirt at Will's feet.

"Seize him!" Gisbourne waved an arm at the shire deputies, but the gesture was incomplete. Beneath him a thundercloud rose up and boiled white against the sky, skrieking a long, furious, wild whistle. He battled for control as his horse bolted headlong into a battery of armed men, crashing them into each other. Pikes clattered, tangled up. Sir Guy shouted, "Get back, you fools! Never mind this! Get Gamewell! Get him, I say!"

But Will had not failed to take advantage of Katie's nipping little dirk. Indeed, he was pleased that she had changed her mind and decided to use it, even if only on a horse's flank. He would not fail her. By the time

Gisbourne untangled his horse with his men, Will was no longer idle in the arena.

Why, no! He was high on a balcony—God knew how he got there—but the people loved it. He ducked away from a hail of arrows, then climbed to a rooftop, tossing a wide smile and a jaunty wave at the crowd below. At the change in their faces from shock to delight, Will realized they were with him. The deputies were forcing their way through, but the crowd was resisting, giving Will time to get his footing in the roof's thatch. His feet went to the ankle in stray matting, but his spirit was as light as a feather on the wind, and he scrambled merrily higher. Another shower of arrows drove him down, two of them catching in his heavy clothes, none drawing blood, and while Gisbourne's men reloaded, Will stood up and cupped his hands around a shrill whistle. Immediately came the answer: a wild, drawn-out scream from the livery around the corner. Then a violent crashing. Hooves against planks. Planks breaking. Then another rain of arrow and pikes sent him ducking, though not before he caught a glimpse of Katie slipping through the crowd. Some of the people were trying to edge away from the sudden danger, jolted by the sight of Urlan's body, a fountain of blood, on its knees in the dirt while deputies swarmed in confusion. Others, however—mostly Saxons—took their cues from the Four Swords, who were merrily tripping, bumping, and poking the deputies to distraction, and a deluge of various foods soon added to the process.

Will scrambled along the rooftops skirting the bazaar, aiming around to where they had first entered the area, to where a great blond stallion stomped his way forward, nose raised and nostrils flaring as he led Katie's horse toward the whistle he worshiped. Will whistled again. Palermo screamed answer, wheeled on his heavy hind legs, and bolted in a new direction. The deputies tried to follow as Will moved swiftly from roof to balcony to shop front. Gisbourne followed with his burning eyes. Will gave him a saucy salute between jumps, salted with that carefree smile, thought secretly his goal was to keep Sir Guy's gaze up, high, away from the crowd, away from Katie. When Will lost sight of her, it did not show on his face beneath the emblematic scarlet bonnet. He'd had it in his belt. Now it was on his head. A sort of signature, an added sting for Gisborne. It was working. Christ, if only Robin could be here! How he would enjoy this!

Black eyes moved with him as he raised his sword to slam off a pike speeding at him. The impact nearly broke his arm. It did drive him head-down into the dusty straw. He came up spitting filth and bits of straw, staggered to his feet, and battled to sheath his sword. His shoulder throbbed. For a moment his arm hung limp and tingling at his side, opening a door for apprehension to sneak in and steal his smile. Staggering through the thatch, he threw himself in a crazed dive at a laundry line, caught it, fighting the numbness in his arm, and when the line snapped under his weight on one end—he had bet it would—it carried him in a wide arc, out, out, down, to land feet-first in a wagonload of vegetables.

"This way, you fools!" Gisbourne raged, bullying his horse through the confusion. His deputies tried to follow, but several Saxons and the Four Swords were adding ample hindrances.

Will struggled up and ran along the wagon's sideboard where Palermo met him. A final leap landed him hard in the saddle—most painful—and he leaned down to catch the other horse's reins, glad he was he'd advised the liveryman to keep their horses saddled and bridled.

Now, to find Katie.

When the scarf that had been concealing most of her hair was torn off in the melee, a thought hardly passed before Katie let her mask follow it into the herd of feet. Sir Guy may or may not have guessed she was here, but it didn't matter. Half a challenge rose in her, anyway, something she would never have expected of herself. It was a sudden wish to be arrogant, to throw down her mask and show Sir Guy the meaning of individuality. And that is exactly what she did. Her blanket of bright hair glittered in the sunlight like a flag. Her desire to hide her way to safety was buried by her desire to show a little assertiveness. A gesture of that breed wiped clean her dirk of a red trickle from Sir Guy's poor horse's flank, though from what Katie could see, it was providing no handicap except to make the horse blazing angry. No angrier, however, than Sir Guy. And the rage redoubled when he spied her as she foolishly wished he would. His eyes grew as big as two sparrow hawks, his mouth falling open in a shout. No word, only a shout. It could have meant anything. Katie felt its bite though the sound never reached her, and when her eyes met Gisbourne's across the sea of heads and hoods, the impact was force enough to knock them both back a fair step.

There was no message to be sent.

She took a deep, sustaining breath and dodged through the crowd again, stopping only a moment later to change direction and realized with an inward laugh that her appearance had sent Sir Guy straight off the back of his angry steed and full into a pool of mud. His men were dragging him to his feet, she saw, half his face plastered with abject rage, the other half with mud. His horse stomped around him, skillfully avoiding hands that caught at its reins. Only imagination gave full value to Sir Guy's delight at his clothes being doused in mud and dust. Katie shared pleasure with her own empathy for him while hurrying back to where she had last seen Will.

But he was gone. Now what could she do? Had he left her here, helpless and alone? She felt the little dirk in her hand. Well, alone, then.

A noose quivered around her neck—for a moment she actually felt it as she heard the shire's army turning to her on Gisbourne's order, felt the scratchy fate awaiting her if she allowed them to capture her.

A quick sweeping glance took in the nearing shire officers and filled Katie with dread. They were men, after all, armed heavily, cloaked in mail, and trained to fight. Her fingers turned the little dirk, striking in her the realization of her own problem: sticking blade to a horse's rump was a high flight away from pushing aside the innards of a human being with intent

to murder. Was self-defense murder? Never
had she studied that point during all the stories of valor she heard and retold. Now faced
with it, she wished the past had made room
for one extra rumination. So escape, not fighting, was her only hope, at least for now.

She dodged down a thin alley, scattering a
flock of eight or ten chickens who promptly
flapped, squawking and pecking, in the faces
of those deputies who followed her. The only
way out was down an even thinner alley, darkened by houses towering it, at the end of which
there was a patch of sunlit street. Down it she
plunged, hiking up the flowing skirts of the
gown Sir Guy himself had given her in a better moment, but before breaking out into the
open, she toppled a pile of baskets loaded with
grain. The furious cries of deputies staggering
through that mess chased her, rippling on her
skin. I have to get out, she vowed. I have to
live.

Her instinct to survive burrowed deep into
thoughts of Will and of Robin, both of whom
had backed her with faith, trust, and action.
To die here would shatter them and leave her
memory soiled; to be captured—for in whole
truth she didn't believe Sir Guy would kill
her—would be worse, forcing Robin's band to
risk all for her rescue. And they would, they
would try, she was painfully sure. Will was
quite truthful about Robin's sense of personal
loyalty.

The deputies flew after her with gritted teeth
and clashing weapons, telling her that womanhood would buy her no favors here. If they
took her, Sir Guy might not be near enough to

stay the blades of brashness. These shallow idiots would pluck her head from her neck without a thought, for her quickness had humiliated them. That much was clear in their viciousness as they caught at her skirts and snatched bits of her hair.

She shook her head, an uncatchable scream tearing from her throat, and a burst of energy put distance between her and them. She had no heavy mail to weigh her down as they did, and she managed to pull away, breaking into the sunlight.

One of the deputies pulled up, raised his pike, and let it fly like some primitive hunting spear at his target. Katie heard the swish and stooped low. Her body shrank in terror. The pike whizzed over her, but the shaft rang hard on her shoulder blade, hammering her to the ground. Her arms flew out in front, slammed into a sea of metal pots for sale near a shop front, and she twisted, helpless, her spine striking the building. She was stunned. Her limbs quivered, but she couldn't make them move. Her ears rang with a terrible deafening hurt, and shaking her head only worsened it. She struggled to her knees, gasping, clutched a nearby wagon, and dragged herself to her feet. The smell of herbs wafted up her nostrils, clearing her head.

What seemed so long took only second. When her eyes cleared, she saw a wall of chessboard emblems moving noisily toward her, feet stomping, belts squeaking, sheaths rattling. So many swords drawn just to save her? What an honor.

Power flowed back into her legs, but it was too late. She was trapped against the storefront.

The deputies ground to a halt twenty paces away. They were waiting for Sir Guy. One of them was calling to him, waving—this way, this way. All around them, townspeople gawked and scattered, most of them still not sure what was going on.

Pikes swam before her. She swallowed a lump of fear.

Within seconds four blades flew in, lined up, and lowered to horizontal thrust position between her and the deputies. Blue tabards lined up shoulder to shoulder in a sparse wall before her. She could only imagine the stubborn glint, the mete of challenge, flickering in those four sets of eyes. Their right shoulders turned evenly to the wall of deputies, blades at equal height.

"The Four Swords at your service, gentlemen," announced Michael.

Christopher blew them a kiss, rotating his sword haft, the blade catching sunlight. "Hello, loves."

"Save yourself, Katie," Nicole called, the sternness shocking her. "We'll hold them off."

"Aye," growled Brian, more pleased than any. With a twisting smile he stuffed his cross and necklace into his open collar. "These Norman curs will eat our dust for a change."

And the Norman curs, not being curs of much brain, really didn't know what to do about it, for although they outnumbered the Four Swords, but with these particular four it didn't seem to matter. Sometimes the fiercest animals are the most easily bluffed.

Time mattered. Katie dared not fail her friends by allowing the deputies to assess the situation. A sudden dodge to her left took care of that.

Behind her erupted a great noise of metal grating against its own kind, and she sent a silent thanks to those who, for no reason, had plunged into her inferno.

Anguish clutched her heart for her friends' safety when she heard howls of effort and pain, and she knew for certain that the fun had gone out of this day for good. The ache in her back reminded her of it as she made way down the alley and out onto another court—straight under the flailing front hooves of a rearing horse. She ducked away, scampering for freedom, only to be yanked back against the steed's sweaty side.

"Let go!" she screamed, kicking hard.

"Katie, don't fight," Will's voice pierced her. "Turn around! Mount your horse and we'll be off while we still have our necks!"

"Mine will be shorter from now on just from the scare," she said, choking. The saddle was stiff and cruel to her thighs where she had struck the ground, but she felt as though a cloud had lifted her. Will's red cap and cloak flashed at her side, and they were off.

Palermo wheeled, Katie's horse following so desperately that she hardly had to steer it at all. Unfortunately the path was blocked every way except the way she had come. So that was the way they went. Down the dim alley and out again into Nottingham's central square, into the sunlight. Katie clung to her horse's withers and saw the wide yellow rump of Will's horse gather before her and rise up, up, higher . . .

A sickening surge in her stomach dizzied

her. Her own horse raised up, crushing her deep into the saddle. She saw the herb wagon pass beneath, then Palermo's flank drop forward. Into a pool of blood.

Red liquid splattered beneath hooves. Wide-eyed, though she wished to close her eyes and pretend this was over, Katie could not avoid seeing the bloody ground and disembodied limbs lying in it—hands, arms, some of the bodies they may or may not have belonged to. She saw, painfully, only two blue tabards now as she and Will sped through, trampling corpses. She clamped her eyes shut, reaching her limit for one day's misery. The horse's steamy mane clung to her face. All she was aware of was the pulsing muscles beneath her cheek, the endless movement beneath her. In her ears drummed hoofbeats. She could hear nothing else.

Nottingham buzzed by, an eternal series of streets and turns, buildings forming and dissolving around them. Then the town gates. Then the open road.

Nottingham's stink peeled away in a sudden breeze from the hills. The thunder of hoofbeats changed in timbre, enough to tell her they were moving off the road and onto rough, frozen grass. The ground rose and fell like a lung breathing beneath them. Foam flecked into Katie's face as her horse strained at the bit to keep up with Palermo, and she forced herself to sit up in the saddle. Her spine crackled, but she was upright again. She searched for the reins, finding them flopping uselessly from the bridle, far out of reach. All she could do was grasp handfuls of mane and cling tight.

They angled around a cliff bottom as they

neared River Trent and the rougher countryside it had carved out of England's face. For a
few seconds their horses ran flank to flank.
Will lunged forward after those flopping reins.
He was insensible to the girl poppet in his belt
as it shivered loose and tumbled to the ground
to be trampled first by his horse, then by those
who followed. He managed to catch one rein
between his fingers, drag it back, and shoved
it into Katie's hand. "Take this! Take it. Steer
your horse left. I'll head right and draw them
away."

"Draw who away?"

"Think, my girl. Off with you, and no turning back!"

The thundering continued, divided, and she
was alone on a foamy, heaving steed, the horse
long since crazed with terror. Once Will de-
parted, she heard the other hoofbeats behind
her, plenty of them, getting nearer with every
breath. Will had been wrong to think the deputies would follow him and leave her free to
escape.

A second later, not time even for a thought,
the ground fell away before her.

Her horse shrilled, scrambling for solid
ground, but there was none. Twigs and icicles
snapped all around her, a scream beginning in
her throat, only to be cut off as she plunged
forward out of the saddle into a jagged grip of
rocks. The world spun like a child's top. Sound
went away.

In complete silence the sky and clouds turned,
became grass, became sky again, then rocks,
bare trees, snow, and a gigantic brown body
smelling of sweat. Her own arms and legs flailed

before her like the limbs of a rag doll. The sky
darkened suddenly. The smelly brown body
rolled over her, crushing the air from her chest.
A hoof scraped her head, ringing off her skull.
Then the ground was gone a second time, and
she was falling.

High above, a gathering of men of horseback
stared over the cliff, and to every face came a
wince of empathy. There were better ways to
die.

• Chapter Thirteen •

Sir Guy's horse reared to a halt at the cliff's edge, kicking away loose rubble. Gisbourne slid out of the saddle. His face was limned in horror.

"Catherine," he choked. He started down the cliff, but his men quickly pulled him back and held him.

"No, my lord, there's no chance!"

"Let me go to her—"

"My lord, she's dead, she's dead. The horse rolled over her. Pray you look at the horse!"

Far down the embankment the massive brown body was stock-still, doused in foam and its own sweat, its head twisted back too far. Its spine was snapped at the withers.

Far below the pitiful creature Sir Guy and his men saw a motionless arm and a leg protruding from the brown overgrowth at the riverbank. White skin glowed pale and deathly against high, dead foliage. Gisbourne would be forever grateful that he could not see her face. It might have destroyed him.

"Katie . . ."

His bodyguard pulled him away. "Best we not stay here, m'lord, come away!" The man turned his master away by force and led him back to the road where others had gathered and were holding the horses.

Numbly, Gisbourne accepted his horse's reins, too aware of the animal's hot, breathy snorts, the signals of life. He clutched the mane and closed his eyes for a moment as misery consumed him.

"Very well," he muttered, blinking reddened eyes. "It was not to be." Clearing his throat did nothing to smooth his voice, nor a deep shuddering breath to calm his body. "Have . . . have they found Gamewell?"

"I know not, master."

"I want him found, do you understand? I want him found and hanged for this tragedy, this outrage."

The quiet tone laden with thorns bit through all who heard it.

Two men climbed back upon their horses and rode away, passing a single deputy who rode to Sir Guy and dismounted. "We lost him, your lordship. He got clean away without so much as a hoofprint. Only this was left behind. God knows what it is."

Sir Guy held out his hand. Into it fell what appeared to be a wad of cloth and yarn. He smoothed it out, brushing off the dirt, and turned it over. A small face looked up at him. There were two gray eyes and a tiny pink mouth, one of the eyes unraveled grotesquely. Long flaxen yarn hung through his fingers. The tiny yellow dress had a tear in it, but a Celtic brooch still held a small cloak intact.

Gisbourne pressed his lips together, gazing into his hand. Gently he smoothed down the doll's hair; gently he curled the gray string running down the face like a gory tear and tried to turn it back into an eye. His big hand closed softly around the poppet's trampled body.

"Your orders, Sir Guy?" someone prompted.

"Find Will Gamewell if you have to burn every Saxon house in the shire. When you have him, I want him brought to me. I will personally tighten the noose around his neck until he dies cold dead. Then I shall dangle the rest for the crows. Find him, do you hear? Those are my orders."

"Aye, m'lord."

"Aye, m'lord."

"Very good, m'lord."

They mounted. Before riding away, Gisbourne opened the front of his tunic, and there, beside his heart, he tucked the remnant of a guttered wish.

There was snow at the riverbank. Cold, rushing water had reflected the sun's light during this recent thaw and had kept the ice from melting. So deep a ravine saw the sun only briefly, except in summer, but this was not summer, and a silent, dripping battle pulsed between ice and sun, river and riverbank. From far into the town church bells chimed upon the wind, clashing and arguing with each other in the throes of Feast.

Dreams of summer came easily upon the breeze that followed the river on its unending course. A winding pattern dictated messages of ways older than old, all folding upon themselves until the runes and letters and scratchings and etchings were polished to near imperceptibility by age.

Was this what it was like to be dying? Or was this what it was like to be dead? Perhaps it was this easy for Edward, this business of dying, slipping away.

Funny how well the sense of smell still worked its unappreciated art. It would be pleasant to die smelling wildflowers. But the only scents now were those of dry winter grass, the crisp running water, the chill breeze, and the snow. Had it been winter? Or was that, too, part of the process, this cold?

The clouds spun lazily, clouds whose faces had turned over England for millennia, the very same clouds, hair of the Huntress Goddess herself, she who had laid down her bow and tamed her dogs to conceal their fangs; they now lay their heaving bellies down upon the cold earth and awaited the hunger.

The Goddess spun down from the sky, which was not her natural domain, and looked into the face of death. Death was not dark nor shadowy but most pale, quite like those shades who walked with her in half sleep from the time of deep magic.

She took a last look at Katie and spun back up to where moments meant nothing. It was time for humans to hold their own keys and turn them if they themselves chose and Katie knew she must try.

"Robin, hasn't this gone on long enough? If they're so determined to be left alone, perhaps we bloody ought to let 'em alone. They look to me like they got nothin' an' want only their lives."

"I'm not after their lives."

"Then why are we standing out in the cold?"

"Why, Tuck, I'd swear you've lost your sense of curiosity."

"And gained a sense of reason. Let's get home."

"Nay, not just yet."

"When, then?"

Robin sighed and looked to either side at the line of Greenwood men standing this odd vigil with him. They flanked the stone fence near the east edge of Sherwood, a fence that once had encircled a house but was now crumbling. The house succumbed to fire years ago, and much of the fence stones had been cannabalized by local folk for their own chimneys and walls, but enough remained to be a defensible little fortress against highwaymen, assuming the highwaymen possessed nominal bloodlust. There were no arrows behind the short fence; only swords—and blood.

"Robin," Tuck entreatied again.

"Hold tight, you old rooster. Their purses might be light, but they need us."

"*They* . . . need *us*?"

"You saw the blood on the road."

"Well, be it then, let's circle around and get it over with. I'm hungry."

From Robin's other side Edmund Bluestocking crowed, "Pity's sake, everybody keep moving. Tuck's hungry."

"Let's send him to London." Will Stutley suggested with his gravelly voice. "We'll starve His Highness out!"

Laughter ruffled across the ribbon of men. They leaned on their weapons, sniffing and scratching, wondering if Robin was going to move against these interlopers before nightfall. Already the air was cooling rapidly; though there had been sun today, it was falling behind the treed horizon and taking its little winter warmth with it. The stones of the fence were very cold now.

"They've held us off long enough, Robin," Stutley said, plucking a twig from his mustache. He had scouted around the other side, through thick, bare bushes, only to return having learned nothing. The intruders had holed up between the fence and a piece of ruined wall. He had seen only bits of movement. "Let's take them by our numbers. If we all went at once—"

"We'd all come back wanting of an arm or two. Stutley, you saw those long blades bobbing there. Would you like to lead the charge?"

"I would if—"

"If someone goes before you," Tuck said, completing his sentence.

"They must be hungry and fair chilled by now," Robin said thoughtfully. He leaned on his bow and eyed that fence. His men shuffled around him, stomping warmth into their feet and sighing rather a lot. "We'll try talking to them." He moved forward, closing the distance between himself and the row of piled stones, flanked by his slapdash army. At roughly the halfway point between where they were and where they were going, a face popped up behind the rocks, blurted, "Scarlet oak!" and vanished again.

Robin and everyone halted.

"What in perdition was that?" Stutley exclaimed.

"Scarlet mote?" was Tuck's question.

Robin puzzled over it for a moment. "Did it sound like a clan war cry to you?"

"Could be," Stutley said. "Which puts us dealing with barbarians."

"If it is, then they mean to fight us out."

"Let it go, Robin," Tuck insisted.

Strolling over to the vast friar, Robin gave him a look too grave to be serious. "And if I do, they toddle out of Sherwood with the message that anyone with a weapon and a quiverload of stubbornness can pass these woods unscathed."

"Some aren't worth the energy it takes to scathe 'em."

Stepping back, Robin addressed his men. "Any suggestions?"

There was a unilateral shrug.

"Such dynamism. Very well, I'll decide. Tuck, take Johnny and Stutley. Hie around back of them and hold off till I give you a signal. Then take them. Mind, I want no blood let until we know what they're about."

The taking turned out to be a quick business. It did not, however, go without a fight. Robin fired an arrow through high, bare branches to draw the adversaries' eyes and also to signal Tuck. The three big men pounced, and there was a great ruckus behind the rocks.

Then out popped a tall sandy-haired youth. He scrambled over the fence, stumbling badly, with a fierceness born of desperation. His left thigh was gushing blood even through a crude bandage, dousing his whole leg, and his pale

face showed a dangerous loss of blood. He bran-
dished a sword and galloped awkwardly toward
Robin. Since Robin was standing out in front,
it wasn't difficult to assume that he was in
charge.

Weapons swept up behind Robin. "Nay,
don't," he ordered. "He's weak as a bird." He
pretended to fumble with his arrow, allowing
the young man to knock it from his hand and
hold him at swordpoint. At the same moment
Johnny and Tuck climbed over the fence, dragging a blood-covered wildcat.

"Call them off!" The blade trembled at Robin's heart.

"Hold. Hold, then, Tuck," Robin ordered.
"Bring that one here."

They were quite near before he realized "that
one" was actually a woman. She kicked furi-
ously, making a vicious handful even for the
two huge men. Her tabard, once blue, was
now red-brown with drying blood. Her yellow
hair was strung with blood and filth, tossing
stiffly as she shrieked, "Scarlet oak, idiots!
Don't you even know?"

"Robin!" Stutley called. "Two more over
here, all cut up."

"Go get them."

His men started to move, but the man before
him pressed the blade point to Robin's chest.
"Leave them alone."

"To do what, die back there? Who are you?"

"Depends on who you are," the girl said,
still yanking against Johnny and Tuck's grips
on her arms, "since you fail to know the
password."

"Password? That scarlet oak? It's no code of mine."

"Then you tell us first."

"I am Locksley, called Robin Hood, and you're in my domain."

"Your domain's limp today," the one with the sword said, jabbing at him and trying to hide the white-knuckled weakness in his hand. His shoulder trembled with the weight of the sword.

Robin made a mental bet with himself. He waved at his men. "Do as I told you."

Several of them went hesitantly to the fence, expecting Robin to be run through. They hauled up two other young men, both severely injured. Cuts and puncture wounds viciously delivered had been badly tended, crammed with wadded cloth and wrapped hastily. Both were deathly pale, one entirely unconscious. They were brought to Robin. He commented, "Your holding off would have killed your friends."

"We'd have killed them and ourselves before surrendering."

"How childishly noble," Stutley said dryly.

"I'll show you childish!" The girl used Tuck and Johnny for leverage, brought both legs up, and delivered Will Stutley a mighty kick. He went sprawling.

"Hold there, girl, enough," Robin said, extending his hand. "What's your name?"

She tossed back her hair. "I am Nicole Beaujoli from Berkhamsted near St. Albans."

Behind her Tuck shook his hand and rolled his eyes at the haughty way she said it.

Robin stepped back from the sword enough

to give her a bow. "Welcome to Sherwood, my lady. What about you, then?"

The one with the sword cradled a useless left arm against his ribs and said, "Brian Landower. From Darley Abbey."

"An abbey?"

Brian refused to apologize. "I gave it up for Lent." He took weight off his thigh. The ooze of blood slackened noticeably.

"Do these others have names?"

The bearded one, who had propped himself up on one elbow as he sat on the ground, unable to move severely damaged legs—he would limp for life if he ever walked again—coughed once and rasped, "Michael Fitz-William of Ancaster." He gestured at the unconscious form beside him. "Christopher Valland. Also of Ancaster."

"What are you doing in the forest in such ravaged condition?"

"Running from a worse condition," Michael Fitz-William said.

"Ah . . . fallen out of favor with the shire? You're in like company. Judging by the shape you're in, I'd hate to think how the losers look. Share meat and stories with us, even if we don't know this thing you say, this scarlet o—" He stopped suddenly, giving a very strange glare to Brian Landower.

"What?" Stutley prodded.

"Scarlet," Robin murmured, "oak . . ."

"Oh, you're not thinking—"

"Could it be anything else?" Robin threw back his head and indulged in a hearty laugh. "Praise Our Lady, he's alive and on the job!"

"What are you prattling about?" Tuck roared.

Robin took hold of Brian's sword, and because of the way he did it, Brian let him. The change of balance made the young man stumble sideways; he would've gone down on his gushing leg had Stutley not caught him. Robin strode past them to Tuck and patted the round man's belly. "It's about a man I love better at this moment than ever before. Hear all of you this: From now on, anyone uttering the words *scarlet oak* may pass undisturbed through Sherwood but for whatever donation they wish to give to our cause. Tuck! Move your great elephant's hide. There are wounds to be dressed and plans to be made."

There was a pain within her breast, and a sweet singing within her head. There was a constant noise—a deafening rumble. It was harsh, like the big forge bellows in the smelting yard, and it filled the universe despite every effort of blood and body to heal itself and calm the discord.

Then a song began, a sweet song with lyrics of lovely, earthy things, portraits of children running, happy; remembrances of gallantries too ancient to remember filled her mind and linked her to life. A small brightness charged her heart.

Finally a new warmth came. It was unexplainable and began at the bottoms of her feet. Yes, she had feet . . . she had forgotten them, but now she felt the warmth there. Coming not from within her body, the heat moved up her legs, filling her thighs and spreading across her belly like a man's caress, until her breasts

swelled to the sensation and her shoulders
moved, languishing in this wondrous feeling.

Deep in her body she climbed a long ladder,
as though her physical self was merely a
receptable, a castle or fortress, a form independent. The ladder at first was cold iron and
very wide, but soon it became wooden, much
like the autumn saplings in Greenwoodside,
and vines began to grow over the rungs. Her
hands folded around comforting broad leaves
now, the greenery sun-warmed and kind to
bare feet. There were songs at the top. She
climbed faster. When she heard her own name
in the songs, she flew.

He met her where the flowers began to bud
on their vines. His arms filled themselves with
her. They spun slowly, smiling into each other's eyes, drawing power, vibrance, sharing the
scents of wildflowers rapidly blooming on the
ladder. After a few moments of caresses she
heard a voice speak to her.

She loved and loved and loved his voice.

"There's my love."

"There's my girl. Here's a bit of broth. This
is good for you. There we are . . . slowly . . . all
down."

"Was it you?" She opened her eyes a sliver,
allowing light to flow in. Soon there was form
within the light. A face . . . Will's face.

"What?" he asked softly.

Her words were a whisper carried weakly
on a breath. "Was it you in the sky?"

Will held a cool, wet cloth against her forehead. His hands had ceased their fearful trembling days ago, when finally he realized that
she was going to live. In spite of the cracked

ribs, the fever, and the terrible, frightening
red-black bruises, he no longer feared the bony
hand of death around her. In the days past he
had watched those bruises spread, swell, turn
deep ugly purple, turn blue and grow veined
with yellowness, then become the most prominent features on her emaciated body. He had
forced liquids into her mouth as he cradled
her, at first only warm water, later soup and
broth for her body to live on as it healed.
Slowly the swelling had gone down, the bruises
had paled to a sickening vein-mapped yellowness, and she moved in her sleep. Death was
no longer his enemy.

As he watched her eyes fight for a coherent
vision, he felt a new fear. Had the fall hurt her
mind? How could he answer a question about
being in the sky?

"Hush, love," was all he said, dabbing the
cloth against her cheeks, her lips, her throat.
"The fever is gone now. I think it will not
return. We're over the blackest moments. We're
safe for now. I've taken care of you."

Katie felt the straw mattress filling up the
contours of her body as she lay upon it and
wiggled her toes to regain contact with them.
"I saw you with the clouds . . . with someone
. . . I wanted to be with you, so I climbed the
ladder."

His hands trembled again. His heart dropped
to his ankles. He struggled to keep it from
showing on his face. She would be afraid of it
if she saw. She would let the fear in, and
death might ride its tailfeathers. "I've set us
up here nicely . . . we're still in Nottingham.
It's an inn called the Boar's Tail. I thought

Gisbourne would never assume we might double back to the town instead of running to the Greenwood. You needed attention. The innkeeper here is Saxon, knew me from times gone by, and was most helpful. You've been so ill, Katie. . . ." A moist swelling came to his eyes, a tightness to his throat, muffling his speech. To hide it from her he stepped away from the bed and fussed with a bowl of broth, doing nothing at all to it while hoping that he appeared busy. Behind him he heard her sigh, a sleepy, waking-up kind of sigh, knowing she was not going to fade away again as she had several times. He heard the mattress rustling beneath her as she tested her battered limbs. Soon the pain would begin for her. He steeled himself for a different kind of fight, one she would have to share with him; could he keep her pain away? If only he knew some magic that would keep her asleep, that would drug the pain to impotence until the day she would rise from the bed whole and healed.

"Will? Will? Where are we?"

When he turned, once he had regained control over his own expression, he saw a shocking clarity in her eyes caused by the pain, but clarity nonetheless, and it amazed him that pain could be so much his ally.

"Will?"

"I'm here. . . ." He sat by her on the bed. "Katie, I'm with you now."

"Where are we?"

"I'll tell you later. We're safe, though. We've been safe for a long time."

"How long?"

So her sense of time passing had fueled itself again. "Nearly two weeks since Feast of Fools," he told her, nodding compassionately, knowing how long two weeks sounded when they had been entirely missed.

"What happened to me on the road?" It was her first truly lucid question. "I fell off a cliff's edge, I think. Yes. Sir Guy's men . . . Will . . . what happened to my horse?"

Empathy showed in his eyes and his tight-mouthed response when he finally did speak, busying himself with washing her bare shoulders with oiled water warmed by the innkeeper at his hearth. Not empathy for the animal but for Katie, who would feel its suffering over again. He forced himself to concentrate on the shape of her bones' soft landscape beneath her skin. "The horse died," he said. "She rolled over you and over her own head. Her neck was broken, Katie. There was nothing to be done about it. When I reached her, she was straining to get up, but only her forelegs were working, scratching at the ground." He dipped the cloth again and squeezed it out. "I had to put her to the sword."

Katie turned her head and blinked into the small window's patch of cloudy sky. Will's caressing hands and warm, oiled cloth soothed muscles first battered then aching from disuse. Two weeks, had he said?

"How badly am I hurt? Is it too terrible? Am I to die?"

"At first I thought so," he said, still with that distance in his tone. Then it suddenly dropped away, and he dropped close to her, his arms flanking hers, his face pressing her cheek and temple. "My love, I couldn't let you die. Many times you began to slip away. I had to call you back—I had to. At times your pain was so bad, I thought to let you drift on to heaven, to your Edward's side and to peace, but I couldn't. I kept talking to you, touching you, and I sang you songs. Stories came to me I hadn't thought of since I was a boy. You heard them all, Katie; these were long days. I told you stories and sang you songs. I couldn't let you go without trying. . . ."

The emotion was too heavy for her to bear at this moment, and she closed his lips with her fingertips. Several moments passed, long and silent.

"What about Gisbourne and the shire deputies? Won't they be searching for us?"

"They have been and still are. You needn't worry, though, my love. I'll take care of you."

Never was there a promise so thoroughly fulfilled. He made her body part of his, filling himself with her hurts until, if not gone, they were shared. His tenderness as he fixed the blankets and dressed her in her linen chemise was evidence of his having cared for her for many days already. Each touch was that of familiarity; he knew every bruise as if it were his own, knew just where on her arms he could take a good grip and just where the bones still ached or cuts stung.

"I want you to have a good meal now that you're finally awake. You've had nearly nothing to subsist on, and nothing solid. Do you think you could eat?"

She smiled tiredly. "For you I'll try."

"Will you be all right? I'll go get something." As he stood she scanned his long legs in their tight fitting trews, his hipbones showing through where his belt had hitched up his shirt's hem, and she wondered if he had stopped eating every bit as much as she had.

She was alone with her thoughts, still peppered with vagueness and half dreams, while he left for a while. Reality slowly filtered back to her, and its edges grew sharp once again. Details trickled in. Even bits of the delirious two weeks past. She let them flow in, even the disturbing ones. They no longer frightened her nor did she resist them. Odd, but her troubles seemed impotent with death so recently beaten off her heels, probably an effect of the light-headedness but a strengthening effect at least. She let it consume her. Will would need help making her well.

Evidently he hadn't gone far, probably not out of this inn. He was back in minutes with hot food—some kind of meat-and-vegetable stew. It was boar's meat, and Katie wondered how much he had paid for the delicacy.

"The innkeeper had this set aside, so I got some for you," he said, nudging the door shut with his heel.

"How nice," she said, stretching gingerly. "An innkeeper who stocks a constant supply of cooked boar's meat."

"Marvelous, isn't it?"

He set the tray down on a stool near her bed, taking time to light two candles since dusk was stealing light from the sky out their window, and sat beside her, gently propping her up on his rolled surcoat. Katie knew she could have fed herself, or at least felt she should, but it seemed she owed him the chance to pamper her through the healing since he had guided her through the hurt. Her time of dreams had been an endless drag of minutes for him, filled not with dreams but with anxieties. For now he needed to see the light in her eyes and the color return to her cheeks after days of death's pallor.

He fed her tenderly, as though it nourished him. All the while he told her of his boyhood at Gamewell. Katie could hardly guess why he was telling her of this, except that he seemed to be continuing a story, not starting one. Had he been telling her this even as she lay unconsious? He said he had, but she hadn't quite believed him until now. He was so sweet and entertaining that she ate three spoonfuls more than she wanted. Her body wanted little to do with sustenance, having done without it so long. Only the hope in his eyes made her force the mouthfuls down. She felt ill. Though she tried to hide if from him, he did see it.

"You'll feel better in the morning," he said, putting the stew down. He tucked the blanket around her and grasped her hand. "Your stomach has something solid to work on. I want you to sleep."

"There's plenty of stew left," she said. "You won't let it go to waste . . ."

"I promise to eat it after you're asleep. I'm not the one who's lying injured." He smoothed back her hair, pulsing through her a rush of sensation. Everything seemed so new!

Katie felt like a child just emerged from the womb. Though her limbs were weak and aching, a strange invulnerability coursed in her veins. With it came a bizarre wish to con-

front Gisbourne, the Abbot Godfrey, Nell—
anyone who had tampered with her life for
their own purposes.

Will was tracing the shape of her lips with
his little finger. "Sleep. The morning light will
waken you."

Sleep was a deep featherbed. Much deeper
than the straw mattress beneath her. It was
made soft by her new distance from danger,
something entirely mental and not physical at
all, since real danger lurked quite close. She
had seen it in Will's evasiveness when she
asked about Gisbourne, and it now pervaded
her dreams, but it was not cowled in fear. In
her dreams she was chasing the danger as
though it had become her prey.

Waking came not with the sun but with a
steamy herbal aroma. It smelled like a combination of tea and flowers. Katie blinked her
eyes open.

And there was Will, pouring a bucket of
steaming water into a huge half barrel already
filled with water. "You're going to enjoy this,"
he said. "Did you sleep well?"

Trying a careful stretch, Katie yawned. "I
drifted away to a place of great power. I was
the moon and queen of all that place."

He dried his hand, came to the bed, and
sprawled beside her, half lying down, his face
close enough to hers that she felt the warmth
of his breath. "And who was king?"

"King? Let me see ... I think it was Alfie
Bloxham's goat. Dreams are funny, you know."

"Mmm ... cruel too. Are you ready for your
bath?"

"Is that what it is? Oh, Will, this isn't proper.

Baths are taken in cool, open ponds with free-running water, not closed up in smelly tubs!"

"This tub isn't smelly," he said, pretending indignation. "*This* tub is a pool of herbs. Dried wildflowers, rose petals, and shepherd's purse, and other good things to help you heal. You're going to make a wonderful pot of tea, m'dear."

"Where did you find all those things?"

"Remember that old poppet-maker? She evidently appeared at the inn's main door, asking to peddle her herbs. The innkeeper was about to send her off, but I happened to be down there after your stew. She said this combination would soothe you, put energy in your limbs, and set your blood to coursing. The faster your blood runs, the faster you'll heal, you know." He stripped off his shirt, leaving bare the trim, hard muscles hewn of the winter life, his chest still shapely and enticing, though his ribs showed below and his waist was too narrow. Katie loved every line, since each meant some sacrifice or other. Slowly he began untying the ribbons holding together the bodice of her chemise, one at a time, savoring each. He helped her sit up, gently tugged the chemise from beneath her thighs, and eased it over her head. It puffed like daisy petals on the floor.

"There we are," he murmured, seeming satisfied as he lifted her naked body into his arms. His bareness was moist against her cool skin, and oh, so warm. . . . "You tell me if it's too hot." He eased her feet into the tub.

"Oh, it *is* hot," she said, clinging to his neck.

"Too hot?"

"No . . . not too hot . . . oh, it feels so strange! Imagine a bath so warm! I always thought hot water would cook a person as it does a hen's carcass."

She sat on the barrel's edge, on a piece of cloth Will had put between her and the splintery wood; for the first time she saw her body—a mass of white skin and yellow bruises marbled with terrible purple veins. Her legs and arms bore a parquetry of scratches. They must have been very bad scratches still to be scabbed after two whole weeks. She snapped her eyes shut and turned away from herself.

"Katie—" Will caught her chin gently. "Never turn away from a good win. These bruises are prizes gained in a valiant joust. Were they mine, I'd count them and tell the world."

A tear trailed down her face through a veil of perspiration from the steam. "I would you hadn't seen me this way," choked a whisper.

"Katie . . ."

"I wish always to be perfect for you."

Will dropped a kiss on her shoulder. "What would perfection be without courage? I've seen 'perfect' women. I didn't like them."

Tears kept coming, but suddenly she laughed. They pressed foreheads and rocked in an embrace for long moments. Then Katie shivered, and Will insisted that she lower into the bath.

"Oh, it feels unnatural!"

"But not unpleasant?" Will sat on a stool and hung over the barrel's edge.

"No," she conceded, "quite savory, really. It cannot be healthy."

"Not for healthy folk. But you are sick folk. On you it will have the opposite effect. Relax completely, and when you feel capable, begin moving your legs—not much but enough to use your muscles and joints. I, in the meantime, intrepid hero that I am, shall set about soothing your fine skin with sunflower oil. If you fail to turn into a flower, I shall be disgraced."

Katie laughed, lying back against the rim and letting her head loll. "Doubtless I'll be forever spoiled to hard work. I'll need a dozen servants to tend me from now on."

Will only grinned as he wadded a stonewashed cloth and poured oil onto it. He'd give her a thousand servants if he could. Yet these bruises might as well have come from his own hand. He should have taken her north. To Sheffield. Or York. He should have insisted. "You need no servants," he said quietly. "You have me." Without meeting her eyes he dipped the oilcloth into the water and pulled it up her body, watching it mold to her floating breasts, then drew it up along her throat, over her shoulder, and down her arm. The process was sensually repeated with the other arm. Steam glossed his bare upper body and crinkled his hair, making Katie wish the tub was big enough for two. She thought back with fond regrets to a time when he had offered himself to her in an ebony pond under the moon.

The steam filled her head, veiling her mind in sensation. Will's hands upon her body became broad, caressing leaves in a luscious garden. Katie gave in to a wave of dizziness and closed her eyes, letting her head drop back. Will's cloth rolled against her throat. The hot water was a tingling glove, consuming her as a lake consumes a floating flower, and Will was the warming sun.

Like a separate being, her own hand broke

the water's oily surface and drifted to her shoulder where his hand was moving the cloth, and her palm lay across his knuckles, finally returning his caresses. In silence she guided his hand along her body and down deep into the dark water, to the core of her womanhood. Her thighs enjoyed him, her eyes enjoyed him, her hand showed him her love. A complete and willing love.

"I wish I was better," she murmured. "I want to be a woman for you."

His thoughts must have been similar, Katie mused. He started a wonderful game—he was planting kisses along her arm, ever so slowly, each kiss a work of art, then afterward he would wipe each kiss off with the oilcloth. He lifted her hair, gathered it over her shoulder, getting across to her bare neck, and his game commenced.

Long citrine hair floated out before Katie, cloaking her bruised body; suddenly that brave, distant feeling returned. Why were they hiding? They had done nothing wrong!

The power of Will's touch made her long for recuperation. She leaned into his hands, drawing strength, her eyes drifting closed in the luxury of his fingers and his lips.

"Will," she murmured, "what was it like at the start? When the regency trouble first surfaced and you took to the forest? The change must have been most drastic and unsettling for you."

He gave a short, dispensing shrug, as though he never really thought of those days. But he remembered them quite easily, more so than he might have anticipated.

"Not so very unsettling," he admitted, and Katie knew the truth was coming. A lesser man would have stretched the opportunity. "In the beginning it was only Robin and me, shivering in the Greenwood. Once Sir Guy and the prince knew of our plans to revolt, there was no safety in returning to Gamewell or Locksley Hall. Gradually we met or recruited others, mostly displaced nobles and ravaged Saxon townsmen who'd been burned out or tortured or taxed out. Robin's burden grew heavier by the day, but he kept saying it was a sweet burden with all of us to help him bear it. You saw the Greenwood children—in faith, now you know them as well as their parents do. Who knows what atrocities might have befallen them had not Robin stuck his neck out."

"Such an abrupt change must have been difficult," Katie said, "going from comfort and wealth to a foresting life. I know. I went from the forest to the warmth of Edward's home then back to the forest."

"Aye, it was. At first I loathed it. It was cold and damp, even in summer, with only our cloaks to cover us. My teeth nearly chattered out of my skull. Robin tried to make me go home, but I wasn't about to let him think he could tolerate more than I could."

"And you'd never have left him alone, anyway."

"Rubbish. I'd have let him rot in a moment for a warm blanket."

Katie laughed. Her ribs ached, but the laughter felt so good, she allowed herself more of it. "Don't worry, Will. I believe you. Of course I do."

"Vixen."

"What is it about Robin that made him give up all he had, to fight such a hopeless battle?"

"Hopeless?"

"Oh, worthwhile, to be sure, at least for now. The Greenwood is a sanctuary for desperate families. But there's little hope for the future. Eventually Prince John will become king, and we'll be back in the same bucket. Even if Richard does return, he'll die someday, and John will have the crown."

"Not if Richard marries and has a child. Once we free him from that Austrian beggar, he'll come home where he belongs and have the sense not to leave anymore. A single big shock is enough to blow a man's brains into shape."

"Or a woman's."

"Pardon?"

"Will, what did Gisbourne mean when he said you were of Norman blood?"

"Exactly that. Why?"

"I thought . . . I assumed . . ."

"My dear, did you really think *Montfichet* was a Saxon name?" he reminded, pronouncing it as it would have been said in Normandy.

"Then Robin—"

"Is Saxon throughout." The puzzlement in her expression made him smile. "My mother was Saxon, but I was raised Norman. Do you doubt me now?"

"You could be a Norman prince and I wouldn't doubt you. After all I've seen and know, how could you ask?"

"I saw the suspense in your eyes. Did you imagine I would support a Plantagenet king yet think only Saxons to be superior? No one is superior. Justice is justice. I don't have to be Saxon to believe that." He paused, dried the oil from his hands, found a comb, and carefully began combing out the lengths of her hair, beginning from the ends.

"You never finished."

"Finished what?"

"Telling me about Robin. Why he feels as he does. Feels for the others, I mean."

"I have never known."

"What?"

"Completely true. Certainly I understand his compassion now and know he's totally right, but where it stems from I've no idea. Since childhood Robin's had trouble tolerating injustice. Perhaps someone was unjust to him. Or he may have witnessed some event, but I never heard it from him."

"And you've never been curious?"

"Nary a whit."

"I would have been. I can't believe you never asked in all your time together. Why would you risk your life without knowing his motivation?"

A light pensiveness came over him as he busied his hands with braiding her hair. Though it was still wet, a tight braid would make beautiful waves later. "I go with Robin. He's never cheated me, and his causes always seemed more noble than mine. So I go along. Besides . . . he needs me. He says I steady him. And life is fun with him."

Katie scoffed, "Now that's less than noble. And I've seen some of the 'fun.' "

"Aye, there are rough times also. A struggle

just to eat. But we have our rewards." He stopped braiding her hair, sat back, sighing once, and squeezed the end of the braid absently. His gaze drifted to the window. "No, I . . . I don't know what drives Robert Fitzooth to become Robin Hood. He went from a soft life at Locksley to the Greenwood with hardly a ruffle. No transition at all. It was as though he merely reentered another life well known from some former existence. He's a fun-lover and a troublemaker from boyhood, more interested in adventure than anything, yet I watched him take on the burden of other folks' troubles as though destiny put him in charge. As though he had no option." Will shrugged then, and the touch of puzzlement left his face. "Nor did he want any. Perhaps generosity has no source."

He finished braiding her hair in a dozen thin plaits, and with no excuse to do more there, he dipped into the water and lifted her left leg, then wadded a cloth on the barrel rim for her ankle to rest upon. Out came more oil from the small bottle. He gave her a mischievous grin before kissing her big toe. These were playful kisses as they traveled along her foot, invested in the roundness of her ankle bone, finally to grace her calf and her bent knee. She smiled at the tickling sensation of his lips and tongue, followed by an oily swipe with the cloth. Her skin glowed now. Her heart shined.

"Promise me a silly promise, though I feel embarrassed even to ask it," she said impulsively.

"You wish to see me run naked through the town square with silk scarves upon my ankles."

"No."

"You wish me to tell you about the time I was hurt so badly that your paltry wounds pale against my pure spirit of survival."

She laughed. "No."

"Well, all right, you demanding wraith, what impossible star must I catch for you?"

"I want to return to Greenwoodside."

He sat back. "You want what?"

"As soon as I'm better, I must go back."

"Katie," he began, then paused to find the best phrases. "You were afraid in the forest. That's why I brought you here. Those people bothered you."

"Only some of them," she defended, "and only because I allowed them to intimidate me. Why did I? None of that is important now. With you beside me and my life in my charge, am I justified in fearing anything? We must go back. Or I must, even if I go alone. I must confront what I've been running from."

Will's hands drifted to his lap, dripping water onto the wood floor. He stared at them, his expression changing several times.

Time rolled to a lazy stop. Outside, even the sounds of the bustling town seemed to drop away.

"If truly you must have revenge," he said dubiously, seeming not to wholy approve. He did not finish.

Katie once might have retreated from his disapproval or from the harsh implications which she knew were his real worries. Today she did not. She remained as relaxed as the hot bath made her, without a quiver of doubt.

"Not revenge," she said. Her voice was a rock. "Respect."

A rap at the warped door rescued Will from responding. Somehow, instantly, his dagger appeared in his hand. He placed his shoulder against the door. "Who is it?"

"Innkeeper."

"What do you want?"

"I got bedding."

"You're alone?"

"I am."

Will opened the door. A hunched old man with gnarled hands slouched his way into the room carrying blankets. He dumped his armload on Katie's bed, then spoke to Will, ignoring the dagger. "You done wi' them bowls? I'll take 'em." He collected the bowl of half-eaten stew. "You want more?"

"No."

"Yes," Katie corrected. Will had not eaten yet, her eyes reminded them.

The innkeeper snorted. "I kin warm this up." He took Will's elbow and pulled him aside, a gesture less necessary than the old man wanted to believe. "They came looking for you again. They wanted to look in all the rooms. I tell'd 'em we had sickness here and best they not. They wen' away, but they'll come back."

A low groan rumbled in Will's throat. His eyes narrowed. "We're no longer safe here, is what you're saying."

"I could move you t'another room."

"Would do no good. I'll arrange to move her this evening. Hold them off as long as you can."

The innkeeper left, never casting a single

glance in Katie's direction. That may have been the possessive power of Will standing nearby or pure common sense—keeping the innkeeper distant from the fugitives he was harboring.

Will drew his shirt back on. If a man would face death, he should be clothed. "Gisbourne is acting out a vendetta against me."

"Not only you," Katie said. "We humiliated him together."

Suddenly Will's tone shriveled. "We were not together in his tent outside Sherwood. I once yearned to know what passed between you then, that night, but I no longer want to know. Whatever did, it seems important to Sir Guy. Few men, apparently, are cold-blooded to you, Katie."

"This is not my doing," she protested. Yet how could she utter such disclaimers when all this was indeed her doing? She hardly remembered what foolishness possessed her to beg Will to take her from the safety of the Greenwood, to run from a danger not truly there. When she wished to leave, she needn't have asked Will to risk his life to take her away. She should have left the Greenwood alone, kept her problems to herself.

This must be remembered. Never again would she shift her own liabilities onto other shoulders.

No matter how robust those shoulders were.

Will stalked to the window, appearing harsh, steeling himself for the conflict lurking at the end of their day. Within himself he knew his sudden disgruntlement was a weapon, a type of armor, as unavoidable in tense moments as anger or love in their proper times. "Aye, you may not be the direct cause of it, but you're lurking at its core." He sighed out a decisive breath. "We'll leave after dark. I know a few Saxon strongholds where we may be safe for a day or two. Places Sir Guy might not think to look." He continued to gaze out the window, not staring but rather watching every movement below in the street, scanning the countryside beyond houses and shops, seeing things Katie could only imagine as she luxuriated in the bath.

"Yes, I see the deputies," Will said, squinting and leaning cautiously over the sill. "Gisbourne must have had the ways out of town blockaded. It's the only way he could suspect I would still be in Nottingham. We have the advantage. He thinks you're dead. He will not be looking for a man and a woman but only for a man. Me." The stool creaked as he sat again, his eyes slimming in thought. "Which urges me to think. Perhaps the wiser course would be—"

"No!" Katie forced her body forward against waves of sharp pain. Bones ground against each other beneath her left breast. She clutched the barrel's edges. "There will be no splitting up. I'll hear none of it!"

His hand opened in entreaty. "I could get away on Palermo. You would be free to escape in some sedate and safer way. It makes great sense."

"No! I won't do it!"

"Katie, I shall be perfectly fine."

She leaned even farther forward in defiance of the pain seeking to swallow her. "You cannot deprive me!"

A force, a demon, a spirit of some breed rose in her, consuming the last vestiges of timidity, fueling itself with the possibility of being left behind, until it raged beyond control in its white heat. Will watched it grow with every bit of the abomination he had felt about her hopelessness when first they met. Was she retreating? Perhaps her injuries had distorted her reason. Or was she moving forward into a deeper horror? Will tried to understand as he stared at her, hesitant to interfere as her battle ensued. Should he stop its flight, or would the wise course be to let this new aspect play itself out? If he stopped it, she might forever suffer from wondering, and that could be a vastly sorer damage than wounds.

Since no cooling could douse the flame he saw, he cleared his throat and carefully said, "We stay together."

The water gushed over the rim. Wet wood accepted bruised shoulders. Katie closed her eyes. Pain filled her.

There was silence in the Boar's Tail, in the upper room, until nearly nightfall. Katie's small tirade had drained her strength, and she slept. The day went away in her sleep. She slept soundly and without stirring, knowing Will watched over her, waiting, tending, allowing her to work through this new excursion in her own time, and knowing he would never leave her here. A less clever man might steal away and lead the deputies off in the wrong direction, leaving her to be angry that he had deceived her and made the decision in spite of her, even though to save her life. But Will knew that Katie's life was her own. He was

giving her the dignity of making her own decisions, however foolish, however deadly. Will's
personal honor was a deep-running river. So
he stayed.

Katie awakened this time not to the gentle
wafting of herbal aromas but to a clamor of
horse hooves on the hard dirt below her window. She bolted to a sitting position. Her spine
clicked, but she ignored it, her attention caught
by a figure crossing the room in unexpected
darkness. Why were the candles not lit?

As she blinked to clear her eyes the dim
moonlit sky disappeared behind one black-on-
black shutter, then the second. The sky winked
out.

"Will?" Her voice was a rasping whisper.

"They're here. Can you walk?"

She felt in the darknes for her chemise, then
for the sturdy support of the bedpost. Her
right leg behaved well enough, but the left
knee would hold none of her weight without
buckling. Bracing herself on the wall, Katie
forced her leg to do its job in spite of pain that
moved to her head, dizzying her beyond sensation. Her eyes adjusted somewhat to the near
total darkness but only enough to navigate into
a corner.

There was surge of air. A dagger hilt was
shoved into her hand.

"You wanted to fight. You wanted nothing
to do with reason. Now you have your wish. If
you were a Christian, I'd suggest you start
praying."

Through the darkness she asked, "Are you
angry with me?"

"With you or your injuries, I've not yet decided. Katie, only a fool resists a good plan. Whatever happens to me, stay in this corner."

He sank into the shadows. Katie squinted, trying to see him, but there was only the outline of a shoulder several paces away.

Within Katie burned the deep desire, the need, to fight, to claim—

Revenge?

She had never considered it. Or perhaps she had never considered it by that name.

The desire gripped her dagger for her. Only that power turned the blade outward, ready for a low thrust to some man's genitals.

There was a shuffling noise outside their window. Something scraped the inn's outer surface.

The two of them sank into the walls. Katie willed her knees to lock, the pain in her body to fuse with fear and become anger. Only if she was ready to die could she fight insanely enough to live.

A creaking noise pierced the silence. The shutters parted, letting in the night. A trace of moonlight. Silhouetted there crouched a cloaked figure, tall, bending over to peer into the room. He pushed the shutters in wide before him.

Katie began to tremble uncontrollably. Her legs and thighs shook until the pain surged back.

The figure dropped into the room and stood to full height. A floor-length cape slipped from the sill and washed around him. He stood still, listening. Katie held her breath, though the pain in her ribs and chest nearly drove her to faint.

The cloaked figure signaled out the window,

bringing in seconds a moving yellow glow like witch light outside. Wobbling like the moon on a lake, the yellowness drew closer and filled the window, drawing its source up behind. Another cloaked being, face hidden in a deep hood, climbed through the window carrying a lantern.

Katie's heart jumped into her throat. In the weak light she saw Will hiding behind the half barrel of water. They might not see him, but in instants they would see her.

The two hoods turned, scanning the room along the lamp glow's rim.

Soon they faced her.

"Ah . . ." brushed a voice, "there you are."

Will sprang up from behind the tub. Katie waited for the smell of blood.

But it was not in attack that Will rushed from his hiding place. His sword clattered to the floor.

In the same thought the first cloaked figure brushed back his hood.

Will rasped, "*Robin.*"

The two came together, embracing hard and for a long time.

"Greetings, scarlet oak," Robin said, clutching him tightly around the shoulders. "Told you you'd get into trouble without me."

Clinging to him, Will wheezed, "I thought you were Gisbourne."

His cousin patted his back, then held him away, maintaining the tactile bond. "I nearly was. They've almost closed in on you, Will. Best we go, and now."

Will's hands were cold as he absorbed Robin's presence. He was no longer alone in his

care of Katie. Now he had help. He sought her
out in the gauzy yellow glow.

Her legs had given up. She lay crumpled
against the wall, her palm pressing the wood,
the fingers of her other hand limp as the knife
lay in them.

Will rushed to her. Robin came with him.

"Katie, Katie," Will murmured. He gathered
her into his arms. "Come, little warrior. We're
going home."

• *Chapter Fourteen* •

A few weeks later, after the frustration of having Will Scarlet and Katie Chenoweth slip through his grasp and escape from Nottingham somehow—Scarlet had always been nearly a shadow when it came to getting away—Sir Guy paced the outer cell of the Abbey of the Sacred Heart in Southwell. He had already waited too long, considering that he was unaccustomed to waiting at all. Few men in these shires had the audacity to set Guy of Gisbourne second to anything else, but this Abbot Godfrey proved a nervy fellow indeed. As he paced, angrier with every step, he replayed that night in his mind. Shadows, fleeing ghosts of riders and runners, swordsmen and archers, all lashing out at him and his men under cover of night. Somehow Gamewell had gotten word to Locksley, and the legions of the forest had rushed to his aid. Even crueller than the humiliation before his men was the loss of a woman he particularly desired. And the loss of her to Gamewell, of all men. In his fury Gisbourne had also learned that Locksley and Gamewell would not be cornered with brute force or open confrontation. He learned he would have to become stealthier, and that knowledge would lead him to the cell of a minor clergyman who had a particularly curious trail of rumors and whispers following after his name whenever it was mentioned.

Gisbourne shoved back his sword as it hung on his crossbelt, muttered an oath on the grave of his mother, and rammed his way through the door as though it did not exist.

"How dare you keep me waiting like common street rabble!" The sound echoed through the high-ceilinged chapel. "I'll have an audience with you and right now!"

The abbot turned slowly, only a half turn, from where he stood with two altar boys near the center of the chapel. He nodded, brows raised, in a most indignant manner, and calculatedly infuriated Gisbourne further by slowly snuffing out one taper, then another; he then cleaned the bells of the snuffers and paused to genuflect. Finally he moved toward Sir Guy but not too close. "Your lordship," he said in a sugary tone, "you risk desecration of God's house. What may I do for you, in His name?"

"In His name, nothing," Gisbourne snarled. "In the name of civil peace, quite a lot. For several months I've tried to vanquish the band led by Robert of Locksley, who lays siege upon the road between here and Nottingham. For months I've struggled in vain. And recently I have discovered an unusually large stream of trade flowing between Southwell and the town of Lincoln, northeast of here. Also curious is the fact that Nottingham pays no tithes to you but to the Bishop of Darley, while Lincoln lies within your sphere of influence. As Lincoln prospers your pockets grow fatter."

The abbot rubbed the great wooden cross around his neck, fondling the silver studs decorating it. "Sir, you malign me most unfairly. I am pledged to holy poverty."

"I see no poverty here. Your robes are silk. Your bed has many coverlets. Your face is fleshy from rich food. Your chalices are wrought of fine metals. Lincoln's merchant guilds are paying you to keep the Cart Road closed. Is that not true, Abbot?"

The abbot smiled, pretending a pious simplicity that turned Gisbourne's stomach. Instead of a halo he wore a sniggering triumph. He was protecting himself well, and Sir Guy knew it. The abbot had let none of his confidence slip, kept his mask securely in place, locked by years of careful practice under stricter scrutiny than Gisbourne's. "Let me offer you wine, my liege."

"The finest coin can buy, no doubt," snapped the nobleman. Beneath his beard Gisbourne felt his skin prickle. "I did not come here to sip your tainted plunder, priest. I mean to get that road open in spite of you. You will cease your efforts to keep it closed. Cease this very day."

"Good master, my daily vespers are filled with prayers that the outlaws release the Cart Road to decent tradesmen. How may I convince you? The folk of Southwell wish to trade with your fair town, but all who pass there are ravaged. Surely this is not *my* fault. Or do you think a simple servant of God might hold sway with the likes of Locksley? Why, I die at the thought."

"Did you also die at the thought of sending Katie Chenoweth into their hands, hoping they would do your dirty job for you and keep a heretic from gaining approval within your parish?"

For a fleeting instant, as quick and as dreamlike as a bird's whistle, the abbot dropped his facade and stood baldly shocked before Gisbourne. In that instant the truth was revealed.

The abbot turned away quickly, to hide his indiscretion, then turned back almost immediately, his mask once more in place. "Mistress Chenoweth volunteered to approach the outlaws. I begged her to reconsider, but she heard naught of my pleas."

"You're a liar, your Grace."

The abbot held up his palms in innocence. "Then I shall burn in hell. I have proof for you to see."

"Evidence, you mean. Evidence you're careful to destroy at every step."

"My lord, the day has been long. I must bid you good—"

"I have found out," Gisbourne plowed on, "that you have a spy living among the outlaws. Living among them, sharing their food, warming at their fires. Who is it? I demand to know."

The abbot waved his hand casually. "You imagine things, good sire."

"I imagine my hands around your throat if you don't tell me. I've sent men to infiltrate them, but without exception my spies are found out. How is it that you succeed where I have failed?"

"I have no spies."

"You have a spy!"

"Who has told you this story?"

Gisbourne grunted. "My spies might not be clever enough to outwit the Hood, but they *are* clever enough to outwit you. They led me to the news and I want to know who it is." Gisbourne watched the abbot's face, reading the hairline sneer of satisfaction there, and knew, beyond doubt, that his information had been correct. His buckle and sword jingled as he paced around the abbot like a circling hawk. "And since you have a spy there, you must know where the Hood's camp is. How is it reached? Through Northman's Pass? By pacing away from the river? By intersecting the sun with two trees? How? Tell me, curse you! I must know!" His hands closed into fists, his arms trembling with restrained rage.

The abbot tipped his head in a mocking brand of submission and put a few carefully measured paces between himself and Gisbourne. "My good sire," he began in a tone as exasperating as it was placating, "you are dreadfully mistaken. You have been led to pawn by someone much cleverer than I. . . ." His hand lay across his heart. "I am merely a servant of God, a shepherd to a small flock, an insignificant—"

Gisbourne thundered across the rush floor, smashing Godfrey up against the nearest wall. "You secondary prelate! Your spy has been living among the outlaws for months! You could have broken the siege months ago by telling the location of Locksley's camp! Dozens of lives might have been saved! Wasted money put to better use! Instead you've lined your pockets with silver from Lincolntown while Notting-ham lies waiting for the road to open and trade to begin again with Southwell. Tell me where their camp is! I command you!"

Through the chapel the echo of Gisbourne's words rang, fading to silence only after engulf-ing the two matched men in their own mutual hatred, power against power, influence versus opulence.

Gisbourne's wide knuckles pressed into the abbot's throat. Pure disgust rolled in his gut for this travesty of holiness.

The abbot tried to swallow, then rasped, "You may murder me, sir, but God alone commands me. He will judge you."

Rumbling with rage, Gisbourne tightened his hands at Godfrey's jugular, closer . . . closer . . .

A growl began deep within him, escaping as a loud shout of frustration and fury. He threw Godfrey to one side and stalked off several steps. Then he rammed his fist into the collec-tion receptacle. A glitter of offertory coins ex-ploded and spun all over the floor at the abbot's feet.

"I wish you would take up a sword and face me like an honorable man," Gisbourne grum-bled fiercely, eyes like ice. "Then I would know what to do with you."

The abbot rubbed his throat, still leaning on the pew where he had been thrown. "My liege would surely wax victorious with sword in hand. I have naught but faith to wield. I am only a poor man of God."

"You are nothing of God. You're a pirate."

Silence crawled like insects between them. Gisbourne could deal with treachery, with troublemakers, with rogues, robbers, knights, landmongers, battlelords, or challengers. But this tidy brand of practiced deceit, this polished corruption made him ill, sapped his ability to defend honor by the sword or obey the proper codes of chivalry. There could be no chivalry here if he was the only bastion of it. No matter how he called upon honor, the abbot would twist his efforts with a simplistic, delicate lace of lies. The abbot had only to wave the cross between them, and he was protected as if by a spell.

"I'll have you," Gisbourne swore. "When I return to this town, I will fight you. I will fill the ears of your parishioners with the truth about you and your dealings against them. Mind that."

The powerful threat showed in the abbot's face only as a defiant twitch.

"The truth will be known," Gisbourne added.

The abbot raised his eyebrows. "I have always striven to instill the Truth in my flock."

"Mark me, pulpiteer. Your trick on Katie was the beginning of your end."

"Good day, my liege."

"Mark me."

"Good *day*."

March twenty-first. It was the year 1194 in the dominance of the Christian savior, and winter was over. Sunshine came more often and longer each time, and what had been snow became rain. The people of Greenwoodside huddled less and less, their fires no longer the centers of their lives, and slowly they began the process of warming themselves and hacking out graves from the thawing ground to finally bury the swaddled corpses of the less lucky. Thanks to Katie and Will, several trade wagons had ventured through Sherwood with "scarlet oak" on drivers' lips, providing at least a meager emergency stock of food or a few extra coins. Now that spring was coming, wagons came more frequently.

Thanks to this glimmer of success, Katie noticed a definite improvement in the attitudes toward her. Part of it was gratitude. Folk realized now that even a pagan could perform nobly and come back scarred. Another part of it was guilt. Katie was treated quite well now, making it easy to ignore the leftover glares from Nell. Nell had once been the leader of antagonism; now she was alone in it, and her prey no longer heard her.

And there were friends in the forest now who cared not if Katie was demon or Druid, angel or dragon; the Four Swords had miraculously survived their endless bleeding and thrown in their lot with the Hood.

Winter had taken several lives, but most of the children, including Edith Small's baby boy, survived. For this Katie was especially glad. Edith's tiny Alexander now stood a fair chance of living to adulthood. Winter's deepest pain had come when Greenwoodside realized the purpose of the baby's survival. He was a replacement, they decided. But this had not quelled Katie's sorrow when, in the ravages of a winter sickness, the intelligent child Gwennie coughed up blood, convulsed in Edith's arms, and died. Life was fleeting here.

Katie's body spent weeks knitting back to health. Each draw of breath was an excursion into pain until the bones in her ribs ceased their grinding and fused to some semblance of their original unity. The ability to walk straight without wincing came even later. After that, weakness had to be beaten. She ate only perforce; her body still resisted food, her stomach greatly shrunken by weeks of unconsciousness at the inn. Recuperation came slowly and only as the result of long walks Katie would demand of herself. She went every day into the woods, moving from tree to tree as far as she could manage until dizziness and enfeeblement left her clinging to a tree trunk, gulping in air. Then she would have to turn and walk back. She always went alone and hid her walks from Will. She wanted no help.

Each day she walked in a new direction. One day to the river. One day to the gorge. One day near the road. But not too near. Never too near.

One day she noticed the smell of a camp fire. Her memory flickered back to the day she and Will had first left the Greenwood, dressed outrageously, when she asked Will who those women were. The women who served.

Thoughts to turn away succumbed to the fire's enticing scent. Curiosity placed its hand in the center of her back and gave that final push.

Four women looked up at her approach. Two of them stood immediately and walked away without even the slightest ceremony. The remaining two glared, silent.

"I'd like to stop and rest by your fire," Katie requested. "My name is Katie Chenoweth."

"We know you," barked the older of the two, a woman thin almost to gauntness, with small green eyes, a wrinkling mouth, and hair gray around her face.

"We know all there is to know," snapped the other. This one was sturdier with drooping breasts and a smooth face, except for two dramatic jowl lines either side of her mouth. She tossed a handful of kindling into the fire and set it spitting. "Sure. Siddown. Warm yourself."

A circlet of head-size rocks ringed the fire. Katie sat down and placed her feet flat against one of them, silent until her toes were toasty warm.

"You be Will Scarlet's woman," the swarthy younger woman said. It did not sound like any kind of question.

"I am my own woman. I do love Will Scarlet."

The woman sat back mockingly and whistled. "Ain't you the little peahen."

Katie shrugged without apology. "I am no one's property. What's your name?"

"Ruth, I'm called. You know. Like in the Bible."

Giving her the smile she seemed to need, Katie said, "Yes, I know. I've always thought it a grand sort of name. Most powerful."

The older woman chortled at Ruth's expense. "Aye, she's got power. When she wraps them chunky thighs around a man, he knows he's been wrapped." She struggled to her feet and tugged her shawl closed at her throat. "Best watch thyself, peahen. You took away Ruth's main customer."

Katie knew Will was a quick-blooded man and had been so long before she came along, yet this unexpected twist of fate dealt her a stunning blow, silencing her in obvious unease until long after the older woman vanished into a nearby tent. Ruth was looking at her. She could feel it. Though she expected some disclaimer from Ruth, none came. Finally she no longer could avoid Ruth's unashamed eyes.

"I'm sorry," Katie said lamely, "I did not know."

"And what would he be if he told you? I never claimed him mine," the rough voice responded. Ruth sat up straight, twisting sideways and lifting her chin. "I done a good job with him. Proud of it I am."

"Do you ... do you eat well enough out so far? Are you able to keep warm?"

"It's a warm business we're in out here."

"Yes, I ... I can imagine. Thank you for your hospitality, but I must—"

"Stay."

"Pardon?"

"You stay. Or you'll never be sure."

Katie quivered unexplainably. "I don't understand," she lied.

"You do," Ruth corrected. "You know how I live. I live off the leavings of them others. Off Will Scarlet. It was him kept me warm nigh since I came to the woods."

This sudden, unaccustomed threat took hold of a pale throat. Swallowing through it was impossible. "I'm so sorry ... I never knew of this. I had no idea."

"That's why, now that you've stumbled on us, you have to stay and listen. I got no stomach for tenderness. If I let it in, it would kill me, so I don't. That Will . . . well, he can make a woman pant, but I ain't got to tell you that, do I? I'm just a stray dog to Greenwoodside, but I know my place. Because I do, Will Scarlet can survive in this wretched piss pot. He's nothin' but a hot supper to me, and I'm nothin' but a hot hole to him. An' that's healthy, my girl. Pity might not get me into heaven when I die, but usefulness won't keep me out. If any woman is the death of Will Scarlet, 'twill be you, not me. Here. Have a bit of bread."

"You must forgive me. . . . This is all very sudden."

"Not so very sudden. I been thinking about it for a long time, wonderin' and ponderin' what I'd say to you if ever you happened along my path." She paused to gnaw a piece of bread torn from a round loaf. With a full mouth she went on. "Never thought of you being his type. You must be smart in the head. He always liked these," she said, flopping her large breasts with one hand, "and you ain't got them like I do. It must be your brains he likes. You must have nice *big* brains."

Katie still had trouble conversing with Ruth. She forced down the proffered clump of bread, thinking only of Will and Will's lovemaking, avoiding, not successfully, visions of him thrashing with this woman. The image was unexpected and totally unsavory. Instantly she called herself to blame for the bad taste of it, a crude vision based on slim knowledge of the woman across the fire; the crudeness reflected more on Katie than on Ruth, who at least carried no pretenses in her unbaked view of the world and of herself.

"Where are you from, Ruth?"

"Me? People like me don't come from nowhere. We hatch under rocks, then we learn to stand up on our own two legs. Or one leg when we have to." She made a vulgar, though vivid, enactment with her hands. "Anyway, I come from Laxton. That's up north."

"I know Laxton. I'm from Southwell, you see."

"And what brings me into this kind of business?"

"On, I don't want to pry." She met Ruth's eyes without timidity for the first time. "You needn't justify yourself to me any more than I need explain my choice of trade to you. This is simply a walk in the woods to me, nothing more. Unless ... of course ... we might be friends."

A chunk of bread fell from Ruth's lips. "Friends? Hah. I'll talk to you, but I don't never want to be your friend."

"But why not?"

"Too risky."

"Then we'll talk."

"Glad to."

"What shall we talk about?"

"You wanted to know how I came to be in this business."

"I never asked, but if you feel I should know ..."

"Every woman should know, peahen. Every woman's in danger of becoming me. As long as there was men, there was women like me. Always been, always gonna be. And a good lucky thing it is. Without us they'd all die."

Katie spoke slowly, curious now beyond tact. "I don't mean to demean your importance but . . . why would they die?"

"Simple. Women like you would kill 'em."

"Are you trying to intimidate me?" Calmness ruled her tone, but it was the same corrupt calmness she had used on Nell. It reeked with pretense. The old shroud. Katie vowed her next sentence would be genuine.

Ruth leaned forward, eyes widened. "Peahen, I don't got to intimidate you. You're a disaster all on your own. If Will Scarlet dies, it'll be because of you."

"How will it be my fault?"

"Never said it would be your fault. Said it would be because of you."

"But I don't understand why."

"Is you planning to marry him?"

"I suppose marriage is in our future."

"Keep it there. Way far in the future. Keep yourself out of his mind. Throw away them brains. Let him play in your lady curls and forget they're not mine. Be his whore. And, girl . . . don't be nothing more."

The advice set an echo tolling. It tolled through every excuse or dismissal or coloration Katie shoved upon it, looking for silence all the way back to Greenwoodside. She told herself Ruth was jealous. Ruth wanted to degrade her. Ruth wanted Will to herself. She told herself that Ruth was greedy. Ruth aspired to be Will's wife someday. Ruth wanted Will's money.

Greenwoodside huddled before her. She

stopped at the first of the tents and gazed at the tiny community. Ruth was not jealous. Ruth didn't want Will's money. Ruth laid no claims to Will's love. By the time Katie forced herself toward Will's tent, the most prominent memory from her conversation with Ruth was the naked affection for Will. It had shown in Ruth's eyes. She had, in her raw manner, been begging for Will's life, even if she never saw him again.

Will was in his tent. When Katie came in, he lit a candle. "Where've you been? It's nearly dark."

She sat on the sheepskin beside their sleeping mat. "I've been taking walks. To bring strength back to my legs."

"Oh? I don't know of them."

"I didn't tell you. Now that I'm nearly better, I can tell you."

"Why—"

"I wanted to do it alone. I needed to work my body. You would have helped me too much."

"Come and lie with me."

He was naked beneath the covers. Ruth's words rippled on Katie's skin as she removed her gown, leaving on her linen chemise, and joined him.

"You feel better," he groaned, snuggling her close.

"Yes, I do."

"I mean you *feel* better. To me. Your arms and legs. They feel solid and strong again."

"Because of my walks."

"Perhaps we can walk together from now on." He guided her hand to his lips and kissed each finger in sequence, then the center of her palm. "Mm?"

"I walked east of the camp today, Will," Katie suddenly admitted, surprising even herself. She hadn't intended to tell him. Evidently the forces, the Goddess, the God, the conflict, all seemed to have other plans.

He stiffened beside her. "You mean, you . . ."

"I spoke to the camp followers. I spoke to Ruth."

Will stopped breathing. When he began again, it came as a heave. He covered his face with one hand. "Oh, dear." Pushing out from beneath her, he sat up.

Katie raised herself on her elbow. "You never told me."

Hesitation chopped his words. "You can see how it would be awkward."

"How could you keep from me something so intensely personal to your identity? I thought I knew you."

"A man has needs . . . I can't, I won't explain to you."

"You need explain nothing to one who has been a wife and knows a man's needs, Will Scarlet."

"Then you must know you've no call to be grudging about Ruth."

"Have you been to see her since I came to the Greenwood?"

"No," he said hurriedly, "not since I first loved you. I swear, not once. Lord, I'm disappointed in you, Katie. Such concerns are beneath you."

"You've never even gone back to her once?"

"I've been faithful to you. But I suppose with

her so near and since you were so ill, you have difficulty believing me—"

"Will, how could you?" She sat up beside him, seeking his face in the candle glow.

"If you must know of every woman I bedded before we met, then I've misjudged you."

"How could you abandon her?"

Will raised his head, eyes squinted in question. "Eh?"

"She helped you. She took care of you all those months. You left her derelict, without so much as a thank-you. Will, you must go back to her. You must show her you're all right. That you haven't forgotten how much she helped you when the tension begged release. It's important. She cares for you."

"My God, Katie, she's a trull. A plaything."

"You know she is not. No man can spend so many hours with a woman and learn nothing about her. Think about those times. There must have been talk as well as whoring."

"Katie—"

"Do I surprise you?"

"Constantly. I hardly know what to say."

"Say nothing to me, then. Think of what you might say to her."

Will turned on his thigh to face her. He felt her shoulder, running his hand down her soft arm, taking the sleeve of her chemise down to her elbow. Her breast tugged against the fallen bodice. "You are the most generous creature I've ever known."

"Not so generous." She lowered her eyes. "At first I was hurt when Ruth told me about the two of you. But I soon reasoned it out. I cannot forever dwell on the needs of your past any more

than you should linger over my love for Edward.
I shall dwell only on your needs now."

Her hands slipped beneath the blankets. They
found and fondled his hips, his belly, his
buttocks, the shifting ridge of his spine as he
arched against her.

"I feel inadequate to you," he whispered
huskily as her mouth worked against his navel,
driving him to grunts. "I berated you—*Katie*—"
Ecstasy was a honey-coated blade striking him
again and again, square in the belly, cutting
toward his loins. He dragged his legs beneath
him, pressing to her moist onslaught, forgetting
that she had never done this to him before,
had never been the aggressor. And he forgot to
wonder where this change came from or if it
was good. He knew only waves of sensation
surging and breaking in his body, the quiver of
his knees beneath him, the killing fullness, the
stiffening of a woman's breasts in his hands.
This wasn't right. It wasn't supposed to be so
fast, so savage. Where was the love? Where
was Katie? This was the first time since her
injury that they moved together in the same
bed— could it be so different? Had he imagined the slow passion of before?

Will tried to speak her name. Only an orgas-
mic series of gasps broke from his lips. Sweat
beaded on his face and shoulders. Passion shuddered through him, out of control. A flashing
hand knocked the candle to the ground, and
darkness flooded in. He tried to reach for Katie, to find her face, to beg for the gentleness,
but she forced him back with a crude mount-
ing. Sensation consumed him then.

All he heard was the roar of his own heart-
beat, his rushing blood, his own throaty groans.

More like the sounds of a man in pain than a man in love.

He was in the blacksmith's furnace.

The heat ate him alive.

And on the coarse brown hairs of his belly hung the remnants of a woman's tears.

"God burn him!"

"Who?"

"My blasted cousin. Look at me!"

Katie tried not to laugh. One of Robin's distinctive black-feathered arrows bobbed from the center of Will's red cap, dangling down before his face and batting the end of his nose.

"It isn't funny!"

Katie literally bit her tongue, holding it between her teeth against the coming chortles, but her cheeks tightened obviously, and she tried to turn away before he saw.

"Recreant," he accused. He plunked down on the fallen tree, which provided the main support for his tent, and yanked off his cap, mourning the hole left once the arrow lay at his feet. "He truly might have killed me with this one. I was bending over. If I'd stood up a thought sooner—he must stop doing this to me! I must find a way to make him stop. Can you think of any way? This has been going on ever since we came to Sherwood. He's pinned every scrap of clothing I possess. And now my hat itself!"

"Has he drawn blood?" Katie asked, still at odds with giggles.

"Never. The odds are closing on me. Any day now some misstep or little breeze will sink one of his arrows into my flesh and we'll both be sorry. Look at my hat! How am I going to mend this hole?"

"Give it to me."

"Can you fix it?"

"I'm a blacksmith, not a seamstress. I could mend your sword or your belt buckles but not this. Marian will do it, I'm sure."

"Mind, I want it done correctly. No visible stitches. This cap's been with me for years."

"She sews beautifully. You know that."

"Something has to be done. It's the only irrational thing he does. I tell you, I truly fear for my life."

Katie turned back to the dead hare she was skinning on a furrowed stump. Blood ran freely down the grooves, all of which led to a wooden bucket. The hare was part of the catch from a recent hunt by Johnny Little and Edmund Bluestocking, to be stewed later with two other hares and fed to the children and the sick. There was food enough now but certainly not summer fare. Better weather brought out the tax gatherers with Prince John's brutal ways abounding, driving more families to seek sanctuary in Robin's protection. Thus Katie divested the hare of every possible morsel. The carcass she carefully put aside. Later she would boil it and the two others for broth. Odd how thoroughly she had become burrowed into Greenwood life. A year ago she would have tossed the carcasses to the birds with nary a backward glance. How sad, she decided, that prosperity must promote wastefulness.

She felt Will at her left shoulder.

"There," he said, "that's what will remain of me the day he misses. Gore and offal." He fingered the hare's bloody ear. "If only I could . . ." A breeze took his voice.

Katie went on cleaving the animal's ribs apart. "If you could do what?"

"Show this . . . to . . . is that its stomach?"

"This? Yes."

"Very small."

"A hare eats rather skimpily."

"But if this end was sewn shut . . . like this . . . perhaps it would hold—"

"A handful of blood. Oh, Will, you wouldn't do that to him."

"There's a hole in my bonnet with precious bare sympathy. I might shock him into stopping his game. I could put it in a cloth pouch on my belt, and you could entice him to shoot at it—"

"I?"

"You'd decline to help me live a longer life?"

"I would decline you nothing I have to give, but what about Robin?"

"What about him? There's not a man alive who appreciates a full-bosomed jest like he does. It's second only to how well he loves a good heart-pounding adventure. Here, I'll hold the offal. You pour a measure of that blood into it."

"Well . . ."

"Don't you agree that his game is dangerous? That he should stop?"

"It is dangerous; of course it is. Weapons should not be used for games."

"As the target, I heartily agree."

Katie sighed. "Hold it open."

"Slippery bit of gore, isn't it?"

So their plan was conceived. Will delighted

in his scheme, and Katie was quickly caught up in his enthusiasm. She desperately needed a bit of lighthearted distraction herself. Too many of her thoughts had turned to confused reflections upon Ruth's dark prophesy, wondering if her love with Will was enhanced and held more precious by the knowledge or damaged by it. With these ruminations also came the awareness that she would never comletely belong to this way of life. She existed in the Greenwood by proxy, not by need. This place provided not sanctuary for her but merely oasis. Eventually she would have to emerge. Whether or not Will would be with her then she dared not guess. After speaking to Ruth, Katie had consumed her fill of prophesies.

Before supper that evening, Katie fulfilled her part of the scheme, and not having any reason to distrust her, Robin quickly accepted the challenge of nipping what Katie described as Will's ugly little belt pouch.

"That black one? Is that the one?"

"Yes," Katie told him. "You can't really put an arrow through it without hurting Will, can you?"

"That vast pouch?" Robin guffawed.

"Vast? Hardly the size of my palm, I'd say."

"Would you like to see me strike it?" He looked at her askance. For a moment she thought he might know her trick. A knowing grin turned his lips up beneath the thin mustache.

"Only if you can. I'd not like seeing Will hurt."

"Neither would I. He's so satisfying a victim when he's unhurt. Well, then . . ." He chose an arrow, shouldered his bow, and climbed into a nearby tree for a better view of Will, who mingled downwind in a hollow at Greenwood-side's core. He drew the arrow into the bow, taking extreme care with its set, while waiting for the folk around Will to provide an opening.

"Wait," Katie called. She should tell him. What scamp had she become to take part in a jest like this? "Wait . . . until I go down there. I'd like to see . . ."

Robin waved a gallant hand. "Of course. There is no hurry. Will inevitably presents himself in the open. He's too vain to hide from me."

Once in the hollow, Katie winked at Will before shooing the children out of the line of aim. Will took care to remain in it as he examined Marian's progress with mending his cap. Though she knew Robin's skill was reliable, Katie could not keep her heart from thumping. She paused at the edge of the trees. A glance behind showed her a near distant figure drawing his bow. She touched her lips in hesitation, her hand raised slowly, her mouth opened to . . .

The forest hissed.

Will spun, struck a tree, and slammed to the ground on his side.

Katie flinched. He made it seem real. Had Robin—

Will rolled over slowly, his arms and head slightly raised, staring at his body and a smudge of blood beneath his ribs. In a chilling performance of disbelief he palmed the blood.

Marian jumped to her feet with a shriek, her knuckles pressed to her mouth. Parents dragged their children back. Katie swore she heard a gasp from deep in the trees.

Robin's voice from the trees frosted Katie's blood. She couldn't force her eyes to the trees, locking them instead on Will as he continued his feint with the glance Katie resisted.

Branches snapped behind her, a bone-cracking kind of noise, a noise of mistakes. Of cruelty. Even petty revenge.

Will's name rang through the budding bushes, over and over.

A brown-clothed form fanned by Katie's right side, skidding to Will's side.

"Christ condemn me, what've I done! Will—" Robin dropped to his knees and pulled Will into his lap.

Carefully covering the bloody pouch with his hand, and resisting Robin's effort to pull it away, Will clutched Robin's sleeve.

"Will!" Robin choked again, "I was sure—the arrow—it was true. . . . Will, by the saints, speak to me!"

"I always warned you." Will made his voice weak, but there was no resisting a faint smile.

The smile hurt Robin. Tears came to his eyes. His mouth fell open, but no sound came through the quick breaths. His arm tightened around Will.

Katie hurried through the staring people to them, anxious that Will might not perceive the whole effect of this game on Robin, knowing now how much more vicious revenge can be than its crime. She knelt by them, her hand pressing Robin's arm. "Will, enough," she said.

He ignored her, collapsing against Robin, whose face filled with torment.

"Perhaps now you'll keep your aim at Gisbourne, instead of me," Will gasped, "if I live—"

"You'll live if I have to go to hell in your stead! Move your hand—the bleeding—"

Was false.

Will's hand gave way to Robin's. In a panic Robin searched for the wound. The search ended at the blood-soaked pouch. And its secret.

Robin stopped breathing.

Katie, too, held her breath.

Crossing his legs with an air of casual roguishness, Will eyed his cousin and said, "Let this be a lesson of what might have been." A small shrug and a grin hoped to dismiss the seriousness but failed. "Robin—oh, Robin, come now—"

Katie watched helplessly as Robin quivered to his feet, staring at the blood smeared across Will's side, only then to walk stiffly away, barely breathing.

"Robin, you can't be serious," Will called after him. He stood up, starting to follow. "Robin."

"No, Will," Katie said. "Let him go."

"But this is asinine!"

"Speak to him later. Our joke was cruel."

"I never intended cruelty, hang it. I merely wished to—blast!" He pressed his hand to his mouth in exasperation, then grimaced at the blood newly smeared across his face. Katie wiped it off. Will stared, confused, in the direction Robin had gone, and a few deep breaths calmed him into awareness. "Blast . . . I never meant any harm to him. I truly thought he might harm me, if only accidentally."

"I know you did," Katie told him. "Perhaps I might tell him that."

"Certainly he'll not wish to see me at the moment. Ah, blast his overripe imagination!"

"You were most convincing," she said ruefully. "I'll see what I can do."

"Pray do it quickly, before the damage burns too deep. He'll ... he'll be all right, he'll recover. He'll ponder it and see that I was justified—"

"You might have been, but I would still rather apologize to him. I feel sure you will also."

"Aye, I'll wager on it myself. Off with you." He chased her with a pinch on the back of her thigh and a sultry smile, rife with contrition.

The lacy green forest was surprisingly quiet. Pale new leaves whispered between branches still stiff from winter. No sun shined through today's dappled cloud cover. The air neither carried warmth nor caused chill, eminently preferable to the cold of recent days.

Now where had Robin gone? Katie's hands clenched together as she recalled his expression. A man with that expression might go down the hill path, then up the slope into the grove of hawthorns where foliage grew thicker and faster. Where the ferns would seclude him.

Down the hill path she went, her feet squishing in moist spring soil and mulch. In spite of preoccupations she stole a moment to close her eyes and inhale deeply the glorious spring air. The Goddess was dominant once again. Her womanhood was in full flower and so should Katie's be. The Hunter God would soon rest and lay down his antlers upon the warm earth. It was a time for women. Katie's time for happiness again. She had cheated Will when they loved last night. That was not love but only passion. Tonight they would have love.

But for now, to find Robin and tend this mess.

There was a sound in the woods, a sound of running or at least of movement. She sought it out and found herself frowning not at Robin but at Nell.

"Get help!" the woman called, stumbling toward her through a nest of tangled bushes. "Get help—"

"What is it?" Katie huffed. Nell was not her first choice of company today.

"The boy—the child—" Nell panted, clutching nervously at her skirts. "At the—the—"

Katie clutched the woman's shoulders and made her stand still. "Tell me. Is something wrong?"

"A child at the gorge! He fell over the side!"

"What child?"

"I don't—don't know—I heard a scream and ran there. I saw only a crumpled child at the bottom." Accusatively she added, "*You* help him!"

Curse this woman's ignorance! "I'll go to the gorge. You get—Nell, are you listening? Go to the main camp. Bring Will and the other men and tell them to bring ropes."

"It's begun again," Nell snarled, "these troubles of penance."

"Do not start that again!" Katie started toward the gorge. "I would think that sense would have come to you by now. Get the men."

"This is your doing."

"A child falls down the gorge. How is it my doing? Hurry along!"

Nell scowled but started toward the camp. Katie spun on her heel and aimed for the gorge at a run. As she approached the thickening tuberous growth at the gorge's rich-soiled edge, she wished she had asked Nell exactly where the child fell. This area was leaping into spring quickly this year, thanks to the early thaw, and a small body could be easily concealed in the coppices below. The gorge was protected from harsh winds, providing a perfect receptacle for delicate seedlings to catch and grow, and Katie hurried along the edge, desperately searching for any sign of a hurt child.

A rustling behind her made her stop. She listened and turned slowly, unsure of the direction. Perhaps the boy had struggled up the gorge's flank and was trying to get back to camp. She looked but saw nothing except winter handing the woodlands to spring. She could only wait for Nell to return and point out the exact place. Meanwhile she continued looking. Perhaps she should climb down into the gorge and search the bottom. She began picking her way down, then heard more shuffling in the forest and hurried toward the hill to meet the others.

Where were they? The sounds had stopped. She went farther into the woods, certain of what she had heard. In anger she slapped a tall bush out of her way. Impatiently she glared through the woods, unwilling to go far from the gorge in case the child cried out. What was keeping Nell?

Behind her, more noise. This time she turned without pausing, to take the sound by surprise. Forms flew out of the underbrush like flushed crows, sinking the universe into a frenzy of arms and bodies. Katie inhaled to scream. A gloved hand crushed her mouth, shoving between her teeth; her jaw was held open, but no sound could emerge.

She struggled. She tried to kick, but her legs were wrapped with heavy cord. Seconds later someone yanked her arms behind her, coiling her wrists with the same harsh cord. With all her energy she closed her teeth hard on the stiff glove. Her teeth barely indented the tough fabric; a voice cried out in pain behind her, and the hand pulled away, another taking its place before half a scream could break from her lips. An arm encircled her waist, and she felt the ground fall away beneath her feet. A strip of cloth passed before her eyes seconds before closing on them, giving her the vivid sight of it shutting out her world. Sherwood blackened to sounds and scents. Then, as sudden as a blink, a hard force rang off her skull, and she sank limp to the cool forest floor.

When she awakened, there were no more scents. Her head knelled till she nearly fainted from pain and dizziness, but a shock of icy water forced her to full consciousness. She grimaced as the water drooled cold trails down her body— her clothes—where were her clothes? Only her chemise, now soaked, clung to her breasts, ribs, and thighs. She was tied to a small tree. It was night; glowing torches ringed the darkness. Robed figures held them. Before her stood a dozen Cistercians and Abbot Godfrey.

"Errant daughter, God has brought you back to us."

Revulsion filled her at the sound of his voice. Soft. Controlled. Syrupy.

Katie responded with only a slight tug to test her bonds. She winced. The ropes chafed her skin raw as she twisted her wrists against them. They were unmovable. She forced herself to stand straight and glare into his small eyes. "In the name of civility," she said, "I ask you to release me. Before things go too far."

"In the name of Almighty God, my duty is to cleanse you of sin and wrest your soul from the grip of the Devil."

"What do you want from me?" she demanded. For men of a peaceful god, the ring of clergymen around her were extremely well armed. Their swords glinted in the torchlight. She swallowed a hard lump of air and said, "I pose no threat to you anymore."

"All witches must be excised if the Kingdom of God is to be made pure."

"Of course, that is your main concern." Katie pulled harder against the ropes. Pain fueled her resentment. "Speak to me! Tell me why you accuse me of witchcraft when you know better."

"The Devil has enticed this woman," Godfrey called to the circle of believers. "She must first be tested as *wiccian*. If the tests prove her so, she must be absolved."

"By you? Who will be my judge?" Her words carried more courage than she felt.

Godrey turned to his followers, raising one hand over his head. A wave of horror passed through her as Katie saw what wagged against the night sky, a blue-black starless sky.

"No! You don't understand!" she cried, but

the only answer was the sound of her fate slamming shut like a portcullis.

"This effigy fell from the *wiccian*'s robes. It is the cloth image of a man. Doubtless he is some poor victim of her *wiccecraefte*, the dark arts of unholy magic that preys upon the weak and helpless in the name of the Devil."

"Devil!" Katie spat. "Your kind took the benevolent antlered god and made him your devil because he clashed with the teachings of the new Church. You took our Mother Goddess, stripped her of her sexuality, and forced her to be your subservient Virgin. *You* created the evil, not my people! Godfrey! Address me! I am the accused!"

"This effigy has been used by the *wiccian* to torment a wayward mortal who could not resist temptation, to control him to do her bidding and her master's." He handed the poppet to another friar.

It was then that Katie saw Nell. The woman hovered behind the line of Cistercians, wary of showing her face to the person she had betrayed.

"Nell!" Katie called. "Come out of there. How can you do this to me? I've done nothing to hurt you! Turn your harm around and fetch Will and Robin before it's too late for both of us. Nell, do you hear me?"

"Mistress Nell is a dutiful daughter of the Church, *wiccian*." The abbot searched through Katie's clothing as he spoke.

"You mean, she is a dutiful servant to you," Katie corrected. "Is that how you found our camp? Did she lead you to us? Nell! Listen to me. If I die, your fate is sealed. You know

Robin Hood will never let you leave Sherwood alive."

"Quiet, heathen," the abbot ordered. He turned to the circle of his brethren and raised high the small scrolled dirk Will had bought for Katie at the Feast of Fools. "The *wiccian* carries this emblem of her phallic union with the devil. You see the black handle with the etched designs. This is called an *athame*. The coven of *wiccians* plunge it into a chalice to symbolize the unholy union they crave."

"You are mad," Katie gasped. "Anyone knows those dirks are commonplace. Where is your real proof of my evil? Nell can no longer do your work for you, Godfrey. This is on your head and no other!"

The abbot glanced at Nell but made no other gesture to her. His robes swept the frost-beaded ground as he turned to Katie, slowly unrolling a parchment. A large wooden cross bobbed on a cord against his chest, mocking her. "You will answer these questions. Remember, you stand under the eyes of God. If you lie, God will cause you to fail the tests. How long have you indulged in *wiccecraefte*?"

"I am not a witch. It is you who are your own evil."

"Which of these names do you call your demon-lover: Cernunnos. Pan. Satan. Minotaur. Incubus."

Weary with cold and the ice of hopelessness, Katie cast her gaze groundward. She tried to think through the hammering ache in her head. "I have no such lover."

"What marks did your demon-lover cast upon your body?"

Katie shut her eyes tight. She sank against the tree. How could she conceal the scars left from her fall? How could she keep him from finding the two-year-old remains of a burn from the forge hood?

"How many sisters of the Devil practice in your coven?"

She remained silent.

"What animal do you become when you change form?"

"You must release me. We are fellow townsmen. We lived side by side. How can you do this?"

"How many babies have you stolen? What oath did you speak to obtain your powers? Whose children have you put under spells? What words do you use to invoke your familiars? Do you sleep in natural or bestial form?"

When she remained silent, one of the monks stepped from the circle and slapped her across the side of her face. She tried to cringe away but not quickly enough. At first the pain was numbing, then it wrenched a gasp from her. Her eyes burned and watered. She slumped, her head lolling.

"You will be subjected to several ordeals," Godfrey went on. "First we must search your body for devil marks and demon bites. We must prick you to determine the extent of your tryst with the He-Beast. At last you will be bound and cast into the river. If God's water rejects you, we will know the truth. Do you understand, *wiccian*?"

Sucking air into her throbbing chest, Katie forced out, "If I drown, I am innocent." Oh, Will if ever we were joined by our minds' mutual love, I beg you—hear me now. Against these men I am helpless. I need you, I need you—"

Her last sight of Godfrey before the cloth strap passed over her eyes lanced her with nausea. He was passive, even haughty. His face held no remorse at all. She shook her head violently as the blindfold tightened. "Not my eyes! Don't cover my eyes! Don't cover my eyes!"

She thought of Edith and the birth of Alexander, the gentle tests folklore put upon the woman before and during childbirth. They were nothing like these. They had not been designed to end in death but in life.

Terror gripped her and she screamed. If only she could see—if only they hadn't bound her eyes—to see the trees—

Hands spun her around, forcing her to hold the thin tree trunk. Her breath came in shivering gulps. Something sharp pressed into the hollow of her soulder, and she felt pain. She defied the pain, shutting her eyes tight, refusing to cry out. She clutched the tree. Her own breath hung on the bark, afraid for its life. Nell's face twisted behind her bound eyes. The pieces fit together too well for coincidence. Fear had graduated its own boundaries. Finally it had become aggression.

She hissed a breath through clenched teeth when the pain retreated suddenly. The sharp instrument stopped pushing against her muscle and tissue. It sucked at sinew and left her body. Blood trickled. She sank against the tree, hanging on, white-knuckled.

Will ... where are you? I am not afraid of death, but torture is a craven thing and it petrifies me.... This is not my choice of deaths—Will, please, please ... don't let him touch me again....

A moan fell from her quivering lips.

Behind her, the hated voice. "O Lord, Heavenly Father, give me the strength to purify this Thy wayward child. She has fallen into the claws of Thine immortal enemy. Let her spirit commend itself into Thy hands. Give me the wisdom to expose—"

Shouts filled the air, wild shouts. The steady drone of Godfrey's invocation drowned in them.

Metal clanged. Swords. Will!

Katie forced her legs to straighten. The friars were heavily armed. Sherwood's men would have a fight to face. But they were here, they were here, they were here....

Someone tore the blindfold from her head. Beautiful night sprawled before her. In spite of the cold air, sweat poured down her face, instantly frosting her skin. There was a jolt on her wrists; they fell free. She blinked, searching out her rescuer.

"Come on, dove, freedom's this way." It was Christopher's voice. And there he stood, sword in hand, plucking the ropes from her legs while keeping a keen eye on the fight in the ring of torches.

"Ger her away, Valland," Robin called from behind her. Immediately after came the snap-hiss-thunk of an arrow seeking its bloody home. "Swiftly now!"

"This way, sweet." Christopher took her arm and drew her toward the line of evergreens, pausing once to fight off an attacking friar. Christopher was the better swordsman. He caught the attacker's blade on the downstroke and twisted it away, following with a killing swipe. The friar slumped to the dirt and moved no more. Katie stumbled away on Christopher's arm. She dared not look behind. The hearing of shouts and clangs and grunts and screams smote her, making her long to be far from here.

Christopher led her away, protecting her when he had to, when one of the corrupt monks followed with weapon raised.

Suddenly Katie pulled away and spun around. "Will—where's Will?"

"He's not with us this time, love. Robin had no time to find him. We're outnumbered but fear not. We're also talented." He smiled, that emblematic, charming smile, a smile that filled his face and eased Katie enough to comply when he ushered her along into the deep woods. He would protect her; she knew it. But how many times could these people risk their lives for her?

Christopher tried to make her hurry. Katie forced herself through the underbrush, ignoring the cut of dry stalks on her bare feet, willing her body to ignore her throbbing shoulder and its sticky flow of blood. Christopher helped her, but the night was moonless and the woods very dark.

Suddenly the evergreens came alive behind her. A hand struck the center of her back and sent her forward through the trees.

Christopher shouted, "Run, Katie, get away!" He vanished into a chime of blades.

Too battered, too frightened to argue, Katie stumbled through the woods toward a campfire. She saw it through the trees and smelled it now. Figures ran toward her. A blanket closed over her shoulders. Arms encircled her and drew her along.

"Help them," she choked, "send more men. . . ."

"No men here to send." It was Ruth. This wasn't the main camp.

The woman led her to the fire and sat her on a rock. Off went the blanket and on went a cold, wet cloth. Katie gasped in shock and agony and tried to writhe away. Two women held her there.

"The bleeding's got to be clotted. Hold still."

Katie dug her fingers into her thighs and endured it. "Where's Will? Have you seen him? Has he been here?"

"Aye, that he was. And I warned you. Didn't I warn you?"

"Has no one seen him? Why was he not with Robin?"

"Love is a curse."

"Leave her be." Marian appeared from the core of night, carrying Katie's cloak. She knelt by Katie and draped the cloak over her good shoulder, leaving the puncture wound bare as Ruth tended it. "Dear Katie. Scarcely you heal from one hurt and you're hurt again. So much badness in the world, I can only wish—"

"Marian . . . Marian, have you seen Will?"

"Will Scarlet? Oh, yes . . ."

"Where is he?"

"Well . . . oh . . . you see, after Robin heard your scream—he was in the forest, you see, not

far away, praying, I think, when he heard you—
after that he came rushing back for help, but
only a few of the men were there and he didn't
want to tell Will because, I suppose, he feared
that Will might rush in to save you and get
killed himself before Robin had a chance to
surround—"

"But where is he *now*? Marian, please!"

"Now? Oh ... I suppose he's with them by
now. He found out, you see, found out that
Robin had gone to save you if you were still
alive—praise God you were—and off he went
just as furious as a bumblebee in the rain.
We've not seen him since. I hope, I certainly
hope he can fight good enough through his
anger. He loves you so much, Katie."

Ruth huffed. "A curse."

The sudden need to feel Will's arms engulf
her nearly squeezed Katie into a faint. She
would never live in peace if last night's lovemaking was indeed their last. . . .

"The swords," she blurted, surprising herself. "I don't hear the swords." She pushed to
her feet.

As though in answer, a handful of Greenwood fighters staggered through the trees, not
one of them without wounds. They passed
through slowly, wordlessly, and went on to the
main camp. Then came Robin, one arm bloodied and closed around his midriff. He looked
ill. He leaned on a tree, bending forward
slightly.

After him came Will.

"I can always find other places to live," he
grumbled.

Robin snapped at him like a badger. "You'll

do better elsewhere if you cannot keep your head."

"Only a fool hesitates when a sword flails at his neck."

"They were men of the Church and due that hesitation."

"Don't feed me your platitudes, Robin. Sometimes your simple heart makes me retch."

"Will!" Katie limped toward him, arms outstretched. Oh, his arms, his body! To feel them now . . .

Seconds before she would have embraced him, his strong hand caught her wrist, careless of the raw skin there, and twisted her away, holding her there. Into her open hand he deposited Abbot Godfrey's wooden cross and the rope it had hung from, both soaked red in blood and smelling of death.

Will's eyes burned her.

"We paid with a bit of our souls for your life tonight," he said, and his tone buried her in despair. "Take better care of it."

Blood dripped between her fingers. Life linked itself with death. Shadows engulfed the forest.

Robin went one way and vanished.

Will went another way. Gone.

White fingers spread wide, streaked red. The wooden cross struck cold earth and stained the Earth Mother's gown.

Katie shivered and stared.

"Now you know why I said what I said," Ruth told her. "If Scarlet had had his mind on his business instead of on you, things might have fared better."

"I'm tired of hearing such words," Katie said, snapping a hard look at Ruth. "What world has no room for love?"

"Fool! Why do you think they let us stay here? What do you think *I'm* here for? You think they feed us out of charity? No! They keep us because we satisfy them and leave them lonely. Lonely men fight better. Have you not noticed? None of the men in Hood's vanguard have women or children."

"I know that—"

"Then know why. A man in love is a distracted man. He don't fight with his whole head. He don't fight *cold*." Ruth put her hands on her hips and turned in a small circle. "And what of you?"

"Me?"

"You, little girl. What if Scarlet dies? Can you get through another dead love? This ain't just another of your stories. That blood's real."

The truth of it crashed down upon Katie. Her love for Will suddenly became an awesome weight on the scale of her own survival. Could she bear to see him die? Would it wrench her heart from her as Edward's death had? If there could be two great loves in a lifetime, could a woman bear two great deaths? If he was killed, how would she know that thoughts of her had not done the deed? He might think of her at that critical moment when he needed to have his mind on his business. The gap might leave room for a deadly blade to enter.

Her fists knotted at her sides as she rounded on the other woman. "You are wrong, Ruth. And I was wrong to listen to you. Your world without love is not life. All you describe is another kind of death. I will love him as fully as a woman can love a man, and if we die, at least we will have lived!"

• PART FOUR •

BELTANE

• Chapter Fifteen •

"Here it is May Eve, and still you and Robin refuse to forget."

"Robin does not easily forget the deaths of holy men at his hands. Katie, it bothers you too much."

"When people I love are hurting, I hurt."

"Oh? Whom do you love?" Will clasped Katie's wrist.

"A select few," she said, raising her nose and eyebrow at once.

"Tell me who you love."

"At Beltane a person should be at peace. Robin is not at peace, and neither are you."

"At Bal—"

"The rite of spring. May Eve," she explained, "for Druids. Today the Earth Mother regains the planet from the Horned One."

"A time of many changes. I can almost smell them when the wind blows." Will lay back on their sleeping mat and watched Katie dress, refusing to let the doubts in. For the past month he had been unsure of her feelings. At first he feared the past, the dead past, thought Edward's ghost might have returned to plague

401

her again, then worried that he might have pushed her into passion too soon, then tortured himself when he thought he saw questions flying in her eyes. The idea that he might have damaged her beyond mending hurt him.

Yet their loving, while distant at times, was now whole. Katie participated with enough adoration for ten men and the cloudy spirit of that one frightening night never returned.

She finished dressing, quite aware that he watched her every move. The sleeping mat was warm as she joined him, lounging across his bare chest. "Since the end of winter Robin has been disturbed. You cannot say you've been unaware of it."

"I have been," he agreed slowly. "Painfully aware. It is the doing of my ill-bred jest. I should have let him potshot me if he wished to. I never realized how that game eased the pressure he feels. Perhaps the good weather will bring him out of it."

"Perhaps I am also to blame."

His fingers found her hair. "We are all to blame. Gisbourne's to blame. Prince John is to blame. The trees are to blame. Blame the shoes on your feet if you wish."

She sighed. "Still . . . I sometimes feel great regret that I ever left Southwell. I feel it when I see the wedges I've driven between you and Robin, the trouble I've caused. . . ."

"Ah, trouble you are, yes . . . but when you wish never to have come to Sherwood, do you wish it with me in mind?"

She plunged forward upon him and kissed him, never meaning to convey that message. The tent, with its ragged animal-hide walls and overgrowth of protective vines, shielded them from the world and its politics, its pasts and futures. She lost herself in his arms, pressing her face into his throat until his plusebeat was her universe.

"Katie," he breathed, "my wish is to spare you all those troubles. I dream of giving you the best of everything. And a title. We of the forest have forgone every comfort, not only luxuries but also the basest comforts, for the privilege of living with our own honor, but honor carries little warmth or peace on cold nights when danger threatens."

"I have warmth aplenty on cold nights, dearest love. Your strength of conviction is all the luxury I need."

He chuckled. His brows raised as his smile brightened the tent. "And I scold Robin for his platitudes."

"And I wonder," she thought aloud, "whatever happened to Nell after that night."

"Is it not enough to be thankful we've never seen her again? She evidently knew Robin would exile her from Sherwood. She left on her own and much the better."

"She acted out of fear."

"I begin to think religious fear is the most vindictive of all. It's what drove Richard to the Crusades."

"Richard's ego drove Richard to the Crusades."

"That I cannot deny."

"Will!" Edmund's voice came from outside. A stick rapped against the tent. "Ho, there. Are you within?"

A low groan sounded in Will's throat. To Katie he murmured, "Not at the moment. . . ."

"Ho, Will!"

"Aye, what's about?"

"Action out on the road. Robin's on his way an' asks for you."

"All right, coming straight away. Sorry, love. Robin calls." He rolled away and got to his feet, reaching for his black tunic.

"I'll come with you."

Will belted the tunic over green trews, then drew on the scarlet cowl to warm his shoulders. "To the road."

Sherwood in springtime hummed. Will rode Palermo to the road, Katie at his side on the brown mare, for the action Edmund spoke of had happened at the distant east end of the forest, in the lower reaches by the River Trent. Katie reined her horse in when she reached the line of Sherwood men, allowing Will to trot Palermo through to Robin alone. Robin was also astride his horse, a nut-colored gelding that blended into the trees as fluidly as moss. Palermo, his blond frame and broad, muscular hindquarters bobbing gracefully, flowed to a halt beside Robin's horse. Will reined him back an arm's length, taking a place just behind Robin's shoulder that seemed to fit Will with distinguished perfection. Katie understood now. Will was not Robin's competition. He was his complement.

Centering the road, in a wide sun-spotted shadow beneath a vast oak, a carriage and a pair of oxen awaited judgment, guarded by a single boy, a youth of nearly fifteen. He defied the outlaws with his eyes, for he had no weapon.

The other men with the carriage, Edmund told Katie, had run off the instant the outlaws appeared. Only the boy stayed.

"Do you think he'll fight?" Robin tossed over his right shoulder. How significant that he had never looked to see who rode up behind him. "I'd hate to hurt a lad so young."

"He's determined more than he's afraid," Will answered, resting his hands on the saddle's high frontpiece.

"What are you called, lad?"

The boy scurried around the carriage, grasping the yoke possessively. "I want to be left alone. There's nothing here for you."

"I asked you your name."

"The monks named me Sebastian. There's nothing for you to steal."

Will lowered his voice. "He spoke no password?"

"Not ours. What do you think?"

"I think the carriage alone is worth a month's sustenance."

"Let's see what lies inside." He nodded to Johnny, who moved in on Sebastian and held the shrieking boy while Robin ordered the carriage opened. A gasp rolled over the road.

Sunbeams hit the sparkling rubies, amethysts, opals, and emeralds. The stones seemed like golden angels reaching with jewel-tipped fingers toward heaven.

"Ahhhh," said the men in appreciation.

"By the heavens!"

"Robin!" Will urged Palermo forward. "We're rich!"

"If the box looks like this," Tuck howled, "what must it hold?"

"A thousand kings' ransoms," one of the men wished, gog-eyed.

"Nothing!" Sebastian cried. "There's nothing in it."

"Whose box is this, boy?" Robin asked.

"Not yours."

Will laughed, a resounding victory.

Robin dismounted, soon followed by Will and a few others. Will stayed just behind him, watching as his cousin forced a blade into the lock and broke it with a snap. Robin opened the box and looked in.

Abruptly he stepped back, flat into Will. "What in creation—"

Will moved forward, dipping only a shoulder past Robin, enough to peek into the box, but finally reaching inside it. Robin tipped his head away slightly, as though he had suspicions or understandings the others did not yet, though he stood his ground.

In Will's hand hung a bony claw, crippled, stained with age, its skin dried to vellum and hardened. Long bones, frozen in place, muscle tissue and several veins reduced to cracked brown string clung to murrey-red, crusted bone. A treasure it was not.

Robin swallowed hard. "Will . . ."

"What is this thing?" Will asked Sebastian. "And why would it be coffered in silk?"

"Replace it," Robin warned. "Put it back."

"And these are worthless." Will dipped his other hand into the box to scoop out two silver coins that appeared to have been chewed on.

"Not worthless. God forgive us . . . priceless." Robin put a hand on Will's arm, steadying himself. To Sebastian he directed, "These are relics?"

The boy opted for dignity despite the cloying grip of Johnny's big hands. "Bound for the sacred archive at Kirklees."

A wince stopped Robin's breathing for a moment, and he paled. "Hallowed vestiges . . ."

Will dropped the coins and the fossil back into the gilt box. "Robin . . ."

Robin's voice shivered a deep disturbance. "We've interrupted a holy pilgrimage." He turned away, staring at nothing.

"Robin." Will rushed after him and pulled him around, grasping his shoulders. "Robin, there's nothing in this. Listen to me."

"What are they?"

"They are bits of nothing, cousin."

"I want to know what they are!"

Sebastian nearly jumped away from his own skin. He cringed into Johnny. "Relics freed to Christendom by the liberation of Jerusalem in the year of Jesus Christ 1099."

"Tell me, hang you."

"Two of Judas Escariot's payment coins—"

"Dear God—"

"And the right foot of Mary Magdalene."

Robin shuddered in Will's grip. "By the Holy Cross we'll burn in hell for this."

"Rubbish!" Will flung himself away and slammed the lid shut on the box. "Keep your head. These are mockeries! That thing looks more like the foot of a dog than a woman."

"Hold your tongue, Will, for God's sake."

"For *your* sake I speak. There are so many silver pieces attributed to Judas that the original thirty must have gone forth and multiplied. Robin, sometimes even faith must yield to logic. Who would think to save, of all things, her foot? You know as well as I the liberation of 1099 turned up three or more heads of John the Baptist and enough slivers of the True Cross to crucify a man the height of Chepstow Castle!"

"Close the carriage. Put it safely at camp center. I want a guard on it. I must think what to do, I must think, I must pray. . . ."

"Robin—"

"Release me, by Christ. We've breached a holy journey. I must seek the Lord's guidance."

"Why do we not simply put it back on the road and let it go on its way?"

"In the hands of a boy?" Robin paced away a few steps. "Indeed, into whose care can I entrust holy items?"

Will's hand sought him again, crossing a line of indelicacy in favor of his cousin's state of mind. "They're sham, Robin. Let God torture me as I stand here if they be genuine."

"I'll spend the night alone. Feed that boy and see to this wagon. I want it inspected for safety, any flaws repaired by our best craftsmen, and a constant guard around it."

"A guard against ourselves?" Will demanded caustically.

He and Robin exchanged intolerant glares.

Finally Robin remounted his horse and drew up the reins. "In the morning I will decide what is to be done."

The forest echoed the sound as he galloped away.

Silence ate at the gathering around the wagon. Katie looked on with remorse as Will stood where Robin left him, and she wondered if their religion had no room for variance of perception. Robin and Will were so different, so antagonistic, yet they maintained their stubborn unity. Living with them all these months had not left her barren of empathy for them, but she would never understand this habit of putting spiritual significance on artifacts and bits of dead bodies. And they called *her* beliefs barbaric!

As she sat her horse in silence her heart went out to Will. At least Robin did not battle with his own religion as Will did.

Will licked his lips and pressed them into a thin line. He looked sharply around. "Well? Do as he says!"

The warm afternoon dragged on; the sun lay pale through the clouds upon Sherwood and was nearly ready to set when Katie found Will thinking alone on a hillside. She wisely said nothing but sat beside him and hugged her knees to her chest. She wore only her chemise and lightweight cream-yellow gown, in spite of remembrances of Sir Guy, for it felt so very good to throw off winter's heavy wools and let the spring air waft about her body and through her hair. She sat beside Will for a long time, neither of them speaking. But the sunset spoke through the verdant trees. Again the air was filled with wildflower scents tossed from the arms of the Mother.

"I have a suggestion." Her voice seemed to echo. She thought she had barely spoken aloud.

"I'm in need of one," he acquiesced.

"You and Robin take the relics on to Kirklees yourselves."

"It would be a great risk."

"No more than letting Robin go on this way. We need him."

"That we do."

"He'll trust no others to guard the reliquary on its journey, will he?"

"I doubt it. Nor would he order anyone to take such a risk. I shall have to volunteer."

"He truly believes in those things?"

"Oh . . . yes."

She paused, thinking. "His beliefs are admirably uncluttered. Yet I am confused by your anger toward each other over this."

"You need not be. I am angry because I'm a stubborn bastard who likes to get his way."

"And Robin?"

"Robin's anger comes not at all from our disagreement. He allows me my cynicisms . . . usually."

"Then why is he so despondent over you?"

Will lay back on his arm, twirling a stalk of grass, and waited until she lay back with him. "Katie, it's so simple. He believes my mortal soul is in danger. He doesn't want me to go to hell." Brown eyes touched the whispering hillside. "And I continue to snipe at him for it."

"Oh, but only because you are trying, in your way, to protect him. Indeed—the foot of Mary Magdalene."

He peeled the grass stalk to bits and cast them one by one to the breeze. "Is that not sobering? Where are the other parts of her, I wonder? Did they remember to preserve the innards as well as the extremities? I wonder what her 'foot' originally sold for. And how often it has been resold to complacent believers like my cousin. Such things make my head pound."

Katie never averted her eyes but held his gaze until he drew her into the warm bend of his body, a line of sinew and skin hammered lean by winter.

"You, however," he murmured thickly, "are my comforting dream. And you make other parts of me pound."

Their lips met, moistly joined, then moistly parted and joined again, savoring. His fingers strayed purposefully into the bodice of her gown, seeking the ribbons tying her chemise over her breasts, and when he had freed them, he filled his hand with throbbing flesh.

She sighed a shudder of arousal and melted against him. "How much can I comfort you," she said, "when danger and trouble seem to follow me wherever I go? All my efforts to escape it have dragged it closer on my trail. When I came to the Greenwood, my plans were only to improve, or at least to maintain, my own life and work. Since that day I've brought nothing but discomfort and adversity to the lives of others. Others whom—now—I love."

He tipped her head back with a tender knuckle and involved himself in dove-gray eyes. "Do you see adversity here in my gaze? Do you see pain? You are the salvation of this man in your arms, Katie. You are heat and light, knowledge and body and flesh, and when you take me between your soft thighs, I feel it more than in my manhood. I feel your entire being in mine. You complete me. It is a thing Ruth could never do for me. I want you to know that. I am aroused as much by your spirit

when I listen to you speak your unusual thoughts
as by your touch, low on my body. There are
women after women like Ruth in the world.
They do a simple thing well, but there is no
filling of hearts." The sun broke through a
cloud, making them squint as it buttered their
faces with cool golden-red light. "When you
touch me," he went on, "I know it is a gift
from your mind."

She caressed his face, absorbed in his love
while not yet dulled to the subtle intricacies of
meaning beneath his words. Oh, true words,
very true for him, but a sweet disguise. "Tell
me what else you are thinking," she urged.

He paused. Had he failed at his evasion or
had he again underestimated her? Or had he
secretly—even secret for himself—wished her
to discover the undertone? "What do you
mean?"

"You have some other thoughts. Will you share
them? Or am I intruding?"

"Nay. They concern you," he admitted.

Katie felt suddenly cold, as though caught in
a portend. "How?"

"Summer is coming. Merchants are beginning to use the Cart Road more boldly now
that the watchword is known to be in the cause
of King Richard. While all this is good, with it
comes a bigger danger of spies and the chance
of being caught. Protecting you becomes harder,
and I will think of it constantly."

"Tell me, Will, if you've thought of something. Your avoidance is making me afraid."

"Katie, I want to send you away."

"Away! Where?"

"I've thought it all out. I have friends north

of York. I'm going to send you to live with them until we can return Richard to England." Whatever else he may have hoped or planned to say went unfinished as the remainder echoed upon the hillside.

Her response seared the grass from its roots.

"And when did you come to own me?"

"Katie, be—"

"When did I ask for cloister?" She rose to her feet. "Have I rediscovered my vitality only to let rot it away up in those bogs? I have survived trials I should never have survived, and my quest begs for fulfillment! How can you say such a thing to me?"

He stood, finding difficult foothold on the hillside. "It's only my love for you that drives me to shelter you. I know what your quest is. I can fulfill it for you now."

"It is not yours to fulfill," she bit out. Rage roared in her astride a tall hurt. She stalked away, but he followed.

He wrenched her around, long hands biting into her arms. "How baffling that you can be so wise and so stupid at the same time. Is your stubborn pride more important than your limbs and your life? By the time we reached you that night, the prelate might have cut your fingers off, or your feet, or violated your femaleness with some unthinkable instrument, for I cannot forever be with you! You might have been mutilated, and where would your honor be then?"

She slapped him away. The effectiveness of it shocked even her. Certainly it was the shock, not the force, that broke his grip. "Love is not possession! *I* choose for myself!"

"Is this what I am to face when we are someday married?"

She wheeled off, throwing back, "Do you expect a wife or a spaniel?"

Young grass submitted under her soft slippers as she left him behind. The dell filled with his voice, but she refused to hear and could not have told a moment later what he said, hearing only the rustling of his approach as he caught up with her. An instant before he yanked her around, she winced in anticipation and steeled up to confront him.

"Leave me alone, Will. Rough handling frightens only butterflies and cowards. I think I am neither."

"And if you think I would handle you roughly to win a disagreement, you're also not sensitive. Stand and speak with me!"

"What should I say? 'Yes, take me to York'?"

"It was merely a suggestion."

"A moment ago it was an order."

She tried to step by him, but ran into a wall of black, green, and scarlet. Beneath the shadowing point of his bonnet a new fury smoldered.

His voice ground like stones in a mill. "No. If I had ordered," he said, "You'd long have been gone."

Returning a glare so acrid with alternative meaning as to be compelling, she pointed out, "More quickly than you know."

He straightened before her, an imposing figure by which she refused to be intimidated, creating a strange illusion of false retreat, but then he advanced upon her with all the force of his gender. He drove her to the ground, fully intending to complete what he had begun. She fought him, landing a good blow on his neck, though no antagonism could push her to harm him in earnest, even if she could.

Nor could any anger hide her love. She buried it beneath rigidity, flinging her face away until he had to grip her jaw and force her mouth to his. His body pressed hers into the soft new earth. His hand dragged her skirts up her bare legs, ignoring the weeds and wildflowers torn up and pulled along to the fine, silky center of her womanhood as he tried to show her who was the knight and who the lady.

Katie resisted as long as she could, but true resistance found no place in her heart. She wanted him; she always wanted him, no matter how their minds clashed. Their bodies could no longer be strange to one another. She knew that as she felt him crush against her, a bloom of manhood and the smoke and fire of pure passion. She put the burden on him. If he found failure, it would be in his own heart.

And there, in his heart, it was.

He made a sound of pain and threw himself from her, leaving her emptier than death could.

"I cannot," he gasped. Elbows in the grass, he turned his head away.

"I thought you had made your decision," she mocked.

As though never hearing her, he went on, "I can't love you this way." Tragedy tore his voice. "I could kill myself more easily than dominate the heartbreaking specter of a woman you are. I don't want to rule you or order you, Katie. I'd be stealing, I'd be a common thief and you the conqueror—perhaps I am vain or weak or too scarred by you—love is only a boiling vat to consume a man beyond pleasure—torture, torture is all it is."

Spilled across the thin fabric of tolerance and desire, her shimmering hair threaded the twilight.

A cool, sympathetic voice followed him across the stillness, a tempering whisper, out of the brushwood like the steps of a fawn.

"Then return me my torture," prodded the earth, the sky. "Together we will turn it to ecstasy."

His eyes caught the tears in hers.

The passion began slowly. The wind whispered apologies, but Katie and Will no longer heard anything. The sweet suction of their kisses provided the only conversation. These meetings of lip to flesh consummated ever so gently, a melody of dulcet tones in lovers' hearts. Deliberately, reverently, Will plucked at Katie's shift until her breasts slipped free and glowed pale in the waxing moon's light. She dipped her head back, baring her throat to his moistening mouth, losing herself in sensation, her hair rolling against her shoulders, Will's hands seeking out skin beneath it, the grass cool and dewy as it braced her body in expectation of him.

"Forgive me," he whispered, a gush of hot breath in her ear.

"Love me," was her response, as simple as the water gleaming nearby. She put her hand over his and guided him in rediscovery of her body, its slim curves, its sumptuous throbbing, its heightened awareness of him at those special places where the signals always arose. He knew the places now but loved to let her introduce him to them, each one—inner thigh, tip of breast, earlobe, hollow of her shoulder—all over again.

He lay her back upon the grassy knoll, on the soft cushion of overgrowth skirting Sherwood Forest, and he became her new clothing, her new coverlet, protecting her night-cooled body with his throbbing fullness and the warmth of his own flesh.

Sorry that she had hurt him but glad to have asserted herself, Katie happily accepted his entrance, man into woman, with self-confidence and deep intimacy. He was part of her now, not overlord or underling, neither guide nor follower, and as passion for his swaying hips filled her and she cupped his pelvis in her hands, she saw a wild specter of the two of them standing together, side by side, on a windy hill. They were endlessly joined, as she never imagined possible. Katie Chenoweth became whole and fulfilled on that grassy bank, beneath the wondrous rotations of a man who truly must be her ultimate destiny.

Kisses rained across the birth of night, a slurred song of trembling desire, a human etching of the River Trent when her waters swelled and hungered against the Earth Mother's bosom, a strange, yearning son that became its own fulfillment. Prowess shook its mane and sank into elusive beauty. The loneliness, the separateness of being human, was only a droplet in their ocean. It heaved against the iron-gray sky. Their bodies, a cloudy mesh of limbs, tautened against each other—breast, thigh, throat, sinew, buttock and belly—and the song became strident. With the enthusiasm of children in bloom they went after each other, and with the ferocity of experience they succeeded. Until desire was spent there would be no turning back. The conquering hero had returned. Candor fell to the wind, breathing a throbbing triumph. Katie Chenoweth took her Will to her breast, and beneath a sunset canopy, there on a Plantagenet hillock wrapped in myths, she was reborn.

Will went to look for Robin. It was still night. Confusion about his feelings toward Katie had not dulled Will's keen awareness that Robin might be in great need of him tonight, or at least of a steadying hand or a show of faith. Had someone foretold the events on the road and the coming of the reliquary, Will himself could easily have taken over to foretell Robin's reaction. Deep down—then not so deep—he knew he should never have argued with his cousin and leader because, first of all, Robin was reacting only to a firmly ingrained piety, and secondly, Robin was right. The reliquary, blessed and considered sacred, had value both in coin and belief, and if its presence brought comfort to someone somewhere, then its disappearance would surely cause anguish. Will thought himself unfair to expect ignorant people to forfeit their relics because he preferred to think rather than blindly believe what he was taught or told. But Robin was not ignorant; he simply had more than his share of faith and cared more to question men than God. Yet this incident was not isolated. It came as the apex of this winter's abundant pressures, the problems of Katie, of Gisbourne, of having no news of King Richard for frightfully long months, of wondering whether the ransom was being collected to free a monarch already dead, of wondering if the Greenwood sanctuary was becoming a holding place for its citizens to await their deaths. For if Richard never returned, cruel and cold death—the death of traitors—would greet them all. Indeed, they were already running from the noose, since Prince John had declared as outlaw every man, woman, and child who abetted Robin of the Hood in any way. And now, piled upon all that stress, Robin also had to shoulder a bit of the Church. No wonder he bent under the weight.

With apology nibbling at his lips Will walked familiar trails through dense spring ferns—Beltane, Katie called this time of year. A haunting word of the Old Language, from an old time. He felt the imperious link of new times to old. Katie's ancestors had worshiped the trees and the shifts of seasonal change, their worship coming not in the form of quivering awe or private mumblings but in knowledge and learning. By knowing the trees, she had told him, the *drui* worshiped. He thought of Katie and Robin and resolved to bury the question of the relics. Instead he would work within Robin's framework of belief.

He went to the tent Robin shared with Marian but found only Marian, who said she had been alone there all night. So he searched and eventually found the master archer lying upon a tossed cloak in a thicket many paces away from the camp. His arm covered his eyes, shutting out the starlight. For several moments

Will watched him, wondering if he was asleep. No ... he was awake. His fist knotted and unknotted.

Will stretched out on his side next to him, propping himself on his elbow. He pressed Robin's arm, creating a mental bridge. "Robin? Are you all right tonight?"

Robin moved very little—small, twitching movements only—but he removed his arm from his eyes and looked at Will. He swallowed as though it were hard to do so. "Do you remember," he began, showing the color of his thoughts, "the time my father took us to Kirklees?"

Temperately Will said, "I remember you didn't like it."

"I felt strange there ... unwelcome." He gazed at the tree-fingered stars. "It was as though I'd died and were returning. My body tingled. I felt so numb, like I was decaying. Like a corpse. Why would I have felt like that? I'm a pious man who always assumed myself welcome in God's houses, yet a cold thing entered my bones and rotted there for a long time after." He rolled over, coiling his arms and resting on them. "I swear to you, Will, I feel it coming again." Beneath shook through him.

"What is it?" Will asked. "Do you know?"

Robin shook his head.

"Perhaps," Will went on carefully, "we might trust ourselves to continue the reliquary on its way."

"What? Deliver it to Kirklees Priory ourselves?"

"Why not? You, me, Stutley, Tuck—Tuck could take it in and confer with the monks—

Reynold and the lads will go, certainly, and I will go."

"Deliver it ourselves," the archer repeated. After a long pause, very long, he sighed heavily. " 'Twould be very dangerous, Will. A trek through bad territory."

"We've faced worse." Will's hand flopped on Robin's shoulder. "My God, you're as tight as coiled hemp!" He got up on his knees, kneading the rocky shoulders beneath his hands. "How long have you been like this? Have not slept at all?"

"How could I sleep? We've forestalled God's own possessions."

"Then God will guard them. We'll travel as far as we can through Sherwood's own fells, overland to the north road. We can get nearly to Sheffield that way, then use the east road to Ashton-under-Lyne. At least then the danger will be confined to the priory itself. Robin, by Christ—try to relax. I can feel you growing more and more tense."

"I feel it too."

"Lie down. Tree branches are more supple than your back. Lie down, I said. Where's the champion of composure I knew, admired, and put up with?"

A grunt rolled through Robin. "He's wondering why Richard thinks he can rule England from the Holy Land."

Continuing evidently useless efforts to knead the fetters of responsibility from his cousin's back and shoulders, Will contemplated the anguished peace, an inarticulate peace at best, that had befallen them. "If you could but sleep," he wished aloud.

"Who can sleep in the hood of a tolling bell?"

At last Robin gave it up and, pushing to his feet in spite of Will, rubbed his face in fatigue and paced the thicket. "Your solution is my only choice." He spoke as though no one listened. He chuckled in a most self-derisive way. "Have I grown so weak?"

Irresolute, Will insisted, "Your conscience knows no limits. You do yourself injustice, and you are not an unjust man. Stop this harm upon yourself."

"It occurs without my permission."

"How long has it been since I've seen you laugh? I know ... we're of a kind when it comes to this damning frustration, you and I. Rather than wait, we would hammer our targes with our sword blades and let the clangor tell Prince John we want a fight, straight out."

Robin folded his arms tight to his body. "You know as I do our politics, those of England in these times—they cannot be won by the sword. They can only be maintained by stealth in some limbo. John is the heir after Richard. We can only hope Richard is alive and pray that he will return."

"Knowing that, you should forgive yourself. I know impatience is cosseting ... I know. Come, then"—he squeezed Robin's arm again with one hand and clapped his back with the other—"ride with me. We'll shake out those chinks in our armor."

The horses were saddled and ready. Robin felt no surprise at their presence but merely landed a grateful, bemused glance on Will before they mounted and struck out across the moonlit hills and fells, through dark, towering trees. Flank to flank they galloped as they had in their boyhood, Palermo and Robin's horse, Gwydion, rising, falling, and bolting beneath them, driving out tension, hammering it to shreds under knifelike hooves. Sleeping birds bolted like jewels from thickets. Half the remaining night they rode across endless countryside, past the boles of dark trees, until their horses beflecked the night with foam and their own bodies glistened with sweat. And Robin once again smiled. It was not much of a smile. But it warmed Will to his very toes.

When daylight flickered over Sherwood Forest with its pink-yellow light and its warmth, the decision had been made and told throughout Greenwoodside. Robin would usher the reliquary on its way to Kirklees Priory himself, and any man who wished to accompany them would be most welcome. There was a real danger, but as the reliquary carriage prepared to leave Greenwoodside, a growing crew of volunteers diced the odds until Robin called a stop to it. By then, before he even realized it, every man in Greenwoodside able of body and mind had rallied to this mission. Loyalty for Robin chimed before his very eyes, as bright as the dawn for all to see, and, most important, for *him* to see. Will remained at his side, befuddling and artfully ignoring the glances of those who knew they had argued. Will stepped away only long enough to bid Katie a tender farewell, drowning her in a single consuming kiss.

"I have no desire to leave you now," he said, gazing squarely into her eyes.

"Then let me go along," she returned.

He smiled at her and drew a strand of her shining hair across her lips. "This is not part of your quest, my love." He carried the strand to his own lips and kissed it symbolically. "Last night was paradise," he murmured. "I wish it had gone on forever. Tonight, when we camp and I try to sleep, my body will fill with need of you, and I'll wish I had begged you to come."

"Last night we were completely joined," Katie responded, her cheeks going rosy as she remembered. "We stepped upon a milestone and crossed together. I too felt the mystery slide away." With the touch of flower petals she caressed his face. "Take care," she whispered, guiding his hand to the swell of her breast. "Take care of yourself for the sake of this heart. It beats for you."

He pulled her close and shut his eyes tightly to block out the time apart that was coming. It would be a long journey. Kirklees Priory reposed near the village of Huddersfield, north and east between Nottingham and York. Since they would travel so far, Friar Tuck intended to continue on north to his own abbey, Fountain's Abbey near Ripon, to greet his brothers and fulfill other duties, promising to return to Sherwood before autumn.

But Katie would not miss Tuck. It was not Tuck in her arms, nor Tuck she yearned to hold closer, to hold endlessly.

Will broke away, not easily, carelessly flinging himself astride Palermo and gathering rein. The big horse wheeled beneath him. Barely a minute later Robin quelled some of the anxious churning in his stomach with a single wave of his arm, starting the entourage forward, closing the distance between God and His trinkets.

Long after they had gone, in a camp supremely empty, Katie found herself inclined to care for young Sebastian. She made him a hot meal and tried to put him at ease. Robin had refused to let him accompany the reliquary, saying the wiser course would be to escourt the treasure only with trusted fighting men and not with a youth they would be inclined to protect before their own lives. Katie sympathized with the boy, but she agreed with Robin.

"I find you brave enough," she told the long-boned youth that night, "that you stayed with your wagon when the other monks ran away. I admire you for it. You needn't be concerned about proving yourself further. And you needn't worry about the reliquary. If Robin Hood says it will be delivered, then it will be."

The timid boy looked at her with squinting eyes, a habit from too often reading in near darkness. He had long, thin hands, and they tended to quiver. When eating, he used only his thumbs and forefingers. "I was not with monks," he told her. "I was with a military guard. They were hired to move the reliquary."

"Military guard? Why would monks hire a guard to move their reliquary without accompanying it themselves? Strange that attitudes could change so much." She sighed deeply. "Sometimes I forget how long away I have been from city life."

Sebastian shrugged, chewed a chunk of rabbit, and swallowed with some effort. " 'Twas not our reliquary, anyway."

"Not yours?" Katie turned. "It came not from your abbey?"

"I am from the monastery of Croxden Abbey, which is small and keeps no relics."

"Then where are they from? Tell me quickly."

He flinched as she advanced upon him. She hardly meant to intimidate him, but such a threat came unbidden with this intense foreboding that suddenly, chillingly, gripped her. "They told me ... it had been held safe at Louth near the sea. I had no reason to question—"

"Did you tell Robin this?" Her voice was shrill.

"He—he did not ask me!"

"You had no reason, then, to question why a parcel would be brought *south* to Nottingham from Louth, only to be turned north again for a journey twice as long as need be?" Driven by pieces of a blackened puzzle suddenly clacking together, Katie clutched the boy's cowl and yanked him to his feet. "Tell me why trained military guards would turn and run and leave a precious cargo they were being paid to conduct?" She twisted around, shrieking, "Marian!"

"Are you—are you," Sebastian stammered, "saying that it was a rouse?"

"We were foolish and blind not to ask why a holy relic would be conducted by one boy and a handful of armed men if it was so dear to the Church." She pressed her hands against her temples, devastated by the rush of questions and wretched answers flying into her mind.

Again she gripped him. "Why would important relics go to a priory?"

"Because . . . of the archives?"

"But why would a priory have archives? Oh, we have been deceived! Robin's piety will be his death! Marian! Marian—Edith—find me a horse quickly!"

• Chapter Sixteen •

They were deceived. By someone who knew
Robin Hood's one great weakness: that he would
not question a manifestation of his Church. He
had seen the cross rise before him and bowed
his head, refusing by sheer weight of habit to
look into the eyes of the specter and demand it
prove itself true. He had seen only the Cross
and none of the ground upon which it stood.
Had he looked twice, he would have realized
the ground was boggy and could swallow a
man whole.

Katie had no trouble concluding who that
someone was. Only a man who desired more
than anything to entice Robin o' the Hood out
of Sherwood's guarding embrace, where he
would be introduced to his coffin could plan
such a trick.

Katie rode after them, hard and long, as fast
as the darkness would allow, with its great
blue hood casting uneven shadows in her path.
She could make and mend bridles, prepare
tools and horseshoes for the farrier, but her
time upon a horse's back was limited to the

times she'd spent with Will. Before that there had been wagons to ride.

Tonight her horsemanship improved. Skill simply came to her and when her thighs ached and her arms and shoulders tingled from holding the reins, she shook her head to clear any fatigue and enticed the animal onward. Countryside rolled out under hooves and trees whipped by as Katie fleetingly thought of life across the face of England—a life so tenuous that possessions were transient, fading things. The forge, the clothing of a successful burghess, any comfort or splendor could easily dissolve. Life was all she had; all anyone had.

Soon the land went from tall hills to jagged clefts, deep gouges cut from the earth and high, ragged territory of mountains called the Pennines. She had no choice but to slow down, to allow the mare's careful picking across the dangerous crags and slopes, but it gave both steed and rider a crucial rest, if an uneasy one. Finally her mare's drenched haunches dipped as Katie pulled her to a halt on a high green promontory. She found herself choking on a terrible sight. Down through rocky, mossy morasses in the throat of a bracken-hedged valley trickled the Sherwood company, moving slowly to the pace of the reliquary carriage. Halfway between her and them, pinned like jewels on a rumpled green cape, lurked Sir Guy of Gisbourne and two score deputies of the shire, armed and waiting, hungrily watching. She looked down upon them from high up. Her stomach turned. They were smug as they hid in the earth's folds, smelling their bloody victory and strutting like stags in rut.

Down across sloping rocks she forced her mare, asking the beast for only a bit more energy, a last stab at dignity, a final elegance.

Her approach was so singular and so bold that Sir Guy's men did not even turn their heads as she rode right through them toward him. Only when she was past did they gasp and gawk, but by then she no longer cared.

In spite of exhaustion the mare jolted and reared up beneath her when she pulled her up suddenly, square in front of Sir Guy's astonishment and the humiliation of his men, white-faced because they had let her surprise them.

"Ambush is beneath you, my lord," she announced firmly.

Sir Guy looked like a stunned fish.

"Catherine!"

"There is dishonour in using a man's blind devotion to his god to lure him toward death."

"Catherine, you're alive!"

Katie, though strung with fatigue, held her legs tight around the mare's foam-soaked sides and felt her own body charge with excitement. Not fear, precisely, but a harrowing kind of omen. She was undeniably afraid, but fierce indignation drummed down any weakness and hesitancy. She faced Gisbourne at a distance of twenty paces and showed him that he would never again be close enough to grasp her.

He regained his composure with some effort, then motioned his men to stay back from surrounding her. Perhaps he read in her eyes that she would gladly steer the mare over the cliff, go through all that again rather than be taken.

"My lord, I beseech you," she began, "to take an honorable course."

Scarcely able to believe what he saw before him, Gisbourne absorbed her presence. "What would that be?"

"Wait for me to ride down into the valley to warn Locksley of your presence."

"That would be an odd form of chivalry."

"One that involves equity. You are not a man to sneak like some lizard behind rocks."

"But I am a desperate man. Robin of Locksley must be forestalled for the sake of the shire's prosperity and for the good of England."

"For the good of the Normans who support Prince John."

"Who else should—"

"I did not come here to engage you in rhetoric," she decreed, holding the reins high as her mare danced, twitched, and snorted funnels of steam into the morning chill. "I have had enough of debate for a lifetime. A hard ride through night's long veils tends to clear the mind of excuses. Sir Guy, once you held me captive. Captive even though you kept me in a gilded cage. For a while I thought I could only reach as far as the ceiling of my cage. I was weaker than you and believed strength had to be the possessor. But I am strong now, too, even though I fit no niche in this world. I am half Saxon, half Celt, loyal to a Norman king, contemptuous of a Norman heir, and I embrace an unacceptable religion. At least I know that no man will ever master me. When you held me at your whim, I mistook that for a possible thing. I was wrong. If I had turned and walked away, you would have had to kill me, and the shame would have been yours, but I would have been free. In fact, I need never have left Southwell in the beginning at all. I allowed myself to be bullied into an unnecessary quest. I did not understand my own power of personhood. Now I do. Never again shall any man control me."

Gisbourne's neck knotted in comprehending rage. "Gamewell does not control you?" came through gritted teeth.

"No man. I walk with whom I choose. Yet gratitude touches me. In part it was you who showed me my whole self."

"Will your whole self reside with Locksley's marauders? Is that what you've 'raised' yourself to?"

Refusing to argue, she merely repeated, "The choice is mine. You might put me to the sword, but I will die Katie Chenoweth. Fare you well, my lord." She turned her horse around. "I hope you find your Catherine." Never had she gambled so with her life as when she lifted the reins high and closed her heels on the mare. The ground wheeled beneath her and groaned beneath broad hooves. She put her eyes on the horizon of hills, her skin shrinking, expecting a crossbow bolt to ram home between her shoulder blades.

Gisbourne watched her ride away—not too swiftly, for she was leaving, not running. He sensed a crossbow lift at his side and slapped it down without even looking away from the vision of splendor and savagery galloping off before him.

"Your lordship, she's going to warn them," his adjutant said.

"Idiot, do you think I have no ears?"

The crossbow again rose. "I can still hit her. I beg you to let me."

Gisbourne's arm smashed horizontally into the man's mouth. Blood spurted across his sleeve, staining velvet. "She will die," he said, "or she will be mine. But if she dies—the morning sun seemed to tremble during his pause—"it will be by my hand, not yours. She merits that." He yanked up his own reins. Fierce black eyes rammed the words home. "And she shall have it." With that he rode out in front of his men. His white stallion's neck twisted in confusion as Sir Guy wrenched around and signaled the storm to begin.

Katie rode down into the valley and plowed right through the shock of the Greenwood band to where Robin and Will gaped at her sudden appearance. Ignoring the lace of questions, she spilled her story to them, every bit, including revelations about the relics that everyone had forgotten to ask. Her hand panned the valley's jaw to where Sir Guy sat his horse high up there, no longer hiding.

"There you are," Will said. "Next time you might listen."

"If we have a next time," Robin answered, connecting glares with Gisbourne over the distance.

"What are we going to do? We're outnumbered by a third."

"Run," Katie said abruptly. "The dishonor is his, not yours. 'Twas he who falsified relics and laid a dirty trap. Robin, he expects you to fight. If we turn now, we can surprise him and escape back into Sherwood. From those crags he and his men must take an indirect route."

"Aye, we'll have a slight advantage," the Hood accepted.

On the horizon, Gisbourne lifted his hand.

"Get ready," Robin said. The warning rippled back through his men.

Will reached over the gap between their horses and gripped Robin's elbow. "What about the relics?" In his eyes showed his meaning. Even if the relics were genuine, were they worth the lives it would cost to save them?

Robin's eyes gleamed, accepting a better wisdom. "Abandon them."

Will smiled broadly at him in danger's spite. He then turned to Katie. "You've ridden the whole night long." The condition of her horse, her cloak snagged with twigs, and the tangled yellow tresses draping over her shoulders to the saddle told the story.

"Never mind me," she said. "But my mare will drop dead if she's made to carry me farther."

"Aye," Robin agreed, motioning the men to drop the provisions from one of the spare horses. "Change steeds quickly, Katie. All you men, listen! We've been tricked. Our only chance is to retreat back to Sherwood. Go in pairs or triplets if you must separate, and care for your own lives. At Sherwood, gather at Three Rocks. Do you understand? Do *not* go back to Greenwoodside. You may be followed. Go now! Save yourselves!"

The air broke into a thunder of hooves. Even from here they could see shock spread on Gisbourne's face. Katie's prediction proved correct; he never thought they would make a mad, impossible dash for home.

Quickly Robin said to her, "When we reach Sherwood, you must hurry to Greenwoodside while my men hold Gisbourne off. Evacuate the women and children. Lead them into the deep woods for safety. We'll take no more chances."

"I promise," Katie said, "on the children's lives."

Will squeezed her hand in silence. The simple gesture shot her with courage.

With a last glance to the crags, where Sir Guy and his men were trying to get to them, the three beat a hasty rear guard for the men of Sherwood. In moments Sir Guy had nothing to surround but a carriage, a jeweled case, and two oxen. He immediately gave chase.

Directly across the cheek of England rode hunters and prey, hot for the kill, desperate for the den. Invasion of Sherwood seemed imminent. The nearer the forest drew, the less Sir Guy seemed willing to give up. He drove them hard, fully intending to overtake them or follow them as deep into the forest as they forced him. Now that the trap was sprung, the old Robin resurfaced. He actually enjoyed the endless, crazed ride with Katie and Will beside him, and Katie flew through her own fatigue on the wings of self-declaration. She had done it! She had told Sir Guy all the things she had dreamed of saying since the day she tried to sneak away from him. Thoughts filled her mind of her personal victory, but they clattered against strategies for evacuating the women and children from camp. Should she take them to the river? Or deeper, back, north to the gorge? Or farther still—into the thickest, oldest oaks?

Three Rocks was a natural fortress of trees on high ground, backed by a precipice that was impossible to climb. Unfortunately the precipice, which would become their guardian to the west, would also be their captor. If they had to escape, there would be no way to do so. Drive Gisbourne back or die. The time had come. Sir Guy had succeeded in his desire to force confrontation.

"How long can we hold them off?" Will asked, skidding to a stop where Robin was directing his best archers to key positions high in the trees.

"Between us we have about two hundred arrows, but only ten archers good enough to score hits. The others will be fair cover, but otherwise, a waste of arrows. Let's pray they don't break our lines and force us into swordplay. I have fewer good swordsmen than good archers." He scanned his men and sighed. "If they could only win by the size of their hearts and the mettle of their spirits." He rapped Will at the belt line and demanded, "What's the situation?"

"We lost three horses to exhaustion on the run back and one to a broken leg. If we run farther, we shall have to go on foot."

"No chance of that. We're committed."

"Gisbourne tried to follow Katie into the thick foliage when she broke off from us, but he couldn't find the opening to the path."

"He will never find it." The trees of Three Rocks, flecked with sunlight, created an eerie peace, a summer sweetness too filled with omen, and it charged them both with incalculable recklessness. "Have you counted his company yet?"

"Nearly forty."

"Strength?"

"He has archers and javelin throwers."

Robin winced. "The best."

"Doubtless. You know Sir Guy."

"If they advance on our ground, we'll take to the trees. Instruct the men to retrieve any stray arrow shot by Gisbourne's men. We can return to their owners with dividends."

"What are your plans?"

"I hope to take out half of his men with arrows. Then we shall have a fighting balance if we must go to the ground."

"Where do you want me?"

"With that good sword hand I want you on the rock where you can see them and relay to us which of his men are the strongest archers and throwers—and their positions. Can you do that?"

"I shall do my best, Robin."

"Bluestocking! String ropes from tree to tree in a crosswise pattern. It will give us mobility."

"Aye, master." Bluestocking's elfin face showed between broad leaves.

Will and Robin gazed down the slight incline to a sparse bunch of rocks and dells, which would betray them by providing cover for the enemy, and sized up the charging distance between there and themselves. They had a chance. Not a chance for victory precisely, but for escape, assuming they could cripple Gisbourne's legion into retreat.

There was a movement at the bottom of the

slope. Behind them their lookout sounded, "To arms! Make ready!"

"Load your bows, men!" Robin ordered. "Fire only when you have a clear shot. Conserve arrows. Make them count." He quickly caught Will's hand in both of his. "Best of luck."

Will tried to respond but couldn't.

Gisbourne's men swarmed at the slope's hem. They attacked immediately. Three Rocks was drenched in a rain of arrows. Robin's archers soon killed or wounded a half dozen of the enemy, but Gisbourne had not surrounded himself with trained men of war for nothing. Within the hour four Greenwood men lay dead in their own blood, twice that many more being stanched of wounds to the bodies and legs. Will's position on the rock soon became obsolete, so he retreated into the trees to wrap wounds and heave javelins back to their source.

"Listen!" Robin called as he stood on a branch high over the ground. "Hold your fire, men! Shoot only when his men advance. Horde all arrows and javelins they send. We'll try to disarm them!"

"Oh, very good," Will crooned from the ground. He stepped around the body of young Conal Reynoldson, whose throat gushed blood from a fatal javelin throw and for whom, regrettably, Will could do nothing. He had taken the extra moment to bind the gore, hoping the lad's father and brothers might be a little less horrified when the inevitable came.

"Robin?" he called, wiping blood from his hands.

"Yes—what?"

"We're in difficulty."

"Yes, I know that—"

"We're down to a dozen or so. Perhaps we should take the offensive."

"And we shall, as soon as—"

A javelin flew out of nowhere, incising the shroud of its long, spiraling shaft and tearing any leaves in its path. Robin dipped close to the bough as the javelin arched toward him, but there was nothing to hold on to for balance.

The shaft hissed. Will heard it though he never actually saw it, nor did he hear it in time to shout a warning. All he saw was Robin's crumpled form cracking through thick foliage and falling. There was a loud thump.

"Robin! Robin!" He ignored whizzing arrows to cut across an open space but had to dig through thorny brushwood before he discovered his leader trying to get to his feet from a supine position in the overgrowth. Will stepped awkwardly through to him and extended a hand. His heart pounded in his throat. "Robin, you all right?"

"Steady, old friend. Just lost my footing." Using Will's arm for leverage, he hauled himself to his feet. "Get the men out of the trees, except two archers for cover. We'll charge them when they have no more javelins to throw."

Will stepped off to carry out the order when Robin suddenly dragged him back. "Wait," he said. "Look."

A wagon rolled to a stop at the slope's bottom. Helpless, Sherwood's outlaws watched as a covering was rolled back by Gisbourne's men; there lay a cargo of arrows, bows, crossbows, bolts, halberds, javelins, mail coats, torches, and a pile of sacks probably carrying foodstuffs. With a bell's sharp knell the skirmish became a siege.

Will felt the blood drain from his face. His ears buzzed, and it seemed a cold knife ate in his innards. "Robin . . ."

The silence beside him was grave.

Gisbourne, they saw, motioned a portion of his men to the wagon, but the weapons remained untouched. Instead they lifted and lit a dozen torches. Robin stepped boldly to the edge of the trees for a better view. Will pressed close behind him, dismayed at the fact that Robin was no longer hiding.

"Locksley!" Gisbourne shouted from below. "Hear me! Surrender yourself to me or I shall burn the forest to cinders and your families with it."

Robin leaned forward. "No—"

Will pulled his arm. "He wouldn't dare."

Yet, without the slightest hesitation, Sir Guy waved his hand. Torches were touched to standing bushes. In seconds flames skirted Three Rocks.

"Will, let go of me!"

"No! You can't give in. He'll not settle for you alone. Robin, trust Katie. She'll take the children to the river. He can't stop the fire now."

"Do you hear, men of Sherwood?" Gisbourne hailed from below. "Surrender now and I shall order my men to save your families. Continue and your children will burn!"

He can hold us here indefinitely with that load of provisions," Robin said. "If I negotiate, we may have a second chance."

"I can take the wagon."

Robin's eyes flashed like steel. "I forbid it. You'd be sacrificing yourself!"

"Then I shall be sacrificed."

"Will, no—no! Come back!"

But even Robin's strong voice failed against desperate rage. Sword drawn, Will charged down the hill under cover of spreading flames and billowing black smoke. In instants came the cover he counted on—arrow after arrow spitting by him, driving Gisbourne and his deputies to the ground or other protection. Onward toward the wagon, through the vent provided by Robin's sharpshooting, Will ran, given momentum by the slope. He hacked away two deputies, ignoring the thud of his blade against flesh and the red, spurting gush and the screams, until the wagon grated under his feet and he felt the reins in his hands. Smoke choked him now. Flames roared across the slope, a wall of heat chewing at Sherwood. Soon the trees themselves would be roaring. Will shouted and snapped the reins. The draught horses, already twitching because of the fire, jolted to life. The wagon shivered, then lurched forward. With no particular plan and no possible escape Will aimed straight for the wall of flames, ducking crossbow bolts as they whined at him.

At the last second the horses balked. Will jerked the reins hard. The horses pivoted violently away from the flames, too sharply for the wagon to follow. It loomed up on two side wheels, pouring its contents into the inferno, finally tipping entirely and becoming fuel for the god of vengeance.

Will hit the ground hard. He had barely managed to keep his footing on the wagon as it tipped over, though choked and nearly blinded by smoke, and finally made a wild leap for safety.

But safety was a subjective condition. He was not burning.

He was facing, instead, a palisade of loaded crossbows. His own sword wavered in a defense position, growing impotent. Gisbourne glared at him.

Will lowered his sword and allowed himself to be taken.

High on Three Rocks, as they watched the fire grow and spread and consume, defeated men became suicidal furies.

"Your lordship, further orders?"

Gisbourne waved his way through the smoke to where his men had Will Scarlet bound hand and foot. The two men, of equal and different pasts, did not speak to each other.

"Take six men," Sir Guy said to his adjutant. He never looked away from Scarlet, nor Scarlet from him. "Go downriver and set a second series of fires. We'll force their women and children out to the riverbank. They will make compelling hostages. Locksley must surrender then."

"For this one, m'lord? Dungeon or gallows?"

The big nobleman's eyes went ironlike with victorious malice.

"Both."

Sheets of flame closed in to the northeast and southwest of the camp with terrorizing speed. Escape very soon became a matter of leaving everything but clothes on backs and children yet too young to run. Katie had not entered Greenwoodside with the same urgency she now possessed to leave it, for she'd assumed there was at least a little time, even if Gisbourne did not decide to invade the woods. But now there was fire. No one expected fire.

"Hurry! Hurry, everyone!" Katie called over the creeping roar. She coughed as she tied a cloth over one small boy's mouth and nose and sent him dashing after his mother, who was struggling with two younger children. "Help each other!"

"Where are we going to go?" Edith asked, also choking as she clutched Alexander and dragged Amlin.

"Follow the others. We'll go to the river."

Tears ran down the older woman's face freely. "Such torture to leave a child behind in a shallow grave. I feel—I feel so—"

Katie hugged her. "You must think of the two you're taking on to life." She caressed the tiny bundle in Edith's arms, the sleeping baby whose name she had chosen. "Are you the last?"

"Ruth and the other women from that side have not come yet."

"Then hurry on."

"But you're coming—"

"Yes, yes, I'll come straight away."

She found Ruth and the others struggling and choking their way through the clinging heat in the wrong direction. She turned them right, helping to drag along those who were made faint by the stifling smoke. Soon they caught up with the Greenwood women slowly picking their way through fire-clothed trees toward the Trent. The women of the second camp soon took part in helping with the children, easing the burden of those who had two and three and four children to guide. The older children graduated to a crude adulthood as they clutched their smaller brothers and sisters, awkwardly driving onward with an invulnerable courage only youth possesses. In spite of the cloying heat, collapsing trees, whose blackened, flaming arms clawed at the smoky sky before crashing into their paths and the smothering fumes, Katie dragged and cajoled the ragtag train forward.

She hesitated only once when two of Sherwood's roe deer surprised her by breaking across her path, heading not toward the river but laterally, toward the gorge, nearly into the fire. *Poor things. The smoke is confusing them. The river. The river is our only chance. Fresh air . . . water . . . freedom.*

Katie stopped short, not breathing, realizing that Gisbourne had started the fire from two different directions. Their only escape lay at the river, but he would be waiting there.

"Wait! Wait!" She ran toward the front of their queue. "Wait! Stop! It's a trap!"

"Trap?" cried Ula.

"What do you mean, Katie?" Marian asked.

"Gisbourne set this fire. He will be waiting at the river to capture us all. We dare not go there."

Melicent hoisted her own child up in her arms, trying to cover the girl's face from stinging smoke. "Where else *can* we go?"

Glynna Mondsey stomped a patch of flame

from her eldest daughter's skirt and demanded, "Do you expect us to go back into the inferno—?"

"What have you seen in your Druid mind, Katie?" Marian interrupted. "I will follow you and your sense of woodlore. What have you seen?"

"I have seen the animals crossing our path, going not to the river but to the gorge. Rabbits and roe deer and birds—all to the gorge. I feel we should follow them. I understand now—I must do what I feel and know and not what I think. Will you trust me? Decide quickly!"

The women stared at her, at each other, at the red, ashy death encroaching upon them. They listened. Roaring flames. Cracking branches. Coughing, crying children.

"I'm following Katie," Marian announced, and turned toward the gorge, ignoring glowing embers that floated all around.

Edith shoved her baby into Katie's arms. "I trust you. Lead us."

The others, doubt crimping their faces, soon gave up and trudged after her, deeper into the face of death. Sweat drained from their bodies, only to be seared off by dry, hot wind. Phosphorescent bits of ash and burning matter floated all around them, burning their faces and making it difficult to see. They moved across the fire instead of away from it, and with every step, doubt jabbed at Katie. As the air grew thick with swelter, each breath painful, she worried. Was she leading them to their deaths? It felt like dying to breathe the fire's breath. It seemed strange how fire could be either friend or enemy. Always fire had meant prosperity, safety. The stifling furnace of the blacksmith sending its waves of profitable chafing heat through Southwell, flushing the cheeks it fed. The warmth of a glowing hearth. A gurgling pot of soup. Fire had once been her partner; now it became a cruel antagonist. Somehow one more step followed the one before. Blinded by heat and suffocating in billows of black smoke, Katie nearly fell down the gorge when it opened under her feet. Clutching the baby to her throat, she staggered back, then inched downward, nearly sitting on the slope, feeling her way wih her heels and one hand. "Follow me," she called, "but take care. It's steep. Help the children and the old ones."

With killing slowness Katie led her bedraggled party deep into the earth's face, away from the sizzling forest. Sparks descended with them, but the fire itself could not follow, could not consume rock and wet ferns, and there were no trees in the gorge to catch flame. The air here was less seething, though by no means cool, and they could breathe better. Katie stumbled to her feet, quickly counting heads. How strange the women looked, wimpled and shawled, dragging children, each other, and the elderly residents of Greenwoodside to questionable safety.

"Dig now," Katie called. "Dig under the mulch. Dig as deep as you can. Bury yourselves and your children in the cool earth and mulch. We'll let the fire pass overhead."

Silent from fear, smoke, and exhaustion, the women numbly obeyed her. They dug with their hands and their hopes. Katie shuttled about, helping, wondering if she had instructed them to dig their own graves.

And she was the last to lie down in the earth. She looked once across the gorge's crotch to the leafy lumps under which the Sherwood family huddled.

Finally she lowered herself into her own hole, where she had laid tiny Alexander, and gathered him into her arms after drawing a blanket of mulch over herself and him. Through the rotten leaves she watched Sir Guy's two fires meet high overhead, caressing like lovers and consuming the whole world. Ever greedy, the flames began to creep down the sides of the ravine.

It was raining.

Water sheeted on the rock walls. Will stared at it longingly, thinking of the fire. The dungeon cold penetrated to his bones, compounding the chilly arms of hopelessness now holding him. For hours—he knew not how many—he had paced this purulent stone cell, only to conclude that there was no way out. The cell was too simple to provide any frailty in its purpose. Walls of poorly fitted masonry came down to waist height, after which began solid bedrock and packed earth. He had only his hands to dig with, and his hands would fail long before the hard crust around him. Up a short flight of steps glowered a door as thick as his thigh, with only a slot the size of a small bowl through which food was passed. Last meals, he supposed. At eye level a window with thick iron bars provided a slight link to the outside world, but the view of the public gallows tree was pitifully poor comfort. Unfortunately the only relief from the stink of human and rodent excrement was in standing near that window.

He coiled his arms around himself and against the dampness. Even now, in the blue of night, the gallows tree glared back at him, silhouetted against gray rain. It was so cold here. . . . He hardly remembered the intense heat at Three Rocks. If he thought of it, only his mind remembered; his body no longer could. The rain mocked him. By now the Greenwood would be nothing but a mat of soaking cinders. No comfort came to the desolation robing him, nor any rest from thoughts of Katie, of Robin, of the fight he had abandoned in a futile attempt to turn the odds.

He shivered from deep within. He would never sleep again.

The bolt slid away outside the door; lifted, it seemed, by the voices of the guards. Torchlight wedged into the underground cell. A massive shadow filled the doorway at the top of the stone steps.

Unwilling to huddle in front of Sir Guy, Will let his hands drop to his sides.

"So you survived," he noted. "Regrettable."

Sir Guy did not answer but descended the steps. Two guards remained blocking the door, holding torches. More fire.

Will stiffened his legs. "What do you want?"

"Not forgiveness," Gisbourne said, "so you needn't worry."

"I thought I knew you. But your ruthlessness reached new heights today. I assume I am to be hanged in the morning."

"You will die at dawn, that is true. However ... I feel I owe you better than the gallows. You shall be executed in the quickest possible manner. By the ax."

"Your lenience is compelling." Will turned to the window. "Why do you feel you owe me anything?"

"You acted nobly. And you have suffered enough for one turn of the sun."

Will's heart dropped to his knees. Suddenly he was cold from within as well as without, frozen by the generosity; its source was so unlikely, there had to be a reason more terrible than pity. Trembling, he asked, "Coming from a man who would gladly hear me moan in agony, that frightens me. Yet I would rather know—"

"You have that right." Sir Guy paced the cell uneasily. "First I will tell you that my inferno turned upon me but not in the form of flame. I underestimated the pure rage of cornered animals. My troops were driven back by a handful of madmen. Your men. Never have I seen such numb fury. I myself put an arrow in a man's chest, only to watch him pluck it out and keep on fighting. I give you credit. For untrained farmers and derelicts your men sent mine floundering."

"They are Robin's men. I deserve no credit for the loyalty that drives them."

Sir Guy grunted his approval. "You've at least retained your integrity."

"If you have any," Will countered, forcing himself to ask, "perhaps you will tell me the fate of our children." The request dried upon his tongue.

"You daren't wish it too strongly. I myself went to the riverbank to await them. I planned to use them as bait to capture Locksley. But the wind changed. The fire closed in." He paced away as though circling a dinner table spent of its food. "Not a living soul emerged."

Will clamped his eyes shut. He turned his back to Gisbourne and gripped the wet edge of the window. He cared not to hide his pain from the man who had caused it. Nor could he have. It was enough to keep from passing out. All the children ... the women ... Katie ... Katie.

He choked. "You bastard." The last syllable failed.

Sir Guy joined him at the window at a discretionary distance, but not so far that Will couldn't have landed a serious blow if he chose to. "Surely you realize the only true differences between us are political ones. Would you like to change places with me?" When Will raised an agonized glare, Gisbourne opened the door to his feelings, but only a slit. "I am a Christian, too, remember. Where do you suppose each of us will spend Eternity? You are going to die in the morning, and you'll go to your maker a hero. I, more's the shame, must go on living and, in the end, face that fire of mine. You see," he said, "I have murdered children."

Pity came unbidden. In his sensitized state Will could not resist it.

Sir Guy went to the steps. The guards parted. "I shall see that you are brought a blanket and a hot meal to better pass the night before you die. A man of noble blood should at least go to the block rested."

Pain could kill a man's heart without a single wound. In the pit of Will Scarlet's being ate that bottomless kind of pain. He leaned upon the window edge, numb to the frigid stone, and wished for morning. Sorrow welled in his eyes and narrowed his throat. If only he was a coward. A coward could take his own life.

The door opened again. The guards were laughing. "Ho, gallows bait," one called, "His Lordship wants you given a hot meal and comfort for the night. There's your hot meal"—he threw a flaming rat's carcass to the cell floor—"and here's your comfort." They dragged in a verminy, drunken old hag, ragged, beggardly, stinking of ale. She spat as they cast her down the steps where she lay in a heap, grumbling, swearing, and burping. "Quench your urges on that morsel," the guard taunted. "Plug your nose and she'll be good as a virgin." Their laughter rang through the cell. The door grated shut.

Will turned back to the window, burying his head in his arms. The stench of the dead rat made his innards churn. In the corner the old hag continued her senseless snorting until the guards' laughter faded, then she lapsed into a stupor.

Outside, the rain faded to a drizzle, then stopped, leaving the night dank.

"Katie," he murmured in his misery, "forgive this fool. Death must be our only marriage." His throat knotted. Tears drained down his face.

From his imagination, from the walls and the sky, her voice drifted through his mind—

clear, confident, and, as always, challenging. "Is this defeatist the man whose resourcefulness I love?"

Will flinched. His fingers constricted on the iron bars. "I hope, at least, you are with Edward now. Save me a place by your other side and may God grant me mercy for loving you so."

Her voice came again, as soft as the rain. "My wish to be with Edward is sweetly gone. Turn around, beloved fool."

Will turned, obeying what he thought was only a dream, and there before him he watched a dream unfold. The old hag, once a crumpled heap of destitution upon the dirt floor, now stood straight as a reed. From the torn sleeves emerged white hands on slim, narrow wrists, which moved to the hood and the face it shadowed. The hood slipped back. Where once there had been only grayness there now gleamed clean, alabaster hair, framing the face he loved and the soft smile he had hoped to see only in heaven. He watched through blurring eyes as the snarled robes drifted to the floor as though they, too, had been given life.

There was a light in the cell. Ivory skin and angel's robes blinded him, shimmering through his tears. His dead love had come to fetch him to heaven. There—yes—there she stood, like a phoenix rising from a pile of discarded rags ... Katie ... white-gold, bright in love, cloaked in her gown and her own gleaming cape of hair.

Will stumbled forward, forgetting that she was only an illusion, forgetting that in a moment he would hit the stone wall.

But—these were her arms! This was her body pressing against him! Her hands caressed his head.

"Katie," he gasped, weeping shamelessly. "My Katie . . . oh, my love . . . oh, my love . . ."

Katie held his head to her breast as they drifted to the cell floor, holding each other. "Poor knight," she whispered. "You thought you were alone."

The clouds parted, and the moon moved in the sky before either spoke again.

"Katie, I don't understand," Will murmured, and more minutes passed.

"The rain saved us. It drove down the flames. We were hiding under the mulch in the ravine. We didn't lose a single child."

"Praise God. Or praise your Goddess—I hardly know what to believe anymore."

"Nor I. Except that I believe in you, in us."

He pulled himself away, holding her arms. "Now we must both die. This cell is our coffin."

She smiled, and the cell was light again. "Did we survive so much, only to die in the morning? I think not."

"Ah, love, your optimism is sweet to me. You forget this is a dungeon, not a tent."

"And you forget that you love a blacksmith." She smiled and pulled around a bag with a long strap that had hung across her body beneath the ragged disguise. From it she withdrew a hammer, an iron chisel, a pair of heavy tongs, and a thick, short chain with an iron handle wrapped in leather.

"Any cage can be made inviolable," she said, enjoying her moment, "but seldom to its builders. Edward and I were commissioned to fortify these cells, to make the hinges and bolts and bars. To a hand without tools the bars look and feel solidly embedded. But when these cells were built, the town of Nottingham scrimped too much to make it truly solid. These bars," she went on, going to the window, "are sunken only a finger's width instead of a finger's depth as they should be. The impregnability is only a matter of illusion." She touched his hands lovingly. "That is why they put no iron cuffs on you in this prison. Cuffs could be used to knock these bars loose. Which is what we will do." She picked up her tools. "We'll be free in moments."

Will caught her and held her tight against him. Freedom could wait an extra moment.

They broke out of the dungeon cell every bit as easily as Katie said they would, and the night opened before them. The wet ground was muddy and slippery but felt like a velvet carpet to Will.

Katie led him in silence to the place where she had hidden their horses, her eyes constantly working against the hurt of seeing his wounds. A scoring across one cheekbone, probably made by a fist. A clotted gash between his thumb and forefinger. A noticeable limp. They had probably thrown him down those steps. She resisted asking.

Oblivious to a danger that seemed to taunt them, they mounted their horses. Will swung his dark blue cape, glad that Katie had thought to bring it—but Katie had thought of everything today—feeling it fall around his shoulders like the grip of an old friend, and a warmth came into his body.

"Go slowly," he said, "quietly. No need to draw attention by running hard until we have to."

From her saddle Katie gazed at him, her lips turning very slightly into a delicate bow. She charged him with her power of life, just sitting her horse and hardly moving a muscle, hardly breathing, beautiful in her bravery and a love he fully perceived.

"I adore you," he mentioned.

"What a coincidence."

"Shall we ride?"

"Let us, by all means, ride."

They were nearly to Nottingham's great city gate before the bell's began to toll, a piercing announcement of prisoner escape, and Will lifted the reins high, whooping, "There! Now we run!"

Nottingham rolled away beneath them. Wind fingered their hair and cloaks as they crashed through the streets and devoured the town gate in a simple snap of the reins, ignoring, even triumphing, in the clamor of men on horses closing behind them. But they had a substantial head start and used it.

Into the deep night they plunged toward the forest. Sherwood's ancient oaks reached toward them with their thick double and triplet trunks, each as big around as two men were wide, trunks that moved off from each other like peninsulas from continents, to reach across whole fields against the sapphire sky. Immediately behind them rode two deputies, the first to realize the escape, and behind them at a mile's distance or so rode another dozen.

Katie glanced at Will only once during the

wild gallop, concentrating on keeping her seat in the saddle as her horse flanked Palermo at breakneck speed. Arrows whizzed by their ears. Her skin crawled at the sound of them. She leaned with the horse around a tight curve but shrieked as the animal crumpled beneath her and skidded to its knees in the dirt. A long arrow shaft protruded from the horse's neck at the base of its brain. The big body quivered under Katie, who still hung somehow from the saddle, and then died. Instantly the two guards descended, but Will was already there. He knocked one man from his saddle before Katie could even think of what happened and, with his bare hands, got the other man by the neck. Their horses twisted around each other in a strange dance while Will quite simply choked the guard into oblivion.

With an impossible leap Katie clung to Will's saddle. He pulled her up behind him, brought his heels together on Palermo's flanks, and they were off. Thunderous hooves from behind urged them onward.

But they were no longer alone.

As the big stallion plunged into a dry creek bed and out of it, the ferns and bushes came to life. A line of hemp snapped taut behind them, and the dozen deputies charged straight into it. Horses and men tumbled into a chaos of bodies. Necks and bones and arrows cracked. Screams filled the night, soon turning to dreadful moans.

On into the bosom of oaks cantered a blond horse, two lovers, and a small, broken collection of misfit heroes, whooping their victory.

• Chapter Seventeen •

"Be sure to attend every meeting, at least one of you, and review the guild rules before you take on an apprentice. Apprentices can be a curse, you know. Spare no one your highest quality wares, no matter how small the details. And be sure to mend that crack in the funace hood before one of you takes an injury from it."

Katie stepped back, heedless of the swish her apple-green gown made around her legs, and surveyed Nick and Gaston. They were a little haggard, but they had survived. The Cart Road was now open to any Englishman loyal to Richard, and Katie had made very sure that the smiths' guild and indeed the whole of Southwell understood it was her doing. A heroine's welcome was not her desire, but that she did get. Half the neighborhood now crowded outside the house she and Edward had bedded, lived, loved, and toiled in, but she took no bows, no matter how deserved. She cared only that her two boys got their due leg-up in the smithing business. From now on the forge would operate under their names, their sweat.

"Are you certain, Katie?" Nick asked her. His ruddy face was ruddier than usual. "You'll nae stay? It's your forge, after all."

She touched his thick arm and Gaston's narrower one. Even Gaston, she noticed, now had round muscles blooming across his shoulders and forearms. "My forge," she agreed, "but no longer my dream or destiny. Oh, I'm no surer what those words mean than you are, of course. I shall not play philosopher for you, but know forever that I made the best choice for myself. The best for you, too, I think. No, don't hug me. This is not good-bye. Be strong. I know you are, as Edward knew. Run his forge well, lads. No one has a better claim upon its success than the two of you. Someday you shall have your own Katies to bring home to the forge." She touched Nick's cheek, then Gaston's, then turned without a backward glance and walked out into the crowded street. All around her the faces of her neighbors—contrite, admiring, a little ashamed, rather proud—begged her forgiveness and wished her well. And there was Will, waiting on Palermo. Like her, he wore clean clothes, much of them new, gifts from Robin—a dazzling new scarlet cap with a red plume, bright leather boots, a logan-green tunic and trews, leather-belted and topped by a flowing red cowled cape. Grand.

Katie was helped onto the pale gray horse beside Palermo by one of her neighbors. For a long time she and Will exchanged a gaze.

Finally she prodded, "Something?"

He was candid. As much in attitude as in words. "I have no comforts to promise. No title, no future. You'll be no Lady Montfichet as I will be no lord."

"I shall be content to be Lady Scarlet," she told him.

"You'll be the wife of an outlaw."

Her chin went up. "I'll be an outlaw in my own right, thank you very much."

Will smirked, quite affected, and said, "Our futures are uncertain."

"Oh, but most bright. And full of purpose. Greenwoodside will be moved and built again. They'll need both teachers and knights, my darling," she said, caring not who heard, "and that is us."

Will reached for her hand. They leaned toward each other and kissed. He started to say something, perhaps to utter still another tidbit of truth, but was kept silent by a sudden *swish-thunk*.

They both looked. His new red cloak lay duly initiated by a shivering arrow, run through the fabric and embedded in the saddle.

There, high over them on the roof of the furnace house, stood the rakish outlaw Robin Hood, his own cape flapping like something out of an epic poem. He smiled, then tipped his bonnet to them in a flamboyant salute and winked.

With a flourish he disappeared over the rooftops.

Hand holding hand, Will and Katie reined their horses toward the south town gate. Odd, but the sun was from the south today.

• *Epilogue* •

Not until 1194 was King Richard freed by payment of the ransom to finally return to England. Robert Fitzsooth of Locksley and those Saxons of the Greenwood still alive had their lands reinstated to them. Richard soon left on another crusade and actually spent less than one year of his ten-year reign on England's native soil.

In 1199, upon the death of Richard Lionheart, his brother, John Lackland, was crowned King John I. He comes down through history as one of the most corrupt, vicious, self-seeking, and licentious rulers of all time. His incompetence eventually resulted in the first major constitutional battle in the history of England. His own feudal barons rose against him and in 1215 forced the signing of the Magna Carta. The document exacted controls and concessions for the merchant class, drastically reducing the power of the monarchy forever.

Earlier on, probably around 1204, either by a small puncture wound in his chest or by poison at a traitor's hand, Robin of the Hood fired his last arrow out a window and declared he should be buried where it landed. Then, in Johnny Little's arms, with Will Scarlet and Will Stutley at his sides, he died. This occurred at the small priory known as Kirklees.

To this day, under England's mists, a grave there lies.

About the Author

Diane Carey holds a B.A. in Classical and Medieval Literature and the history of the theatre from Alma College in Michigan, and a Master's Degree in English from the University of Michigan. She has played Highland bagpipes for fourteen years and enjoys studying the Celtic culture of the British Isles. She shares a "charmed life" with husband Gregory Brodeur, and daughter, Lydia Rose. A lover of world cultures, she loves to include all the colors of history in her writing, and writes in several genres. "Tall ships, medieval festivals, and, of course, writing," she says, "all keep reality safely at bay!"